Deeper Evil

The Evil Secrets Trilogy
Book Two

Vickie McKeehan

beachdevils
PRESS

Deeper Evil
The Evil Secrets Trilogy

Published by Beachdevils Press
ISBN: 978-1-4524-0848-4 eBook
ISBN: 978-0-6156-4480-6 Paperback
Printed in the USA

Cover art design by Vanessa Mendozzi Design
www.vanessamendozzidesign.com

Visit the author at:
www.vickiemckeehan.com
www.facebook.com/VickieMcKeehan

For Deep, my favorite Oompa Loompa,
and the best lunch buddy a girl could have.
Not everyone is willing to share their fries without
complaint.

Deeper Evil

The Evil Secrets Trilogy
Book Two

CHAPTER 1

Sunny Southern California was turning out to be better than he'd originally thought, much better. It was warmer, for one thing, late May with spring still blossoming and coming to life around him.

Even though the locals kept mentioning something they called May Gray and grumbling about the upcoming June Gloom, he hadn't really noticed. The days seemed no more overcast than the ones he'd grown up with in his native Ireland.

But Los Angeles definitely had its advantages. From his little hotel patio, he could sit and enjoy the beach as it slowly filled each morning with female bodies slicked with oil baking in the bright warm sun. Like this morning. He had started his day watching six gorgeously toned women play a game of beach volleyball wearing, God bless them, tiny little strips of fabric that barely covered tits and ass. Who needed Aruba when he had only to kick back and enjoy those hot bodies mere steps away from his own door?

He was living in paradise, enjoying the fruits of his labor.

And he hadn't felt this invigorated in twenty years.

Weeks earlier, he'd been burned out, ready for Prozac. But now for the first time in years, thanks to this last mission, he was actually enjoying life. In a way, helping Kit Griffin last night made him feel as if he were making up for all of his mistakes.

And there were plenty of those. But he wasn't going to waste time dwelling on them.

At his age, this might be his last chance to do something positive, make a change, and maybe take that first step toward cutting back on his nicotine and alcohol intake. God knew he loved the ten cigs he allowed himself daily, as well as his late-night measure of Jameson.

Had the media not labeled him an overnight hero, he might not be thinking about taking better care of himself. Amused at his own thoughts as well as the swell to his ego, he did his best to imagine himself as one of the good guys.

And just couldn't bring the image into focus. He'd crossed over into the dark too many years ago for that picture to fully take shape.

Last night, as part of that first step, he'd promised Kit Griffin he'd keep her and her friends safe, a different direction for him to be sure. It wasn't like him to promise anyone anything. The less involved you got, the better. That had been his motto for decades, something he lived by. He made very few promises.

But those made were always kept.

In his line of work that might be unheard of. Hit men rarely lived by a code of honor. But then, the few the proud, hadn't been trained by Noah Parker.

As he glanced across the cobbled Main Street in the direction of the Book & Bean, he realized the role of protector might be new. A hero he wasn't.

But even now, he knew Baylee Scott was inside the store alone with her baby daughter, working in place of Kit this morning because Kit Griffin was still trying to recover from her kidnapping ordeal from last night.

From the moment he'd opened his eyes that morning, his instincts had kicked in. He'd learned long ago never to ignore a gut feeling. Something was up. Years of tracking the quarry had him feeling antsy. It was the reason he'd driven up to San Madrid at the crack of dawn, the reason he'd left those hot bodies playing on the sand.

And even if he happened to be wrong this morning, because he'd seen no signs of the Boyd brothers, there was no way he could walk away now. No, the last couple of weeks had already set the wheels in motion. There was no going back. He'd been prepared to accept the consequences then, whatever they were.

And he still was. Today was no different. Looking back would get him nowhere.

He could not have predicted the chain of events the past few weeks would set in motion, nor the rippling effects. Who knew the three Boyd sons would throw down an entirely different kind of challenge, one he wouldn't be able to walk away from now?

Add in the fact that he still had a score to settle with Collin Boyd for kidnapping Kit last night and he had all matters of unfinished business with the Boyd clan.

Collin had a nasty wound to his shoulder. He ought to know, he'd put it there. He intended to finish the job first chance he got just as soon as the bastard came out of hiding. And if he didn't crawl out from under his rock, he'd go in and dig him out. It was just that simple.

It was true he still had a few things left on his to-do list before he could call it quits in L.A. The remaining law partner for one. At some point, Frank Geller would have to be taken down. It wasn't fair to let him off the hook, to escape payback when he'd been in on the ground floor of the plan from day one like his sister Jessica and her husband Sumner.

They had already paid the ultimate price for their greed. He'd seen to that. In time, so would Frank Geller. But now was not the time to get impatient or careless or tip his hand too early. He might be unaccustomed to this role of guardian, but he intended to do whatever it took to see this thing through to the end.

The way he saw it, quite a few lives depended on it.

⚜ ⚜ ⚜ ⚜ ⚜

Standing behind the scarred oak counter inside the Book & Bean, the only coffee shop in San Madrid, a tiny fishing village north of L.A., Baylee Scott put the finishing touches on a latte.

At just after seven in the morning, she glanced at the line snaking out the door and wondered how many of the customers were there for the coffee and pastries or how many were reporters or curiosity seekers who had watched last night's newscast and wanted to catch a glimpse of the kidnap victim.

Baylee shook her head at the idea of people coming to gawk at Kit Griffin, her lifelong friend and owner of the Book & Bean.

What kind of people did that? She wondered. Because she didn't recognize most of the people as regulars, that alone told her the people in line were more than likely reporters of one sort or another, who had made the trip hoping to get a quote or pick up some glimmer of gossip they could pass on, and sate whatever audience they attracted.

The whole media circus didn't sit well with Baylee. Not only did she feel incensed at the intrusion on Kit's behalf to her friend's personal life, but she very much feared this entire ordeal would bring to her door a person she'd been trying to evade for more than a year.

As she steamed milk for another latte, she did her best to calm her nerves and think like practical Kit did. She tried to concentrate on how much extra business these prying parasites might bring in today.

But it was difficult to tamp down her fear in lieu of how good this would all be for the bottom line.

Baylee recalled yesterday's mad house when the media had invaded the little town with their crews and cameras in tow, hoping to edge out the competition to get an exclusive interview with the prime suspect in the Alana Stevens murder. She was sure the police had purposely leaked the fact that Kit had suffered years of physical abuse at the hands of her mother—or rather the woman who had merely raised her. That had brought the reporters swarming like vultures over a dead carcass in the road. And once they'd discovered that Kit was involved with Jake Boston, the software mogul who was still the prime suspect in his wife's slaying two years earlier, the media had played that relationship angle to the hilt.

Two separate murder cases, two murder suspects linked together as a couple; the press had gone wild, Baylee mused now, as she poured coffee into an oversized mug and plated a couple of cinnamon rolls for the next customer.

The way the media had portrayed Jake and Kit, one would have thought the two presented the biggest single threat to the greater Los Angeles area since The Hillside Stranglers.

But as ludicrous as it had seemed yesterday, the store had experienced its most successful day money-wise since opening four years earlier.

Even though Kit and Jake's connection to each other had created a firestorm of interest—at least it had for about forty-five minutes—the news of Kit's kidnapping last night had changed everything.

Baylee shook her head just thinking how fickle the media could be. She glanced at the wild-eyed, sleep-deprived reporters waiting in line. Some of them looked as though they had been up all night. Funny what a difference twenty-four hours could make, she thought.

It had taken a kidnapping to put another twist in the story and brought them back full circle to the Book & Bean for Round Two.

Today, they seemed to be working the sympathetic angle, convinced Jake and Kit had been wrongly accused. She could laugh now because they certainly hadn't been convinced yesterday of the couple's innocence.

But once they discovered the wealthy Collin Boyd, son of slain murder victims Jessica and Sumner Boyd, had taken Kit hostage, the story had dominated the six o'clock newscast. Then at ten o'clock, those same news reporters had announced her rescue. And that was before anyone had known about the faceless, unknown stranger who had come charging into an abandoned warehouse in Thousand Oaks where Collin had been holding Kit, and saved the day. He'd shot Kit's captors, including Collin, and then called Jake to come pick her up.

By the time Jake had arrived, the stranger had already disappeared. Jake had found Kit still unconscious. Luckily by the time she woke up in the hospital, she hadn't remembered a thing about the kidnapping other than the role Collin had played in the whole thing.

The fact that Jake had found one of those mysterious gold cowboys that had been left with each of the other victims clutched in the palm of Kit's hand suggested that the man who had come to her rescue was the same one who had murdered Alana as well as all the others—and now for whatever reason had decided to play hero.

No one close to Kit felt like complaining.

Kit was alive, thanks to the stranger, and tucked away in her little bungalow along the water's edge.

As Baylee waited on yet another customer, she thought the whole thing sounded like the plot from one of her father's action movies.

No wonder the media had shown up again, she thought moodily as she absently wiped down the counter once more before taking another order.

Looking out over the strange faces in the crowded shop, Baylee thought she recognized some of the same on-air television reporters from yesterday. As more news vans pulled up in front of the store, it was clear they were staking the place out, hoping to find out more about Kit's mystery savior.

Even now, they were clamoring to get another story for the noon newscast. It made her stomach burn to think the sharks were circling. They were obviously waiting for Jake and Kit to make an appearance so they could jockey for a quote on camera, no less.

Well, they'll be sorely disappointed on that score, thought Baylee, as she expertly worked the espresso machine, mixing together java with steaming milk, working on making the perfect blend. She doubted Jake intended to let Kit out of his sight for days yet.

Baylee sighed. She hoped they weren't staking out Kit's house at this very moment. Her friend desperately needed some downtime.

That was the reason why she'd offered to open up for the next couple of mornings even if it meant she and Sarah had to get up extra early to make the drive in from Agoura Hills, from the sweet little guest cottage she'd rented from Gloria.

Baylee didn't mind. Kit was more like family, more like a sister than her best friend. They would do anything for each other. The least she could do was mind the store to keep Kit away from the prying eyes and the inane questions of the pesky media. Even though it might mean she and Sarah risked wandering into the spotlight right along with Kit and Jake.

She shook off the alarm that wanted to creep in. Chancing a quick look at her almost six-month-old daughter, who sat in her swing behind the counter, content for the moment to chew on a red plastic teething bracelet, Baylee sucked in a breath. Knowing Collin had been desperate enough to kidnap Kit last night was bad enough and sent chills down her arms in spite of the heat from the espresso machine.

But as she methodically passed the finished product, the latte, to the waiting hands of her customer, she fought off images of what Collin's brother, Connor, might do if he found out she was here in San Madrid, and had been for months.

She needed to think about leaving L.A. for good. The problem with taking off again though, meant she'd be leaving behind her dying father, not to mention the fact that she'd have to go on the run with Sarah.

How could she keep doing that to her baby daughter? Sarah deserved better. To Baylee it seemed she'd been on the move ever since the baby's birth, unsettled, moving from place to place.

She had to get her life back on track. But how could she do that when she was so terrified Connor would find out about the baby? The idea put the reality of her situation front and center.

As she wiped down the counter again for the twentieth time that morning, Baylee thought about what she wanted. She wanted for her and Sarah to be left alone, to feel secure again; she wanted her life back the way it had been before Connor Boyd had crossed her path and shown her the dark side of his life. She wanted to be left alone to raise Sarah on her own. And she'd do anything, absolutely anything, to ensure he never learned Sarah existed.

Was that asking too much? If she hadn't had to come back to L.A. because of her father's cancer, she would still be living in Denver, where she'd given birth. Living back with her friend, Blair Rafferty, the person she'd turned to during her pregnancy, and who had given her a job.

She knew she'd hurt her friends, Kit and Quinn, by doing that. By shutting them out, they had been excluded from participating in Sarah's birth. But how could she explain what had happened? She couldn't take the chance that Connor wouldn't have followed through on his threats.

No, she thought, she would continue to keep her secret. Kit had too much going on in her life right now, too much to deal with to get bogged down with her problems. And Quinn, Quinn was a brand new resident doctor, just a month into her first year of residency. Others might not recognize her as "Doctor" Tyler just yet, but as far as Baylee was concerned, Quinn had earned the right to focus on her future, her career, without the added problems she brought to the table.

Baylee sucked in a nervous breath and made a promise. She'd been handling the stress and pressure of it all for the past fifteen months—by herself.

She would handle this on her own as well. She had to.

☘ ☘ ☘ ☘ ☘

Dylan Burke didn't mind the drive up the Pacific Coast Highway.

In fact, as he made his way north to San Madrid along the PCH, he sat behind the wheel of his classic muscle car, a spiffy convertible, a brilliant metallic blue 1968 Chevy Camaro he'd restored himself from the shell out, and jammed to Springsteen, drumming along as The Boss sang about having a hungry heart. Enjoying the scenery, Dylan absently reached over and cranked up the volume.

On one side of the road he watched the waves lap up against the shoreline, moving lazily in and out. On the other side, he enjoyed a glimpse of fast-moving rolling hills dotted with clusters of purple lupine, California orange poppies, and sand asters in late spring bloom.

The ocean breeze lifted the loose blond hair Dylan hadn't bothered tying back into his usual stumpy ponytail. As he took in the scenic drive, he decided doing a favor for his best friend, Jake Boston, who also happened to be his employer, had its own rewards.

Today the VP of research and development at Billing-Pro Software was playing errand boy. He'd promised Jake, who was basically babysitting Kit Griffin and working from her house in San Madrid, that he'd drop off some much needed computer equipment to make telecommuting a little easier.

And after last night's kidnapping, Dylan knew Jake had no intention of letting Kit out of his sight for even a minute. So he knew the state-of-the-art scanner, the extra modem, as well as the laptop computer he carried in the trunk of his car would be a welcome addition to Jake's virtual home office.

Dylan didn't dwell on the fact that he could have simply shipped the equipment via same day delivery. No, he had volunteered to make the trip for one purely selfish reason. The side benefit stood about five-three with shoulder-length brown hair and had the most alluring pair of aquamarine eyes he'd ever seen.

He didn't even want to linger for very long on the way Baylee Scott filled out a pair of jeans. If he was completely honest with himself, he'd been captivated by her since that first night at the hospital, the night Collin Boyd had run Kit's car off the road.

Just thinking about Baylee made him grin. No, he didn't mind making this side trip at all.

By the time he reached the city limits sign, denoting San Madrid, population four thousand and seventy-five, he left the four-lane PCH and headed due east away from the ocean.

Turning onto a genuine cobblestone Main Street, Dylan drove through the quaint fishing village, past a picturesque town square complete with a free-flowing fountain, past an assortment of shops until he reached the outskirts of town. By the time he realized he'd run out of shops and businesses, he was headed north again, out of town, connecting back to the PCH.

In the blink of an eye, he'd completely blown past the heart of the little town. He looked for a place to make a sharp U turn and headed back the way he'd come. A half a mile or so back, he hit the business district and noticed the old-fashioned street signs, the gas streetlamps, and realized the town looked more like a scene out of the 1950's.

Pulling the car to a stop into a slotted street parking space directly in front of the Book & Bean, Dylan hoped this spur-of-the-moment visit wasn't a bold move on his part. The other times he'd been around Baylee, she'd been skittish. And that was putting it mildly. He might not know a lot about this particular woman, but he did know she showed all the signs of having been hurt. Big time.

As he got out of the car, he began to have second thoughts. To top it off, she was a single mother—a woman with a baby. In all the years of doing the backstroke in the dating pool, he'd never once so much as gone near a single mom. It hadn't been something he had purposely avoided; it just hadn't come up before.

The women he usually dated were a far cry from mother material. If he had an ounce of sense, he'd get back in his car right now and head on over to Kit's house, drop off the equipment, head to the nearest beach and grab his surfboard before the tide changed.

But something in Baylee's beautiful eyes had pulled at him that first night he'd met her. And weeks later the woman was still doing a solo drumbeat in his head he couldn't shake.

Refusing to listen to his inner voice of reason, Dylan opened the door of the bookstore and stepped inside. Immediately he removed his Oakley Spikes, looping them in the V of his shirt.

The minute his eyes adjusted to the inside light, he took in the rows and rows of shelves filled with books, everything from romance novels, suspense and thrillers to science fiction, true crime, self-help, and a wealth of cookbooks. When he spotted the mystery section, he moved that way to check it out, telling himself he might as well pick out a couple of thrillers while he was here.

And then Dylan heard the baby babble. There was no other way to describe it.

He fixed his eyes on the small bundle of kicking feet, wearing cherry pink overalls, gurgling away in the Pack 'N Play set up by the cash register in the middle of the store.

He watched as the tiny little thing flopped on her stomach, those big blue eyes, so like her mother's, trying to zero in on a plastic spoon-looking thing. As he stood mesmerized, she reached out a chubby little fist trying to make a grab for the spoon thing. As she made the reach she rose up as if to crawl, but landed back down, flat on her belly.

Fascinated, Dylan stood there entranced until he heard voices. His eyes drifted to Sarah's harried mother, dressed in a form-fitting blue sun dress, a shade lighter than those aqua colored eyes.

☦ ☦ ☦ ☦ ☦

Baylee was in the process of helping a difficult customer, trying to locate a particular hard-to-find second book in a trilogy, when she looked up at the man standing beside the Pack 'N Play. Their eyes met. She stopped what she was doing long enough to wave at him. He saw her absently brush a few loose strands of hair off of her face, a gesture he recognized as a habit she had when she was uneasy, which was practically twenty-four-seven.

When the customer decided she'd buy another book by the same author, Baylee cheerfully rang up the woman's purchase, trying to keep her mind on the transaction instead of on the tall, lean, muscular man with blond hair that hung loose to his shoulders. The hair made him look more like a surfer instead of the vice president of a software company.

Dylan watched her work the register, but noticed that all the while she kept a nervous, watchful eye on the baby. She might be jumpy, thought Dylan, but the woman was an energetic little package and then some.

As soon as the customer turned to leave, Baylee shoved the cash drawer closed and charged over to the Pack 'N Play. She leaned down and picked up Sarah, snuggling the baby into her body. Turning to Dylan, she asked sweetly, "What brings you to San Madrid? Are you lost?"

His mouth curved into a cocky grin. "I'm playing delivery boy this morning, dropping off some computer equipment for Jake. After what happened last night, the man's determined not to let Kit out of his sight for two seconds. I'm on my way over there now. But I couldn't pass through town without stopping by to check out the legendary Book & Bean, now could I? Not when I might be able to talk you out of some more of that mouth-watering chocolate cake, the kind you brought the other night to Gloria's."

If it were possible, Baylee's smile widened all the way to her cute ears where a pair of huge silver hoops dangled prominently. "So you liked my cake. The secret's in the cinnamon. I mix cinnamon in with the chocolate. Of course, I'm not as good at baking as Kit is, but let's face it, since her accident, she gave me the go-ahead to try my hand at some of her tried-and-true recipes. You know, just so the customers won't go elsewhere for their baked goods while she was on the mend.

"And after what happened last night... I offered to open up this morning. Give her some extra time to recover from her ordeal. Thank God someone came along when they did and rescued Kit from Collin and then called Jake. Collin threatened to kill her, Dylan. If that stranger hadn't come along..."

Baylee realized she was sputtering like an old car out of tune. For Pete's sake, could she just shut up for a minute? Why did she always let this man with the surfer body, the blond hair and the bedroom blue eyes make her so nervous? She needed to get a grip.

Even though her rambling only reflected how grateful she was to the unnamed man who had come along at just the right moment, she just couldn't help but marvel at the miracle of that.

She looked up and saw Dylan grin at the fact she'd finally stopped talking.

"Come on, we'll take care of that sweet tooth of yours, Mr. Burke."

As he followed her lead into the coffee shop, he tried to get his mind on something besides the woman's legs. It was the first time he'd seen her wearing a dress. And disappointed, he wasn't. In fact, if it were possible he thought she looked better than he'd ever seen her, more rested, more relaxed, not as jittery as usual. In fact she appeared downright happy.

As he looked around the shop, the place was empty, not a customer in sight. But it was spotless. The weathered oak counter was buffed to a glossy shine that matched the one on the hardwood floors. The half a dozen small round oak tables had been bussed and the chairs neatly pushed underneath.

There were four overstuffed chairs that looked like you could hunker down and get comfortable in them and stay a while to read a book. He noted the glass display case was polished to a shine, didn't have a smudge on it, and held a rather stark assortment of various baked goods, including a couple of leftover cherry tarts and four paltry cinnamon rolls. The inventory had either been picked over, or hadn't been there to begin with.

"Slow day?"

"Now it is. The media with their camera crews cleared out about thirty minutes ago. You just missed them. They ate everything Gloria and I baked last night. Gloria's guest cottage doesn't have much in the way of a kitchen, but with Kit out of action until recently and the coffee shop still needing a supply of pastry, Gloria and I have been teaming up using her kitchen to make sure there are plenty of baked goods to sell.

"But it just so happens I saved back the chocolate cake. I planned to drop it off at Kit's with the other leftovers when I closed up."

He sucked in a breath, blew it out. "Glad to hear the media got tired of waiting. Those two don't need any more hassles."

"They didn't. Get tired of waiting, that is. They took off after getting a tip about some mega superstar who tried to surf off Malibu and had to be rescued by lifeguards. The fact that he had to be rushed to the hospital topped the Jake and Kit saga. The mega star's unfortunate mishap had all of them scrambling out of here like ants after sugar, cleared the place out. Kit and Jake can't compete with that." Her lips curled in a wide grin.

"The vultures are like pond scum, aren't they? You wouldn't happen to know who called that tip in, would you?"

She grinned and gave him a wink. "Don't have a clue." She hadn't grown up in the heart of Hollywood for nothing. She knew well how the paparazzi prized a good celebrity sighting, especially when there was the chance the "star" might have suffered injuries.

"You must have been swamped here by yourself."

"For a little while it was chaos, but we're used to a line out the door. There's a rush here almost every morning. We don't officially open until seven, but Kit has the locals spoiled. The early birds commuting into Ventura and L.A. know if they drop in around six-thirty or so she'll go ahead and fix them up with coffee and fresh Danish.

"This morning I opened the doors around six-forty, had a line out the door waiting. The locals usually get here early, but this morning... the press beat them to the door. But you should have seen it here yesterday. The whole town came out to support their local girl. The media showed up to get the lowdown on Jake and Kit. But what they got instead was how much the townspeople loved and supported her. It was a kick to watch. Every time a reporter asked one of them what they thought about living with a murderer in their midst, each one of them reiterated how Kit would never hurt anyone. The support of the townspeople just blew her away."

"I was there last night after Collin and his two thugs grabbed Kit. Jake blamed himself."

"Oh, he shouldn't have. It wasn't his fault Collin and those horrible men broke in and waited for her inside the house. And they gave her some kind of drug that knocked her out. Fortunately, she doesn't remember a thing. Well, other than it was Collin who kidnapped her."

Dylan watched as she stepped behind the counter and removed the lid from a cake pedestal. With the baby sitting happily on her hip, she worked one-handed to cut him a wide slice of chocolate cake brimming with thick double fudge icing. He watched in wonder as the woman worked single-handedly, holding the baby in place.

Out of habit, she asked, "Would you like some coffee with this?"

Exasperated, he couldn't just stand there and watch her serve him like that no matter how adept at it she was. "Baylee, why don't I either hold Sarah for you or pour my own damn coffee?"

Surprised that he'd offer, she arched a brow and looked at the man thoughtfully. "Do you know what you're doing? Do you know how to handle a baby?"

He shook his head, rolled his eyes, and reached for Sarah. "Women. What's to handle? My sister has a kid about this size. First you pick them up by their legs, swing them around a couple of times..." He hooted with laughter when he saw the look of horror come into her face.

"You are so easy," he pined as he joined her behind the counter.

Baylee surrendered Sarah into his waiting arms and watched as the man seemed to know what he was doing.

By Dylan's calculation the baby weighed maybe twelve pounds, but that was probably an eighth of what her mother weighed. Small-framed, petite, and long-legged was what she was, thought Dylan as he took a seat at one of the tables. Jostling the baby up against his shoulder, he rubbed her back like he'd seen Baylee do.

He couldn't help it. He inhaled the way Sarah smelled in waves of talcum and lotion.

"She really is a cute thing, isn't she? How long has she been rolling over?"

Relishing the opportunity to talk about her daughter, Baylee all but glowed when she told him, "A couple of days now. It's like she's trying to swim, flopping her little arms around grabbing for everything."

She took out one of the over-sized cups and filled it up with a Hazelnut blend. As she brought his cake and coffee over to the table, she studied his good looks. And sighed audibly. The man had to be a heartbreaker. She might be a single mom, but she still had a healthy libido.

She'd noticed Dylan that night at the hospital even before he'd gone out of his way to find her a place to feed Sarah. What woman, even a single mother, wouldn't take notice of a blond-haired, blue-eyed, six-one Adonis who would go out of his way to do something sweet when he didn't have to?

Then he'd been just as nice to her when they'd all met up at Gloria's the night they'd gone over how Alana and Jessica must have murdered the Parkers. The man had gone out of his way yet again to make sure she was comfortable. He'd sat down next to her to ask baby questions about Sarah's development as if he'd really been interested. Of course, Baylee knew he was just being nice. A single guy like Dylan wouldn't give a hoot about a baby, or her for that matter.

But who couldn't resist the guy's charm?

Whoa there, Nellie, thought Baylee. Do NOT go there. Stoplight dead ahead.

Baylee stretched out her arms and said, "Here, I'll take her back while you eat." But just as she started to scoot into a chair and take Sarah out of Dylan's arms, she went dead still in mid-motion.

She froze in terror.

Dylan saw the color drain from her face, saw her hands drop in mid-air, saw her whole body tense as she stood erect, facing into the bookstore, body language on full alert.

Even as he tried to make some sense of her demeanor, he saw her cool blue eyes fill with stark terror. There was no other way to describe the panicked look that came into those pools of liquid blue or the look of sheer horror on her face.

The look of fear was so blatant that for an instant Dylan thought that maybe the place was about to be robbed, so he turned to follow her gaze and saw she was looking beyond the coffee shop into the bookstore. With her having the better vantage point, it occurred to Dylan she could very well be staring down the possibility of an armed thief.

But the words out of her mouth didn't match that scenario.

Without looking at Dylan, Baylee whispered so only he could hear, "Don't ask me any questions. Just do what I tell you. Get up and leave." She took a step forward as if to block both of them from view. It was an obvious protective gesture.

"Get up. Now! Take Sarah to Kit, Dylan. Leave right this minute. Go. Get out of the store and take Sarah. Don't come back in the store with her no matter what you hear or see. Understand?"

When he didn't immediately move, Baylee snapped, "Just do it, Dylan. Now!"

Dutifully, Dylan did as he was told. He got up from the table and made a hasty retreat outside through the front door of the coffee shop, clutching Sarah to his shoulder. Once he hit the sidewalk he kept walking, past the front door of the bookstore. As he ambled by the window, he glanced through the glass and saw a man dressed in a suit and tie, a man he recognized as Connor Boyd, standing to the side of the counter with an intense expression on his face.

As soon as he was sure he was out of sight, Dylan pulled his cell phone from his back pocket, pushed speed dial one-handed.

Jake and Kit needed to know Baylee was in trouble.

And they were only five minutes away.

As soon as he heard Jake pick up, Dylan didn't wait for pleasantries or pretense. "I want you to listen to me, get your ass over to the Book & Bean. Now. Don't ask questions because I don't have any answers. All I know is that Baylee is in trouble. She went ballistic the minute she saw Connor Boyd set foot in the shop. She wanted me out of sight and she insisted I take Sarah."

Sitting in her living room on the sofa, Kit noticed Jake's demeanor stiffen. Without any explanation, she watched as he began to gather his keys and head for the front door, leaving her to try to grasp the gist of the conversation. But when she heard him say, "I'm on my way. It'll take me less than five minutes," she grabbed her handbag and followed.

Without disconnecting the call, Jake continued to ask questions, pressing to get as many details as he could while Kit trailed at his heels, both of them heading out the front door to his car parked in the driveway.

"You're sure Baylee didn't want Boyd to see Sarah?"

At the mention of Baylee and the Boyd name, Kit's attitude changed from merely curious to alert. Her head snapped up as she followed Jake down the steps to the car.

Before crawling behind the wheel, his first thought was to let her stay home and not drag her into any more drama. But with one look at the stubborn set of her jaw, he realized that wasn't going to fly. Besides, the memory of what had happened to her last night at the hands of another Boyd had him pushing her through the passenger door of the car, saying, "I'm not leaving you here alone."

"Damn straight, you aren't," Kit muttered as she jumped in the front seat. All the while Jake held the cell phone pinned to his ear with his shoulder, listening to Dylan's play by play, as he backed his Mercedes out of the driveway.

Dylan paced up and down the alleyway behind the Book & Bean. "Baylee definitely did not want Boyd to see the baby. And I feel like an idiot leaving her in there alone with him. But you should have seen the look on her face, Jake. She was scared for herself, but she was terrified he might see Sarah."

Jake gunned the Benz past the harbor, through the four way stop, toward the Book & Bean, all the while relaying what was going on to Kit, who sat eagle-eyed in the passenger seat about to burst open with dread.

♧ ♧ ♧ ♧ ♧

Inside the Book & Bean, the minute Baylee saw Dylan was safely outside with Sarah, she went into slow motion stall. She had known this confrontation was inevitable from the moment Collin had stopped by the store that day looking for Kit. She'd known he'd eventually say something to his older brother about seeing her here. Her dyed-brown hair hadn't fooled him and now the man she'd feared for the past fourteen months had finally found her.

She should have run like a rabbit when she'd had the chance.

But it was too late now.

Connor hadn't yet realized she was in the coffee shop. She decided to let him come to her. She started wiping down tables that didn't need wiping. Her heart raced with a fear that up to now she'd only predicted.

She held Sarah's image in her head, determined not to let Connor Boyd get the upper hand ever again. When the man with jet black hair and eyes so dark they looked black finally made his grand entrance, an image popped into her head.

An evening more than a year ago.

To put some distance between the two of them, Baylee walked behind the counter, searching underneath for a weapon of any kind. She came up with two things. She could either hit him upside the head with a seriously heavy ceramic coffee cup, or scald him with hot coffee. The second option had more appeal. She reached for the ever-present pot of hot coffee.

Connor came up behind her, took the pot from her fist. "Did you really think you could hide from me, bitch, and that I wouldn't eventually find you? You try to run from me, and I'll find you every time. Don't you understand that?"

"Why would you want to…find me, that is? I've served your purpose once, why would you want to look my way again? In fact, Connor, why are you even here?" Play it cool, Baylee-girl, play it ice cold, she thought, as she asked, "You must be looking for Kit?"

But of course, she knew better.

Towering over her at five foot ten, Connor's coal-black eyes bored into her as he calmly set the pot back on the burner before grabbing her around the waist. "Don't lie to me. You've been running. I told you more than once to keep what happened between us—private."

He tugged hard on a strand of hair behind her ear, pulled, and leaned in to whisper, "Although, remembering how much you enjoyed it the first time, I can always arrange Round Two." When she continued to struggle, he added, "That's it, baby, I like that feisty spirit when you fight me. You enjoyed yourself as much as I did that night. I'm here to remind you, Baylee. Not for a minute do I think anyone would take your word over mine, but it won't hurt if I tell you again what will happen to you and your friends if you don't keep our little secret—between friends."

"Friends?" Baylee struggled again to loosen his grip. "We are not now nor have we ever been friends. And I haven't been running. I simply went…out of town…to visit a relative. Then my father got sick and I came back to L.A. That's all there is to it. Once again, your ego is getting in the way of reality. I told you I didn't want anyone finding out—about what happened. I've kept it…to myself just as we agreed. I have no plans to tell anyone. Ever."

Connor pushed her back against the counter. One hand wrapped around her throat. "Don't think you can fuck with me on this, Baylee. There's no running from me. I'll track you, wherever you go. Is that understood? You tell anyone, you know what I'll do, what I'm capable of…"

Dylan, carrying Sarah, continued his pacing up and down in the alleyway around the corner from the bookstore. And felt like a heel for leaving Baylee in there. Every so often he peeked around the building. Still on the phone with Jake, he bellowed, "I'm standing out here like an idiot while she's in there alone dealing with Mr. Asshole. Why aren't you here yet?"

"We're just pulling in now."

Once again, Dylan stuck his head around the corner of the building and saw the car pull into the slotted street parking in front of the Book & Bean and park beside a huge black Hummer. As soon as the car came to a stop, though, he watched as Kit bolted from the vehicle on the run before Jake even had a chance to put the gear into Park.

The first thing Kit saw when she tore open the front door of the coffee shop was that Connor was behind the counter with Baylee pressed up against it, his body blocking any chance she had to move.

But the minute Connor heard the bell jingle over the door he instantly released Baylee, and took a step backward in retreat. Out of what seemed to be a nervous habit, he adjusted his tie. Baylee took the opportunity to step away from him and move toward Kit and the front door.

Baylee's eyes met Kit's.

A lifetime of being best friends, of knowing each other's moves and nuances had Kit looking for facial gestures, an expression in the eyes as they stared at each other from twelve feet apart in complete agreement.

Placate him, Kit. Just get Connor the hell out of the store the quickest way possible.

"Were you looking for me, Connor?" Kit squeaked out, trying to keep her voice level.

Connor morphed from enraged bully to puppy in the blink of an eye. "Of course. Baylee here was just telling me about your harrowing ordeal last night when Auslo and Taft kidnapped you—weren't you, Baylee? Obviously, I heard what happened firsthand from Collin. The news junkies got it wrong, but then that's nothing new." He adjusted his tie again, never taking his eyes off Baylee. Then as if coming out of a daze, his eyes slowly left Baylee to hone in on Jake as if he'd just realized he was outnumbered.

By the time his eyes finally drifted to Kit, he adjusted his tie again and transitioned once more into concerned lifelong pal. "I wanted to stop by, talk to you about that terrible misunderstanding you had with Collin. I shouldn't have to tell you that he feels just awful about what happened. You know he'd never hurt you on purpose, Kit. It's absurd to think otherwise. You should be grateful he overpowered Auslo and Taft and called Boston here to come get you."

Kit's eyes widened at hearing him repeat the same bullshit story Collin had told the police last night. Wanting very much to call him on the lie, she breathed in and out, never letting her eyes give anything away.

"We're all just glad you weren't killed. I drove up here to personally see that you were all right. There's been so much death lately, don't you think? We need to put this behind us. Be the kind of friends to each other we used to be. This misunderstanding should bring us closer together not farther apart. We've both lost our parents, Kit; we're both dealing with a great deal of loss lately. Obviously, we have a nutcase out there who's exterminating our families."

What a crock, Jake thought as he positioned himself between the man and Kit. He wasn't sure what to expect as he watched Connor move from behind the counter toward them, toward the front door of the coffee shop. Jake took hold of Baylee's arm, nudged both her and Kit further behind him, shifting their positions so that he stood planted like a steel rod facing Connor down. The men eyed each other with all the primal instincts of two coiled vipers sizing each other up, waiting to strike.

But Connor continued moving and talking as he made his way past Jake toward the front door of the coffee shop. "I'm glad to see you're on the mend, Kit. I wanted to check and see for myself just how you were getting along. I can't have someone trying to kill my surrogate little sister, now can I?"

What a performance, Kit wanted to say, as she simply picked up the game in progress. "What was it you wanted, Connor?"

"I can't emphasize how important it is for you to sign those papers and get them back to me without interrupting Alana's real estate business. Remember, I am the attorney of record in your mother's probate proceedings." He adjusted his tie yet again.

After what he'd been about to do to Baylee, Kit wanted to slap Connor upside the head and tell the man what he could do with his papers, instead she went with cool. "I certainly wouldn't want to disrupt Alana's business. But if you aren't already aware, Connor, let me just say, I'm the number one suspect in Alana's murder." That wasn't entirely true, at least not since last night when Holloway, one of the detectives working on Alana's murder, had stopped by the hospital and finally, officially, cleared Kit. But Connor didn't need to know that now. "I don't think the police will let me run her business from a jail cell."

Some forced, unexplained emotion flickered across Connor's face. "If you need a defense lawyer, Kit, don't hesitate to let us know. Boyd Boyd Geller & Gatz provides the best legal defense money can buy. You remember that." His eyes narrowed. "No one messes with a Boyd, a Geller, or a Gatz. Surely, you recall that from our childhood. You let me know, though, if you need our services. I'll be heading out now."

He looked directly at Baylee when he said, "You take care."

His message crystal clear and delivered with force, the reason for his coming here finished, Connor walked through the door and out to his Humvee.

The trio watched, holding their collective breath, as he backed the vehicle out of the slotted space and into the street. When the Hummer screeched away, Baylee practically dropped to the floor until Jake reached out and steadied her. She latched on to his arm, but then turned to Kit, all but plunging into her body, wrapping her arms around her friend.

Kit puffed air into her cheeks, blew it out before telling her, "That was a close one. You want to tell me what that was all about, Baylee-girl? And don't even think about making something up. That man had you cornered…"

But Baylee, in full-out mommy-mode, paid no attention. "Sarah, where's Sarah? If you'll just give me five minutes I'll explain everything. Right now, I need to see Sarah, make sure she's okay."

Jake, who had never turned off his cell phone, held it back up to his ear and told Dylan, "Did you get all that? The coast is clear. You can head back in now."

Dylan stepped through the back door from the alleyway bouncing Sarah in his arms before Jake could disconnect. Baylee, still shaking from the experience, took off like a shot and met him halfway there. Cradling Sarah in her arms, she snuggled the baby tightly to her chest, and then drifted to the back of the store where she could be alone with her for a few minutes.

Baylee knew she had to face all of them, but she needed to hold Sarah for a moment, get her head on straight before coming clean.

Dylan traded curious looks with Jake, who in turn shot one of the same in Kit's direction.

"Hopefully, when she comes back, we'll get her to open up." Kit said as she shrugged her shoulders and headed toward the counter. After making up a tray with cups of fresh coffee, a basket of cinnamon buns, and plates, she brought it over to the table where Jake and Dylan were huddled in conference.

For an instant, when Jake's eyes met Kit's it seemed as if they were the only two people in the room. But then the reality of the situation took over and when Kit took her seat, she put her hand on top of Dylan's. "I'm not sure why you were here, but I'm grateful you were. Thank you, Dylan."

"I didn't do a damn thing but take the baby outside, and leave Baylee in the store by herself. I stood out there for what seemed like an hour and a half before you guys showed up not knowing what the hell was going on in here. What if...he'd done something to her while I was playing babysitter in the alley?" He was still unnerved at the idea of Connor Boyd being alone in the store with Baylee. She'd been terrified. And he hadn't done a thing to help.

"No what ifs, Dylan. You were here to take Sarah outside. I have a feeling right now, that's what mattered the most. I have my suspicions and if I'm right, the last year is starting to make sense."

CHAPTER 2

"And what exactly are your suspicions, Kit?" Baylee asked, nervously standing in the doorway between the coffee shop and the bookstore, wringing her hands with a disgusted look on her face.

"Okay." Kit stood up, walked to where Baylee was, and folded her arms over her chest. It was time Baylee enlightened them all with the truth. "I think you and Connor must have gotten together some time last spring. I think he's Sarah's father." Just saying the words scraped Kit's throat raw. "And he doesn't know Sarah's his."

"Got together?" Baylee sneered. "I guess you could call it that, although that's a stretch."

The inference went over Kit's head. She went ballistic at the notion Baylee had been holding back an affair with Connor for more than a year. "How could you, Baylee? You know what all three of them are like. You were right there with me when we tried to persuade Quinn to stay away from Cade. She didn't listen and look what happened. At one time, Quinn thought Cade was different, too. But she soon found out they're all exactly alike, evil through and through. What were you thinking?"

The minute Baylee broke down, started sobbing, Kit's anger fled. She went to her friend and threw her arms around her. "I'm sorry, Baylee. I didn't mean to yell."

But when Kit led her over to the table to sit down, Baylee shook her head. If she was going to have to tell them, she needed to pace, needed room to move around. She locked her arms around her chest trying not to look at Dylan and Jake.

"Let me just get this out once and for all." She sniffled. "Remember a year ago in March, when I went to that charity fundraising event at the civic center in Malibu hoping I'd run into Elaine Fairchild, convince her I finally had enough jewelry pieces for a show?"

Kit nodded, knowing how much work Baylee had put into her jewelry design business. At one point it had been her passion. Designing jewelry had been for Baylee what medicine had been to Quinn. But after Baylee had disappeared for seven months last year, Kit had wondered why she'd given it up. It was as if Baylee's heart was no longer in it. She'd been back in town since Christmas and hadn't once brought up her dreams of designing her own line of jewelry one day. Of course, she'd been a new mother with a dying father. Kit had just assumed Baylee no longer had time for a demanding business.

But Baylee wasn't really looking at Kit now or anyone else in the room for that matter. She was locked in a world of her own. "I ran into Connor at the reception. For a while over canapés we made polite conversation about the people we knew, people we had in common, mostly reminisced about childhood, you know, about the times I'd visited the Enclave with you for birthday parties and such when we were kids, about school functions even though there's a huge age difference between us.

"We talked about how brilliant Quinn was for finishing up med school so quickly. Just small talk really, this and that, polite party conversation. He offered to get me some champagne, I said sure. When he brought it back I took a few sips of the drink and immediately started feeling sick to my stomach. I decided I needed to leave, get out of there, get some fresh air.

"Connor offered to walk me to my car. I was feeling so sick I let him. I remember getting to the car. And that's it. I don't remember anything afterward. The next morning I woke up in a hotel room in Malibu. Alone. Connor was nowhere around. He called me later that day to tell me what a great time we'd had."

"That son of a bitch." At the sound of Dylan's comment, Baylee's voice broke.

She took a deep breath just to force the words out. "About six weeks later I found out I was pregnant. I was scared, Kit."

"Of course you were scared, anyone would have been. But you could have told me, come to me with the truth. We could have gone to the police, Baylee. That bastard needs to be in jail."

Baylee shook her head. "You said it yourself about Collin. When you have enough money to buy a third world country, you aren't going to do jail time—for anything. Look at what Collin did to you last night, kidnapped you right out of your own house. Is he sitting in jail this morning for kidnapping? No, he's not. His family's already bailed him out. He's back at the Enclave, probably lounging at the beach, working on his tan. My guess is Collin won't spend a day in jail for what he did to you."

She spared a glance at Jake who'd gone a little white at the reality of that.

"And what would I have told the police about that night, Kit? What details would I have shared with them? That I left a party on my own woke up the next morning in a strange hotel room, not able to remember anything about what had happened. Connor was right, who would have believed me? It was my word against his.

"It's true; I knew what they were like. I'd seen how violent Collin was with you a year earlier. I knew Cade's history with Quinn. But the only thing I did wrong was trust Connor to bring me that stupid drink. There was something in that drink, Kit. I'm convinced of it. When I thought about it later, the champagne tasted too salty, too bitter. He'd spiked it with something."

"I'm sure he did. He probably used that date rape drug, what's it called… "

But it was a furious Dylan who spoke up. "Probably Rohypnol, also used to enhance the effects of cocaine, or maybe GHB. Gamma Hydroxybutyric, commonly known as liquid ecstasy. In a safe dosage both have minimal effects. But if you bump up the dosage of either one, add alcohol to the mix, either drug can induce a deep sleep and it's difficult to remember anything. In extreme cases a person might not even wake up at all. You're lucky you did, Baylee."

Hearing that only made Kit's blood boil more. But for Baylee's sake she tabled her anger and concentrated on her friend. "You had no way of knowing he'd do that to you, Baylee. Stop blaming yourself. I'm so sorry I jumped to the wrong conclusion. I should have known better."

"But the point is I wasn't thinking straight, Kit. I got out of that room and couldn't get back home fast enough. During those six weeks, I had myself tested for STDs half a dozen times before I found out I was pregnant. I didn't go to the police, didn't say anything to anyone, and kept what happened to myself."

Wringing her hands, pacing back and forth, Baylee went on, "He kept calling me for a month after it happened just to threaten me, remind me not to say anything. He doesn't know about Sarah. On her birth certificate I listed her father as unknown."

Baylee's eyes darted to the men, shame filled her. But she couldn't deal with that now. There were other more important aspects to point out now. "And that was before I ever knew anything about what Alana did to Gloria, her own sister, before I knew what part Jessica played in taking you away from your birth mother. I've been scared to death ever since I found out what they did to Gloria."

"Oh Baylee. I'm so sorry. What a burden this must have been for you to carry around all this time. No wonder you left L.A. Where did you go, anyway? Quinn and I were worried sick about you."

Shaken, Baylee closed her eyes. "Do you remember Blair Rafferty from college? She lives in Denver now. We still keep in touch." Her shoulders slumped.

"I didn't know where else to go. The only reason I came back at all was because Dad got sick." She looked Kit directly in the eye, shook her head, and said sadly, "If it hadn't been for that, I wouldn't have come back at all. When Tanya called me about Dad, told me about the brain tumor, I felt guilty that I wasn't here for him. Like an idiot, I thought enough time had passed and Connor wouldn't give me a second thought.

"But that day Collin stopped by, that day he was looking for you, Collin must have said something to Connor. I should have left then. I've been so terrified he'd find out about Sarah, want visitation rights or custody. The fear's only gotten worse knowing what Jessica did to take you away from Gloria all those years ago."

"Jessica's dead. She won't be taking another baby away from its mother." There was some satisfaction in that Kit thought gamely.

"I'm not worried about. But she taught those sons of hers every trick she knew. And with all that talk the other night at Gloria's about how they have a habit of producing false documentation in court, I'm scared Connor might do something devious like that to get Sarah. I won't let him near her. Ever. You all need to understand that right now."

Her voice grew sharper laced with steely determination when she emphasized, "He can't find out about Sarah. I don't want that man around Sarah, not for any reason. I can't share custody. I won't. It's that simple. I can't handle that."

She finally looked at each one of them, her blue eyes piercing, making sure each of them understood. "I'll do anything. I'll live in Alaska; I'll live in Mexico; I'll go to the ends of the earth before I'll let Connor Boyd anywhere near my daughter. He may be her sperm donor, but that's all he is. He isn't father material. He's violent and he's mean. I don't want that for Sarah. I grew up with an alcoholic, a verbally abusive man, a man who refused to let go of the past. I won't allow Sarah to grow up like that in an explosive, volatile environment. Ever."

Tears welled up in Kit's eyes as she took both of Baylee's hands in hers. "Baylee, I promise you I'll take you to the ends of the earth myself before I let that bastard get anywhere near Sarah. I'm sorry I talked you into staying in L.A. I should have let you leave. But I didn't know the circumstances then. If you'd just told me what was going on, I would have driven you out of town myself."

Hearing that, Baylee broke down again.

Jake and Dylan exchanged looks across the table. Dylan wasn't sure what Jake was thinking or feeling, but he knew he felt like hitting something. He wouldn't mind landing a couple of blows on that smug bastard's face. After two seconds contemplating Connor's demise, he pulled himself together enough to ask, "So he doesn't suspect a thing about Sarah, right Baylee?"

Baylee dried her cheeks with her fingertips, shook her head. "No. That's why I wanted you to take Sarah out of here, take her to Kit. But I don't know how much longer I can keep her a secret. If he finds out…I'm afraid he'll fight me for custody or something. Sharing custody of my daughter with a rapist is not an option."

"But as long as he thinks he's gotten away with it, as long as we keep Sarah's existence unknown to him, you're okay, she's okay. Right? You don't have to make a mass exodus out of town."

Jake turned to Dylan. "What are you thinking?"

"Well, it's like this. If Baylee needs to disappear with Sarah for a while, make it look like maybe she's living with someone else, Boyd wouldn't have a reason to come looking for her in my direction. He doesn't even know I exist. He may be able to track credit card receipts, a money trail if she's on the run in some other city, but he can't track what doesn't exist. If she lays low at my place, until the son of a bitch gets tired of looking for her, or maybe like I said just thinks he's gotten away with it, he'll go on with his life and leave her alone."

"I couldn't move in with you. I couldn't ask you to do that. Sarah's a great baby, but she's teething, and she cries, and she isn't sleeping through the night yet. Besides, I've just settled into Gloria's little cottage. I can't keep moving around once a month. Oh God, I just said I'd do anything, didn't I, to keep Connor from finding out about her? I need to sit down."

With that Baylee dropped into the nearest chair.

Kit grabbed Baylee's hand. "No, listen to him, Baylee; it isn't such a bad idea. You're planning on leaving anyway, right? So, why not hide out locally? We'll see to it that there isn't any money trail he can follow, no credit card receipts to track. Keep your Range Rover parked at Gloria's guest house as if you're still there. If he comes looking for you there, Gloria can stall him, let us know he's looking. And if he comes back here, he won't find you. This time we're the ones who'll be keeping tabs on him."

Kit turned to Jake. "What about that private investigator, Jordan Donovan, you hired to look into Alana's murder? Since I'm no longer the main suspect, he could keep tabs on Connor. This is more important."

"Hell, if that's what it takes to keep the two of you safe I'll hire a whole team of investigators to keep an eye on all three of those bastards."

But Dylan wanted Baylee back on track. "Look, worst-case scenario, he finds you at my place. He sees Sarah. It'll look like you're living with me, that we're together. I could claim to be Sarah's father then. To prove otherwise, he'll have to get a court order for DNA. That will take some time. Even if he were to use the Boyd influence with a judge, it still takes time to get the results. Being with me will buy us some time, Baylee, until we figure something else out. By that time, if we have to, we'll smuggle you and Sarah out of the country."

Baylee sniffed. "But I can't keep hiding. He'll find me again and again. He said so. He won't give up. And why would you do something like that, Dylan? You don't even know me."

"Because I don't want the bastard getting his hands on Sarah any more than you do." Dylan wasn't even thinking about what he was offering. His heart seemed to be leading his mouth down a perilous road. But the idea of Connor getting anywhere near that baby or near Baylee made him sick to his stomach. It was plain as day for anyone to see the man was a ticking time bomb. Plus, he had cold, violent eyes.

"Is this what my life will be like from now on, looking over my shoulder until he…until he finds out about Sarah? And then what? What happens then? Hiding out at Dylan's isn't the answer. I should leave town, maybe head to Europe."

But Dylan wasn't convinced. "And what makes you think he wouldn't find you wherever you go Baylee, with no friends around for support? You'd be alone in a foreign country and he might track you down anyway. Think about it, it isn't so much about hiding as it is about giving him the impression, the illusion that you're with someone else, someone that could just as easily be Sarah's father."

He stopped long enough to get up and pace. "The bogus idea works if he sees you with me. We give him the impression we're a couple with a kid. If we pull it off, we give him no reason to suspect Sarah is his, but rather mine. Think about it. He'd be less inclined to go digging around if he thinks the baby belongs to someone else. That someone might as well be me."

Kit put her arms around Baylee. "Think about it Baylee, you can't keep running every few months with a baby. This way, you won't have to leave town and you'll be around the people who love you. Dylan's right. You won't really be hiding out, more like hanging out at

Dylan's place for a while. And you can't work at the Book & Bean now that he knows you're here."

"But I want to work. I have to. I'll go crazy sitting around worrying."

"Then Jake and I will figure something out, work on a way to get you and Sarah safely back and forth from Dylan's every day. But until we do, you're on vacation."

Jake got to his feet, slapped his friend on the back. "That's not a bad plan, Dyl. Way to go."

Dylan blew out a heavy sigh. "Yeah, the look on Baylee's face tells me the plan is sheer genius. It would appear that we'd be living together, Baylee, but we wouldn't. Understand? You and Sarah would have your own rooms, your own space. It's a temporary fix. For now it gets you out of Gloria's guest house—a place he knows about—and into a place he doesn't know exists. I've got the space. We can move you in tonight."

࿋ ࿋ ࿋ ࿋ ࿋

Dylan's Pacific Palisades beach bungalow had been built decades earlier, but the upgrades he'd put into it just a couple of years ago, like new cabinets and modern appliances in the kitchen and new plumbing in both bathrooms, made a huge difference in the comfort of the mid-century house.

The place wasn't overly big, but then a single guy with a demanding job didn't need much room when he spent most of his downtime at the beach, swimming, surfing or playing volleyball. He liked his little house that backed up against the Pacific Ocean, where he could play on the surf on the weekends if he wanted, roller blade with the neighborhood kids, or just walk out his back door in the evening to watch the sunset or the waves on the water.

He had a fifteen-mile commute through the canyons to work in Westlake Village, a commute that sometimes might take as long as forty-five minutes to an hour depending on the traffic, which he utilized well enough by listening to his favorite CDs. On the days the trip grew wearisome, he'd remind himself how much he loved waking up to the sound of the surf, and somehow the amount of time he had to spend in the car didn't seem so bad.

As he wandered from the kitchen to the living room, making sure the doors were locked, something that was definitely out of the ordinary for him to do, Dylan considered how much his life had changed in the span of a few hours.

She was here in his house, a mother with a baby.

He couldn't help wondering what in the world had made him offer Baylee a place to stay. He was a nice enough guy, a man his friends could count on when the going got tough, but he wasn't stupid. He'd known how much work a baby could be from his sister's kid, who was just about ready to turn the big one. Even though the little guy was a real cutie, the baby took a lot of effort and commitment.

What in the world had he been thinking?

But then, one look at Baylee's face, one look into those aqua eyes, had answered that question in a heartbeat. He was starting to wonder what was wrong with him. He hadn't gone all in over a woman since Sherry Ann Connelly in his freshman year of high school. And that probably had more to do with pheromones and the fact that he'd just discovered firsthand what caused Sherry Ann's cheerleader uniform to poke out so nicely, rather than the depth of his fourteen-year-old infatuation.

But Baylee had him feeling—different. It had been that way from the first moment he'd laid eyes on her standing in that hospital waiting room, surrounded by at least fifty other people crowded in around them. Throw in the fact that she'd been standing there holding a baby, a fact that hadn't deterred him in the least, and he knew for certain this was unlike the way he'd felt about anyone else.

Right now, she slept right down the hallway, steps away from where he stood.

Earlier that evening, he and Jake had gone back to Gloria's guest cottage, parked her Range Rover in the driveway, and switched the car seat to Jake's boxy G500 Benz, before loading both of their belongings inside.

For a woman who had been raised in Beverly Hills, the daughter of William Scott, one of the most successful action-film directors in Hollywood, Baylee didn't seem to have all that much stuff. Her clothes had barely taken up half a small closet. This was a fact Dylan had a hard time understanding. He was hardly an expert on women, but the one thing he knew for sure was that most women collected clothes and shoes and accessories, those little baubles that rounded out the outfit, like prized art. At least the women he'd known did, and that included his mother and sister.

But what Baylee lacked in material possessions for herself, the baby made up for twofold. Sarah seemed to have every baby gadget available on the market, everything from an infant carrier, a state-of-the-art car seat, a swing that played music, a fancy stroller, a high chair, right down to a very classy, cherry wood baby bed, which had taken him almost a damn hour to put together. And if it hadn't been for Jake's help, he would have had a bitch of a time trying to install the high-tech car seat into the backseat of his vehicle.

But despite having second thoughts for the better part of the evening, the move had gone fairly smoothly. Sarah was fast asleep.

All seemed quiet on the western front.

As he turned out the living room light and headed to bed, he passed by the hall bathroom. And came to an abrupt stop.

He backed up a few steps when he thought he heard soft weeping coming from inside. He waited several long minutes listening at the door to see if she settled down. When it didn't seem like that was going to happen any time soon, he knocked lightly on the wood. "You okay in there?" He heard a low moan, and then serious sniffing, before he heard Baylee blowing her nose. Then silence. Then the crying started up again.

"Baylee, can I come in?"

He heard her groan again and the crying grew even louder.

He cracked open the door an inch, just in case she wasn't decent. But she was wearing a low-rise pair of purple flannel pajamas with a black-and-white dog pattern design that looked a lot like mini Snoopy characters. He got an eyeful of skin and belly button as the wild-eyed woman sat on the lid of the toilet, clutching a very thin roll of toilet paper in her hand as if the cardboard cylinder were her only lifeline. A pile of used, wadded up tissue several inches deep covered her feet.

Step carefully into this quagmire, Dylan thought, as he made a tentative move further inside the small space. "What's wrong, Baylee?"

She blew her nose again. "I...I...I'm such a ter-rible mo-ther."

That was the last thing he expected her to say. Dylan took a cautious step further into the room, went over, and sat down on the ledge of the bathtub, letting his hands drape from his knees.

"Now why would you say something like that?"

"You. Don't. Know. Me."

"You're right, I don't. But from what I've seen I think you're a good mom."

"Oh no. No, I...I'm absolutely hor-rible." She sobbed louder.

He hadn't considered when he'd offered her a place to stay that he'd be sharing his house with a hysterical female. But he needed to say or do something now; he just wasn't sure what. He scratched the side of his face, thinking. Finally, he decided on the direct approach. "Okay, tell me why you're so horrible."

"Since Sarah...was born, since she got here, I...I...I've moved...a lot. I can't seem to stop moving."

"That doesn't sound so horrible to me."

"You don't under-stand. I...I've moved fi...fi...five times. She's only fi...fi...five months old. She's had fi...fi...five different places to sleep. That's...just...unacceptable."

"Baylee..."

"No, it's true. We started out in Denver, and then we came back to L.A. and stayed with K...K...Kit for a while...and then...I moved in with my Da...Dad and Tanya...and...then we moved into Glo-ria's little house...and now...we're...we're living here with you. That's fi...fi...five moves." She held up five fingers on one trembling hand. "I...I feel like such a trans..." She sniffled. "Like such a trans..."

She hiccupped before she sniffled again.

"Transvestite?" Dylan teased.

"Tran-sient." She surveyed the heap of tissues hiding her feet. With her shoulders slumped, she kept her head bowed, staring at the mess on the tile floor.

"Baylee, you've had a lot going on in the last six months, more like a year, more than most new mothers. Stop beating yourself up for trying to keep Boyd from knowing Sarah exists. Your moves were necessary."

"Oh, Dylan, it isn't just that. When I found out I was pregnant I left L.A. I gave up my apartment. So when I came back, I didn't have a place to stay and I moved in with my father and that was a terrible mistake and I've been moving around just like a trans..."

"Transvestite," Dylan grinned.

"Noooo. I...I...I can't keep moving around so much. Don't you see, I'm such a bad...mo-ther."

"Hey, stop that. Hush now." He moved closer to her just to see if she'd let him. He knew she was upset when she didn't inch back the way she usually did. He put a hand under her chin and brought her head up to make her look at him. Her red nose looked like Rudolph's. Her crystal blue eyes were red-rimmed. Her face was flushed. But to him she still looked beautiful.

"You're a great mother. Fantastic even. These last five months with Sarah, you've been carrying around the weight of the world on your shoulders. I think it's time you cut yourself some slack."

"I'm…so…scared. What if Connor…"

"Well, don't be. If Connor comes looking for you here, he'll see a man and a woman living together with a baby and move on with his nice tidy life." At least Dylan hoped that's what would happen. He took the almost-empty roll of toilet paper from her and twirled off the last of several sheets. "Now dry those eyes."

She sniffled. "I'm a mess."

"You are. But you're such a beautiful one," he agreed lightly.

Through bleary eyes, she looked up. His blue eyes speared hers. A fleck of need kindled. But only for a second until Baylee's dimmer switch clicked on. It wasn't hard to picture this man with his surfer good looks keeping a bevy of women dangling on his own personal string.

"Won't the fact that we're staying here put a major crimp in your social life?"

"Yeah, but I'll live. Maybe I'll take Sarah out in that stroller thing, walk her around the neighborhood, show her off, cruise around the beach some, pick me up a couple of new women. That baby's probably a real chick magnet."

Baylee's mouth fell open. She looked appalled.

Dylan laughed. "God, woman, you are so easy."

But Baylee's sense of humor was a bit out of whack. She still had that solemn look on her face when she offered, "I'll help with the cooking and cleaning…and…"

"Baylee, I don't expect you to be my damn housekeeper."

"But I want to carry my weight around here, Dylan. Kit says I can't even go back to the Book & Bean. I have to do something."

He grinned and tried to lighten the mood. "Baylee, are you nervous because we're attracted to each other?" He saw her swallow…tremble a little at the idea. Always a good sign.

"Not nervous. Surprised maybe?" Baylee answered.

"Surprised. Why?"

"Why would you be attracted to me of all people? Right now, I'm in this mess. It's not my best moment." She laughed. "Not only that, but I don't feel very attractive. Look at me."

"I have." His tone turned serious when he realized she wasn't playing a game with him or fishing for a compliment. It was time to level with each other. He tucked a strand of her hair behind one ear and went from the gut. "Well, for starters, you're beautiful."

Dylan thought she was beautiful, what a concept. "But I have a baby. I thought you single guys avoided all women with kids like we were some kind of combined pestilence better left alone."

He laughed. "I admit I've given some thought to that. Sarah definitely changes things."

"And?"

"And I think it's doable. We're doable."

"Are you serious?"

"I admit it's awkward, you living here now. But we can take it slow. Get to know each other first. That's the part I haven't done…for quite some time, maybe never. Usually…"

Baylee nodded in understanding. "Usually, it's hop in the sack first. I get it. But I can't do that with Sarah. I have to be careful."

"I know. This is definitely not the norm."

She sniffled. "I'll say. Thanks for letting us stay here, Dylan."

"No problem."

"I'm sorry I'm such a mess." She blew her nose again on a soggy piece of tissue that came apart in her hand. "It's embarrassing."

"You've had a rough day."

"Thanks for pretending to be Sarah's father." She sniffled again. "You're a nice person."

"Yeah. I'm a saint."

"Well, I wouldn't go that far." She smiled weakly.

He smiled too and picked up one of her hands, stood up. "Now, what do you say I walk you to your door? You'll feel better about things after you've had a good night's sleep."

Baylee stood up. "Dylan?"

He angled his head and looked down at her. At six-one he was a good eight inches taller, toned and athletic, but the woman looking up at him was just as fit, just as toned. Probably from hauling around Sarah in that infant seat thing, he thought, as he waited for her to go on.

"Tanya called. She's my… she's the woman who raised me." She was actually the closest thing to a mother Baylee had, but Dylan didn't need to know that. "She takes good care of Dad. Apparently, he isn't doing too well. I need to go…see him."

He noted the guilty look on her face. He remembered what she'd said at the Book & Bean about her alcoholic father being verbally abusive. Never known as reticent, he wanted to know more. "Talk to me, Baylee."

She bit her lip. "I have some issues with my father." That was an understatement, but at least it was an honest first step. What would Dylan think when he actually met the man? "He's difficult."

"You want to tell me about it?" He couldn't imagine what it was like for her to grow up with an abusive father.

She shook her head. "Maybe some other time."

"Okay, no problem. Just let me know when you're ready to see him." The visit would be their first foray into this fictional scene they'd created. And he would see what the legendary William Scott was like for himself.

"Look, Dylan, I know you have a job, work to do. I can go over there by myself."

He let out a weary sigh. "We've been all over this. For this to work, we need to make sure people see us together, see us as a couple, that is until we're comfortable being one. And Jake is onboard with this.

"I'll work from the house and do whatever it takes, for however long. Until Jordan Donovan puts a team together that will keep an eye on the Boyd brothers, the job falls to Jake and me to keep an eye on the two of you. So forget it, Baylee, we stick together…like superglue. Your Range Rover's back at Gloria's. If you need to go anywhere, any place at all, we go together. And stop acting like you're a visitor here, like you're intruding."

She'd been doing it all evening, asking if she could use this or use that, hesitant about settling in.

"I want you to feel at home here, be comfortable with the situation, and be comfortable with me. I know you're bummed about not going back to the Book & Bean, but if you're working at the store, you're more vulnerable now that he knows you're there. Next time he could zero in on the baby. If it means that much I suppose you could work at the store without taking Sarah with you, and leave her with a sitter. Is that what you want?"

"I was upset at first. But after I thought it through, I understand. It's better this way until things calm down." She wiped her nose. "You have a lovely home here, Dylan. I can't help it if I feel like I'm intruding." She was intruding. Then she looked up into his blue eyes. Even though he towered over her, she felt no fear, not like she had with Connor.

She was so petite, thought Dylan, and so close. He tipped her chin up slightly just before he stepped into her body and brought her up against his chest. Touching his mouth to hers, lip to lip, the kiss started slow, gentle. In an instant it began to build hotter. A tender touch of lips became open-mouthed tongues bursting with flare and heat. Baylee angled her head for better access, allowing Dylan to taste and sample while she began to climb.

Her body was on fire. She felt slick and warm, heated from head to toe. She had no idea why the small space was suddenly so hot. She was burning up. And she wasn't the only one; she could feel Dylan's body vibrating with the in and out, the give and take of the kiss.

And what a kiss.

They came up for air.

Immediately missing the contact, Baylee muttered, "That was…" Incredible, she thought.

He continued to hold her as her body clung to his. He finished her thought in a hoarse whisper.

"Hot. Somehow I knew it would be like that."

"You did?"

"Yeah."

"You don't sound too thrilled."

"We just agreed to take it slow. And yeah, thrilled, I'm not. But I'll live."

CHAPTER 3

Since watching the sun sink into the water, Connor had downed an entire bottle of Rey Sol Anejo along with snorting several lines of coke. Outside on the terrace of his Malibu beach house, he'd been sitting alone for hours casting an occasional glance out to sea into the black night trying to feel—something, anything at all.

The tequila hadn't helped, nor had the drug. They never did, at least not the way they once had. The only emotions he mustered these days began and ended with blind rage. Today had been no different. He thought about Baylee, tried to conjure up a sense of caring. Instead, anger bubbled up. Lately, he couldn't seem to control it like the old days. Rage, anger, there was no mellow. He wanted to hit something, preferably that little bitch Baylee.

The image of them that night at the hotel blurred with so many images of other women. Baylee should have felt glad to be included in his own personal private club of sorts. She should be grateful he had kept himself under control in that backwater little coffee shop today. She'd been lucky. If Kit and Boston hadn't come in when they did he might have had to teach her another lesson... The Connor Boyd life lesson.

When he heard footsteps behind him, he glanced up to see his uncle, Frank Geller, walking toward him. He turned, catching the smug look on the man's face. It pissed him off. Connor took a deliberate puff on his Cuban cigar and bellowed, "It's about goddamned time you showed up."

He'd been expecting Frank two weeks ago. But then he'd been conveniently out of touch on yet another honeymoon, somewhere on the Riviera with his fifth wife, a busty blond tart half his age.

Connor intended to give Frank as much grief as he could for it. "Just now getting back into town, Frank? Took your sweet goddamned time about it, didn't you? We buried the only two sisters you'll ever have last week along with my father, your business partner, you dumb fuck. We couldn't very well put off having three funerals long enough for you to decide to show back up again, now could we? Three goddamned funerals in two weeks. Why the hell didn't you answer your cell phone?"

In his late sixties with the dark brooding eyes that ran on the Geller side of the family, Frank did his best to look sheepish. The nervousness was real though. Knowing full well he didn't like to tangle with his volatile nephews, especially this one, he'd taken his sweet time finding a flight back to L.A. after receiving the news about the murders.

One didn't rush back into a cesspool when you were enjoying all manner of perversions, the best money could buy, in an exotic foreign land. That would have been incredibly foolish. And Frank Geller was many things, but foolish wasn't one of them.

It was no skin off his nose if someone had finally taken matters into their own hands and dealt with a few vendettas from the past. Settling a few scores was to be expected. No one knew the risks of doing business like they had over the past forty years better than his own two sisters, Jessica and Eva. And certainly Sumner Boyd had made his own enemies throughout the years.

Even in the dark, staring into the soulless eyes of his nephew, Frank wasn't about to be so bold and forthright to share those feelings now. That would only feed deeper into

Connor's instability. Frank snaked an unsteady hand through his dyed-too-many-times slick black hair and merely stuck his hands in his pockets, tried to look chagrin.

"We were staying at an exclusive resort. When we booked our accommodations, cell phone service wasn't exactly our primary concern at the time, if you know what I mean. How was I supposed to know some nutcase would be back here in L.A. exterminating my family?"

"Yeah, well, if I were you I'd crack open my wallet and hire a personal bodyguard, one that isn't too smart and is willing to take a bullet for you because this nutcase isn't just brilliant at what he does—he's seriously pissed.

"Because Frank, my friend, of the four original partners you're the only one left standing. Do you have any ideas what the hell is going on here? Other than the fact he's discovered that our little family law firm started its roots and all with a double murder."

Frank tried the deep-in-thought look and scratched his chin. But he didn't dare talk back to this one. He knew better.

"I understand Alana's murder triggered this whole thing. Why would anyone wait so long for revenge though? Did you consider that? Forty years is a long damned time. I can't imagine who could have found out. And Cade tells me Auslo and Taft couldn't locate the incriminating piece of evidence."

Connor's eyes flashed.

Even though Connor was seated, Frank took a step back.

"You aren't in court, Frank. It's just the two of us here. You don't have to tippy-toe around the word. They couldn't find the gun, the .357. They tore up Alana's house, Kit's, Gloria's, even searched Boston's software company. Didn't find a goddamned thing in the process, total waste of time, total waste of money. And Auslo and Taft were two total wastes of excuses for lackeys."

Frank saw Connor starting to work himself up. "We've no idea if Alana even still owned the thing. She could have gotten rid of it ages ago."

Connor snorted. "Didn't know the bitch very well, did you? She kept it for leverage, Frank. Blackmail material, you stupid fuck."

Frank tried reason. "Now we don't know that for certain, Connor. It's probably long gone by now anyway and nothing to worry about. I certainly couldn't find the damned gun when I was married to said bitch, and believe me, I looked. We don't even know if, in the larger scheme of things, the gun is that significant anymore."

"Frank, the gun is the least of our problems," Collin pointed out, as he sauntered outside to join them, wearing nothing but jeans, bare-chested except for the large bandage covering an obvious wound to his shoulder. Other than being a little pasty-faced from blood loss, a fact that stood out because his coal black hair was still wet from his shower, Collin showed no signs of having stared death in the face twenty-four hours earlier. In his macho way he looked rather cocky, pleased with himself that he'd survived a bullet.

He walked over to the outdoor bar, uncapped a bottle of Johnny Walker Blue, and poured a generous portion into a crystal goblet.

"What the hell happened to you?" Frank asked.

At Frank's obvious stupidity, Connor laughed. "Haven't you heard? The nutcase tried to take him out—and missed."

"Missed? To hell you say. What does this look like, a paper cut? It was the same SOB who took out Auslo and Taft with deadly accuracy." Collin suddenly remembered the bullet hitting him, the searing pain, and how lucky he'd been just to get up and run out of that warehouse.

But like the immature man he was, Collin made like he was target shooting and formed a gun with his index finger, sent it jabbing through the air in Frank's direction. "You're next, uncle of mine. If I had to put money on it, you're the one's he's gunning for next, old man. I'm lucky his aim was off, so lucky I might even go out and buy a lottery ticket." Aiming his finger in a mock shot, he added, "Pow!"

Connor turned slowly to face his brother. "You can be such an idiot some times. How can you joke about this? The doctor said one inch the other way and we'd be planning another funeral. I'm surprised you're up and at 'em and not milking this for all it's worth. Did you get a good look at this guy?"

"Are you kidding? It happened too fast. One minute I was body-shielding Kit, the next my chest was on fire." Collin said this with all the guile of a man playing his part to the fullest.

Connor shot a disbelieving look toward Collin. "Save it, bro. You don't have to pretend in front of Frank. That may be the official story for Jacob and Adam. And knowing our less than brilliant-cousins they'll never figure it out. The Gatz branch of the family has always been more than a little slow on the uptake. But when it's me, I don't want your bullshit. You were supposed to let Auslo and Taft handle the abduction while you waited back at the warehouse where no one would be able to connect you. That was what we agreed on."

Collin fidgeted from the line of coke he had consumed along with several of the pain killers the doctor had given him. "And you and Cade were supposed to get there in time to finish off Auslo and Taft."

"And you were supposed to wait until it was dark. Going off trying to act like Mr. Tough Guy almost got you killed. Now if they compare bullet wounds…"

"Believe me, I provided the good doctor with enough financial incentive, he's already lost my chart."

"Next time, follow the plan. This guy has to be a pro."

"That's an understatement. One good thing though, he took care of our problem for us. Taft and Auslo won't be offering us up and turning state's evidence."

At that moment, Cade stormed outside through the terrace doors in a huff, obviously angry, headed straight for the bar, and poured a generous glass of whiskey. "If you guys are talking about our killer, you might want to take a look at this." He shoved a folded sheet of paper into Conner's chest. "I found that inside my locker this afternoon at the country club."

"Shit," Connor uttered, as he rubbed his forehead.

The note read: *I know about the Parkers*.

"He must have followed me to the club."

"Or hired someone to put it there."

"Either way, he's too close, sticking too goddamned close for comfort. I don't like it, Connor. This guy is playing for real. I don't think he plans on stopping with mom and pop either, not when that note was shoved in my face."

He turned to Frank. "You, my friend, are in serious shit. If I were you I'd get out of the country, take that lovely new wife that's thirty years your junior, and get out of Dodge before she's collecting your life insurance. Although, now that I think about it, knowing Charlise, she probably won't shed too many tears over you, just cash the insurance check and start perusing the clubs for your replacement. Just so you know this guy is quick and deadly. He doesn't mess around. Collin here was damn lucky he missed."

"The hell you say. Why does everyone keep saying that? Hello. Shot here, bullet taken out of my goddamned chest. The son of a bitch did not miss me."

Frank ignored Collin. "So far, he hasn't gone after Eva's kids. I know Adam and Jacob and Elle are taking precautions. As soon as I was apprised of the situation, I alerted my kids to do the same thing. Garrett, Scott, and Taylor are heightening their personal security. But I must say, for now, the man seems to be content with just you three."

Connor's brow tightened. "So you're throwing us to the wolves, is that it, Frank? Think again, pal. You think it will end with us. Well, don't count on it, buddy. I think you're full of shit. Let's count the ways, exactly what we know." He held up his fingers and ticked off the points. "First, he must have been especially pissed at Alana. I mean, twenty-one fucking stab wounds says, 'I'll show you bitch.' And don't forget, for the first few weeks he had the police convinced Kit offed her own mother. That was pretty fucking clever of him if you ask me.

"Then, right after Alana, he takes care of Mother in the middle of the damned street, makes it look like a suicide. Then let's see, he takes Eva's body all the way out to a fucking abandoned strip shopping center which we know has a history, kills her there to make a point. And then, not a hundred yards from this very spot where we're sitting, he takes out Dad on his own damn stretch of sand. I'd say, since you weren't around so he's pushing us up to priority one, going after Generation Number Two. I don't think he's gotten around to our cousins yet. But it's only a matter of time before he does. Why you say? Because I don't think he plans on stopping with us three."

Frank's face showed Connor's words had hit home. He looked pale and worried. "Maybe we should get everyone together, have a little family meeting."

"You think? Dumbass. Of course we get everyone together, apprise them of the situation. We're in serious shit here, Frank. Either get with the program or, like Cade said, get the fuck out of Dodge."

Frank started to pace back and forth. "If all this comes out, the scandal would ruin us. The legacy we've worked so hard for over the years would be destroyed. If this guy knows about the Parker murders it stands to reason he's out for revenge. It won't stop with just me or you three."

Connor finally stood up, pointed a finger at Frank. "You stupid son of a bitch, fuck the scandal. If he's successful, there won't be anyone left to run the damned empire. Don't you get it? He's exterminating each of us one by one, the whole damned family. Kill the legacy."

Frank pulled out his cell phone and punched in a phone number. "I think we could use Jankovic on this. He owes me a favor. Let's see how our nutcase likes going up against a real professional killer."

"That's fine, Frank, but first he has to find the son of a bitch. And if you don't think this guy's real. Think again."

Collin calmly pointed out, "I hate to add to the pot, but Kit and Boston will have to go. They can't be around to testify against me. That Holloway detective didn't look as if he bought my side of the story. I'm not spending the next twenty years in San Quentin for kidnapping that bitch. Can this guy, this Jankovic, take care of Boston and Kit, too?"

Cade shook his head. "If you had stuck with the plan, your beloved Kit would be history by now anyway. We can handle her and Boston." Cade studied Collin. "You wouldn't have done it anyway, Collin. You aren't fooling anyone. You're still too much in love with her to do it yourself."

Collin bristled at the accusation. But he didn't deny it. He should have offed her when he had the chance last night. That would've shown Cade the way things were with Kit.

Cade laid a hand on his brother's shoulder. "Leave it to me. I'll take care of Kit."

Frank looked around the terrace at his three nephews. Thank goodness his own sons weren't like these three.

When he noticed Connor had walked to the railing, had distanced himself from the others, and was once again staring out into the horizon, Frank shuddered at what the man might be contemplating. He walked over to where he stood. The last thing he needed was to be on the outs with this one.

He started to lift a hand to Connor's shoulder and knew better. He let his hand drop away in mid-air. "It'll all work out. You'll see. We'll get Jankovic out here and take care of the situation. Cade won't have to lift a finger toward Kit and Boston. Jankovic will take care of them too."

Connor wasn't really listening to anything Frank had so say. His father had been right. The man was an idiot. But he realized now, he'd have to take care of Baylee. He turned back to the group, thoughtful. "I have a personal problem, a loose end that needs handling as well. But I'll take care of it myself."

Curiosity peaked, Cade asked, "What loose end?"

"It's personal."

"Aren't they all?"

"It's all for one here. Remember?" Collin threw in.

"I'll see to the matter my own way," Connor said with finality, which meant the subject was closed. But he realized that after today, Baylee might go on the run again. For all he knew she could be gone at this very moment. So he'd have to find the cunt first. And if she was on the run, he'd track her down. He couldn't leave that particular loose end around to talk just as Collin couldn't leave Kit around to testify. He had no wish to spend jail time over something that amounted to a one night stand. He should have taken care of it before now anyway. He'd taken matters into his own hands before. He could damn well do it again. Women were nothing but trouble, couldn't be trusted no matter who they were. Hadn't his father taught him that?

When he noticed all eyes were on him, he looked over at Frank. With a cold, hard glare, he reminded him, "You just make sure Jankovic knows the extent of the problem. If he can't handle the job, make sure you find someone who can. I don't want any fuckups. Is that clear?"

Frank nodded, knowing full well he'd better see to it that Jankovic succeeded or suffer the consequences.

Trevor Dane listened in fascination.

Installing the bug in Connor's house hadn't been easy, but it had been necessary. He couldn't be in three damned places at one time, could he? The listening device leveled the playing field somewhat. Plus, he'd installed a GPS tracking device on each of their vehicles to keep track of the bastards. Knowing what they were up to beforehand would give him the edge he needed.

So it was Jankovic, was it?

He shook his head. Leave it to them to bring in a classless, bumbling goon. It made him wonder how these people had gotten so much in life with so little sense for so long. And then he remembered exactly how. Killing an old couple in their beds in the middle of the night might have seemed easy enough back in 1969, kind of like ducks on a pond, but Trevor didn't plan on making it easy for them now to get to anyone. Not if they were going after Kit. Not if Connor were going after Baylee. And right now he could only surmise that she was the loose end Connor had mentioned.

Goon or not, he decided he wouldn't let his guard down. He couldn't get lazy at this point. There was still too much to do.

He had a purpose, a reason to put one foot in front of the other, a reason to get up in the morning. It could be nothing more than feeling his years a little too often, for a little too long. But whatever the reason, he only knew he didn't want to lose this natural high. It was better than drugs, better than booze.

A new feeling for an old sniper.

It was true he'd been a busy boy the last few weeks. He'd personally put an end to four of the five people responsible for the senseless murders of Pete and Mary Parker back in 1969.

Knowing how losing his parents had haunted his mentor Noah, the man who'd befriended him during the darkest days of his own life, made Trevor even more determined.

Suddenly he remembered the terror on Alana's face as he'd driven the knife into her heart. He recalled how frightened Jessica Boyd had been just before he'd put the gun to her head and pulled the trigger. It had been the same with Eva Geller Gatz, Jessica's sister. And he would cherish the smug look on Sumner Boyd's face and the fact that it had vanished the moment the man realized the bill had come due for a long-forgotten debt.

Yes, Trevor had been a busy boy. He'd made them all pay the piper and in his own way. They thought they'd gotten away with cold-blooded murder. But they hadn't counted on Noah Parker surviving his captivity in a Viet Cong hell-hole prison camp and coming back six years later.

Trevor might be the only one on the planet who knew Noah's story, the only one who cared, the only one who was committed to seeing that Noah found justice for the murders of his parents—forty years after the fact.

At the close of the war, Noah had made his way back home to L.A., back to the Sundown Ranch high in the Hollywood Hills, looking to take his life back. But the man had found nothing. Everything had been gone, wiped away as if it had never existed. His parents, their beloved ranch, their home, the land, the cattle, the horses had all just disappeared. Where horses had once roamed and fat cattle had grazed on sweet grass, a developer had put up an ugly strip shopping mall.

After serving his country, Noah had wanted nothing more than answers.

It took him a week to track down what had happened to his parents, to discover they had been brutally slain in their beds one hot summer August night, leaving a macabre death scene to tell the tale of a violent, senseless crime with no obvious suspects.

One detective had even suggested that the crime scene looked eerily similar to several other murders that had taken place during the same hellish week back in August 1969. The cop had believed the deaths might have been part of the Manson family crime spree. And since they were already locked up in jail, what was the point?

After spending months hounding detectives at several different jurisdictions, one sheriff's deputy finally suggested he learn to deal with the fact that the killers were already sitting in a jail cell serving time. Case closed. But without positive proof, Noah had refused to accept that, refused to let go.

But what he came to know as fact was that no one seemed to care about a double homicide that had happened six years earlier to his parents. No one but him.

After wandering aimlessly around L.A. for months flat broke, he had re-upped in the army. The military had used the rage burning inside him over the deaths of his parents to make him the best the army had ever seen, the best he could be, the best sniper, and later, the best soldier of fortune money could buy.

Over the next twenty years, Noah would play amateur detective on his own time, never able to let the murders of his parents rest for long.

But it wasn't until he retired that he began to camp out at the county court house, began searching through old court records, poring over old probate documents, old archives that he found the answers, answers that had eluded him for two decades. Noah had discovered through court records that the law firm of Boyd Boyd Geller & Gatz had basically inherited everything his parents had ever owned through a trust set up three months before their deaths to the tune of some fifteen million dollars. Turns out, the trustee had been Jessica Geller, and she had been married to her law partner husband, Sumner Boyd.

His naïve parents had trusted the wrong attorneys.

His parents been elated when BBG&G had won them a settlement in excess of fifteen million dollars paid out over three years. Noah had known about the court victory, had been happy for his parents. But it had been the partners in the law firm that had betrayed them.

Through persistence, he discovered that Jessica Boyd had not been the only one to benefit from the deaths of Pete and Mary Parker. No, it had been a family affair, a conspiracy between all of the law partners, which included Jessica's husband Sumner, her sister Eva Geller Gatz, and their brother Frank Geller.

A mere four months after the deaths, the Parker Estate increased in value to the tune of fifty million dollars when the law firm had sold off the Sundown Ranch and the surrounding land to a local developer named Carlton, who happened to be the new husband of Alana Stevens. Then, nine months after the murders, in May of 1970, the four conspirators had formed a partnership and using a portion of the trust to purchase a sizeable chunk of Malibu real estate, which they immediately developed into a compound of family-owned mansions clustered together. They called this compound The Enclave.

As Noah finally unraveled the mystery, he had to admit sixty-five million dollars wasn't a bad take for a night's work murdering two defenseless old people in their sleep. He just couldn't be certain which of the five had been the ones to pull the trigger.

But then, one day, to test his theory, he decided to make an unannounced visit to the law offices of Boyd Boyd Geller & Gatz. And suddenly the rest of the tumblers had fallen into place.

None of the partners had been happy to see him. In fact, they had put up roadblocks at every question, refusing to answer the most basic of questions about the Parker Trust. They had threatened to call the police on him. It was clear to Noah then that they simply thought themselves invincible, beyond reproach where the murders of his parents were concerned.

They'd gone on with their lives thanks to every asset that had belonged to his parents.

From there it had been simple really. Noah had followed the proverbial money trail, followed the lawsuit his parents had won two years before their deaths, a lawsuit the firm had handled from the onset, followed the disbursement of the three year court settlement, the fifteen million dollars that led straight back to BBG&G.

All of the original partners had profited. Over the years they'd gotten richer and fatter, the same years he'd struggled to survive in a prison camp, barely eating, barely living, and barely getting by. Then to get out at war's end, hoping to come back to his life on his father's ranch, to pick up some semblance of his old world, only to discover that greed had obliterated his old world and he'd never be able to get it back again.

In retirement Noah had time to keep watch, tally his evidence, and make sure his theory made sense. Knowing the ranch land had been sold a mere four months after the murders and that Jessica's best friend, Alana Stevens, had brokered the deal, there was yet another money trail to follow. And this time he dug deep, bribed a few bank officials, and documented every aspect of how the money led not only to every member of the law firm but to the Stevens woman as well.

Going over the police reports, which he'd obtained through a series of bribes to a county sheriff's deputy, he'd discovered the murder weapon had been a .357 magnum. He'd taken that information to every gun dealer in L.A. and found that two days before the murders Alana Stevens had purchased that particular caliber weapon from a pawn shop in the San Fernando Valley. He didn't think she'd bought it for protection.

Believing he'd solved the murder of his parents, Noah had taken what he had to the authorities, document by document, piece by piece. They'd listened—politely. Called his evidence, his theories mere coincidence, and in the end they'd been less than interested in pursuing the bad guys, especially when these particular bad guys were now movers and shakers all over Beverly Hills, all over the state.

Just when Noah had been about to take things into his own hands, mete out justice the only way he knew how, the way he'd been trained, he had discovered he had pancreatic cancer.

Noah had turned to his old friend Trevor Dane to pick up the task at hand.

And Trevor had no intentions of letting him down, especially now that he knew the evil ran so much deeper.

CHAPTER 4

Baylee heard Sarah begin to fuss through the baby monitor, rolled over in bed, blinked through a fog of sleep, and stared at the clock, 5:45. Her body felt like it was five-forty-five.

After waking up around midnight Sarah had stayed awake for almost an hour playing, until her bleary-eyed mother had finally gotten her to go back down again. At this point, she wondered if her daughter would ever sleep through the night. Baylee slid out of bed and grabbed for her robe. As she did she caught her reflection in the mirror hanging over the dresser. She paused long enough to stare at her mousy brown hair. For months now, ever since coming back to L.A., she'd dyed her damned hair and for what?

Connor had found her anyway. And it hadn't been difficult at all.

At the first opportunity she planned to put it back to its original blonde.

When Sarah's fussing grew louder, she hurried next door to the bedroom designated as Sarah's nursery before the baby woke up Dylan. Pushing open the door to what used to be his office, she wondered why he had insisted setting up Sarah's crib in here and not her room. She hated the idea of intruding on Dylan's personal space, kicking him out of his own office seemed rude. She wasn't even paying rent. He had refused to take a dime. And she was grateful for his generosity. Now that she'd had time to think about it, she wondered how she could have ever thought going on the run with a baby was the answer.

But thank God Connor hadn't seen Sarah.

Thinking about him had her wondering if her life would be in turmoil from this point forward, hiding, running, moving every time she got scared he might find out—about the daughter he didn't know existed—and take her away.

Just because Jessica was dead didn't mean that she hadn't trained her sons well. Her death didn't mean that if he found out about Sarah he wouldn't try something just as underhanded out of spite. Baylee knew the whole family was well-connected and capable of almost anything. She couldn't take the chance. No matter what she had to do to keep Connor from finding out the truth, she'd do. If it meant hiding out here at Dylan's for a while, if it meant pretending Sarah belonged to Dylan, she'd do whatever it took.

Thank God, she'd had the foresight to leave the father-line "unknown" on Sarah's birth certificate. Maybe she could talk to Dylan, see if he'd be willing to put his name on the document now, just in case. It was asking a lot from someone who'd already been far too giving. But this was no time to let pride get in the way of what was best for her baby daughter.

She was embarrassed about her breakdown the other night in front of Dylan. But she'd been so tired to face yet another move, to face how often she'd failed as a mother over the past few months. Sarah had been born nine days before Christmas on the sixteenth of December. Baylee hadn't even left the hospital yet when Tanya Lincoln had called and told her about her father's brain cancer. She'd been torn as to what to do. In the end, she thought she'd done the right thing when she'd packed up and brought her eight-day-old baby back to L.A.

They'd spent the holidays with Kit in San Madrid. From there she'd moved back in with her father. But the past month he'd started drinking heavily—again. And when William Scott, the infamous director, drank, he was not a happy camper. Baylee had refused to expose Sarah to that kind of verbally abusive environment and had packed up again and moved into Gloria's guest cottage. She'd only been in the cute little house a little more than a week. She sighed. She'd miss living there.

She had to admit, it was downright strange to be sharing a house with a man. Four years at UCLA, she'd shared an apartment with Kit and Quinn but it wasn't the same thing. After that volcanic kiss the other night, the two of them would get to know each other in a hurry.

He'd probably get tired of having them around anyway, she thought, as she walked over to the crib. But she had no intentions of staying long enough to get kicked out. It had been days since the incident at the Book & Bean. Maybe Connor had gone on with his own life just as they all hoped he would. As soon as this mess with him was over, when the coast was clear, she intended to get her life back.

Over the next few weeks she had to figure something out and stop all this moving around, maybe buy a little house of her own, somewhere near the beach, like the one Kit rented from Gloria. A little house like that would be perfect for her and Sarah.

She liked San Madrid, and house-wise, the little town was certainly more affordable than anything in L.A. She didn't mind working at the Book & Bean, even though it wasn't her first choice for a career. But how could she make a living designing jewelry when it was nothing more than a hobby? She hadn't been able to completely support herself in the design business before Sarah. Now that she had two mouths to feed she couldn't depend on a sideline business for security no matter how much she enjoyed the work.

She had to start thinking in terms of what was best for Sarah. Baylee didn't mind hard work. She'd been working since she was sixteen, just like Kit and Quinn had. Living with roommates, she'd saved quite a bit of money during college. She didn't require flashy clothes, or four-hundred-dollar shoes. That was one trait she shared with Kit and Quinn and one of the reasons they got along so well. They were not generally materialistic. Well, at least not much.

Even going to an exclusive Beverly Hills private school, the three of them had known from the beginning they were not like the other girls. Life at home had been too difficult for all three of them to spend much time at the mall obsessing over what expensive clothes or shoes to buy.

The reason had been simple. With Quinn, she hadn't wanted to ask her father's lawyer for money for things like that. And forget about asking her stepfather to pay for anything except the necessities. With Kit, she had resisted Alana's efforts at every turn, of anything that even hinted they might make her into a carbon copy of Alana, because nothing would have pleased Alana more than if Kit had spent hours shopping at the mall. So they all three girls had their private reasons for not spending much time there. Instead, they had shared a love of sports, from beach volleyball to rollerblading to riding their bikes to hanging out at the miniature golf course or spending time riding go-carts, or any other outside activity that would get them out of their respective houses for any length of time.

They would spend hours hanging out at the beach, or the pool, any place would do as long as they didn't have to spend time at home.

When Baylee spotted Sarah's little arms and legs kicking the air in a furious motion with all the energy of a kick-boxing ninja warrior, she smiled.

Maybe she could work a deal with Gloria to buy the house Kit lived in at the beach. After Kit and Jake moved into the Crandall House, the little Spanish bungalow would be vacant.

And Baylee reminded herself when it came to trying to find work; she did have a college degree. Maybe it was only an art degree, but hey, it looked good on a résumé.

She needed to get her act together. Sarah deserved better, better than what she'd given her the last few months.

Baylee knew Kit and Quinn would help her any way they could. But Sarah wasn't their responsibility. She needed to step up and do better as a mother. Just looking at the little angel in the crib, Baylee resolved to get her life back on track.

And she needed to do it now.

"Good morning, angel-face. Are you wet? Let's get you out of that wet diaper." In a move that came with months of practice, Baylee had Sarah changed and powdered in a flash, then reached in and scooped the squirming baby to her chest. "Are you hungry? Did you wake up hungry?" As she settled Sarah to her breast, and the baby began to nurse, she decided she needed to find out exactly when Kit and Jake planned to make the move into Crandall House, which would leave Kit's house available and ready for a new tenant.

Baylee didn't intend to waste any more time.

♣ ♣ ♣ ♣ ♣

Dylan sucked in a weary breath and rolled over in bed. Listening to Baylee's soft voice over the baby monitor as she nursed Sarah was killing him, especially after the heated lip lock they'd shared.

But it was impossible not to hear every syllable, every word she said what with the baby monitor he'd hooked up in his own room. Glancing at the clock, he wondered if he could maybe get back to sleep for an hour or two before he had to get up and start work. Working at home was new to him, but essential if he planned to keep an eye on Baylee and the baby.

After several minutes listening to mother and daughter interact in such a personal way, he decided there was no way he'd be able to get back to sleep. He'd be better off taking a cold shower.

He had, after all, agreed to take it slow. But slow with a woman who looked like Baylee was proving to be tougher than anything he'd done in recent memory. What was he supposed to do about his feelings toward her now that she was living with him? How the hell was a guy supposed to date a woman with a baby when he listened to her breastfeed? Or for that matter, a woman who'd probably gone through one of the roughest years of her young life?

Common sense had him checking off the points of taking things slow. But slow was killing him. He wasn't a man used to taking anything at a slow pace. He liked fast cars. He liked surfing, moving through the water fast. He liked rollerblading on the quick. He certainly was not used to taking things slow when it came to a woman.

Oh hell, why lie, he liked fast women, was attracted to them. When he saw a woman he wanted, he acted on the impulse, always making sure she understood there was no long term outlook, no strings, no commitments. They'd have some fun; have a few laughs, do the dance between the sheets, and then move on. No damage. No foul. That was Dylan's dating playbook. Use the fast lane—get in and out quick, keep it light, and keep it fun. It had always worked well for him.

But this was different. Baylee was different. The situation was different

He threw back the covers and crawled out of bed.

🛆🛆🛆🛆🛆

Thirty minutes later, the sun drenched Baylee's back as she stood in the kitchen at the counter, drinking coffee and still trying to wake up. A bright-eyed Sarah sat happily in her infant carrier, a steady stream of baby babble filling the air. And Baylee carried on an animated conversation with her daughter as if she understood every word of baby-speak.

When Dylan strolled in fresh from his shower, wearing a snug pair of jeans and an old Pearl Jam T-shirt, those surfer good looks had Baylee wondering why the women weren't lined up at the backdoor, three deep. He'd kept his hair loose, letting it fall around his shoulders in soft curls.

She'd known women who would have killed to have his hair. "Hi. Sorry we woke you. Again."

"Stop apologizing. I told you I get up early." The lie sneaked out with a straight face. He poured himself an oversized mug of coffee and sat down at the table next to the baby carrier and stared at its precious cargo. "Look at you, had your morning shot of caffeine yet, sweetheart?"

The minute Sarah spotted Dylan, heard his voice, she started squirming and kicking harder. Her baby babble turned into sincere efforts to get his attention.

"I think she wants me to pick her up."

"Of course she does. She's no dummy, Dylan. Every time she sees you she's figured out you'll hold her."

Willing to oblige, Dylan set down his java and started unhooking the straps of the baby carrier. He then hauled Sarah up to his shoulder like a pro. "She likes me, knows a good thing when she sees it."

"More like a soft touch, that's for sure. You're spoiling her, Dylan."

"And you aren't."

Baylee laughed. "Okay, you got me. Want some breakfast? I made French toast."

"French toast? Really? You bet." He sat back down at the table with Sarah on his lap. There were a few advantages to having a woman in the house. Especially this woman. And looking at Baylee in her snug Capri jeans this morning, he decided cooking was the least of them.

"What time do you want to leave to see your father? It is today, right?"

She sighed. "I'll call Tanya and find out what's the best time to drop by. She tries to keep him on a schedule if she can."

"How bad is he?"

"The doctors think he might have another three months if we're lucky."

"I'm sorry, Baylee." He saw the sorrow come into her eyes. "How about before I get on the computer and check my e-mails, we take Sarah for a walk? You look like you could use some fresh air."

Her eyes danced. "That sounds wonderful."

He grinned, knowing what to dangle as bait to get on the woman's good side. Kit had after all, given him a heads up about Baylee when he'd been curious enough to ask. "And why not grab one of my boards out of the garage, hit the surf? Kit said you were the best of the lot. Why don't you show me what you've got? I'll keep an eye on Gidget here."

She arched a brow. "Gidget?"

"Yeah. She looks like a Gidget to me. After that, we'll head over to see your dad?"

An hour later, Dylan stood on the beach, holding a sleeping Sarah to his shoulder. He had no idea when he'd offered to watch the baby while her mother took a turn on the waves what an excellent athlete Baylee was.

Concentrating on the shapely form in the water, as she effortlessly navigated the waves, Dylan realized she moved with all the grace of an Olympic-trained competitor. He loved sports of all kinds, appreciated the effort it took to compete at even an amateur level whether it was a company softball game or playing in a pickup game of beach volleyball. But he knew one thing watching Baylee; she was good. Kit had been right about her ability. And if he'd thought she had toned arms from lugging around an infant carrier, he shouldn't have been surprised now to learn how physically fit she was. Her petite frame had her handling the water like a dolphin.

He stood there riveted to every move she made. When she finally started paddling in on her board, coming out of the water, walking toward him, his mouth went dry.

Baylee stepped out of the surf, spotted Dylan, and waved.

"That was some ride out there. You're pretty good even if you are goofy-footed," Dylan said, as he handed her a towel with his free hand so she could dry off her hair.

"Goofy-footed, huh? You aren't the first to notice. I'm a little rusty though. A couple of times I was up too far on the board, had to remember to glide back. The water was fantastic though. You've got good natural breaks here. Thanks for watching Sarah. She's still sleeping."

"Like a rock."

They started walking back to the house at a leisurely pace.

"There's something I meant to ask you, a favor really."

"What's that?"

"It's big. You may not want to do it. If you don't, I'll understand completely."

"Just ask."

The words lodged in Baylee's throat. She choked, could she really ask this man to do something so huge? She shook her head. "No, I'm thinking it's too much."

"Spit it out."

"Okay. But it's a bad idea."

"Baylee."

"Okay. If Reese Brennan could legally amend Sarah's birth certificate, would you be willing to put your name on the dotted line so to speak, willing to be listed as her father? I wouldn't want child support or anything like that. It wouldn't mean financial support in any way, zero; none because I'd sign a waiver to that effect or whatever."

Dylan stopped walking. Humbled at the offer, he tried to act casual. "I'll call Reese when we get back to the house, get him working on it."

"Just like that? You should take some time to think about it. I'd insist on signing anything Reese suggests to make sure you aren't obligated to pay child support in the future. But even with that, this is serious stuff, Dylan. I'm no lawyer, but I know what I'm asking. It would mean lying, lying on an official state document. You shouldn't take this lightly. And Reese would have to take care of it in Colorado since she was born in Denver. I'm not even sure Reese could do that in another state. But I have a copy of her birth certificate if that would help."

"I'll tell Reese. I don't know why I didn't think about the birth certificate angle first. It's a perfect solution. If I'm listed as her father, Connor wouldn't even consider she might be Dylan." At least he hoped not.

"I've thought about this all morning. I know what I'm asking is huge. But her birth certificate might be the one convincing document that Boyd would respect in court if it comes to that. Of course he might make you take a paternity test and then the jig would be over."

"But it would buy us time. I'll get Reese working on it."

As soon as they reached the deck, Baylee hung the wet towel on the railing and turned to get out of her wetsuit.

Dylan heard the zipper go down from five feet away, and made the mistake of turning around.

Living at the beach, he scoped out scantily clad women all the time traipsing around in bikinis, women of all shapes, all sizes, and all colors. But staring at Baylee, he found he couldn't form spit.

Even though her yellow string bikini top didn't match the red bottoms, it didn't need to. It did the job just fine, giving him a glimpse of her wet, sun-touched skin, her flat stomach, her cute little bellybutton. The sight was enough to hold his gaze until his eyes drifted upward. Apparently, she'd gotten cold in the water because her nipples stood at peak attention. Dylan stood there like a schoolboy fighting for control. Luckily for him, she quickly disappeared inside the house to shower off the saltwater, totally oblivious to the effect she'd had on him.

Yeah, taking it slow definitely sucked, he thought, as he ducked inside with Sarah, wondering why the hell he'd wanted to take it so turtle-moving-slow in the first place.

CHAPTER 5

Two hours later, Dylan found himself sitting down with the infamous William Scott in the director's study, a massive room filled with shelves that held books and awards from days when the man ruled Hollywood's list of elite directors.

He looked over at the man sitting in a wheelchair now and was struck by his appearance. Even though he'd never met William Scott until today, as a bit of a movie buff, Dylan had seen interviews of him many times on TV, and was reluctant to admit before the meeting, he'd Googled the guy on the Internet and memorized his impressive bio just in case.

But as he sat across from William, who slumped now in a wheelchair, he could tell the man was barely hanging onto life. It didn't look as if he had three months to live, but rather three days.

After he had undergone brain surgery in January and endured months of chemotherapy, the cancer had taken a toll on the man's body. Frail and emaciated, his pallid skin hung loosely over his bones. His eyes were glossy. The man looked nothing like the photos Dylan had found on the internet.

William sat quietly, content to hold his granddaughter on his lap, even though it looked as if it took every ounce of strength he could muster to keep the wiggling infant in place. As he sat there cuddling Sarah, Dylan noticed the man had tears in his eyes.

"I'm so glad you came to see me, Baylee-girl. I was worried when Tanya said you had to leave." He pointed a bony, accusing finger at Dylan. "Is he the reason?"

When a small, primly dressed woman in her early sixties with toffee skin, entered the room carrying a tray with tea and cookies, Baylee got up to help her set it down on the coffee table, if for no other reason than to delay getting into the reason she'd left.

Her father would never in a million years admit she was no longer living here because of his verbal abuse. And trying not to stare at his sorry state, she doubted the man was up to an argument about anything in his weakened condition.

Quietly, she answered, "No Daddy, he isn't the reason."

"He's Sarah's father though, isn't he? I'm not stupid, I can see the resemblance."

Baylee bit back the comment that almost slipped past her lips and sighed instead. She gave Dylan a slow smile. This was the test. The lie hung in her throat. The wishful girl inside wanted this blue-eyed man with the all-American-surfer-good-looks to be her baby's father, not Connor Boyd. That same want, deep inside, had her choking out the words, "Yes, Daddy. He's Sarah's father." The lie slid off her tongue as easily as ice on glass.

Dylan couldn't help it. He sat up straighter in his chair. His chest swelled with some nameless pride. He was more than a little surprised that she'd actually stuck to the lie, especially with her family, even after they had agreed to do just that.

At the time, he had no idea he'd be sitting here furthering the fictional story along to her father. As he sat there he told himself she'd gone along with it simply because they were in Beverly Hills, virtually sitting in Connor Boyd's backyard, and it was prudent they keep up the ruse. The Scott estate at 15202 Bel Green was five houses away from Alana's, after all, and with Connor handling the woman's probate he could easily stop in at any time, ostensibly to check on things.

Dylan told himself this was the reason she'd stuck to the plan even though, the more he thought about it, the more he realized he wished it were true. He wanted to be Sarah's father not the monster who'd raped a defenseless woman and then threatened her into keeping quiet.

"Young man, do you plan to marry my daughter? I haven't got much longer, you know. Don't wait too long. Is there any chance for another grandchild any time soon? I'm convinced I'd make a better grandfather than I ever did a father. It takes cancer and old age to make a man see his mistakes, admit to so many regrets."

"Dad! That's none of your business. Dylan and I haven't even discussed getting married let alone having more children. We have no plans to marry. He'll be a part of Sarah's life, have visitation, but…that's it." As the lie got more complicated, Baylee felt six again, as if Tanya were reminding her that good little girls do not lie. She glanced over and met Tanya's stare. She was surprised when Tanya winked as if to say when little girls lie they can expect their noses to grow longer with each one. Baylee couldn't help it. She smiled and winked back.

So far Dylan hadn't said much, but now he spoke up with a twinkle in his eyes. "I'm working on that, sir. Can't let the right woman slip through my fingers just because we sort of put the cart before the horse, so to speak. Your daughter is no pushover. She's picky. I'm trying to measure up."

William's shoulder shook with laughter, pleased. He liked this young man. "And got your work cut out for you with this one. She's a good girl, always was. I can tell you this she deserved a better father than she got with me." But then suddenly, as if he'd just thought of something, William's eyes misted over again. "You named her for your mother."

They'd been over this again and again at least once a week or so since she'd surfaced back in December. After all, she'd lived in this man's house from January to her recent move-out in May. But she knew that since the brain surgery, and with the cancer eating away at him more and more by the day, William's mind sometimes came and went, hence the verbal tantrums.

Because of Dylan's presence, she indulged her father once again, smiling ruefully, telling him, "After hours of labor, as soon as I knew I had a healthy little girl, I tried to come up with the perfect name. I thought of her then, my mother, and it seemed like naming my little girl Sarah, I had a second chance at something."

Dylan wasn't sure what they were talking about, but there was a sudden, tense undercurrent going on between father and daughter. He tried to recall whether or not Baylee had mentioned her mother that day at the bookstore and decided she hadn't.

He glanced around the room, noting all the pictures of Baylee the man had sitting on his desk, lining the mantel over the fireplace. Nosy by nature, Dylan got up to take a look. He saw photos of a little curly-headed, blonde girl beaming back at him, some with gap-tooth smiles, and others with teenage braces from eleven to fourteen. There were various pictures of Baylee with Kit and Quinn, even pictures of Baylee with Tanya, but there were none of her with anyone that looked like she might be her mother. He made a mental note to ask her about that when he got her alone in the car.

William nodded absently, and then without warning, started to ramble. "If it's possible, I love you more for that. Sarah Moreland was a beautiful woman. And a damn fine actress. You were always the spitting image of her, look just like her, in fact. Did I ever tell you that? You do. Maybe that's why… that's why I'd get so upset whenever I'd think about my lovely Sarah. I loved that woman with all my heart." But look what he'd done; he thought now, he'd ruined everything. He couldn't change the past. He couldn't go back. The past was too painful to think about, and too sad; it made his head hurt. He started to shake. "And now I have a beautiful granddaughter. I'm so sorry, Baylee, so very sorry. All those years of drinking, all those years wasted, without my Sarah."

Tanya passed Baylee a knowing look. "William, you look tired. I think it's time you rested now. Why don't you give Sarah back to her mother?"

Just as William's body began to give in to any more tremors, the tears fell in earnest. Baylee took one look at her father and snatched Sarah up out of his lap. The baby looked as if she was ready to pucker up and cry.

Tanya made her way around the back of the wheelchair. But before she could push him from the room, confusion rained down on William Scott like hail from a haunted past.

Years of verbally and physically abusing his daughter for some phantom infraction had his voice rising in fear as he looked into Baylee's eyes. He began to rant, "I'm sorry, Baylee. I'm sorry I took Sarah from you at such a young age. I'm sorry Sarah, my love. So sorry. I never meant to hurt you. I didn't mean it. Please, Sarah, say you forgive me. You must forgive me. I have to know you forgive me before I die."

Baylee didn't know what to think. The man was getting worse by the day, rambling on and on without making much sense. She glanced over at Dylan, who was watching her with wide eyes.

By the time William's wheelchair had reached the hallway, Baylee's eyes were misting over. Noting she was visibly shaken, Dylan walked over and put his arms around both her and Sarah. She let him comfort her because it felt good to have someone hold her for a change. She blotted her damp eyes. "You see why I needed to come. He's going downhill a little more every day. He's worse today than he was a week ago." At least Tanya had somehow managed to keep him sober for the visit.

"You want to talk now?"

She sunk down into a wingback chair, adjusting Sarah on her lap. "Oh, Dylan, it's hard to talk about." And something she hadn't done since spending three years in group therapy right along with Kit and Quinn, recalling the awful incidents from their childhood with twice weekly sessions at Dr. Strasburg's office in humiliating detail. "Where do I start?"

He gave her a quizzical look and then shot her one of his charming smiles. He put his hands in his pockets to keep from wrapping her up. "How about at the beginning?"

She was too tired to put up much of a resistance. "My mother, Sarah Moreland, was an actress, a good twelve years younger than Dad. He directed some of her early pictures beginning with one when she was only seventeen. But they didn't marry until she was twenty-one. I came along when she was twenty-two. According to what little I know from Dad, I guess she had a restless spirit. Their marriage was rocky from the start maybe because of the age difference; I just don't know. He's never talked about the specifics." Only ranted like a raving lunatic at times when he drank, Baylee thought.

"When I was three, she was only twenty-five. The same age I am now." Baylee stopped talking. An image popped into her head. The same one from the same recurrent dream she'd had often since she was a small child.

The grainy scene always played the same. She'd been in bed. She'd heard an argument. When she'd gotten out of bed to see what the commotion was all about outside her bedroom door, she thought she had seen her mother fall down the stairs, no not fall, but rather being pushed after a violent struggle with two women, one who had light hair, the other dark.

In a child's mind, she'd always pictured the woman with dark hair dressed like an evil witch. Her therapist had said the evil witch represented a very common manifestation in the mind of a small child. According to

Strasburg, she had the recurring dream because it was better to see her mother die like that than to accept Sarah Moreland had so easily abandoned her. The dream with the "mean people," as she so often thought of the two women, was simply that, something she had learned to deal with and accept over the years.

But even now, Baylee shuddered just remembering the images that frequently played out in her head from time to time. Then suddenly, she realized Dylan was waiting patiently for the rest.

"Anyway, one day my mother walked out on my father, ran off to Europe with a tennis pro. After that, my father started drinking heavily. Whenever he drank, he got mean, verbally abusive, sometimes physically. To this day the man is a mean drunk. You don't want to serve him a little wine at dinner. No, Dad can't stop with just one glass of wine, or anything with alcohol in it for that matter. During the times he was sober he could be animated, funny, charming even, and absolutely wonderful. We'd do things together; maybe go to the amusement park or to the beach, normal father-daughter outings. He was fine as long as he didn't drink. But the moment he opened the bottle, the moment he took that first drink, he changed into someone else. During the times he drank, he could get violent at the drop of a hat. Anything might set him off. I never knew what it would be. But the older I got, I got pretty good at avoiding him. I'd go down to Kit's or over to Quinn's house. We'd ride bikes or drift down to the beach, anything to get out of the house."

She rubbed a hand over her face. "We'd go anywhere just so we wouldn't be here." Of course she didn't mention that sometimes she'd have to sneak out of her own house, sneak around their various parents to get to spend time together because so often they were grounded or punished for some small infraction.

"Then there were all the times he'd be in a drunken rage and Tanya would hide me, tell him she didn't know where I was. Sometimes she knew where I was, sometimes she didn't. But Tanya saved me more times than I could count."

Dylan winced thinking how many rotten memories she must associate with living in this house. And then suddenly it struck him how much she and Kit had in common. Hadn't Jake told him virtually the same thing about the house five doors down? Hadn't he told him about Kit's childhood filled with abuse? Lamely he said, "I'm sorry, Baylee."

Baylee nodded and clutched Sarah tighter. The baby squirmed in her arms. "My mother abandoned me, Dylan, left me without so much as a backward glance. I never saw her again, never heard from her over the years. Not once did I get a birthday card, or a Christmas card, no presents from a mother who was just too busy partying in Europe with her boyfriend to take time out to buy a graduation present. I don't even remember her very well, just images really from some early photos I found buried in Dad's bedroom closet and confiscated."

She didn't mention the scenes she relived over and over again ever so often from the dream. "Tanya basically raised me."

Alarm bells went off inside Dylan's brain. "Let me understand this. In all those years, your mother never bothered to write? No letters, no phone calls?" For some reason that didn't sound right.

"Not one letter or phone call in twenty-two years. One night she put me to bed." At least Baylee thought she had. "Then she was gone, just disappeared from my life."

Dylan put his hands in his pockets and walked over to stand at the terrace doors, looking out into a perfectly manicured garden setting. These houses, he thought, mansions really, had to go for millions. Who said growing up in Beverly Hills was a walk in the park?

But something about the story didn't seem right to him. Maybe he'd watched too many CSI shows, or read too many crime novels, but how many women, especially mothers, disappeared off the face of the earth without even saying goodbye to their children?

He thought about all those mysteries he had watched and remembered how many spotlighted women who'd vanished without a trace, only to be the focus of an intense search. It always ended the same. The police couldn't find any activity from their credit cards or cell phones after they'd gone missing. They just vanished into thin air. The whole thing with the tennis pro sounded strikingly familiar, like one of those phony stories a husband might come up with to explain why his "cheating wife" mysteriously disappeared, a convenient story to cover up something much more sinister.

Without putting much more thought to it, Dylan made up his mind to find out whatever he could about Baylee's mother.

The actress Sarah Moreland could be Googled.

☙☙☙☙☙

Once in his room, after Tanya had left him alone, William Scott calmed down. Today was a lucid day, one in which his memories were vivid as glass—and therefore his memories haunted him.

He remembered being on a soundstage in Burbank, probably inside Studio D, in charge of every actor, every stage hand. He recalled how the place hummed with activity as he watched two set designers go about the business of turning three blank walls into a very believable, attractive living space that when they were done resembled an actual living room.

Gaffers adjusted rows of lighting, testing equipment, while a cameraman got ready to shoot the next scene.

William loved everything about directing, loved being in charge of a film, the action scenes, everyone and everything revolved around him.

At the break, William took in the noise of a busy soundstage as he moved several yards away on the same lot, past rows of trailers that housed the actors biding their time between takes.

Then the memory shifted, the scene was inside one of the trailers. It flashed quickly, brilliantly in color. The sexual scene unfolded as if he were watching his image appear on the big screen like one of his finished products.

Alana Stevens lay back on the bed in her trailer with her arms and legs entangled around the director of her latest film, *Growing up Dead*. For the past four weeks, she and William had ended up between the sheets more times than not as a way to relieve the stress that came with making a movie. Alana ran her hand up and down the length of his chest and purred, "William that was wonderful. How'd you get to be so creative both in bed and out?"

William laughed, brushing his hand in a circular motion on one of Alana's breasts, tweaking her nipple. "Baby, you inspire a man to take all manner of creative license."

She smiled. Men were so predictable. But she had to admit this one was rather special. They'd been together on and off for the past three years, mostly on, whenever they were doing a picture. "As long as you're aware that I'm the one you take creative license with and not that little marshmallow tart Sarah Moreland. She wants you."

And Alana was so jealous she couldn't spit.

William grimaced and sat up in bed, suddenly losing all interest in Alana's ample assets, and more in tune to her acerbic tongue.

Most of the time he could concentrate on her body and the sex and forget about her mouth, especially when she used it for annihilation—like now. He looked around for his clothes, scoping out his escape route.

"Sarah's a child, barely seventeen and playing your little sister in this film. I've hardly had time to notice her.

Although, when she's in front of the camera, she does have that natural sparkle on screen."

It was the wrong thing to say and he knew it the moment the words shot past his lips.

Alana bolted up like she'd been burned. "William, that child has been after you from the moment she stepped foot on the lot. And I won't allow it, do you hear me?"

She made a last grab at William's thighs just as he moved out of reach. "Why is it men are absolutely oblivious to the obvious? Sarah wants you. She's told everyone on the set that will listen. And she's stealing all my good scenes. And you're letting her."

Ah, there it was, he thought, as he retrieved his shirt and started working the buttons. He'd expected jealousy from Alana because that was who she was, but when it came to her career, the woman was usually more subtle about manipulating him into giving her more lines, more scenes.

This was the third time they'd worked together and it was always the same. Alana was a piranha both in bed and out. She rarely stood for anyone usurping her "star power" during a shoot. He reminded himself that he wasn't stupid, just taking advantage of the situation, her body, the sex she'd provide over the stressful weeks of filmmaking. But this time, her clinging vine act was becoming tiresome—and more than a little scary.

"Alana, Sarah isn't stealing anything. You're the star, baby, as always. No one's taking anything away from you. Sarah's simply playing her supporting role as the bothersome little sister to her fullest potential." And was doing a superb job of it, he thought, as he pulled on his pants, tucking his shirt in with some haste, anxious to get the hell out of Alana's trailer. He looked around for his shoes.

But the woman rose slowly, seductively out of bed with purpose, looking like Lady Godiva with her long blond hair billowing around her shoulders. Comfortable with her body, she slithered out of bed and made her way to stand in front of him, cupping his groin with one hand, and expertly unzipping his fly with the other. "Darling, if I won't permit Sarah to steal my best scenes, I certainly won't allow her to take you away from me. You of all people know how very much I count on our time together."

God, the woman was Venus in heat. There wasn't anything she wouldn't do in bed. His brain disintegrated as it so often did when she touched him. He went stone hard. Alana was tall, almost as tall as he was, with the body of a perfectly toned athlete, not an ounce of extra flab anywhere. She smelled like sex. He grabbed her, pulling her back into him and was inside her before he could think about the consequences.

A knock on the door ten minutes later reminded William he had a film to finish. He backed up and sat down on the bed to slip on his loafers and look around for his sunglasses.

Allowing a glance at the woman lying behind him on the sheets, noticing the pout that formed on her lips, he hurried his routine. When she started to speak, he was caught off guard by her change in tone.

"William, I know what you're thinking. I'm petty. But I'm just trying to protect what's mine." How could she dare let him know how much she cared for him, what was in her heart for the first time in her life? If he found out she felt more for him than she'd ever felt for any other man what would he do? What would his reaction be? She couldn't take the risk. She wouldn't leave herself open and vulnerable like that, so she gentled her voice even more, made it sound as if it were all about her work.

"It's hard for a woman to succeed in this business. I've already got a backup plan. I took some real estate courses. My friend helped me get my license some years back. I'm not stupid, William, I know I don't possess that much talent for acting. I know why I get the roles I get. With selling real estate in this market, the money's so much better than acting and I bought a house—in Beverly Hills.

You should see it. I could get you into a house there too, William. For once, I'm making plans for the future, a future that could be so much better if we were together." There, she'd said it, she thought as she ran her fingers along his back, and then up through his hair.

Alarms went off. This was news to him. Alana didn't care for anyone but Alana. And make plans? She'd always been an in-the-moment kind of woman, never considering consequences or the ramifications of what her actions might bring to anyone else. "What are you saying, Alana? You're ready to give up acting?"

"My friend Jessica thinks I could make a fortune selling real estate. I could make a lot more money in sales than I ever could in this heartless business." She'd already made a small fortune from the commission from her first sale, but William didn't need to know how much money she had in the bank.

The sex had obviously addled his brain or his hearing. Alana leave acting behind? It was true she wasn't that talented. She got roles because of the way she looked, the way she was built. But she had more ambition and drive and determination than anyone he'd ever seen. And depending on the role, she could light up the screen with the best of the sex kittens. He couldn't imagine her giving it up. "Real estate? You're kidding right? You'd be happy selling houses instead of the attention you get from acting?"

"Selling real estate gives me security. I just want some financial security, some continuity for once. Jessica's convinced I could open my own office right here in Beverly Hills. Right now, I just want to know about us."

Us? What us? He had to get the subject back on track. "I can't imagine you doing anything but acting, baby. But it's your life. Obviously, you don't need my blessing. Sounds like your friend's already talked you into it."

Her heart sank. Had she really expected him to declare his love? The feeling of despair coupled with rejection was fleeting as Alana's temper burst into full-blown fury.

"At least Jessica has my best interests at heart. For once, I need someone to think about what's good for me." When he stood up, she tugged on his hand, the gentle tone gone completely while her demeanor turned back to demanding. "Just remember, William. Be a very good boy, or you'll pay big time for being mean to me."

That comment, as well as the shoe she aimed at his head, had him finally moving toward the door. "William, do not piss me off. People have been known to pay when they do."

He paused before opening the door. "What the hell does that mean? Is that a threat?"

"Not at all. I'm just telling you like it is. I won't put up with you making time with Sarah. As long as you're sleeping with me, don't even think about going near her."

"You are some piece of work, you know that? She's seventeen, a child." He let the door slam behind him. But he wasn't far enough out of earshot to miss her parting shot. "You have no idea who you're messing with. Cross me and you'll pay."

William flinched. The scene in his head faded to black, bringing him back to the present, back to his bed, and the room where he remembered his lovely, innocent Sarah.

He shuddered at the memory.

No, the frail old man he was now always hated remembering what he'd done. Because ultimately, even as a young man, he'd had no idea what Alana Stevens, or her friend Jessica Boyd, had been capable of doing until it was too late.

CHAPTER 6

Kit and Quinn agreed that no one needed a little TLC more than Baylee, the sooner the better. Since Memorial Day was still a few days off, they decided not to wait. And being the lowly first year res at the hospital, Quinn was pretty sure she had to work the holiday and wouldn't get to spend Monday with her friends anyway, but she did get the Friday off before the holiday, so it would be a good time to get together with Baylee and boost her spirits.

Because of Quinn's shift at the hospital, unable to get together face-to-face, both Kit and Baylee had burned up the minutes on their cell phones over the past forty-eight hours rehashing the fact that Connor Boyd was Sarah's father. Chewing on that sickening disclosure had them troubled over what that meant for Baylee.

Quinn still couldn't believe it. "We should've held her down and made her come clean months ago. The minute she took off we should have hired a private eye to track her down. That way we'd have known about her pregnancy and been there for Sarah's birth. I never believed that hokey story about her heading off to Europe in search of her mother anyway. As her best friends, we should have been more proactive."

"Okay, I didn't believe the story either. We should have done more. But that's in the past, Quinn. You should have seen her face. She's terrified of him. He must have put the fear of God in her for Baylee to have let the bastard get away with this. I mean, we're talking Baylee here, tried and true Baylee, who never so much as jaywalked; the one who is constantly the voice of reason, always the one after us to do the right thing. She didn't go to the police then and I think she regrets that now. But that part is over. Now, we need to make sure Connor doesn't find out about Sarah. Concentrate on protecting that baby from him. Period."

"I know. I know. I'm with you there. I just wish she'd told us. We could have helped her in so many ways. That's what the whole brown hair thing was about. And next time I talk to Blair I'm going to kill her. We e-mailed each other during the entire time Baylee was right there in Denver. And she never said a word. Not a word."

"I know. I know. You have to give it to Blair for keeping her secret, though. You know, Sarah doesn't look a thing like Connor, no dark eyes, no black hair. I thought brown eyes dominated. But that little fact is in our favor. Can you imagine what he would do if he found out he had a daughter? Think Jessica and Alana here. You just know he would find some way to take her away from Baylee, you just know that, Quinn. He's like his mother; he'd never allow anyone to get the better of him. That's what is so horrifying for Baylee in all this, knowing what Jessica and Alana did to Gloria."

Kit kept talking into her cell phone as she tallied the day's cash receipts from the store while sparing a glance in Jake's direction. He was hard at work on his laptop computer still searching database after database, trying to get a hit on Benjamin Griffin, her brother, the brother she'd never laid eyes on who was supposed to be living in Ireland. When he looked up from his search, she grinned and mouthed the words 'I love you' at him before turning her attention back to Quinn.

"Thank God. She's the spitting image of Baylee, blonde, blue eyes. But what's up with this arrangement with Dylan? Why pawn her off on him? What were you thinking?"

"I didn't know what else to do. It sounded reasonable when Dylan offered her the opportunity to stay in the area. It was selfish of me because she was ready to bolt, take off for parts unknown. At the time it sounded like a good way to keep her safe, a spur-of-the-moment decision. But now, I'm not so sure."

"Neither am I. We'll just have to keep an eye on him, that's all. Make sure he doesn't hurt her. I talked to her the other night; she sounds like she's doing okay. Working on the Jessica slash Alana timeline angle we started is a good excuse to get together. And I think she bought it. I mean why wouldn't she? It's what we've been trying to do, trying to link those bitches to the Parkers, enough so that any good detective can take the information we've gathered and run with it, finally bring some closure to this whole thing."

"Do we know more than what we found in those boxes from Alana's attic? We've gone through them until I'm tired of looking at that stuff."

"We'll go over all that. Look, if you're bringing the food, how about we do Mexican for a change? I haven't had fajitas in forever."

"Fajitas it is then. But Quinn, promise me, you won't give Baylee a hard time when you see her. Not about her lying to us or the fact she held everything back."

"It isn't her I plan to give a hard time. If I ever catch Connor Boyd near her again, so help me God, I'll make him pay for what he did."

☙☙☙☙☙

With Sarah fast asleep in her car seat in the back, Dylan concentrated on making certain they weren't followed from William's house. Call it caution or paranoia, he didn't care, but he wanted to be thorough.

Every so often he checked the rearview mirror and listened as Baylee talked about her plans for tomorrow.

"Quinn called. Tomorrow's her day off. If it's okay with you, I'd like to have them over for lunch. She and Kit want to work on that timeline thing they put together, see if we can make it a little more solid linking Alana and Jessica to the Parkers. Kit's offered to bring the food. Afterward, we can work on the documentation, work out the kinks, make an afternoon of it. The plan is to get our act together and then ask Jordan Donovan, since he's the ex-cop, if he'll take our evidence to the sheriff's department, see if they'd be willing to re-open the Parker murders as a cold case. Once we get their attention, we convince them Alana and Jessica are the killers."

Dylan was in on the plan and thought it sounded like a good idea to him, anything to get Baylee's mind off Connor. "It's fine with me, but does Jake know about this?" No one could accuse Dylan of not playing his part to the max.

"Knowing Jake won't let Kit out of his sight right now, I'm pretty sure he knows. It's Reese that thinks we're nuts."

"Reese is just being a lawyer."

"I'm sorry, Dylan. I should have mentioned it to you before now. But it was the only time we could get together and include Quinn. It's a rare day off for her. Who knows when she'll have another? I don't think we'll see her on Memorial Day."

"I'm not upset, Baylee. You don't have to clear everything you do with me."

She thought she did; it was his house after all, but she changed the subject. "Can you believe Jake and Kit are moving in together?"

"No. This thing between them moved really fast."

Baylee laughed and shook her head. "Men. Glaciers move faster than Jake Boston. Think about it, they've known each other for ten years. Kit's been hoping this would happen since she was fourteen. Personally, I think it's great he finally got off the pot. Kit's the best. She's loyal and loving. She'll be wonderful to him."

"Hey, if it works for them, I'm all for it. His first marriage to Claire was a disaster, a joke. The woman was a..." He tempered his words. "Claire slept around. It's always been Jake's theory that she was sleeping with whoever killed her."

Baylee was no prude, but her mouth fell open. "I had no idea. Were they ever happy?"

Out of the corner of her eye, she saw Sarah's pacifier fall out of her mouth and Baylee reached into the back seat to retrieve it, stuffing it down into the diaper bag. When she turned back around she pointed out, "Jake won't have to worry about that sort of thing with Kit. Like I said, she's loved him for such a long time, she won't hurt him. Does Kit know that about Claire though? She thought Claire was the love of his life."

Dylan laughed at that and shook his head. "Oh God no. Claire told him she was pregnant, so they got married. Two weeks after the wedding he caught her taking a birth control pill. There was never a baby. There was, however, Claire wanting Jake's money. But Jake suspected she was never faithful. So, when she ended up murdered, the police thought he had motive."

"How terrible for Jake. He was never charged, though. You know Dylan, Kit isn't really into the whole money thing. She isn't into material stuff. She's about as down-to-earth as you can get. But I'll tell you right now, Kit wants a family more than anything. That's what I think is behind this whole idea of finding her long lost brother in Ireland."

Dylan had grudgingly revised his opinion of Kit somewhat as he had gotten to know her a little better over the past few weeks. Okay, Kit wasn't the money hungry viper Claire had been.

He also didn't think Baylee was into the whole material thing either after inventorying her clothes. The clothes weren't out of style exactly, they just weren't the latest in trendy fashions, no designer labels or flashy party dresses for Baylee.

But then he realized she was staring at him, waiting for him to say something. "I take it you aren't sold on the idea of Kit finding the long lost brother."

"I wasn't at first. But I see her point. Family means a lot to her. Now that she knows Alana wasn't her real mother, I think she'll want to start a family with Jake. Right away."

"You mean she didn't want kids before?"

Baylee shook her head. "Sadly, no. She was convinced that she might...she was afraid she might turn out like Alana."

"Ah, got it. The whole child abuse cycles theory."

"Something like that."

"And you don't feel that way even though your father..."

"Knocked me around. It's okay to say it, Dylan. That's why I was in therapy for so long. I can say it. As bad as things were at my house, Kit had it a hundred times worse. At least my father didn't lock me in a closet."

Dylan's eyes drifted from the road and zeroed in on Baylee's. "A closet? You're kidding?"

"I wish I were."

"Jesus. After finding all the porn in Alana's attic that day I can only imagine what it was like for Kit to grow up in that house."

When Baylee didn't say anything, Dylan realized she had her own childhood demons to fight off. He changed the subject. "So Kit hasn't seen hide or hair of Collin?"

"No. All of them seem to be keeping a low profile or as Quinn says, it's as if all three roaches have gone underground or something."

It was the "or something" that had Dylan glancing in the rearview mirror once again to make sure no one trailed them from Beverly Hills.

⚛ ⚛ ⚛ ⚛ ⚛

True to his word, that night Dylan got on his computer, Googled the name Sarah Moreland, and was disappointed in the lack of hits. After trying several websites that promised they kept the best bios and trivia on celebrities, both past and present, he found an article that gave a four-line history of Baylee's mother, but not much else.

One thing Dylan couldn't get past was the vanishing off the face of the earth thing. A talented actress doesn't just give up on her career. And couldn't she have picked up her acting career once she got to Europe? But there was no mention of Sarah's work or films after the year she vanished.

The bio told him that Sarah Moreland had been born in Glendale, California. She was a local girl who had gotten her first break in show biz when she'd landed a small part in the movie *Happy in Love*. From there she'd been cast in a supporting role in the comedy drama *Growing up Dead* with Alana Stevens playing her older sister.

The article went on to say that she'd given up her promising career for marriage to director William Scott, and later had a child. The footnote to the story said that she'd given it all up to run off with a young tennis pro with aspirations of joining the European circuit. The article didn't elaborate on the tennis pro.

But for some reason, Dylan refused to buy the story. It just didn't add up.

⚛ ⚛ ⚛ ⚛ ⚛

Connor had spent three days trying to locate Baylee, only to come to the conclusion she wasn't in San Madrid, wasn't at Kit's, wasn't with Quinn. Her Range Rover was still parked in the driveway at Gloria's guest cottage but hadn't moved in days. That left staking out her father's place. He would have to send Cade out to do it. If she spotted him lying in wait, she'd take off for sure.

A bit distracted, his hard, cold eyes chanced a glance down at the nude, petite woman lying on the bed, waiting for him, waiting for him to get into the mood, waiting for the Viagra he'd taken to kick in.

Since he'd first experienced sex at the ripe old age of fourteen, he had had a penchant for a particular kind of woman. They had to be very feminine, very petite, almost delicate-looking—and beautiful. A therapist had once told him his taste in women probably had something to do with the fact that the women he desired were the polar opposite of his domineering mother.

Connor didn't doubt the guy had nailed it on the first try, because it wasn't so much their coloring that got him hard, they could be blonde or brunette or redhead, it made no difference to him, but they absolutely had to be petite—and lately they had to be young. At thirty-seven, he had a penchant for this particular call girl, who was barely nineteen. He knew that for a fact since he'd been using her services for a year. As he stared down at Lola, he didn't care what name she used, he did his best to focus on her body.

He had to concentrate. His headaches were back. The blackness wanted to descend. Through the black edge of vision, he realized how much Lola resembled Baylee.

He'd had a fondness for Baylee Scott since the first time he'd looked at her that way. At the time she'd been fifteen, a visitor to his parent's house, and a guest at Collin's birthday party. Connor had been twenty-seven.

He remembered that brown shit she'd had all over her hair the other day and settled on the memory of her golden blonde hair, her fine-boned features, and those sultry deep aquamarine eyes.

Once again, he did his best to focus on the image of Baylee's natural B-cup breasts, not the augmented ones under him. He remembered the one night he'd spent with her in that hotel room. He'd made it count. After all, after years of trying to get close to her, he'd finally played out his fantasy, a fantasy he'd been savoring in the back of his mind for years.

The Viagra finally kicked in, or it might have been the memory of having Baylee in bed beneath him that did the trick. But the more he thought of Baylee now, the more he wanted to strangle the bitch.

Through the migraine beating its own drum in his head, his mind wandered to the e-mail he'd received that morning. The message had been simple and direct and effective, a one-line threat that read: *You will die just like the Parkers.*

The e-mail had royally pissed him off. Things were spinning out of his control. He didn't like feeling out of control. When that happened he sometimes blacked out and didn't remember doing things.

But the e-mail made him all the more determined to protect what was his. They would all be better off when Baylee and Kit were out of the picture. But first, they needed to find the hit man, the killer responsible for bringing this whole thing to a head. The guy seemed to know everything about them. Jankovic was supposed to work on that. As soon as the son of a bitch got into town— he was taking his sweet time getting his ass to L.A.

Connor's mind was on other things, splintering into pieces in fact. His migraine came back with a vengeance. The blackness descended as it so often did these days, and he lost himself inside the hole that the blackness brought with it.

By the time he'd come back to reality and looked around the room, he'd already finished fucking the hooker. He crawled out of bed and went into the bathroom to flush the condom.

When he came out, he walked to the bar in the bedroom and poured himself a stiff shot of Johnny Walker Blue. He stood there drinking, letting his mind clear. It would all work itself out; with planning, with precision, he would find Baylee. He'd let Jankovic deal with Boston, Kit and maybe even Quinn. That's another bitch that had caused them problems in the past and would definitely pitch a fit when her two best friends ended up dead.

After downing the drink in one swallow, he felt a little better. He grabbed a robe, threw open the door to the bedroom, and told Cade, "Your turn, little brother."

CHAPTER 7

The mean people had come back.

Terrified, three-year-old Baylee Scott cowered under the covers, clutching her blue bunny.

Her little body shook as the shrill angry voices coming from outside her bedroom door grew closer—and louder. To block out the noise, she put both of her hands over her ears to muffle the sound as the shouts grew meaner.

She huddled further down in the bed. But the loud, mean people wouldn't go away. And she could still hear the words as they got uglier. She could hear two women yelling bad words at her mama, words she knew she was not supposed to repeat.

Every so often, Baylee recognized her mama's voice as her mama shouted back at both women to leave, to get out of her house before she called the cops. But both women were so angry they yelled right back at her mama. Baylee could tell by the tone in her mama's voice that she was really angry. But despite her mama getting madder and madder; the mean people weren't leaving.

Baylee thought the argument was about her daddy. But that couldn't be right because her daddy wasn't even at home. He'd gone to some place called Francisco to make another picture. That's what her daddy did; he made pictures for Hollywood. People could see his pictures if they went to theaters or they could sometimes watch them on television.

The day he'd left to go out of town, he hadn't taken her with him, even though she had cried and begged when he had loaded his bags into the yellow car that had taken him to the airport.

He had promised if she stopped crying and helped her mama while he was gone, he would buy her a superstar Barbie. Even though she wanted the doll more than anything, she still would have liked to have gone with her daddy.

As she listened to the grownups continue to scream at each other, the little girl desperately tried to get her mind on something else. She missed her daddy. She closed her eyes and remembered the time he had taken her to the studio with him. She had eagerly crawled into his lap while he sat in his director's chair and watched the other people he called actors say their lines. Then her daddy would yell "cut" and the actors would stop talking until he yelled "action" again, and they'd say more lines until the picture was done.

But this time he'd gone out of town and Baylee had stayed home with her mama. She loved her mama, but she wished her daddy were here now. If her daddy were home he would make the mean people stop yelling at her mama.

She closed her eyes tight to shut out the argument. She tried hard to picture the superstar Barbie at the toy store. Her mama had promised they would go shopping tomorrow to pick out the doll. The only reason they hadn't gone today was because today had been Mother's Day and you weren't supposed to spend mother's day at the mall shopping but doing stuff together, spending time together.

That's why Baylee and her mother had spent the day baking cookies and planting seeds in the garden and making pretty construction paper cut-outs.

At that moment, the little girl heard hitting noises, a slapping sound. It sounded like her mama was in trouble and needed her help.

She bit her lip, trying to work up her courage to crawl out of bed. When the argument grew louder, she slowly made her way out from under the covers and ran to the door, opening it just wide enough to peek out.

Sure enough, she saw her mother arguing with two women. The taller woman had blond hair. Baylee recognized her as Kit's mother. But Kit's mother was mean. She almost slammed the door shut because she didn't like Kit's mother at all.

Wide-eyed, mesmerized by the scene on the landing, the little girl kept her eyes locked on the other woman with long black hair and dark eyes. She'd never seen her before, but she looked mean because she was yelling mean things in her mama's face.

Baylee knew she needed to move, to go outside into the hallway to help her mama. As the three of them stood on the upstairs landing, Baylee could tell her mama was mad. Her mama demanded they get out of her house again, or she'd call the police.

And then all of a sudden from the other side Kit's mother moved in and slapped her mama. Terrified, Baylee cringed. She wanted to move, to run out into the hallway to make them stop. But her stomach tightened. Fear locked her throat. Her feet refused to budge. She tried to push the fear away. But she couldn't move.

Just as she started to open the door further and step out into the hallway to yell at them to stop, the woman with black hair shoved her mama, and Baylee watched her mama fall backwards down the stairs.

She heard her mama scream, a shrill cry that lasted all the way down to the bottom step. She heard a dull thud hit the floor. And then nothing. She saw the two women look at each other. She saw them smile before they turned to walk down the stairway.

Baylee opened her mouth to scream. But no sound came out. Instead, she ran back to the bed. Terrified, in a desperate attempt to hide, she scooted underneath the bed just in case the mean people came to get and hurt her, too.

She only hoped they wouldn't look under the bed.

Trembling, Baylee stayed hidden like that for a long time. She finally fell asleep.

At dawn the next morning, when she opened her eyes, the first thing she remembered was her bad dream. It still scared her to think about the mean people. But despite her fear, she crawled out from underneath the bed. She listened, waiting to hear any little noise outside her room. Slowly she opened the door and peeked out into the hallway. She didn't hear a sound. The mean people from her nightmare were gone.

She crept to the landing and looked down, fearful of what she might see. But her mama wasn't there. Baylee rubbed her eyes and looked down at the bottom of the stairs again.

All of a sudden Baylee started crying, "Mama. Mama. Mama. I want my mama."

Alarmed, Tanya Lincoln, the housekeeper, appeared at the bottom of the stairs. The small black woman started walking up the steps toward the child. "What's the matter, baby girl? What's wrong?"

"I had a bad dream."

As soon as Tanya reached Baylee, she crouched down in front of the child and lifted her chin to get her full attention. "Well, for goodness sakes, baby girl, tell Tanya all about it. What happened?"

It was then she noticed Baylee shaking like a leaf, trembling so hard as if she were scared to death. She scooped her up. "It's okay, baby girl. Bad dreams can't really hurt us. They're just dreams and not real."

Baylee rubbed the sleep out of her eyes. "My mama fell; she got hurt."

"Oh baby." Tanya brushed the hair from Baylee's face. "We'll find your mama. Let's go see if she's still sleeping." Tanya hugged the child to her chest and tweaked Baylee's nose. "It's still early. I bet your mama's still snuggled down under the covers just where you should

be. It's not even seven o'clock yet. I just got here myself a little while ago."

As Tanya made her way down the hall toward the master bedroom, she told the little girl, "You'll see your mama's still sleeping, that's all. And then you're going back to bed for a little while."

As Tanya knocked on the door of the master bedroom, Baylee's arms snaked around the housekeeper's neck. If only her mother were on the other side of the door. They waited and waited, but her mother wasn't in bed at all. In fact, she wasn't anywhere in the house.

She and Tanya looked and looked and looked, searching every room.

But little three-year-old Baylee had seen her mother for the very last time.

☙☙☙☙☙

Baylee woke in a sweat, in a panic mode that made her gulp for air. The dream was back. It had stayed away all during her pregnancy, and then afterward, she'd been too exhausted and sleep-deprived from new motherhood to do much sleeping or dreaming about anything other than her newborn.

It had to be at least two years since she'd dreamed about that night. She thought she'd put it behind her for good. But the visit with her father, the stress-filled time spent in the house today, Dylan's insistence she talk about her mother, must have brought the nightmare back again.

Feeling uneasy, she crawled out of bed to check on Sarah. As she tip-toed down the hall, she couldn't help but think even after all these years the imaginary mean people had certainly left their mark behind.

CHAPTER 8

Just before noon the next day, Jake and Kit pulled into Dylan's driveway and parked behind Quinn's red Miata. As they unloaded the car with all the food Kit had brought, she turned to Jake. "When do you think the house will be ready to move into? I'm getting anxious."

Even though Jake had been glued to her side, never letting her out of his sight for the past couple of days, Kit kind of liked it. Inseparable, she decided, sounded a good deal better and more romantic than babysitter. And that's what he'd been doing since the kidnapping.

If it hadn't been for a faceless man she wouldn't know if she passed on the street, she might be dead now. And because of that, she had a renewed appreciation for life. In fact, there was no better attitude adjustment than staring death in the face, or in this case, a furious, crazy Collin Boyd, and getting a brand-new outlook on the future.

She didn't intend to waste a precious second getting on with her life, which included moving into the Crandall House, the old relic Jake was revamping from the inside out.

"Getting excited about moving in?" The two extra crews Jake had added to the remodeling job had accelerated the progress considerably, but the work still had a ways to go. They had both chewed fingernails down to the quick watching the place come together enough to look like an actual home, instead of a rundown rattle trap built in 1888.

Looking over at Kit's willowy body, her long silver hair pulled back in a ponytail, Jake still couldn't believe his good fortune. He was so close to having what he wanted it scared him shitless. "You still want to have the Memorial Day cookout there even with all this going on?"

She'd thought of nothing else, except maybe Collin and her upcoming testimony at his hearing. Add in worrying about Baylee's situation with Connor and little Sarah and some days it was all too much to deal with.

But the get-together might serve one purpose. It might get their minds off things even if it was only for a few hours. "You bet. And I think we should go ahead and move in," she pointed out as she unloaded the first few trays of food from the back of the car.

He wanted to give her the world, but his practical sense kicked in as he picked up an additional tray of food. "Kit, we can't move in if they're still updating the wiring and the plumbing. I'm certain we won't even have electricity for another week."

As they made their way up to Dylan's front door, she glossed over what she saw as a minor inconvenience. "Silly details. It'd be like camping out. Think about it. As long as the shower in the bathroom downstairs works, which it does, that's all we'd need. Think how it will feel waking up in that round master bedroom." Even loaded down with the food, she did a happy dance before wiggling her butt. "I promise I could make you forget all about wiring or plumbing. And we could make our own electricity."

"You're crazy, you know that?"

"That's me. Crazy Kit. I thought we established that already."

He sighed. "Actually the downstairs is further along than the upstairs is. I guess we could move in a bed, christen the master bedroom. You really want to go ahead and move in?"

In the light-hearted vein of a woman in love, she teased, "Jake Boston, do I hear a hint of hesitation? Are you trying to backtrack, get out of this whole thing already?"

He laughed. "Nope. I'm committed. Definitely committed."

"You make it sound like a death sentence. If it doesn't work out, we can always…"

"Uh-uh, no backing out for me. I was thinking more along the lines of—when do we set a date?"

"Oh Jake." She almost lost her hold on the food containers.

At that moment, Baylee opened the front door with all the enthusiasm of a woman who had been waiting for male strippers to show up.

"Hey, what took so long? Sarah's been asleep for twenty minutes. And a hungry Quinn has been here for half an hour grumbling about no food. You know how she gets when she doesn't eat." But then Baylee noticed the bewildered expression on Kit's face. "What's wrong?" Baylee reached to take the food Kit was holding.

Kit shot a look at Baylee. "So what if the man of my dreams has lousy timing? He chooses now to bring up setting a date for the wedding."

Baylee stared at her friend. "Ohmygod. Well, that's better than evading the subject entirely, right?" Eyeing the terror-stricken look on Jake's face, she chuckled. "Better come up with a date before he changes his mind."

"Good thinking," Kit decided, looking over at Jake.

Dylan joined Baylee at the door, and she automatically handed off the food to him and took several of the other containers from Jake. Baylee turned to Dylan. "Looks like we have a wedding to plan."

"Okay. I'll go dig out a bottle of champagne. We can celebrate over lunch. This smells great, by the way. What's on the menu?"

As Dylan turned to go find the champagne, Jake dumped the rest of his food containers on Baylee, who rolled her eyes and said, "Looks like you two need some alone time. I'll just go set some of this food in front of Quinn. Surely there's something in here that will tide her over until we get to the main course."

Jake followed Kit into the entryway, and immediately grabbed her arm, pulling her back from the rest. "I'd planned on putting the ring on your finger without an audience. Honest. It's just that if we're doing this now, here..." He pulled a small box out of his jeans pocket. "There's no candlelight, but the sentiment is heartfelt. I had this delivered this morning."

"Ohmygod." Kit reached up to touch his cheek. "I've been waiting to say this for years; Kit Boston, Mrs. Jake Boston. Let's get married, Jake." She threw her arms around his neck. "I don't much care when or where or how."

He wrapped her up, touched his mouth to hers. "I love you, Kit." He handed her the box. "I went with a traditional rock. But if you don't like it, if you'd rather have something else, you can always..."

"I want this one." Her vision blurred with tears. She sniffled and took the box, opening it in one motion. But nothing about the ring was traditional to her. Tucked inside was a white gold ring with an emerald setting surrounded by a cluster of diamonds.

"Jake, it's beautiful." She held it out to him and said, "Here, you slip it on my finger." Kit snuffed back tears. Just then, a woman with long black hair and exotic looking almond-shaped eyes stepped into the hallway. When she saw Kit crying, the woman shot Jake an accusing look and asked, "What's this? What did you do to her?"

Kit held out her hand. "Quinn, it's official. We're getting married."

Quinn pulled her in for a hug. "Make it an outdoor wedding on the lawn at Crandall House. Fall would be perfect."

About that time Reese Brennan walked up to the open doorway, joining the crowded foyer. He'd overheard just enough to add, "I call dibs on best man. I say Dylan gets to ride shotgun as the lowly groomsman."

The groomsman in question appeared peeling the paper back from a bottle of champagne. "It's time to get this party rocking. And we'll see who gets to stand up as best man after we go one-on-one in a game of horse."

"Like you could beat me," Reese snorted, as he leaned in to Jake's ear so only he could hear. "You sure about this?"

Jake's grin was wide when he answered, "Never more sure of anything in my life."

Kit beamed. "I like the idea of an outdoor wedding at Crandall House. What better way to christen the entire place than with our very own wedding?"

"Okay, now that we have the mushy stuff out of the way," Quinn suggested, "let's eat."

Over steak fajitas outside on the deck, the six of them bounced around ideas for the wedding, discussed the renovations on the Crandall House, and came up with the idea of having a painting party there as soon as possible to make the move-in go a little faster.

After the meal, they all collectively cleared the table and dealt with leftovers. But when it came time to talk among themselves they did what men and women have been doing in social gatherings since junior high; they split up into gender. The women hovered in the kitchen to talk, leaving the guys to drift back outside on the deck using the excuse that they needed to clean up the grill.

As soon as they'd settled down in deck chairs, Reese turned to Dylan. "How's it working out with Baylee and Sarah in the house? I can't believe you offered her your place."

"I knew it would be different having a woman in the house, but it's a whole other planet with a baby. Sarah woke up this morning at four o'clock. Four o'clock. She's often awake in the middle of the night. The key is to sleep when she sleeps. Sarah's a good baby, though, even the way she cries is kinda cute."

Jake exchanged a disbelieving look with Reese that said, "I'll bet that wears off in a couple of days." But he dropped the idea to needle Dylan about it when Reese wanted to know, "Do you think this little get-together was such a good idea? What if we were followed?"

Reese gave a nod in the direction of the strip of beach behind Dylan's house. "What if the bastards are out there lurking, watching, waiting to make their next move?" He knew it sounded paranoid, but after the last few weeks, he was beginning to think all three of the Boyd sons might have a screw loose.

"Then they'll know we're right here and not going anywhere," Jake uttered convincingly. He took a swig of his beer. "Kit wants to act like business as usual, go on like nothing's happened, thinks I can't be with her every single minute of every day. But there is no more business as usual. That just isn't going to happen until this thing is settled."

"Yeah, same here. Baylee's jumpy. She reacts to every little thing, every little sound." And now that Dylan knew why, it explained her demeanor. "It's sad to watch." Then to Reese, he asked, "Did you take care of that restraining order?"

"Sure, Baylee officially has a protective order against one Connor Morgan Boyd, for all the good it did Kit with Collin."

Jake pointed out, "That's why it can't be business as usual."

"Connor isn't getting near Baylee while I'm around."

Jake sent a sad look toward Dylan. "Yeah? That's what I said about Collin and look how that turned out." It still irked him that he'd been stupid enough to walk into the house blind like that.

"You can't let your guard down for a minute, Dylan, not for a second. That's what I did. Kit could have been…" His voice trailed off as he stared off in the direction of the water. The memory of waking up and finding her gone would stay with him for some time. He needed to be the one that kept her safe, not some stranger, or rather some faceless killer. "I called Holloway this morning. The ballistics confirmed his suspicion. Collin wasn't shot by Auslo or Taft, that's for sure. According to Holloway, he had to coerce a very uncooperative doctor into talking. The doc who treated Collin dug out a large caliber slug from his chest that matched the ones from Auslo and Taft."

Dylan nodded. "That means the same man who saved Kit's life, the one who showed up and played hero, shot all three of them. Wow, that's like gunslinger city in the twenty-first century. The man has to be a pro—with something to prove. And since he left one of those toy cowboys in Kit's hand, it links him to not only Alana's murder but the others as well."

"Exactly. That means Kit's savior hero is also a ruthless killer with a grudge, a man who is responsible, by my count, for six murders. And if he'd been a better shot, if he hadn't missed his mark, Collin would have made it seven. Not exactly the hero type ready for a medal ceremony." He paused before adding, "But I owe him for saving Kit's life."

Reese couldn't believe this latest bizarre turn. "Depends on who's pinning the medal, don't you think? Who is this guy?"

"No idea. But I think he has some connection to the Parkers. What connection I don't know exactly. The scary thing is he had his chance to hurt Kit but didn't take it. With her connection to Alana he could have easily taken his grudge to the Second Generation thing. I'm thinking he didn't for some reason." At least he hoped that was true. "He had the perfect opportunity that night. Instead, he charges in and saves the day, saves Kit."

Jake was both eternally grateful for that and irritated as hell that it hadn't been him doing the saving. Ego, he supposed, was a fragile thing. But as he watched the waves, he knew he was indebted to a man he wouldn't know if he passed him on the street. "I just hope he knows who the good guys are in all of this."

Reese looked like he had something on his mind. "Collin's violating the restraining order pales in comparison to the kidnapping charge. His pre-trial hearing's set for July. Jacob Gatz got it moved up on the docket. Kit already knows her testimony and yours could put Collin away for a long time. This isn't over, guys. Not by a long shot. And then there's Connor to consider. Why doesn't the man just leave Baylee alone? You'd think he would want nothing more to do with her after what he did. He's gotten away with it, why doesn't he just move on?"

Dylan shook his head. "That's what I can't figure. Jake and I saw the guy's eyes. I think he's unhinged. But it's like the rapist is infatuated with his victim. If it isn't that, I'm not sure what his angle is. All I know is he can't find out about Sarah. Did you have time to take care of that other matter?"

"That's something else I wanted to talk to you about in person, face-to-face. Are you sure you want to go through with this, Dylan? Once I amend the birth certificate naming you as the father, you are committed financially, buddy, for now and all eternity. That's a big step up from offering the two of them a place to stay."

This was news to Jake. He turned to stare long and hard at Dylan, knowing he was a nice guy, but even nice guys had their limits. "I'm with Reese on this, why would you want to do that? You're stepping into the middle of what could be the custody battle from hell if Connor ever finds out she's his daughter."

Rare irritation showed on Dylan's face. "You're kidding me, right? Weren't we just talking about how deranged this guy is? Are you saying that you want that baby to split time with him where he gets her on weekends? In terms of custody, isn't that the norm? Try to picture that guy picking her up on a Friday night and willingly returning her every Sunday afternoon back to Baylee like the nice reasonable sort he is. Does that sound like we're talking about the same guy who raped Baylee? You guys talk a good game, but I'm not letting that man win here, not when it comes to Baylee, or that baby."

Jake slapped Dylan on the back. "You're right. I wasn't thinking. Reese, can you do it?"

"Yeah. I've already set the wheels in motion, sent someone to Denver this morning before the weekend. As Dylan's attorney, I just wanted to make sure he knew what he was getting into."

"Thanks, but I've thought this through. It's the only way I know to keep Boyd at bay if he gets wind of Sarah and starts nosing around birth certificates."

"Then congratulations, daddy. You're the proud father of a blonde, blue-eyed baby girl that looks amazingly just like you. How you managed that without all the perks is classic Dylan Burke."

They toasted the occasion by knocking their beer bottles together and then draining the last drops. Dylan looked out over the water, grew serious though. "This isn't the way I planned to become a father."

Reese slapped him on the back. "No perks yet, huh?"

"I'm working on it."

"Well then, that's different. It's just a matter of time before the woman succumbs to that infamous Burke charm and drops down at your feet like every other female does within ten feet."

"Yeah well, she's a little different there."

Reese grinned, enjoying himself. "Yeah, I noticed. I like her. She's been through a helluva ordeal." He left it unsaid that the same statement could be applied to Quinn, who was turning out to be an intriguing challenge. Or Kit for that matter. They were almost like three identical peas in a pod.

"Just because we've figured out the birth certificate angle doesn't mean this is over. Connor Boyd might be a raving lunatic but he's a damn cunning lawyer. If he finds out about Sarah, the recently amended birth certificate won't fool him for long. The man isn't stupid, Reese stated."

"I know that. But next time it won't be so easy. I don't intend to let my guard down."

"None of us will," Jake agreed.

While the guys plotted on their own, Quinn and Kit cornered Baylee in the kitchen wanting to know every detail about her living arrangement with Dylan.

"Is he as nice as he seems?" Quinn wanted to know. "I'll bet he has women coming out of the woodwork. I bet he doesn't even surf; it's probably an act just to hang out at the beach and add to his score card."

Kit shook her head. "No. I saw the surfing photos in his office. The guy's been all over the world, surfed the best beaches."

Determined to keep Baylee from walking into quicksand where Dylan was concerned, Quinn stubbornly added, "Let's face it, surfing allows him to have his pick of women lazing at the beach, sample all the pink taco he can get without buying the meal."

Baylee couldn't help it; she spewed out the Diet Coke she'd been sipping. "Quinn, you never cease to put things in perspective. I really love that about you."

Just like they'd done when they were younger, when they'd first discovered boys weren't completely gross, Baylee took the conversation in stride. These two were like sisters, the closest thing to family she had.

"Since you insist on the deets, I've overheard a few phone conversations. Women call the house, leave messages on his machine, his cell phone, and leave assorted TM's day and night. That doesn't even address the e-mails he must get. I know they aren't all work related, either. But guys, Dylan's unattached, a free agent. He's playing the game. No single guy in L.A. lives the celibate life. Why he asked me to move in is a mystery to me. Go figure."

Kit sighed, remembering those days of L.A. dating. "God, I am so glad I'm off the market. I wouldn't go back to that world again for anything."

Quinn bumped her shoulder. "You finally landed The Jake. Come on, Kit, admit it. You were never into the game the same way Baylee and I were. We knew you always held out hope The Jake would come around."

"Maybe," Kit agreed as she took a long look at Baylee. "When I was in the hospital Dylan asked me about you," Kit admitted with a wide grin.

"He did?" Taken aback, Baylee crossed her arms over her chest and leaned against the counter, feeling a lot like this was junior high again. "Are you sure he meant it that way, maybe he just wanted to know because he..." Her voice trailed off as she stared at the comical look on Kit's face.

"He wanted to know if you were with anyone." Kit jabbed Baylee in the ribs. "He's definitely relationship interested."

"More like interested in another conquest," Quinn added.

In spite of that kiss they'd shared, Baylee didn't want to admit she'd had doubts that a man like Dylan could really be interested in her of all people, a single mom. Why would he be when he could have any woman he wanted?

Although he seemed to like Sarah well enough and enjoyed being around her, the fact that he had women calling him all the time was something she couldn't ignore. She wouldn't. The guy was a major player. It seemed to her that if Dylan had so many women in his fan base, women of his own choosing, women he didn't even have to work to get, he certainly wouldn't zero in on her.

Before she'd had Sarah, she knew firsthand the L.A. dating scene could be brutal. She'd seen Dylan's kind a hundred times. The typical player didn't own a beating heart where women were concerned.

Quinn narrowed her eyes, stared hard at Baylee. As if reading her thoughts, Quinn warned, "Don't go there. You can't change a guy like that. You're here in his house temporarily. Don't start getting ideas that you can tame him. It's not possible. If you're uncomfortable here, say the word; you know you and Sarah can bunk with me."

They'd already had this discussion, but it was nice to hear the offer again. "I'm fine. The idea of moving again makes my stomach hurt. I'm not falling for Dylan. He's a nice guy, but that's it. I have to think of what's best for Sarah. That's first and foremost. And not just in that arena either. Besides, this is nonsense, a guy like Dylan is not interested in someone like me."

Sensing a dip in Baylee's self-confidence, Kit shot a quick look toward Quinn before reminding Baylee, "Hey, he'd be lucky to get a woman like you."

"Damn straight," Quinn agreed. "You're too good for him." Then just as they'd done since they were eight, Quinn held out a curved pinky on each hand, the gesture a symbol of their unity. Kit held out hers and Baylee did the same. In a circle, in unison, the three repeated the chant. "Together we let no one hurt us. We are most powerful when we are one. We draw strength from each other. One."

They fist-bumped each other as they always did.

"You guys are the best."

Quinn laughed. "We're fucking awesome."

But the idea that Dylan could be attracted to her niggled at the back of Baylee's head the rest of the afternoon and refused to budge. Surrounded by her friends she tried to concentrate on why they were there, and put Surfer Boy completely out of her mind.

By the time they'd all gathered around the dining room table, Jake had opened up the boxes of stuff they had acquired from Alana's attic, the stuff Quinn had used to develop her timeline.

As they all turned their attention to Quinn, Baylee decided that Dylan was just a nice guy trying to do a good deed. The fact that he seemed to be a giving and generous soul cemented her belief that he obviously felt sorry for her and was more than likely confusing pity with attraction.

Baylee forced herself to focus on Quinn, who remained standing. They were there to go over the evidence she'd memorized in her spare time. When Quinn picked up a whiteboard that she'd brought to make her points and adjusted it on an easel, Baylee settled down to listen.

"After our last meeting at Gloria's, I didn't feel comfortable with Reese's 'sheer speculation' remark. Let's face it, I took exception. It hit too close to home and got me to thinking about all those times, all those steps you have to take to convince the authorities a crime has taken place. I know from personal experience how skeptical the powers that be are when it comes to looking at someone who has wealth and power as a suspect—for anything."

An image of her stepfather flickered through her mind. Years of practice had her quickly pushing the memories out of her head. "So, I redid the major points on the timeline—twice. It took me some time before I felt good about linking Alana's cashier's checks worth half a million dollars to the same timeframe as the settlement the Parkers received from the lawsuit against McKetrick Construction. But then I called Reese and asked him to get me the exact date of the court win and when they actually received their first payment. He provided the dates you see here." She pointed to the figures written on the whiteboard. "May 1967, the Parkers were awarded a fifteen-million-dollar judgment to be paid out over three years."

Reese took it from there. "But the first five million didn't hit their bank account until December. The second came in November of 1968, and the final payment was delivered in August of 1969. Even though by that time the Parkers were deceased, the money went directly into the Parker trust, which we now know Jessica Boyd controlled."

"Why were the installments so erratic?" Dylan asked as he tried to follow the diagram Quinn had drawn on the whiteboard.

Reese explained, "The settlement sent the construction company into bankruptcy. They had a little trouble meeting the payment schedule. They had to liquidate a few of their assets along the way. The court made sure that the schedule was met, even at one point refusing a motion from the company's attorneys to prevent them from filing for bankruptcy until the final payment had been delivered. I can only speculate as to who might have put pressure on the court."

For clarification, Baylee added, "And by pressure what you're really suggesting is some judge took a bribe?"

Before Reese could answer, Quinn piped up, "Let's not ask the lawyer to speculate about something we can't prove. After all, we wouldn't want to put him on the spot and actually have him offer an unqualified opinion in favor of our side."

Noting tension beginning to build between Reese and Quinn, Kit quickly concluded, "And the Boyd lawyers were particularly greedy. They weren't content with getting their cut of say, thirty percent from the lawsuit. No, they wanted all of it, the entire fifteen million. So they devised a plan of action."

Reese ignored Quinn's dig and suggested, "Let's back up to when this whole thing started with the Parker lawsuit. At some point during trial, the Boyd Boyd Geller & Gatz team realized they were in over their heads. They weren't winning; the situation looked grim. They needed a new plan."

Quinn handed out several more pages of documents. "A good plan, Counselor Brennan. In order to get a better idea of the conversation Jake had with Will Forrester, Alana's first husband, and an obvious pawn in the whole scam at trial, I needed the gist of their conversation. With Jake's help I transcribed what was said. According to Forrester's own words, there were no documents left to show up at trial to prove McKetrick Construction was guilty of anything because he'd personally shredded them all at the behest of management. What's a smart lawyer to do without documentation? If you're the clever little shysters at BBG&G, you pony up some fast even when they don't exist.

"With Alana having the inside track because she married Forrester, the environmental engineer, she got close enough to him on a 24/7 basis, knowing he holds all the key phrases they needed to make duplicates look real, like the toxicology lingo. Smitten with the sex kitten Alana, Will Forrester admitted to providing the key phrases, the key words. Alana passed the info on to good old Jess and Sumner. And before you know it they had documents that looked good enough to fool even Forrester.

"In fact, the lingo was so convincing they produced documents good enough to fake out McKetrick in court. They bluffed their way past the other side to victory. Score points for their side. It's as simple as that.

"My guess is those cashier's checks the guys found in the attic were Alana's payment for her role as Forrester's wife." She held up a staying hand as Reese started to object and said, "Speculation. Sure. But at some point you have to concede the fact that Forrester said there were no other documents. Who gets close to Forrester and finds out there are no papers proving the dumping, even goes so far as to marry the guy? Alana.

"If you read what Forrester says, one day the documents just show up on his desk." She cast a sneer Reese's way and added, "Unless, of course, you believe they were delivered by the document fairy. I suspect they had to test the waters, find out whether or not the forged docs looked real enough to pass muster in court. So they forged a few, left them on Forrester's desk for verification. When he panicked, they knew their documents looked good enough and started applying some pressure on the engineer.

"Then they forced the guy into testifying at trial, and dropped the bomb that he shredded what he thought were the only documents. Defense panicked, called for a recess, settled out of court, again victory for their side.

"Who dumps him as soon as the trial ends in their favor? Alana. And Forrester was there, caught up in the trial, our only living witness that we know of. That's his theory as well, and I'm buying into it right along with him." Quinn turned to stare at Reese. "The Parkers won fifteen million. BBG&G got thirty percent of the take. Somewhere down the road they got greedy. When they realized this old couple's only son is missing in Vietnam, they saw an opening. They hatched the murder idea and used the Manson killing spree to cover their tracks. Fortuitous creatures to be sure. For forty years it worked. So Counselor Brennan, who are you going to side with, those bloodsuckers at BBG&G and the deadly Alana, or Will Forrester, a guy caught up in the whole thing, a guy who loses the woman he thinks loves him and his career all in one fell swoop?" She had him there, Reese thought. "Did you ever consider a career in law, Dr. Tyler?"

She grinned in spite of the dislike for the man.

"Okay, I'll concede the fact you make a plausible argument. But we need something concrete."

"That would be the gun," Baylee pointed out.

"For safekeeping and to get it out of the trunk of Jake's car, I turned it over to Donovan, who's prepared to take it to the sheriff's department just as soon as we can get someone over there in the cold case department to return our calls. It hasn't been easy." In his courtroom voice, Reese warned, "But guys, just because…"

Quinn didn't let him get any farther before she lost her temper, glaring at Reese in disgust. Cutting him off, she pointed out, "You know, I'm getting kind of tired of your gloom and doom attitude. It's one thing to be the voice of reason, but to be a constant horse's ass, against all reason, against everything we're trying to do here, that's getting old."

Reese eyed the fireball that was Quinn. Those exotic almond eyes burned a hole through him. He was determined to get past the fact that the good doctor didn't like him very much. And he hadn't become the best criminal attorney in L.A. without storing up plenty of drive and determination along the way, with a steady supply of stubbornness thrown in for good measure.

So he gave her a patient look. "The point I was about to make is simple. We need the actual police report from forty years ago. We don't even know if the gun that killed the Parkers was a .357 without the police report. That means we'll need to get them to sit down with us at some point, persuade them to dig through their evidence room."

When Quinn started to speak, he quickly added, "At this point we don't even know that the evidence still exists. Like I said, Jordan Donovan and I have called a number of times and left messages. Getting the sheriff's department to take another look at a forty-year-old double murder case is tougher than you might think. And remember, if we think Jessica Boyd and Alana killed the Parkers, the suspects are dead and buried at this point. What motivation do the police have to care about this case now? It's just us, or rather, Kit that has the greatest interest in this, so we need to do some fancy convincing to get them moving. Baylee's right, the gun is it. The Parkers have no family to prod the police along. After all this time, it's forgotten. If the evidence is still sitting there gathering dust in a box, it's still just us. It doesn't mean it's impossible, just that we may have to go the extra mile to make it happen."

The expression on Quinn's face said she was mollified with his response, but her demeanor remained stoic. "I guess that's as close as I'll get to getting you to admit I did my homework on this."

Looking through the papers, Dylan admitted, "I'm impressed with the work, Quinn. But if we get them to reopen this thing and it points to Alana and Jessica… " His voice trailed off as he sent Kit a sympathetic look.

Kit picked up on what he was thinking. "For me, knowing for certain would close that chapter of my life for good. I know what kind of person Alana was. Knowing what happened to the Parkers and believing in my heart Alana was responsible, if that gun ties her to the crime, then the money, that money she got from the sale of the ranch and the land was just wrong. She lived very well on her portion of the Parker money. Let's face it; they all did, Jessica and Sumner, Frank Geller, and Eva Gatz. They founded a legal empire with that money, not to mention developed a sprawling estate on the shores of Malibu. Knowing that, do you think I could live with myself if I took a dime from Alana's estate? Before I knew about the murders, I didn't want the house or anything she owned, but now, knowing she might have benefited…from the murders of that old couple, there isn't anything that'll stop me from getting to the truth when we're this close…"

But Jake reminded her, "I have a feeling the Boyds will give it one helluva try. And we have to be ready for whatever they bring." He didn't throw out his belief that Collin would do anything to prevent both of them from testifying, but then he was pretty sure she had already lost sleep over that.

"At the risk of being labeled the voice of gloom and doom again," Reese gave Quinn a look of pure lawyer-like scorn before going on, "I have to caution all of you that just because Alana hid the gun in the attic doesn't mean she used it in the commission of a crime. She could have been holding it for someone or…"

Again, Quinn interrupted like a volcano. "Spoken like a true criminal defense attorney. Look, we aren't stupid. We know all that, Reese. We aren't here to send Jessica Boyd and Alana Stevens to jail." She leaned toward him and said emphatically, "You yourself just admitted they're dead. They aren't going anywhere. But for Kit's sake, and Gloria's, since they are the ones who've been living with these nightmares about the Parker murders for weeks now, I think we need to find out what really happened to them.

And it would be nice to solve a forty-year-old murder mystery. I know in a way this is all based on speculation, but I think to do this we need to be able to step outside the box from time to time. If you can't do that…"

Like two sparring boxers exchanging blows in the ring, it was Reese's turn to cut her short. "I can think outside the box. I can come up with a reasonable explanation as to what really happened to the Parkers. I can buy into the theory. I don't have a problem with that, but keep in mind we've done a lot of assuming here. You can't solve this thing based on assumptions only. At some point you have to have hard evidence. That's all I'm saying."

"Agreed," Quinn said without a trace of hard feelings.

Reese turned to stare at her. "I must have misunderstood."

"Not at all. We're all trying to come up with something concrete. And you just keep knocking it down. Of course I know that at some point we will have to find hard evidence pointing to Jessica and Alana connecting them to the murders. But can we agree if the gun turns out to be significant that has to count in the grand scheme even if we can't put it in the hands of Alana or Jessica or Sumner Boyd for that matter."

"Absolutely."

"Well, now that we have that out of the way," Dylan said a little too cheerfully as he pushed back from the table and stood up. "Let's have some of Kit's chocolate cheesecake."

※ ※ ※ ※ ※

Later, after Reese and Quinn had left and it was just the four of them tidying up Dylan's dining room, Baylee was putting all the papers back into the boxes when she picked up Kit's birth certificate, examining it line by line.

"You were a skinny little thing. Look at this, you only weighed five pounds when you were born. How can someone who weighed so little at birth grow up to be such an Amazon woman now?"

She waved the paper in the air at Kit and added, "As hard as this thing was to find, don't you think you should keep it in a better place?"

"Let me see that. I haven't seen my birth certificate since that day at the hospital. I was pretty out of it."

"Let's face it, you were blitzed," Jake teased, thinking back to the day they'd all found out Kit's mother was really Gloria Chambers Gandis.

But Baylee wasn't listening to the chatter. She'd only thought to pick up the paper and hand it off to Kit. But now what she read had her jumping back. "Oh, my God. Kit, did you look at your birth certificate? I mean really look. Did you see this? We were so focused on looking at what it said about your mother we completely overlooked Box 3 and 3A." Kit peered over Baylee's shoulder. When Baylee pointed to the box in question, and Kit saw what it said, she snatched the paper out of Baylee's hand.

Now it was Baylee nudging Kit to show her where to look. "It says you were a twin. Skip over to the right of the box where it asks, if twin, what was the order of birth? See the 3A box is marked 2ND. According to that, you were a twin, Kit, born second."

"Could that be right? Could they have made a mistake?" Kit blinked, and kept trying to focus on the paper, including every box until she got down to Box Number 3 and 3A.

Everyone gathered around Kit, who stood there, speechless, trying to determine if Baylee was kidding or not.

When her eyes found the box in question, she dropped into one of the dining room chairs. Over her shoulder Jake studied the birth certificate line by line. "Alana and Jessica didn't just steal Kit, but apparently there were two babies. What happened to the other baby?"

Kit finally found her speech. "Jake, could that be Ben, the one you found living in Galway, the one you've been looking for on the Internet, the same one Quinn remembered my father mentioning that day when we were kids at the beach? Did you look at his date of birth? Could it be him, or is there yet another brother out there somewhere I've never seen?"

"It didn't occur to me to look at his birth date. But I will." Jake turned to Dylan. "I need your laptop."

"No problem." The two computer geeks headed out into the living room where Dylan had set up his makeshift office area after giving up his personal space to Sarah.

After booting up, and logging on, Jake furiously tapped keys, searching, hitting database after database until he found what he was looking for.

"I'll be damned. He's twenty-four years old just like Kit, and won't turn twenty-five until the eleventh of October. They're twins, Dylan. I should have spotted that before now."

"So this brother, this Ben Griffin, was taken to Ireland? Jake, that's crazy. Let's say Alana and Jessica just decided to ship the kid to Ireland. Why would they do that?"

But Kit had already formed her own theory. Standing off to the side with Baylee, she concluded, "My father had to be in on it from the beginning. He didn't just show up after the fact and take the baby out of the country. He did it so Gloria would never know she had a son. How despicable can two people be?"

Baylee pointed out, "But you were born second. When Jake and I confronted Gloria that morning, I'm positive she didn't say a thing about another baby. She was pretty convincing, Kit. Gloria only knew that she'd had a little girl. She said nothing about another baby." She turned to Jake for confirmation.

Jake nodded. "She didn't say a word about giving birth to twins, that's for sure." He kept staring at Baylee. "We would have remembered something like that."

"I haven't been through childbirth. But you have," Kit said turning to Baylee. "Could she have lost consciousness at some point, passed out during delivery and only heard them talk about the baby girl, not the boy."

"It's possible, I guess."

"She told me that at one point she kicked up quite a fuss because they wouldn't let her see me. Maybe shipping Gloria three thousand miles away was to prevent some nurse from slipping up and mentioning twins."

"So you're set to give Gloria the benefit of the doubt on this?"

"I am. This needs to come from me. And I don't think it's something she should hear over the phone." Kit turned to Jake. "I'll give Gloria a call. Tell her we're stopping by with some news. Tell her we've set a date for the wedding. Somehow I'll work this latest bomb into the conversation, sort of like good news bad news. Good news is we're getting married. Bad news is you've got a long lost son, my twin, who's living in Ireland, a baby boy you've never set eyes on.

"For God's sakes, is there anything else those people have done that we should know about? What kind of person does this sort of thing?" She looked at Baylee. "I trusted my father, loved him, and the fact that he could be a party to something like this just makes me ill. And if it makes me sick, think how Gloria will take this latest news. This is going to hit her hard."

Dylan exchanged looks with Jake, who acted perplexed by her calmness. "I'll say one thing for you, Kit, having all the chaos going on in your life makes you one helluva woman in a crisis situation, a woman who without a doubt thinks on her feet."

And that was an understatement, thought Dylan as he walked both of them to the car. All three women were unlike any he'd ever met before. According to them, they'd all had difficult, abusive childhoods, and yet, all of them were incredibly strong. Baylee joined him on the driveway with a wide awake Sarah just in time to wave them off, wondering how Gloria would take the news.

"I can't believe those two would steal Gloria's babies like that." She thumped her head with a free hand. "Duh. What's wrong with me, they were cold-blooded killers who murdered an old couple in their sleep for the land and the money and I'm having trouble wrapping my mind around them stealing babies. Those two were capable of just about anything, weren't they?"

"You're a mother. It's hard to understand how women could be so…"

"Heartless?"

"Cold."

"Same thing." She thought of her own mother, who'd left her without so much as a goodbye, and decided that maybe women back then were all cut from the same callous, merciless mold. Certainly not fit to be mothers.

As they watched Jake's car back out of the driveway, Dylan thought of something. "How about we go out for dinner? I know a great French bistro a couple of miles from here that looks out over the water."

The dimmer switch clicked on. Baylee didn't get many offers, especially these days. In fact it had been almost two years since she'd gone out on a real date, an honest-to-goodness sit-down-to-dinner date. But she wasn't stupid. She knew that trusting this player came with a warning label. She looked over at him standing there in his driveway and saw the charming, self-confident look on his face.

Oh, what the hell, she thought, she hadn't been to dinner in forever. It was just dinner for chrissakes.

Grateful for the invitation, without having to think it into oblivion, she looked him straight in the eye and said, "Dylan, you've got yourself a date."

CHAPTER 9

In Agoura Hills, Gloria Gandis poured another glass of wine in celebration of the news that Jake and Kit had a wedding to plan. When she turned to hold up her glass in a toast she noticed the dour look on their faces. It was obvious they had something else to say. "What aren't you telling me?"

Kit took the glass of wine from Gloria's hand and set it down on the end table next to the sofa. "Come sit down. This won't be easy."

"Then you aren't pregnant."

Jake chuckled in spite of the somber mood. He looked at Kit.

"Not yet," Kit said, as her cheeks flushed pink. "We haven't been trying all that long."

Gloria's heart dropped a little learning Kit wasn't pregnant. The idea of having grandchildren to spoil filled her with warm and fuzzy vibes she couldn't hold back. But looking at their faces now, a bit of her intuition kicked in. This wasn't that kind of news.

"It's about Ben Griffin." Kit finally forced out the words.

Gloria knew Jake had been trying to find Kit's long lost brother, a brother that had surfaced when Jake had stumbled on information that he was the one receiving

John Griffin's residuals from his acting days instead of Kit.

But now, Gloria sat down as Jake went into what they had discovered reading Kit's birth certificate. "There were twins, Gloria. You delivered twins."

"What? Oh God, that can't be. No. No. That just can't be. How is that possible? I don't remember that. They made a mistake."

"I'm sorry, Gloria." Kit took out the birth certificate, handed it off to her. "Ben Griffin shares my date of birth. He was born first."

For several long minutes Gloria stared at the paper. "Alana and Jessica took two babies away from me."

"Yes. But there's more. I don't see any other way for the baby boy to have gotten all the way to Ireland without my father being in on the whole thing. John Griffin had to know, be part of it, because he had to arrange to get him there for an adoption or something."

"My guess is he left him with relatives. Ever done a family tree?" Jake asked.

Kit looked stunned. "You mean..." She looked at Gloria. "Did he have family in Ireland, Glo? You knew him better than most."

Tears welled up in Gloria's eyes. She simply nodded in answer and dropped her head in her hands. "Could he truly have been that mean, that callous, to be in on the whole conspiracy with Alana and Jessica from the beginning? My God, there was a time I thought he truly loved me. Instead, he must have plotted right along with them to steal you away from me. Only they got a huge surprise when it turned out to be not one baby, but two. And a boy at that. Alana wouldn't have wanted anything to do with a boy. She used to say such disparaging things about Jessica's sons. She'd have insisted John take the boy."

"We'll know more when Jake finds him. Maybe this Ben holds the answers to so many of our questions. The truth is we may never really know why my father helped them do this. But it's obvious to me he did."

"I've been unable to locate this Ben. If it comes to that, we'll take a trip over there and do some legwork on our own. We'll find him, Gloria, I promise you that."

The words were meant to be comforting. But kind words didn't do much to harness the rage Gloria felt. If Alana weren't already dead, John too, she might have considered doing both of them in, one after the other, slowly, she thought now, and let them suffer.

They had taken away so much from her. She'd never been a vicious kind of person, never as cold and heartless as Alana had been. But how could her own sister, mean as she was, and the man she'd loved conspire to take her babies from her? How could they have been that calculating?

The thought had no more than formed in her head when the house began to shake; the ground moved and rumbled beneath her feet. "Oh lord, what's happening," Gloria groaned as she became increasingly lightheaded.

"Earthquake," Jake declared, right before he grabbed Kit's hand and Gloria's arm to drag both of them over to stand under the dining room doorway. They stood there while the house shook and pictures fell from the walls and hit the floor. The rumbling lasted no more than twenty seconds but seemed a lot longer.

When it finally stopped, Gloria looked at both of them and announced, "I guess that teaches me about thinking murderous thoughts, especially when it comes to my own sister and John Griffin, the man I loved and trusted. They're both gone now anyway. If there's a hell, I can only hope they both feel right at home there."

After Baylee fed the baby, she placed Sarah in her carrier and brought her into the bathroom with her before jumping into the shower, where she carefully shaved the fur from her legs, and tried to come up with an outfit to wear. She finally decided on a simple, white sundress she hadn't worn in over a year.

After the shower, as she studied the mirror, she realized it was time for the chestnut hair to go. But for tonight, she gave it a few twists and turns with the curling iron, before sweeping it up with a clip, leaving a few wisps of hair framing her face.

She diapered and dressed Sarah in an apple green dress with purple gingham trim and clipped a matching bow to what few strands of hair the baby had on her head. When Dylan knocked on the bedroom door ten minutes later, she was as ready as she was likely to get. And as nervous as if she were going to her first dance instead of out to a simple meal at a restaurant.

When she opened the bedroom door, Dylan took an appreciative look and whistled. "This is the first time I've ever taken such two beautiful women out at the same time on the same date."

Baylee put her hands on her hips. "Do you practice that bull or does it just flow from the tongue naturally? You really know how to lay it on thick, don't you?"

He grinned.

And didn't he look nice, sporting a pair of snug-fitting jeans with a light blue buttoned-down shirt and a navy blazer.

But after they walked out to the living room, things got serious.

Dylan watched like a rookie from the sidelines as the veteran mom prepared for departure. She loaded the diaper bag, making sure she brought an extra outfit, additional diapers, baby wipes, and a bottle of breast milk.

Novice that he was, Dylan soon learned that taking a baby out for the evening was anything but a spur-of-the-moment event. Making reservations was a waste of time.

A genius at code and no dummy, he caught on rather quickly that the exact time of departure depended on several things. The timing had to be right, preferably just after a feeding, which was spontaneous. Then there was load time to factor in, especially if you brought along the stroller, which added to load time, depending on how much the thing weighed and how easily it folded down and traveled. And if the infant carrier doubled as the car seat you were ahead of the game.

By the time they got to the restaurant at seven-forty-five, they were both hyped up. And Sarah must have sensed their stress because she immediately went into a hissy fit. The louder Sarah got, the more keyed up Baylee became.

Trying to think fast, she suggested, "She can't be hungry; I fed her before we left. Could you get her pacifier out of the bag there, Dylan?" Dutifully, he dug into the bag with vigor, searched around before finally pulling the thing out, quickly handing it off to Baylee, who immediately tried to get it into Sarah's wailing mouth. But the infant wanted no part of the pacifier, and let her feelings be known to everyone in the dining room and some that were dining in the restaurant across the street.

After five long, loud embarrassing minutes, unable to calm the baby, and near tears herself, Baylee gave Dylan a frantic look and admitted, "I'm sorry, Dylan. I guess we need to take her back to your place."

"No problem," Dylan conceded. To the bewildered waiter, who recognized him as a longtime patron, Dylan simply handed him a generous tip and said, "Grant, I think we'll call it a night."

With that, Dylan promptly gathered up the infant carrier, grabbed the overstuffed diaper bag and followed a humiliated Baylee out the front door of the restaurant. But getting Sarah into her car seat while she was still squirming and crying proved to be almost as mortifying to Dylan and Baylee as the scene inside had been. The patrons coming and going in the parking lot looked at both of them as if they were a couple of child abusers bent on causing harm to a defenseless six-month-old. Why else would a baby carry on so?

Once the car began to move, a red-faced, hot, and sweaty, Sarah finally stopped screaming. Dylan took advantage of the break and made a hurried exit out of the parking lot. Thankfully, on the way home, she calmed down all the way enough to fall asleep. The ten-minute drive was completed in stony silence. But for Dylan and Baylee, the excitement of the evening had disappeared in a huff.

To make matters worse, as soon as they opened the front door and stepped inside, the first thing they both heard was yet another woman's voice leaving a seductive message on the answering machine. "Dyl, this is Melissa, if you aren't busy tonight why don't we hook up at The Cove, maybe make a night of it? What do you say, sexy? Call me."

Baylee tried to make a fast exit to the bedroom, but then she realized Dylan still held the carrier with a sleeping Sarah nestled inside. Baylee was mortified to hear her own voice quiver as she whispered, "Here, I'll take her, Dylan. I'll go put her down. You go call Melissa, salvage the rest of your evening."

But Dylan refused to relinquish the carrier. Instead, he stubbornly countered, "I've got her." He declined to hand her off. Instead, they both marched solemnly down the hall to the room designated as Sarah's and made their way to the crib. But it was Dylan who undid the straps on the carrier, picking up an exhausted Sarah and slinked her little body down into the depths of the bed before Baylee slipped a blanket around her.

Once tucked in, the screaming child from the previous half hour took on the appearance of a miniature, sleeping angel. They both stared down at the baby as if seeing her for the very first time that day.

The golden silence was a side benefit.

Outside in the hallway, even though Baylee looked like she was ready to weep and make a mad dash into the spare bedroom, Dylan made the best of it. "How about Chinese? They deliver."

"Look, Dylan, I'll be fine. It isn't even eight-thirty yet. In L.A. the evening doesn't even get started for hours yet. There's plenty of time for you to hook up with Melissa." She turned to dash into the room next door to change clothes. Instinctively, he latched on to her hand, entwining his fingers around hers.

Dylan had no interest in Melissa. He wished to God he did. Melissa was uncomplicated, unlike Baylee Scott, who was dealing with more issues than Lindsay Lohan.

He followed Baylee into the spare room and stood in the doorway. "I'm ordering Chinese; what do you want?"

Disheartened, Baylee's shoulders slumped. "Anything really. Surprise me."

After staring at each other for several awkward seconds, they separated slowly, unwillingly.

While she got out of her dress and into a comfortable pair of cotton shorts and a tank top, Dylan headed into the living room. He slipped out of his jacket and reached for the phone to place the order for food.

Ten minutes later they met back up in the kitchen.

"Food'll be here any minute. How about a glass of wine?" He knew she was nursing Sarah, and even though he hadn't seen her take a drink of anything alcoholic since he'd known her, tonight she looked like she could use something stronger than tea or juice.

Baylee took down plates, started setting the table. "Actually, I wouldn't mind a beer."

A little surprised, Dylan moved to the fridge, twisted off the cap, and handed her the bottle, turning back to open one for himself.

She took a seat at the table, studying her hands. "I'm so sorry about the restaurant."

"Hey, don't be. My sister says it's hard to go out to eat with a kid. And Sarah's just a baby. Who knows what set her off?" He took a seat at the table. When he glanced at her and saw her chin trembling, he laid his hand over both of hers. "Baylee."

"I'm a mess, Dylan. My life's a mess. I shouldn't be here. I should call my friend in Denver." She certainly didn't want to move again. But this arrangement wasn't working. The two of them living here together was awkward. It was obvious she was getting in the way of his social life. This was never going to work. Any other Saturday night, Melissa would be here instead of her.

"You're just tired. I know you haven't been sleeping. New mother, new baby doesn't sleep through the night. That's all it is, fatigue. You're worn out."

"I never should have tried to do this by myself, raise Sarah by myself. I thought I could do it. I was so sure, but I'm so tired." She leaned her head down on the table. The waterworks began in earnest.

Dylan swallowed hard. He moved to put his arms around her. "Cry it out. You'll feel better." He got up to get her a paper towel. When she took it out of his hand, he noticed both of her hands were shaking.

"When I first found out I was pregnant, I was about six weeks along. I was pretty sure of the timing because I hadn't been with anyone else. I haven't been on a damned date in almost two years. Anyway, when I found out I was pregnant; I knew it had to be from that night with Connor, after the charity event. There was no other explanation. So I made an appointment at a clinic, sat there in my car for about half an hour in the parking lot; I even opened the car door and got out once. But then, I decided I wanted this baby.

"My own mother didn't want me, Dylan. I had this chance to be a mom. It might be the only one I ever got. I so needed to confide in Kit and Quinn about all of it, but I just couldn't. Connor was calling me every day, threatening me, reminding me I better not tell anyone about what had happened. How could I remain here in L.A. and not be able to explain how I got pregnant without telling Kit and Quinn what really happened?" She sobbed harder. "I had to leave, don't you see?"

That son of a bitch, thought Dylan. Fury raged through him as he realized Connor had manipulated Baylee by using how close she was to her friends, using it as the hammer. He'd known exactly what to say to make his threat carry more weight.

"He put you in a tough spot. But from what I've seen Kit and Quinn would have been there for you through your pregnancy. He knew how close you were to your friends and used that, forced you into a corner."

"They would have too. I knew that. But I let him run me off. I was scared."

"Anyone would have been."

"Once I decided to have the baby, I went to Denver. I told Kit and Quinn I was heading to Europe to try and find my mother. Despite everything, I had a good pregnancy, a little morning sickness through the fourth month, but I was happy. My friend, Blair Rafferty, managed a temp office. She got me a job at a travel agency answering phones. I worked there up to three days before Sarah was born. I was so sure I could do this. But now…"

"Why are you questioning yourself now, Baylee? Just because she cried at the restaurant, kicked up a fuss? She was tired, keyed up. You both were, still are. That isn't your fault."

"We made a scene. Everyone was staring at us. You could tell they wanted us out of there. You were embarrassed. Don't deny it, Dylan. I could tell."

"Maybe, a little." He chuckled. "It was a new experience for me. And apparently it was for you, too. I've learned that when taking a baby anywhere you should expect anything. I won't deny I was embarrassed. I kept thinking they were looking at us like we were the ones causing her to cry like that."

"I couldn't get her to stop crying. I just wanted to go out to dinner. Was that so wrong?"

The doorbell rang.

Dylan brightened, relieved to be back on track. "Dinner's here. Let's eat outside, listen to the surf. I'll grab the food and the baby monitor."

Baylee sniffed. "Okay. I'll take the plates outside."

On the deck, they watched the waves, and ate Kung Pao chicken and Moo Goo Gai Pan. Baylee's mood lifted. How could it not? Looking out into the remnants of the sinking sun, they actually had a conversation without her breaking down and weeping all over him.

He learned she was a sports fanatic, like Kit and Quinn. She liked hockey, but was crazy about football, specifically the Oakland Raiders.

"No way. Bay area native here. The Raiders are my favorite team."

"Dad had season tickets to the Raiders when they were here in L.A. Before the team moved back to Oakland, we went to a few home games at the Coliseum. And Kit and I were at the Super Bowl in San Diego when they got blown out by Tampa Bay, lost 48 to 21. They embarrassed themselves. The only reason Quinn didn't make the trip was because she stayed behind to cram for a major exam."

"You're kidding? I was at that game with Jake and Reese."

"You were at Qualcomm Stadium for the 2003 Super Bowl? Where were you sitting?"

"Between the forty and fifty yard line, South side, up a few rows. What about you?"

"South side. Between the forty and fifty yard line, midway up. We must have used the same ticket agent."

"That's incredible. We were at the same Raider game. Not many women enjoy watching football." He remembered it hadn't been all that difficult to get a date for the game, but it had been damned near impossible to find a woman who would watch the action with him for the full four quarters.

"Hey, all of us love watching football, UCLA games, of course. We try to get tickets when the Bruins play Cal every year. But I never miss a Raider game on TV. I keep thinking one day we'll get another NFL franchise in the L.A. market, but it doesn't mean I'd stop rooting for the Raiders."

"Cal graduate just like Jake and Reese. I can see rough times ahead whenever Cal plays the Bruins."

"I know. I saw the pictures on your desk in Sarah's room."

"Interested enough for a little wager when the season starts this fall?"

"Absolutely."

They tidied up after eating, and moved into the house, settling into the living room on the sofa. Dylan automatically turned on the TV. "How about a movie?"

She wasn't sure she could keep her eyes open. But after he had stood up good old Melissa this evening, she felt like she should at least try to make an effort to be sociable. This was his house after all. And he'd been a good sport during her meltdown. Two, actually.

"Sure. What have you got?"

He pointed to a cabinet where he kept a collection of DVDs. "Ladies' choice."

She went over and started thumbing through the titles until she came to the original 1968 *Night of the Living Dead*. "How about this?" It was the Thirtieth Anniversary Edition. How cool was that?

He'd been ready for her to pull out the only chick flick he owned, *Sleepless in Seattle*, which women seemed unable to pass up while he found it boring as hell. But she surprised him. "Are you sure you want to watch sci-fi, bloodthirsty zombies?"

Taking a seat on the couch, she kicked off her shoes and got comfortable. "Technically, I consider this horror, not sci-fi, and it's a classic. But yeah, I like cheesy horror, like *Shaun of the Dead*. Priceless."

Was she putting him on? "I loved that movie. How about a double feature, what say, we make it zombie night?" The woman watched football, liked cheesy horror flicks, looked like a swimsuit model in a mismatched bikini, and filled out a pair of jeans in a way that made a man weep. How lucky could a guy get?

Dylan found that watching a movie with a true film buff, a movie he'd seen twenty times previously, brought a new dimension to it because Baylee knew all the cool trivia. "A lot of people don't know that since it was filmed in black and white the director used chocolate sauce for the blood. The actors playing the zombies had to eat so much of the stuff they got sick from all the chocolate. And the scene where the undead eat the burning flesh, they were actually gnawing on ham."

Dylan laughed at the details she provided; he couldn't help it. Nothing like behind the scenes trivia to spice up a true film buff's enjoyment.

During the break between movies, despite the baby monitor, Baylee went in and physically checked on Sarah just for her own peace of mind. When she came back, she got comfortable on the couch again and announced, "I have to do something about my hair."

As he loaded the second feature into the DVD player, he absently asked, "What's wrong with your hair?"

"It's brown."

Baffled as to what the color of her hair had to do with anything, he turned to stare at the hair in question. It looked just as good down around her shoulders as it had when she'd had it up at the restaurant. Rubbing his chin, he pondered the dicey path before him. Women were indeed strange creatures, information from the data bank that came from sharing a bathroom for so many years with his older sister. And his mother had her own little nuances that a sensible son never questioned. Carefully, he tested the waters. "So?"

"I have to bleach it back. I'm a blonde, as blonde as you are, or was."

"Blonde?" He tilted his head to give her a long once-over. "You dyed your hair?" And then the tumblers clicked into place. Since her hair was no longer up in that twisted knot she'd worn earlier, he picked up a few loose strands, ran them through his fingers. "This was your version of a disguise."

"Obviously, it didn't work."

When she yawned his eyes remained on her mouth. She felt his gaze. Her eyes locked on his. Her pulse bumped up. Baylee felt the tug of warmth, the pull of heat move through her like an electric current. Before she knew what was happening, he had her drawn into his chest.

Need kicked in. She responded in an instant, clinging to his shirt.

His teeth nipped, tugged on her mouth, urging her to open. He was practiced, skilled. When he moved from her mouth to nibble that sensitive part just below her ear, he felt her body tremble. It was his undoing. Her little panting breaths sent him further down that measured slide toward a burning inferno.

The pull in her lower belly had her thinking how long it had been. His hands roamed over her back, her rear. They fell back against the couch cushions. He found her mouth again. With his tongue he began to explore the textures within.

They came up for air. "Baylee."

"Dylan. What was that?"

"Heat." But he tried to make a joke. "Has it really been so long you don't recognize a kiss?" He had no choice, but to make light of it. The kiss had been electric. Better than he thought. And he had thought about it in detail. When she started to speak, he put a finger to her mouth. "Don't say anything. We're just gonna sit here and watch another movie, that's all. Take it nice and slow." He tried to convince himself as much as her. For several long seconds, he repeated this mantra over and over to himself. He could just as easily have led her to the bedroom now. But she was a guest in his house. And he was lusting after a mother of a little baby sleeping just down the hall.

"I'd forgotten what it was like." Had a kiss ever punched through her libido like that one?

When he pushed the button on the remote, starting the DVD player, he tried to sound casual and act like it was no big deal. "Anytime you need a reminder, just let me know."

"Are you just feeling sorry for me, Dylan?"

"That's unlikely. There's the fact that I'm attracted to you first of all. But, I think you're the strongest woman I've ever known."

"Is that why you offered me a place to stay? Because you're attracted to me?"

"A little. Maybe. I want to get to know you. I want you to know me. I don't want Connor to find you. Any man, who did what he did, is perverse, twisted." And the thought that Connor had probably done it to countless other women several times before Baylee nagged at him. "You needed a place he didn't know about. Now what I don't understand is why you'd think I'd feel sorry for you?"

"Because I was a blubbering idiot earlier. Because I've got Sarah. Because I'm a…"

"Mess," he finished for her. "I know. And Sarah is the reason we're going to take it nice and slow." And he'd do it if he had to cool this need inside him several times a day.

When the movie credits rolled, they turned their attention to the screen, but they remained locked together in an embrace.

It felt good to have his arms wrapped around her, she thought, as she tried not to drift into that fantasy-land where this man would actually love and care for her and Sarah. Even though she had no business going there, she floated along on gossamer wings toward a world that didn't really exist—and never had, at least, not for her.

☖☖☖☖☖

Across town, the tremor went virtually unnoticed, mainly because Trevor focused on the new game in town. His name was Uri Jankovic, a hit man the Serbian mob favored. It wasn't the first time Trevor had crossed paths with this particular hired gun. Ten years earlier he'd shown up in Moscow when they'd both been after the same target. Trevor took some comfort knowing Jankovic was a shoddy hack who made frequent mistakes and had over the years been known to inflate his skills to land a job.

Just before midnight, Trevor watched from a distance as a rented, big-ass Chrysler 300 sedan pulled up in front of the gates at The Enclave. Once past the security guard, the Chrysler crawled along the path to Connor Boyd's place. When Jankovic finally emerged from the car, Trevor noted the man looked like he'd gained at least forty pounds. He'd been a sloppy mess before, but now the man was overweight and out of shape, not exactly a sterling opponent. But there was no mistaking this was the same man he'd seen bumble so many jobs around the globe.

Knowing Geller had hired an incompetent like Jankovic told Trevor everything he needed to know. Frank Geller was either desperate or had taken the cheap route. Jankovic was far from the best. In Trevor's world, the man was known to have bungled more jobs than he'd completed. Obviously, Geller hadn't asked for references.

The listening device told Trevor they were indeed panicking. It didn't take long for their byplay to annoy him. Did these people ever take responsibility for their own behavior? He doubted any of them ever had. But at least he didn't have to guess what they were planning. What a bunch of clowns!

There was no doubt in Trevor's mind who would win this round.

And it wouldn't be Jankovic.

CHAPTER 10

Through a haze of sleep, Dylan thought he heard baby babble. But his focus, without opening his eyes, was on the sinuous female body nestled on top of his from chin to toe.

He smelled her hair, moved his head slightly to nestle further in its softness as each strand fanned out over his chest. He felt the curvy shape of breasts and nipples as the points touched his belly through his shirt. Hard as iron, all he had to do was...

He felt something damp on his stomach. He blinked awake about the same time Baylee's head popped up. They were still on the living room sofa, stretched out lengthwise. Baylee's body rested atop his. The last thing he remembered from last night was looking down at Baylee and realizing she'd fallen asleep. They had cuddled together and now...

Mussed from sleep, he watched as she touched her hand to her tank top.

"Oh my God, what time is it?"

He saw distinct wet spots on the top where her nipples sat erect. He was suddenly aware that her breasts had leaked through her shirt and onto his stomach. As her face turned several shades of pink, she too, was aware of that fact. Lifting his arm so he could read his watch, he struggled to zone in on the time. "Six-thirty. I think."

Her embarrassment turned to joy as she pushed her hair off her face and leaned up at him. Her lips curved. "She didn't wake up. Sarah finally slept through the night."

In this split second, her joy suddenly became his. He grinned. "I guess she was as worn out as we were."

As she shifted to crawl off him, Baylee felt the evident bulge in his jeans. Without meaning to, her eyes drifted downward, stayed there as desire warmed her from the inside out until deeper color flushed her cheeks. Her breasts dripped even more.

Then more baby babble filled the air.

Baylee pushed the rest of the way off, trying to get her mind off that bulge. "I…I have to go feed…Sarah."

He lifted his head in time to see her bolt down the hallway. Through the baby monitor, he heard her go through the motions of tending to the baby, changing her diaper, getting her dressed, settling her to her breast.

Maybe the monitors positioned all over the house were a bad idea, a really bad idea. He could still feel Baylee's small, delectable body on top of his. He sucked in a breath.

Lying there, he knew one thing.

He was a man who'd traveled all over the world. After college he'd taken off across Europe before settling into his job as Jake's lead programmer. Over the years, the success of Billing-Pro Software had allowed him to explore a number of exotic destinations in places like Wales and Japan in pursuit of both business and pleasure. He'd bedded dozens of women, all shapes, all kinds. He'd enjoyed every one of them. But he'd never wanted a woman more than he did the one down the hall with the baby—the one living in his house.

He needed a cold shower, or better still, a dip in the ocean. He was up off the couch in a flash. In his bedroom, he changed into trunks before zipping into his wetsuit. On the back patio, he grabbed his surfboard and made his way across the beach to the water…and dived in.

While Kit worked the constant stream of customers coming in and out of the coffee shop, Jake took care of the flow in the bookstore. Waiting on customers, helping them find the books they were looking for might seem like a completely different world than his, but over the last few days he'd found that it wasn't that dissimilar to selling software. The product was different, but you still had to make a sale.

He had just made his tenth sale of the morning when he decided to take advantage of the lull in traffic to surf the Internet once again for Ben Griffin. As he waited for his laptop to boot up, he decided he might as well check his e-mails once he was logged in.

After waiting for startup he logged into his account and found fourteen messages in the inbox, all work-related, but one message with the subject titled "Claire's Murder" had his pulse beating faster. The sender read Anonymous.

Who was messing with him now? He wondered as he automatically scanned the e-mail for viruses. When it came up clean, against his better judgment, he opened the message—and seethed. Pulled in by the content, he almost didn't hear Kit's footsteps on the hardwood floor as she came into the bookstore.

He quickly closed out of the program and turned off his laptop just in time for Kit to wrap her arms around his shoulders. He felt like hitting something. Instead he took comfort in Kit's body.

Sucking in a breath, he vowed to get his mind off the e-mail, at least for now. But nothing could take his mind off the message. And why anyone would be sending it now, two years after the fact? That was just wrong. As he held Kit, his mind ticked off a quick mental list of people who might be toying with him.

Top of the list, of course, was Max St. John, the lead detective in Claire's murder investigation. Next was Collin Boyd. But considering the content, it wouldn't be Collin. He wasn't that clever. That left St. John, which made even less sense.

As he contemplated his next move, Kit wanted to know, "There's a lull in traffic. Why don't we lock the place up and head up to my office upstairs? Whaddaya say we finally christen the top of that desk?"

He tried to get into a playful mood but fell far short. "Lock up the Book & Bean in the middle of the day? That might be asking for more gossip than you could handle."

He didn't fool Kit, nor did his demeanor. "What's wrong, Jake? The day you aren't interested in christening my desktop upstairs, something's wrong. Did you find Ben?"

He shook his head. "Look, it's just a work-related problem. I'm not ready to talk about it." That was partly true.

She eyed him doubtfully. After knowing him for so long, she didn't buy his performance. He was hiding something. He'd been on the computer when she'd rounded the corner; if it wasn't about Ben, then what was it? "Why is it, that I don't believe you? But this is one of those times you don't want to tell me because you think I might worry, isn't it?"

He grinned in spite of himself. "You know me pretty well."

"Like a book. Okay, for now I'll let it go. You can keep your secrets to yourself. But don't think you can freeze me out just to keep me from worrying. We're a team now. You can't hold back everything, just like you can't be with me every second of every day. It's impossible. But because I'm madly in love with you, you get a pass—for now." She kissed him soundly on the mouth. "But just one. Maybe when you get your head out of your ass, I'll be around to christen that desk upstairs."

⚭ ⚭ ⚭ ⚭ ⚭

Baylee was at the stove scrambling eggs as the smell of bacon wafted through the air when she turned and saw

Dylan standing in the doorway fresh from his shower. She knew he'd left earlier to go surfing. "How was the water?"

"Great." He bent down to Sarah's eye level as she sat quietly in her swing, gumming a yellow plastic ring. "Way to sleep through the night there, Gidget. Your mama needed the sleep." To Baylee he said, "Breakfast smells good."

"I thought you might be hungry. And I wanted to thank you for last night when you talked me through my meltdown. You've been great since I've been here." Baylee set on the table a large platter filled with pancakes that had been warming in the oven. "Dig in."

He was just about to when an incredibly tall, gorgeous blonde appeared on the deck, waving through the open back door to get his attention. She wore a wetsuit zipped down to the waist, showing off a red hot bikini top that revealed ample breasts. She carried a surfboard. "Hi Dylan! I thought you might have time for a ride." The invitation was no more subtle than the bikini.

What the hell was Angie doing here?

Dylan moved with the speed of a wide receiver toward the blonde standing on the deck. As he passed by Sarah's swing, an idea formed. In one fluid motion, he scooped Sarah up to his shoulder, talking as he went. "How's my girl this morning? Whatddya say we go see what Angie wants?"

The movement startled the baby so much her teething ring went flying. Dylan didn't notice, didn't stop to retrieve the baby's toy. His main objective was to get rid of Angie as fast as he could. "Hi Ange, how's it going? Thanks for the invite, but I've already been in the water this morning. Would you like to meet Sarah and Baylee?"

"Sarah and Baylee? Sure." But Angie didn't look like she was sure. She looked downright crestfallen. But she leaned her board on the side of the house and stepped through the back door and into the kitchen with a wariness that spoke volumes.

Dylan jostled the baby like a proud father showing her off for the first time. "This is Sarah, my daughter."

"Daughter?" Angie took a step back in retreat. "But she's a baby."

From the kitchen table, five feet away, Baylee could see the woman doing the math in her head. Oh, this was priceless. Baylee crossed her arms and watched the major player test out his infinite charm. His performance made her want to grab the popcorn. How did he plan to talk his way out of this one?

"Yep, five months old, almost six really, she's gorgeous, isn't she? Looks just like her mother, too. And this is Baylee, Sarah's mom." He left it to Angie to figure out the semantics.

Angie didn't know it, but she had Baylee's sympathy—for about ninety seconds. It occurred to Baylee that these two were both equally involved in the same game she'd walked away from more than two years earlier. She wouldn't go back to those days for anyone, not even for Surfer Boy.

To Angie's credit, she made a fast exit.

When Dylan turned from the doorway, though, Baylee stood there with her arms outstretched to take Sarah. She walked back over to the swing where she adjusted the baby into the seat.

Then she quietly turned and let Dylan have it, never raising her voice an octave. "First, you joke about using my daughter as a chick magnet, then you blatantly use her as chick repellant. What kind of a person does that?" And the memory of the kiss they'd shared less than twelve hours earlier had her adding, "I'm not a player here, Dylan. I can't afford to be."

She picked up Sarah's teething ring from where it had landed on the floor and went over to the sink to rinse it off under the tap. Then she calmly walked over and handed it back to the baby, flipping on the switch on the swing that sent a Barney song lilting into the room.

Dylan's temper spiked. "What's that supposed to mean? I got rid of her, didn't I? I didn't invite her over here. She dropped by unannounced."

"And she's never done that before."

"Well. Yeah. But things have changed."

"Oh, I can see that. Let's not forget Melissa, the one you blew off last night."

"Melissa does not…matter. Hell. I'm single, unattached. I don't need…"

"No, you don't, but if I remember correctly, that's the way the game's played: a lot of them just don't matter. It's better that way. Although admittedly, I am a little rusty, I still remember the game. Your personal life is none of my business, Dylan, until it concerns my daughter. Sarah is not part of the game, nor a pawn to be used in yours."

He sighed, and ran his hands through his wet hair. "Angie and I went out—a couple of times months ago. She's a flight attendant for US Air who lives in Tempe and merely stops by from time to time whenever she's visiting her mom and dad who live across the street. Melissa is," he sucked in a breath, "a friend I see on occasion when the mood suits both of us." He glanced at Sarah before leaning into Baylee to whisper the rest.

But Baylee held up her hand for him to stop. "I get it, Dylan. I'm not that rusty. You don't have to spell it out."

"I'm sorry."

"For what, doing what thousands of other unattached, single people do in this town? I'm not passing judgment, Dylan. It's just that for me that life is long gone. You're obviously still on the roster. Do me a favor though. As long as I'm living here, do not kiss me again the way you did last night. Now enjoy your breakfast." With that she walked back to the swing, hauled her daughter out of it, and headed outside leaving him listening to the strains of a tune that sounded a great deal like, "The Itsy Bitsy Spider."

After choking down the breakfast Baylee had fixed, and not because it didn't taste good, but rather because it was difficult to eat crow when you were just flat wrong, Dylan cleaned up the kitchen. He'd done some thinking during the meal and realized he had a phone call to make. Melissa deserved to know things had changed. Since they had never really been in a relationship, he thought he could get by with explaining things to her over the phone.

△△△△△

Baylee and Sarah hadn't gone far. They'd taken a walk along the beach. She had to admit she liked being this close to the ocean. The waves calmed her and made her think. She wasn't really upset about Melissa or Angie or any of the others she was sure were part of Dylan's life.

A couple of heated kisses between the two of them didn't give her squatters' rights into the man's love life. It wasn't Dylan she was upset with anyway, but rather, herself.

How had her life become such a mess, a mess that had her living a lie? She needed to do something about it, get her act together, and start thinking about the future, the long-term of what to do. She needed to get her jewelry business up and going and not as a hobby either, but rather earning real income.

She had dozens of designs she'd created just waiting for launch. Quinn and Kit had been wearing her creations since high school. There had been plenty of interest in her designs before that charity event, before Connor Boyd had entered her orderly life. She'd sold off a lot of her inventory, but since Sarah's birth, she hadn't worked on her designs much. There had been too much chaos, too much moving around, too much instability for her to concentrate on creating earrings or necklaces.

But no more. She needed to get her ass in gear and design a website or something to get back that portion of her life, if for no other reason than to tell herself that not even Connor Boyd could take that away from her.

And she needed to think about a permanent place to live, stop all this upheaval. If Gloria, didn't already have plans for the house Kit rented in San Madrid, maybe she could move in there. She dug in her pocket and pulled out her cell phone, dialed Gloria's number. "Hey Gloria it's Baylee."

"Baylee-girl, How are you doing? How's that baby? Kit told me what happened with Connor. I'm so sorry, honey. I guess the Boyds are all the same—evil to the core."

"Sarah's fine," she said quickly, not willing to get into the whole Connor thing. "Actually, I had a reason for calling. I wanted to know what your plans were for the rental house you have in San Madrid once Kit and Jake move into Crandall House."

"You're thinking it would suit you and Sarah."

"Exactly. I need to think about a permanent place to live, Gloria."

"You don't mind that the house has only two bedrooms? And the second bedroom on the middle floor is tiny. And what about all those stairs? Those three levels will get old real quick with the laundry room on the ground floor. That's a lot of running up and down stairs with the baby."

"I've thought of all that. I'd put Sarah's crib in with me in the larger bedroom on the third floor so I wouldn't have to go up and down the stairs in the middle of the night. Look, Gloria, I really need a place to live, one I can call my own."

"I don't mean to discourage you, honey. I just want to make sure you understand the house has drawbacks for a woman with a baby. As cute as it is, the house isn't perfect. When I lived there I hated climbing all those stairs. That's one of the reasons I moved out. But if that's what you want, honey, the house is yours whenever Kit moves out."

"Thanks, Gloria. That's one big weight off my shoulders. Now, I just have to kick-start my jewelry business."

"You could go back to doing a booth at the farmer's market on weekends. That worked well before Sarah came along."

"It did. But I was thinking about something a little more substantive, like maybe a website, doing Internet sales. If I got it going I could have my own business at home."

"That would work. Aren't you staying at Dylan's? You know, he might work on the website for you."

"I couldn't ask him to do that. It's awkward here, Gloria. His house is like a beacon for women coming and going, calling at all hours. I'm intruding on his life, like a fifth wheel."

"Really? Then you'll want out of there as soon as possible."

"That's why I'm working on it now." She paused, thinking about the information Kit had been forced to tell her. "How are you doing, Gloria? I know about Ben Griffin. I think it's terrible what those two women did to you." And what Connor might do if he found out about Sarah.

"I'm so angry at them, Baylee. They ruined my life. They took my two babies away from me and robbed me of being a mother. I've been so upset about it I had to increase my blood pressure medication. I didn't sleep a wink last night. And finding out John knew, that he knew all along, just breaks my heart."

"I know Gloria. It's a betrayal of the worse kind. That's what Kit thinks too. I'm so sorry. But it isn't too late. You have Kit, and Jake's doing everything he can to find Ben. It's just a matter of time before you have both of them together."

Gloria started to cry. Baylee felt bad. How could the people Gloria had trusted, the man she loved and her own sister, have been so mean to her?

It was then Baylee realized what she'd known for years.

Having family didn't have to come through blood.

CHAPTER 11

When she got back to the house, Dylan was waiting on the deck with a hang-dog look, hands in the pockets of his olive green shorts. He met her at the railing prepared to do a little groveling. "I owe you an apology."

The walk had cleared her head. Baylee shook her head and grinned up at him. "You don't owe me anything. Your sex life is none of my business."

"I'm sorry I used Sarah for chick repellant."

"More like Angie repellant."

"It worked didn't it?"

"More effective than Raid."

He laughed, bumped her shoulder on purpose, and offered, "Whaddaya say we hop in the car, go get the stuff you need to put your hair back to its original color? Then we bring it back here and get the job done. I'll help."

"Really? We don't have to make a trip to the store. I already have everything we need." She gave him a dubious stare. "You really know how to work with hair?"

He gave his head a very feminine shake, fluffing his hair back off his shoulders with exaggerated gestures. "Hey, how do you think I keep these tresses the envy of every woman within a fifty-mile radius? Leave it to me, darling. Your hair will look fab-u-lous."

"You're so full of yourself; you know that, Surfer Boy."

Dylan ignored the slam, concentrated instead on Baylee's brown dye job. "How blonde are you? Now that I look at it, this brown stuff just doesn't look natural. Are we talking Marilyn Monroe platinum or maybe Debbie Harry gold?"

"Kit's the silver platinum with all that gorgeous straight hair. Kit's is so straight I've envied every strand on her head my entire life. My hair's more golden in color, more like Sarah's, and curly, very curly."

Dylan reached out and touched Sarah's topknot. The baby was still mostly bald but there were a few wisps of light hair on the top of her head. "I can work with this."

Baylee giggled. She actually giggled. "You are such a ham. But I think between the two of us, we'll manage to find the right shade."

Later, while Sarah napped, with the kitchen smelling of hair colorant and bleach, with Baylee's head covered in pieces of aluminum foil wrappers, the two of them waited at the kitchen table for the timer to ding.

Dylan looked over at her and smiled. He couldn't help himself. He had no idea why this woman appealed to him so much—just that she did. Maybe because she didn't seem to have a pretentious bone in her body. Here she was with her head covered in spiky sheets of tin foil and yet she acted so natural about it. What other woman would let a man see her like this without freaking out?

She was just so different than any of the other women he'd known. Maybe for the first time in a long time, he was attracted to something other than the outside, the surface stuff, to something genuine within. He knew one thing. He adored watching her with Sarah. He couldn't discount the fact that she was such a good mother. Her kind and gentle spirit also played a factor in how he felt. Okay, so the woman was hot as hell to look at, even now with her hair wrapped in tin foil.

As Baylee sat in the kitchen chair thumbing through the latest fashion magazine, she knew she must be crazy. What woman in her right mind would want a man like Dylan to see her looking like this? She was definitely not at her best and hadn't been, it seemed, since he'd stopped by the Book & Bean that day. In fact, now that she thought about it, Dylan had seen her at her absolute worst. Repeatedly. Oh well, she sighed, as she put down the magazine; he seemed to be okay with all of it. And wasn't it better this way that he see her true self rather than for her to try and pretty up a false impression that he'd find out about eventually?

The timer dinged.

"Let's see what we've got," Dylan said as he stood up to check the color. "I think you're done."

"How does the color look?"

Dylan started removing the tin foil sheets one at a time. "Honey blonde, just like those pictures in your father's study, the ones on the mantel, the ones that show you with Shirley Temple curls and no front teeth."

"I was six and had the misfortune to lose my two front teeth at the same time. The Shirley Temple curls were Tanya's doing. She wasn't happy unless she could enhance my curls with a hot curling utensil. But you know what, I always hated sitting there getting my picture taken. I could never work in front of the cameras. Wouldn't be an actress if you paid me. I'd be too bored with all of it. I used to go to the studio with Dad. In the early days, he'd pick me up and sit me on his lap while he directed another blockbuster." She sighed, remembering some of the better days with her father. "Those were the good times."

"You're right. You have too much energy. I can't see you sitting still for that long." As he finished removing all the foil, they talked and laughed like they'd known each other forever. Comfortable with each other. They chatted on about hair styles, fashion, football, and babies.

Later that afternoon they put Sarah in her stroller and walked down the street to an old-fashioned hamburger stand on the beach. With Dylan at the helm, pushing the stroller along the sidewalk, Sarah was a perfect angel, never once resembling the infant who'd had the crying jag in the restaurant.

At the burger stand, it was obvious Dylan was a regular. The young brunette behind the counter flirted with him all the while she took their order. The same was true with the plump, middle-aged, red-headed waitress who brought the food outside to their table. Obviously a popular guy, Dylan Burke's charm knew no age limit.

Over burgers and fries, while Sarah sat in her stroller, they enjoyed their meal in relative peace until two women, who were introduced to Baylee as Tara and Kendra, stopped by their table to say hello.

Even though the encounter went smoothly and Dylan handled it with grace, it became apparent that his friends and neighbors couldn't quite wrap their arms around the idea that the single man about town had an infant daughter. The concept threw Tara and Kendra into cross-examination mode. During the exchange the two women did everything they could to glean the ultimate amount of information from the man they'd both gone out with numerous times.

"So you're a daddy? You never said a word. What's her name?"

"Sarah," Dylan offered proudly. It did not escape Dylan's attention that Tara and Kendra totally ignored the baby's mother, as he watched her sit stoically by, taking in the whole ridiculous scene. Nor did he fail to notice how the women grew distant right before his eyes at the very idea he had a child. He didn't think good old Tara or Kendra would be eager to call him any time soon, nor would they be leaving him any messages offering to hook up in the foreseeable future.

"She does look just like you, Dyl. Don't you think so, Kendra?"

"I do. Same blue eyes, same blonde hair. How old is she?"

"Almost six months."

"And this is the first time we've seen her."

"Oh, she's been around. I just haven't felt like sharing her with anyone else. Baylee and I have been keeping a low profile." He leveled both women with a dazzling smile. He was almost starting to believe the story himself. Maybe he should try his hand at acting, start with a few of the local stage productions before moving on to more serious auditions, make the rounds in Hollywood.

When Tara and Kendra finally moved on, Baylee burst out laughing. "You are some piece of work, Surfer Boy. You almost had me believing your spiel. Have you ever thought of taking this act on the road? You'd be a natural."

"Funny how great minds think alike. I was just sitting here envisioning fame and fortune beyond my wildest dreams when I'm discovered as the next Matthew McConaughey."

"In your dreams, pal."

"Hey, a guy can have delusions of grandeur if he wants. I bet he scores with a lot of babes on all seven continents." He wiggled his eyebrows up and down.

Baylee playfully punched him in the arm.

"Ow, that hurt."

"I hardly think you have room to complain. No matter where we are, no matter where we go, you seem to have an overabundant supply of available women."

He'd walked right into that one. He quickly steered the stroller toward a frozen yogurt shop. "How about dessert?"

Dylan ordered green-tea flavored yogurt with pineapple and coconut while Baylee opted for an original mixture filled with blueberries and strawberries. As they sat outside eating their own favorite concoctions, Dylan suddenly realized he didn't know much about Baylee's pregnancy and decided to change that. Curious by nature, the more he sat there, the more he wanted to know about anything and everything that had happened to her over the last fourteen months.

"Did you have a lot of cravings when you were pregnant?"

"Mexican food. I couldn't get enough cheese enchiladas or chicken fajitas or tamales."

"What, no Chinese? My sister craved sweet and sour pork until it was sickening to watch her eat the stuff. How long were you in labor?"

"Eight hours."

"That doesn't sound so bad."

"Really?" Amused, Baylee retorted, "Then you try squeezing out six pounds."

He winced. "Point taken. Is that how much Sarah weighed?"

"Just under six. Five pounds, fourteen ounces to be exact. And don't you dare say that's small. She was big enough."

"How much weight did you gain?"

She gave him an incredulous look. "Is there a question you won't ask?"

His mouth curved. He knew how to get out of a jam. "All I'm saying is you don't look like you had a baby six months ago."

"Good recovery. You think on your feet."

"My sister is still trying to lose the baby weight. She gained almost forty pounds."

"Wow! That is a lot. I gained about twenty. And for some reason the weight just poured off."

He laughed. "That's probably because you can't sit still for five minutes."

"Maybe."

"When will Gidget here be ready to eat solid food?"

"She has her six-month checkup Tuesday, the day after Memorial Day. I'm hoping he'll tell me it's time to introduce some cereal into her diet."

"Tuesday? Why didn't you say something?"

"Forgive me, daddy, but it never occurred to me that a single guy would be interested in making a trip to the pediatrician with us. I'm still getting used to this whole daddy act of ours anyway."

He had a serious look on his face when he said, "Yeah, well, next time give me a heads up. What time?"

"Ten o'clock." Baylee was starting to think the man was taking this daddy act a little too far. She could easily chalk it up to the man's amiable disposition, but it could also be the start of an uneasy obsession. How much did she really know about the guy anyway? "Dylan, I think I can get Sarah to and from the doctor by myself. I've handled it just fine for months now."

"No way. We're a team now."

But for how long, she wondered, as she tried to decide how much of Dylan's act was fake and how much was genuine.

"She was born the sixteenth of December, right? What time?"

His curiosity knew no bounds. "Three-twenty a.m." She cocked a brow.

"Who was with you?"

"My friend, Blair. Look, Dylan, is this interrogation going any place in particular? Am I allowed to have my attorney present?"

"Very funny. Look, there's a lot I don't know, okay? I'm just trying to be thorough. And you opted for breast feeding because it was healthier for the baby over the bottle. Good choice. That's the way my sister went too. Even as we speak, she's trying to wean the little guy, but he's stubborn and not too happy with the sippy cup." He suddenly wished he'd been there when Sarah popped into the world.

Baylee couldn't help it; she laughed. What other single guy would possible know anything about a sippy cup? Okay, so it was his good nature front and center making him so curious, not some bizarre or weird fixation. She relaxed and decided to get more into the spirit of the questions. Two could play this game.

Playfully, maybe a bit more suggestively than she should have, she said with a straight face, "Because Sarah was so small, she had trouble at first getting the hang of the whole nipple thing." When she saw the tight look form on his face, she went on, "It took her a couple of days to get the hang of what she was supposed to do, but she finally figured it out. We both did."

She'd said on purpose to shut him up and put an end to the questions. But she should have known better. Dylan Burke didn't have a shy bone in his body. He just kept right on talking about the benefits of breastfeeding over the bottle until finally he asked, "Isn't it getting about that time?" His eyes automatically drifted to the front of the shirt she wore as if he were trying to see if the answer were written on her boobs.

Now she was the one who was self-conscious. "Uh, yeah. We probably should go. And tonight's bath night so we need to factor in some extra time."

"Really? Can I help?"

Baylee didn't know whether to be thrilled or wary at the offer. She forced herself to remember this was a temporary situation. When this whole thing with Connor was over, she would move on. And so would he. She couldn't—no, she wouldn't—get used to having him in both of their lives. She reminded herself he was simply acting the part of daddy; it was a role he was playing with relish. She had no illusions or fantasies that he'd actually be interested in stepping into that role for real.

As soon as they got back home it didn't take long before Sarah grew tired from having been out all evening and began to fuss. As far as the bath went, Dylan took his cues from Baylee.

While he held the unhappy Sarah, Baylee, who seemed to take Sarah's fussiness in stride, ran water into a yellow plastic thing that looked to him like a bucket. On Baylee's command he reluctantly sat the squalling infant into the water and wondered how on earth Baylee intended to bathe a very unwilling participant. But to his surprise, Sarah's demeanor changed as soon as Baylee began to turn the bath into more game than chore, complete with

Vickie McKeehan

splashing noises and bubbles that not only entertained Sarah but got the job done as well.

He couldn't help it. He was bowled over by Baylee's technique—and not for the first time. Everything about her spoke to the woman's love for her child. She seemed to have a handle on what Sarah needed, when she needed it, and what the baby would or would not tolerate. Considering that the kid couldn't talk, Dylan thought Baylee seemed to know exactly what to do in any given circumstance.

The longer Sarah stayed in the water the more she kicked and oohed over the bath toys. Caught up in the game, he picked up a Dora Explorer bubble maker and began to shoot bubbles into the air. That got Sarah's attention. She slapped for the bubbles, and with every reach of her little hands, water sloshed over the sides of the tub. Dylan didn't mind. He was having too much fun watching her enjoy the water. Imagine, a little pint-sized fish like this having as much fun as he had had just that morning in the surf.

When Baylee announced bath time over and done, he watched with rapt attention, trying to pick up as many pointers as he could as she dried, diapered, and dressed a wiggling Sarah with such a knack. She never broke stride.

As soon as Baylee had the last snap in place on Sarah's pink pajamas, sensing freedom from her restraints, Sarah promptly rolled over, grinned from ear to ear, pleased that she'd survived the ritual bath process. Her mood went from weary to recharged, as if she'd found her second wind.

Dylan reached down and picked her up, settling her on his shoulder. He picked up the soft bear she slept with from her crib and started going after her belly, telling her, "Mr. Bear is going to get you." He proceeded to make Mr. Bear dance until she giggled. When she began to squeal with delight at each playful gesture, he didn't stop until he got a genuine belly laugh out of her.

Baylee watched in fascination as Dylan charmed her daughter. She tried to harden her heart against his appeal. And then like a rock through a window, her mind crashed, wondering how she could help but not fall for this guy. Watching the two of them sit down on the floor and continue their playtime, it seemed that to her, Sarah was as captivated as she. What would happen to both of them when he tired of the daddy role, when he saw that being a father was more than fun and games?

She decided to end the day on a high note, one that didn't require thinking too far into the future. Connor was still out there, no doubt looking for her. She couldn't be distracted from that, couldn't forget that keeping Sarah's existence a secret was first and foremost, the priority. The feelings Dylan brought out would have to be put on the backburner. There could be no doubt Sarah's welfare came first.

CHAPTER 12

In the dream, she was twelve.

Baylee tiptoed to the door, checked the hallway. She wouldn't let him see her, catch her. If he did, in his present state, she knew what to expect. She hated him when he was like this. Her hands shook just thinking about him finding her hiding place inside Tanya's bedroom closet. And now, just to Baylee's luck, Tanya was out running errands. Otherwise, the woman always acted as her go-between, her protector. But at times like this, Baylee couldn't rely on anyone but herself. Any other time her father could be a decent human being, but when he drank, like today, forget it.

William Scott was a mean, drunken bully.

As she stood just behind the closet door, she strained to listen. Maybe he'd passed out by now and the coast was clear. If she could just make it to the backdoor, she could run down the street to Kit's house. Even though Kit had it far worse than she did, Kit would hide her in the pool house for the next few hours until her father either passed out and sobered up or exhausted himself searching for her.

She sucked in a breath and found the courage to open the door. She stuck her head out a few inches and listened again. Deciding the way was clear, she crossed the width of Tanya's bedroom right off the kitchen and stopped at the door again to listen for any sign her father might have wandered into the kitchen. Sucking up her nerve, she opened the bedroom door and peered out. The room was quiet. It looked like she was home free. He had to be somewhere else in the house. She ran like a deer across the room, threw open the back door, and stepped straight into her father's chest.

"There you are, Sarah."

The open-handed slap snuck out like a snake to sting her cheek. "I'm not Sarah. It's Baylee, Dad. I'm Baylee."

"You aren't sneaking out of this house, Baylee Diane. You aren't going down to that goddamned woman's house. Not today; not ever again; no way. I've told you a hundred times to stay away from that bitching viper." Backing her up in the kitchen, William yelled in her face, "You'll stay away from her or I'll know the reason why."

Baylee lied with conviction and not for the first time. "I...I...wasn't. I was going over to Quinn's house."

"Don't lie to me." He grabbed her arm and twisted it back. "I don't want you around that woman, you understand? Kit might be okay, for now. But if she's around that mother of hers for any length of time, she'll turn out just like her. You need to...find new friends."

"Kit is not like...Alana. She isn't."

"Yeah...well, she will be. Living with that evil woman will make her turn mean. You wait and see. No one can trust 'Lana Stevens. Believe me, I know." He swayed as if it were a struggle to remain standing.

Silently, she willed him to pass out. If he passed out, she had a reprieve. But when she looked into his rheumy eyes, saw his resolve strengthen, she said quietly, "Daddy, I'm not my mother. Remember where you are. I'm not her."

"Damn you," he groused, as he staggered further into the kitchen, dragging her along with him. "Don't bring your mother up to me. You always do that. I don't want to talk about your mother."

She didn't want to remind him that she hadn't been the one to bring up the woman earlier. He did it every time he drank, talking nonsense. But she knew better than to dispute anything he said now in this condition. "I'm...sorry." Would this be one of those times when she could avoid taking another punch? She held her breath as well as her tongue. She took a chance and reached out to touch his hand, trying to get him to realize where he was, who was standing right in front of him. Sometimes it worked, sometimes it didn't.

It didn't work. Within seconds, quick as lightening, his hand struck out again and slapped her across the face. Defensively her arms came up to block any more blows as he grabbed her arm. "Get out of my sight, you little..."

He never got to finish. Tanya Lincoln stepped inside the kitchen, all five feet two inches of her, dressed in faded jeans and a loose white blouse. "William, let her go."

William dropped his hand in mid-strike at the sound of Tanya's voice. "She's in trouble. I caught her sneaking down to Kit's again."

"Then ground her, William. Send her to her room, but do not hit that child again." The diminutive woman sat down the bag of groceries she was carrying on the immaculate kitchen counter and stepped over to where William held onto the child's arm. "Baylee, there are more bags in the car. Go help carry them in, please."

Baylee didn't have to be told twice. She'd been saved again. When Baylee scooted out the back door, Tanya calmly touched William's sleeve, placed her other hand on his chest, and stared into his glassy eyes. "You can't keep doing this. You need to get some counseling, and stop the drinking, stop hitting her."

"I don't want her around that Stevens woman. She's the very devil. I don't want Baylee hanging around Kit, either. I don't care how long they've known each other. You let her go down there behind my back. I know you do; don't even try to deny it. And I won't have it; do you hear me? You work for me, something you seem to forget often enough around here. You see to it Baylee doesn't leave

this house tonight. And stop Kit from coming down here so much. Let me run my own damn house for once."

"William, the girl comes down here most of the time just to get out of the house. Don't begrudge Kit a place to come to when that woman gets mean, which is almost all the time. You have no idea what that woman is capable of." Tanya knew only because Baylee had confided a secret in her, but she wouldn't break that confidence, especially with William. *"And you know Alana doesn't allow Kit's friends in the house that often. That means Baylee doesn't go down there as much as you think she does. You're being unreasonable."*

He grumbled and sauntered out of the kitchen, wobbling his way out of the room, and holding on to the wall for support. Tanya heard rather than watched him stagger down the hallway to his study, where she knew he'd be passed out in five minutes time and would probably never remember this conversation when he sobered up.

But despite that, Tanya sighed in relief. It tore her up inside how that man treated his only daughter, his only child. Tanya looked around and saw Baylee standing in the doorway, her aquamarine eyes darting around the kitchen in fear before she set foot inside the room, as if scouting it out.

"Coast is clear, honey. He's probably already asleep. Lord, that man is a piece of work. If I'd known he'd picked up the bottle I never would've gone to the store when I did."

"I hope he passes out and never wakes up," Baylee said hatefully, touching the cheek where she'd been smacked.

"You hush up talk like that. I know you have every right to feel the way you do, but you don't go saying things like that about your father." Tanya gently touched the girl's cheek. *"That needs ice."* She reached into a kitchen drawer, pulled out an ice bag, walked to the freezer, and

began filling it up. After tightening the cap, she held it out to Baylee's face.

Baylee responded by wrapping her arms around the petite black woman, a woman she thought of like a mother. "Thanks, Tanya. What would I do without you?"

"I'm not going to let you find out, child. I've been taking care of you since you were born. You're like my own daughter. And I'm always going to be here for you. You might want to stay clear of Kit's house for a while though. Who knows, when he wakes up he may not even remember this rant, but to be on the safe side better not go down there, especially today. Is Kit doing okay these days?"

Baylee shuddered, remembering that just a month earlier Kit had gone through a horrible ordeal. Baylee snuggled further into Tanya's embrace. At least she didn't have a mother like Kit had, a woman that would shoot her own daughter. Kit had sworn Baylee and Quinn to secrecy. But it had been too heavy a burden for Baylee, and she'd been so scared for Kit that one night last week, after hiding from another one of her father's rages, in a vulnerable frame of mind, she'd confessed to Tanya the secret of what Alana had done.

Alana had shot her own daughter with a .22 caliber pistol. Thank God the bullet had hit Kit's shoulder and nothing vital. She had a bad scar on her shoulder, but at least she was alive. Baylee hated to think of Kit dying. Even though Alana hadn't even seen the need to take Kit to a hospital for treatment, she had found a doctor who came to the house to remove the bullet.

Money, it seemed, could buy silence, even when it involved the shooting of a child.

⚜⚜⚜⚜⚜

Baylee slowly came awake, disoriented, sweating. At least it wasn't the other dream, the one where she saw her mother pushed down the stairs. She got up to wash her face. As soon as she opened the door to her room, she noticed a light on at the end of the hall.

Someone was in the living room. Before she rounded the corner, she saw the flicker of light like that of a computer, heard the typing of keys. From the doorway she saw Dylan, who looked deep in concentration, hard at work.

"I always heard Internet porn was addictive, but it's two-thirty in the morning; shouldn't you give it a rest?"

Dylan jumped out of his skin. "God. Scare me next time, why don't you. It's not porn." He narrowed his eyes, staring. "What are you doing awake? You look upset."

"Just a dream. It's nothing."

He suddenly looked uncomfortable. "You want to talk about?"

"Childhood memories. I've had it before. Really, it's nothing." Baylee noticed that now he looked distressed. "What's wrong, Dylan?"

"I'm not sure how you'll take this. But…I did some research. I was planning to tell you in the morning."

"Tell me what."

"Were you aware your father never got a divorce from your mother?"

"What? Of course they were divorced. She left him when I was about three. They were divorced the following year."

"Was that your father's official story?"

"I guess. No. Wait. Tanya told me. I think. If they weren't divorced that year, it was definitely the next."

"Not according to public records." He hit the computer keys in rapid-fire succession and pointed to the screen. "Here, take a look."

Her eyes locked on the screen as she read the information from a public records database he'd managed to find. The website confirmed there was a marriage between William Scott and Sarah Moreland, but an additional search found no divorce. Even staring at the screen, she was adamant. "Well, the records are wrong."

"I don't think so." When she started to object, he explained, "Hear me out. If your mother disappeared like he said, why wouldn't he get a divorce? Have you ever considered…" This part was a lot tougher.

"Considered what?"

"What if your mother didn't run off with anyone? What if something happened to her?"

Baylee went white.

"I know she was a local girl; I looked up her bio. Does she still have family living in L.A.?"

Baylee's hand went to her mouth. "Who asked you to do this?"

"No one. But something isn't right about the story. Haven't you ever wondered why your mother never got in touch with you over the years? Twenty-two years is a long time to go without ever trying to communicate with your only daughter."

Baylee shrugged, trying to look bored with the entire conversation. "She probably had a dozen kids with the tennis pro. They're probably living in a French villa somewhere growing grapes, getting fat off the land. I got the impression from Dad she was quite selfish. She didn't want me. Why can't you accept that, Dylan? I have, years ago."

But her bravado came out weak.

For the first time since he'd known her Dylan realized she wasn't being honest. Her performance didn't ring true but rather came off more like a defense mechanism that kicked in to hide the hurt.

"I thought you might want to know where she is, find her. If she's alive wouldn't you want a chance to question her about why she left? Find out her reasons for staying away all this time? Or, maybe she couldn't for some reason contact you. If it were me, I'd want to know. Either way, don't you want to know the truth?" He turned back to the computer. "By the way, who was the tennis pro? They don't mention his name on the website I found."

The question caught her off guard. She looked even more annoyed. When she'd moved out of her father's house at sixteen, she'd tried to find out where her mother had gone, wanting to give her a second chance if she could locate her. She'd always been curious, more curious than her father that was for sure. But even though she'd tried, she'd found nothing on her own, not a trace of Sarah Moreland.

But did she have to go down that road again now, visit every time she'd been fragile to the point of breaking? She didn't like to think about those times and especially not with this man. He seemed to always see her at her very worst, her most vulnerable. She took a seat on the sofa and drew her legs up to her chest, so she could rest her chin on her knees.

But Dylan seemed to understand. "You've looked before, haven't you?"

"When I was sixteen, I found out she had a sister living in Glendale. Karen Nash. One Saturday morning I talked Kit and Quinn into jumping in the car, going over there with me to play Nancy Drew, maybe see if this woman, who was also my aunt, had any idea where her sister had disappeared to. I hoped she might know where my mother was living and with whom, maybe give me a last known address, a phone number, something, anything."

Baylee bit her lip. "It was a waste of gas. Karen swore up and down she hadn't heard a word from Sarah in more than thirteen years. I remember I didn't believe her. I thought she was covering up. My mother just left me, Dylan. It's hard to understand how a mother could be so callous, but it happens."

As Dylan listened, the hairs on the back of his neck stood up. Didn't she see that her father's story kept getting weaker and how feeble the story sounded in the first place?

"Does it? Think about it, Baylee. Sarah Moreland runs off after putting you to bed one night and no one, I mean no one, not even her sister, not her little girl, not her husband, ever hear from her again. Not once in twenty-two years. Honestly, and you may get mad at me for this, but I find your father's story bordering on the unbelievable. What was the name of the tennis pro, Baylee?"

"He was French. Luc Delaine. I got that tidbit from nosing around the tennis club one summer. And enough time had passed that people were willing to dish the dirt, so to speak, on what they remembered about their affair. It was kind of a folk story by that time, these two lovers running off so they could be together, leaving behind her movie career, a famous director-husband, and her own daughter. Exactly where are you going with this, Dylan?"

He turned his back on her and started hitting his laptop keys. Right before her eyes, Surfer Boy turned into a genuine computer geek.

"Let's see what we can find out about this Luc Delaine." After several searches, Dylan sighed. "The man seems to have disappeared right along with your mother. What little bio I found said he once had a promising tennis career and then just vanished. If the couple got to Europe, why didn't the tennis pro pick up his career where he left off? There isn't so much as a mention of him finishing in the top hundred tennis competitions after the rumor hits that they run off together. Looks like Luc Delaine disappeared right along with Sarah Moreland."

"Wasn't that the point? Secretively run off in the middle of the night to be together, start a new life."

"You're kidding, right? You mean these two were so in love they gave up their fantastic lives so they could be together? And do what? Your mother never went near another movie set in Europe. Luc Delaine stayed away from all competitions and never walked onto a tennis court again? Come on, Baylee. Think about it. Sarah deserts her acting career. Luc drops tennis like a hot potato. His bio says he was once ranked number four in the world. How is it that these two would give up everything they loved to be together? Everything. Does that make sense to you, Baylee?"

She had to agree when he said it like that it sounded incredible. "Not a bit."

"Have you ever point-blank asked your father what really happened?"

"Now who's being unrealistic? Every time someone inadvertently mentioned my mother's name, he always went ballistic. His attitude about it made questions impossible since he made it clear the subject was off limits. I didn't dare bring it up."

"That's convenient."

Her brows knitted together. "It is, isn't it?" She gnawed on the side of her mouth. "You think he might have done something to her?"

"Maybe. Somebody did."

"You know I'm not sure it's worth mentioning, but… I've had this dream ever since I was little. Never mind, the idea's crazy."

"Go ahead. Tell me."

She told him how the dream always played out and never varied. How her mother had been arguing with two women upstairs on the landing. How in the dream she'd overheard the argument take place outside her bedroom door. Then she repeated what she'd seen after she'd crept to the door and peeked out, what the two women had looked like, one blonde, the other with dark hair. "And for some reason, in the dream, the blonde always reminds me of Kit's mother. Well, not Kit's real mother, Gloria, but Alana. But you know what I mean we just found that out. The blonde woman in my dream always looked like Alana. I always thought the other one with dark hair as the evil, wicked witch."

Dylan sat there looking at her, stunned. "Did your father know Alana?" Then he answered his own question, as if he'd just worked it out in his mind. "Of course he did. They lived five houses down from each other. They were neighbors. Were they friends that you know of? And that bio I read mentioned Sarah's role in *Growing Up Dead* playing Alana's younger sister."

"Get real, Dylan. Dad and Alana were not friends. Dad hated Alana. Now that I think about it, he really hated her. You know, every time he got drunk he'd forbid me to see Kit or play with her; he didn't even want me around Kit because of the way he felt about Alana."

Dylan turned back to the computer. In less than five minutes, Baylee saw the information appear on the laptop screen. Over his shoulder, she began to read aloud from a list of William Scott's film credits. Dylan pointed to the part he wanted her to focus on.

"Alana made three films with my father directing. In one of them Sarah Moreland played Alana's little sister. They all worked together once. They were neighbors. What does that prove?"

"It proves they all knew each other rather well, and apparently your father and Alana had some sort of falling out. Baylee, what if your dream isn't a dream at all? What if you actually heard your mother arguing with two women, one of which might have been Alana, and she pushed your mother down the stairs?"

Baylee looked at him wide-eyed, and then shook her head. "No. In the dream Alana slaps my mother, fights with her, but it's the woman with dark hair who actually does the shoving. I'm sure of that."

"Okay, but Alana was there. Think. Who was the other woman?"

It didn't take Baylee five seconds to pull in the image. Horrified at the revelation, her hand flew to her mouth. "Oh. My. God. The woman looked like a young Jessica Boyd with long black hair. She had dark, deep-set brown eyes. Is it possible?" She got up to pace. "This is crazy, Dylan. I feel like I'm getting caught up in a hallucination. Are we really having this conversation?"

"We are. When did you say you started therapy?"

"Freshman year of college. Dr. Strasburg. Santa Monica. Every Tuesday. I was seventeen. Why?"

"Did you ever mention your dream to this Dr. Strasburg?"

"Sure. Kit and Quinn and I talked a lot about our dreams, good dreams, bad dreams, disturbing dreams, and definitely our recurring dreams. It was all part of group."

"Could you go back there, get him to open up his files, maybe get a transcript of what you said back then?"

"Sure, but why?"

"I'm thinking when you first started talking about it, remembering the details your memory might be much clearer when you were younger, from a much younger perspective than it is now. Because, frankly, what you remember now is a little jaded. As we get older, our memories fade, lose their clarity. It might be worth it to take a look at his files."

Impressed, Baylee let out a sigh. "You really are good at this, you know that?"

He grinned. "Just part of the full service treatment here at the Burke B & B." His eyes narrowed as he suddenly looked, really looked at what she was wearing. How had that gotten past him? His gaze fell on the thin cropped top and the pair of incredibly short shorts.

Baylee saw him swallow as his eyes descended on her body, at same time trying to stay fixed on her mouth.

"You can't walk around like that and expect me not to notice."

"I'm…sorry. I wasn't thinking. I saw the light in here and just…"

"Don't apologize. You know this is going to happen as well as I do. I called Melissa this morning after you read me the riot act. She won't be calling here anymore, at least not to—go out."

"Dylan, that isn't necessary. I didn't mean for you to break up with her."

"I didn't. Break up with her that is. We were never together. You said you remembered how the game was played, Baylee. Fuck buddies. That's all it was." It shamed him to admit that.

"I got that. But if you're expecting me to fill that role…"

He stood up and stressed, "Don't insult me or you. There's something more going on here. Don't deny it. What happened this morning was inevitable. I don't like the fact that I've become a little too careless with people."

"You mean women."

"Yeah, I guess I do. If it would put your mind at ease, I'll get tested."

"Tested? You'd do that?"

"If that's what it takes. I had an insurance exam in January. Jake insists all his key employees have one every year. They took blood, the whole package. It all came back fine. But since that was months ago, I'll go in for another blood test first chance I get."

He stepped closer. "We're attracted to each other, right?"

"Yes."

"I'm not looking for a quickie here, Baylee. Am I wrong to think we could have something special together?"

She shook her head. "You aren't wrong. But it's too soon. You can't pressure me and expect me to just jump in bed because I'm sharing your house and I'm convenient. I can't help it if things get—a little heated between us sometimes. Living here wasn't my idea, it was yours. The three-date rule doesn't apply here, either. You can't rush me on this. I have Sarah to think about first."

He chuckled, rubbing the stubble on his chin. "The three-date rule, huh? Is that what I'm doing?"

She sighed, laughing as well. "Seems like."

"Will you kiss me like you did last night before you go back to bed?"

She blew out a breath. "Do you think that's wise?"

He grinned at the idea of a challenge. "I think I can control my primal urges long enough to enjoy the kiss the same way I did last night without us ending up in bed."

"You're making fun of me."

"Maybe." He reached behind him to shut down his laptop. "Why don't we take a ride out to Glendale tomorrow, spend some time talking to this Karen Nash? I found her address on the Internet. We'll give her a call in the morning. Make sure she's the right Karen Nash with a sister named Sarah Moreland. Maybe Karen can tell us more about the tennis pro."

How sweet of him, she thought. A chunk of doubt fell away. She was already standing close to him and simply stepped into his space, reaching her arms around his waist. "Oh Dylan, that's the sweetest thing. I had to beg Kit and Quinn to make the trip that one time we went out there. And yet you'd go on a whim."

"I'd go because you need to find out what happened to your mother once and for all. Look Baylee, I had a pretty normal childhood, no abusive mother or father, no alcoholism to deal with, no beatings. I can't imagine what it would be like to grow up that way."

Her last bit of resistance melted away. She stood on her tiptoes and touched her lips to his. He grabbed her around the waist, bringing her the rest of the way in, wrapping her up. His hands moved down to cup her rear end. Her body melded into his like it had been waiting to find purpose. The instant their lips touched the warmth spread. His tongue parted her lips, began probing, sucking, tasting.

The heat came in layers, soft flame first before building to liquid fire.

Somewhere a cell phone rang. They broke apart, looking around trying to locate the ringing. It was Dylan who got to the phone first. It was Baylee's cell, which she'd left on the coffee table. Picking it up, Dylan checked caller ID. The lateness of the hour and the untimely interruption caused him to bark at no one in particular. "Who the hell would be calling at this hour?"

"Maybe it's Tanya. It could be about Dad."

He held up the phone while the thing kept ringing. "With a blocked ID, I don't think so."

He flipped open the phone. "Who the hell is this?"

The last thing Connor Boyd expected was for a man to answer. But that wasn't enough to deter him. "I need to talk to Baylee. Now. Who is this?"

Dylan recognized his voice. And it made his blood run cold. "You stay away from Baylee. Lose this number, asshole, and never call her again."

"I want to hear that from her. She doesn't have the guts to say that to my face."

"She may not, but I do. You're the sick pervert who's stalking her."

"Did she tell you that? Don't you what to know why I'm calling?"

"I don't give a shit."

"Are you going to tell me who this is?"

"I'm the boyfriend, Einstein. You always call and threaten women at three in the morning."

Over the monitor, Sarah started to cry.

"What is that noise? Is that a baby?"

"What kind of asshole calls someone at three in the morning? You woke up my daughter, you jerk." Out of the corner of his eye he saw Baylee dart down the hall to quiet Sarah.

"Your daughter?"

"I don't appreciate your calling my woman at three in the morning either. You got that?"

Click. The line went dead.

"Shit." Not thinking straight, he quickly punched in star sixty-nine, but was not surprised when the call did not go through. He knew star sixty-nine didn't work with cell phones. Frustrated, he threw down the phone and went in search of Baylee. He didn't go far.

When he got to Sarah's room, Baylee was sitting in his desk chair with the baby at her breast, shaking from head to toe with a panicked look in her eyes. "That was Connor, wasn't it?"

"Yeah. How'd he get your number?"

"I have no idea. The only people that have it are Kit, Quinn, Blair, Tanya, and Dad. Maybe Gloria."

The list was short. "Well, he managed to get it from someone."

For Sarah's sake, Baylee tried to stop shaking, tried to calm down. "I didn't realize I'd be this scared."

"You mean you expected him to call."

"He's called before, Dylan. But not since last year. And not using that number. I've changed my cell phone number twice, once when I got to Denver and again in December before coming back to L.A. trying to avoid this very scene. The only people that have this number are the ones closest to me."

"You're changing it again first thing in the morning." He realized he was shouting when Sarah stopped nursing long enough to turn her head to stare at him. At the gruff sound of his voice, her lips started to pucker into a cry.

Instantly remorseful, Dylan went around and knelt down in front of both of them. He placed a gentle hand on Sarah's head and said softly, "Hey there, Gidget, I'm sorry. I didn't mean to yell. Getting a little hungry, needed a little snack, did you? It's all right. I wasn't yelling at you. I didn't mean to scare you."

He placed a tender kiss on the top of Sarah's head before looking up into Baylee's eyes. His hand reached out to touch her knee to stop it from moving up and down so much. Gentling his voice even more, he told her, "He has no idea where you are. You have to believe that. He reached a cell phone. For all he knows, you could be in Siberia."

"But I'm not in Siberia."

He smiled. "No, you aren't." But damn it, Connor could check cell phone pings from the nearest tower if he had the right connections.

"It's unnerving, Dylan."

And that was an understatement, he thought. "It's a good thing Reese took care of amending Sarah's birth certificate Friday afternoon. As far as the world is concerned, I'm Sarah's father, legally. There are only a handful of people that know the truth. And Connor Boyd isn't one of them."

"That was quick."

"Reese had a paralegal make the trip to Denver, took care of it right there in person. Considering the circumstances, Reese pulled a few strings before the three-day Memorial weekend."

"You didn't say a word."

"I was going to tell you tonight over dinner and then Tara and Kendra showed up. We got sort of sidetracked."

"How do you feel about it?"

"It's not exactly the way I pictured becoming a father, but hey, I'm cool with it. What about you?"

"I wish it were true." She hung her head because she truly did wish that with every fiber in her body. But nothing could change the truth.

"I don't expect you to believe this, but I do too." He didn't think this was the right moment to mention that Connor had heard the baby's cry over the phone. Nor the fact that like an idiot he'd admitted that the call had woken up his daughter.

As if Baylee had read his mind, she said quietly, "He heard Sarah, didn't he?"

To ease her mind, he did his best to put a positive spin on it. "That worked in our favor, set the tone right up front. I told him his call woke up my daughter. I was pissed and it was no act." The guy had an obvious screw loose, but he wasn't going to remind Baylee of that now.

She was already tense and upset. Even though she had every right to feel that way, this constant state of being on alert couldn't be good for either her or Sarah. He thought he might be making her uncomfortable, so he asked, "Do you want me to leave?"

She shook her head. "You can stay if you want to. Daddy."

He grinned.

"Did you ever think that when we met that night at the hospital, we'd be right here like this?"

"No. I thought Jake was exaggerating this whole thing out of proportion when he said someone was trying to kill Kit and then..." He stopped short when he realized what he'd suggested. "I'm sorry Baylee. I'm not saying Connor is trying to kill you." He rubbed at his forehead. "I'm just making this worse."

"It's okay. He has no reason to want to do that. I just don't want him thinking for two seconds Sarah might be his. It would be much better if he doesn't suspect anything. The good thing is she doesn't look like him at all, no dark hair, no brown eyes. Actually, she looks a lot like you."

"No, she looks exactly like her mother." He tenderly touched the baby's head again. "Look at this blonde hair." At his touch, Sarah stopped nursing and looked up at him, giving him a wide smile. "God, she's something, isn't she? Look at these little fingers and toes."

"I think most parents have this conversation right after birth."

"We took a different route, got a late start."

"You want to try and put her back down. She should go back to sleep now."

"Should being the optimum word." His lips curled into another grin and he held out his hands. Sarah willingly came into his arms. Immediately, she put both hands on his face, squishing his jaws together, giggling. "She doesn't look sleepy to me. In fact, it looks like she's wide awake and ready to play."

"Pat her on the back so she'll burp."

Dylan proceeded to pat and rub. Pretty soon, Sarah let out a loud, very unladylike belch. "Whoa, there. Good girl." At the praise, Sarah responded with a string of incoherent baby babble. Like he'd overheard Baylee do, he acted as though he understood every foreign syllable and carried on a pretend conversation with the child that the state of Colorado and now California considered to be legally his.

⟁ ⟁ ⟁ ⟁ ⟁

At 6:55 Sunday morning Quinn was just finishing up a thirty-hour shift in the ER. Standing in front of her open locker, she stared at the mess inside. Someone had gone through everything, including her purse. Even the emergency box of tampons she kept stashed here had been dumped out and the box left on top. Who would do such a thing? She wondered, as she reached for her purse.

Checking her wallet and finding the twenty-two dollars and some change still inside, she realized her credit cards were also tucked into their slots, as was her driver's license. She dug out her cell phone to check her messages and was surprised to see it already on. She could have sworn she had turned it off the last time she'd checked her phone, which had been around midnight.

After straightening up the contents of her locker, she left the fifth floor doctor's lounge and headed for the elevator, an uneasy feeling starting to creep up her spine. On the first floor she made her way past the security desk, waving at Andy, the guard on duty, who smiled and waved back. She hopped on the elevator that would take her down to the parking garage. As soon as the elevator doors slid open, she stepped out and spotted him with his arms crossed over his chest waiting for her next to the Miata. She took a deep, cleansing breath, and prepared to do battle.

"What the hell are you doing here, Cade?"

He grinned at her and it reminded her of the snake inside the man. "The TRO expired four years ago, sweetheart. It's a free country. I'm not violating any laws."

"What do you call breaking into my locker? Now that's a stretch, even for you. How did you manage to get past security? Why go through my locker?"

Acting all innocent, he asked, "Now why would I do something like that?"

"Don't be coy. What are you doing here, Cade?"

"Where's Baylee?"

The question was like a punch to the stomach. Quinn tried to mask her surprise. "Well, that's subtle but honest. Something new for you. Why do you want to know about Baylee?" She played dumb as dirt. "What's going on, Cade? Why do you care where Baylee is?"

"Personally, I don't. She isn't my type. My type is about five-foot-seven, with a sexy voice and that sultry Native American look about her." He had the gall to wink. "But for some reason Connor's looking for her, wants to find her real bad. And as we all know from experience what Connor wants, Connor gets. Save us all some time, darlin', and just tell me where the hell she is, okay?"

"You son of a bitch. You broke into my locker to help Connor find Baylee. Do you ever think on your own, Cade, or do you always do everything Connor makes you do? Of course you do, the two of you share half a brain."

Quinn saw the rage come into those black eyes quick as lightening.

He took a step closer. "I came here to talk, to find out where Baylee's hiding. Level with me, do you know why Connor's so interested in finding her?"

"Why don't you ask him? Why sneak into my locker for information?"

"Don't push me, Quinn."

"Or what?" She called his bluff, pointing to the security camera positioned in the far corner of the garage. "These little things are great technology and they work like a charm. Usually they keep out the riff-raff."

Cade took another step and was now in her face. But instead of the fist or the slap she expected, he simply leaned in and said, "You know you want me, Quinn. You remember how good it was between us. Why don't you just admit it?"

When she tried to push him back, she had no time to react before he had jerked her up against him, kissing her wildly on the mouth. She began to struggle, trying to push him away, trying to wriggle free. But just as quickly, he flung her back and away from him.

He started walking backwards. "We'll find her it's just a matter of time, Quinn. And when we do…" His voice trailed off as he strolled away.

Despite her bravado, Quinn slumped against the car door, shaking like a leaf. Finally, she managed to get the car door unlocked, and slid in behind the wheel. Automatically, she locked the doors. Without paying much attention to what she was doing, she absently reached into her bag and dug out her cell phone.

⚚ ⚚ ⚚ ⚚ ⚚

It hadn't taken too many days for Dylan to learn that with a baby, sleeping late in the morning was virtually nonexistent. Sarah had gone back down around three-forty-five or so but had only slept for three hours and was back up again at six-forty.

By the time he got out of the shower, he heard Baylee moving around in the kitchen, heard the gurgle of the coffeemaker start up before he heard the lilt of music that he recognized was coming from Sarah's baby swing. And then he heard the baby babble that was becoming almost second nature, an entirely different life than he'd had just a month earlier. He decided he liked having them around. And that fact alone was some kind of a signpost, an indication that life had thrown him a curveball when he'd expected a slider. On what planet would he have traded in his carefree life for a complicated woman with a baby? It just showed that life was most often unpredictable.

She was sitting at the kitchen table trying to wake up, sipping a cup of steaming coffee, when she looked up and saw him standing in the doorway dressed in jeans and a T-shirt. She grinned. "What are you doing up? You should go back to bed."

He grinned back. "How do you do it, with no sleep, I mean?"

"I got almost three hours. You get used to it. Sort of."

As he poured himself a cup of coffee, he told her, "Why don't you go grab a shower? I'll watch Gidget."

"Do I smell that bad?"

"No, but you look like you could use more than a little wakeup juice. Five minutes in the shower works wonders."

Baylee's cell phone rang. She instantly went on alert, giving Dylan a stricken look before he reached for the phone. He eyed Quinn's name on caller ID and flipped open the phone. "Hey Quinn, how's it going?"

Her voice sounded shaky. "Dylan, I'm glad you answered the phone. I don't want to upset Baylee, but she needs to know. I just found out Cade broke into my locker at the hospital sometime after midnight. He found my cell phone. I think he might have gotten Baylee's phone number off of it. I'm not sure what Connor can do with that but there's a reason to everything Connor does. So, you can probably expect…"

"So that's how the son of a bitch got the number." He told her about Connor's call.

"I'm sorry, Dylan, I had no idea they'd go to such extremes. I'm not sure how he got past security, but since it involves a Boyd I'd guess money exchanged hands. He didn't even try to hide the fact that he'd done it. Cade was waiting by my car." Strutting like a peacock, she thought now.

He sat up straighter in his chair, shaking off the last dregs of sleep. "Did he hurt you?"

Quinn did her best to take the fear out of her voice. "I'm okay. But it's never easy going one-on-one with

Cade Boyd. He just rattled me, which was exactly his intent. He got his point across."

Their conversation had Baylee reaching for the phone. "What did he do, Quinn? Tell me the truth."

"Baylee. I'm fine, really. I'm just tired and the son of a bitch surprised me. Change your number, kiddo."

"Plan on it. I'll e-mail you with the new number."

"Maybe that isn't such a good idea either until we figure out what they're up to. You need to call Kit, give her a heads up. She needs to know, too. This means they're getting more desperate, as if that were possible."

"I'll take care of it. You go home and get some sleep. You sound exhausted."

After they hung up, Baylee called her cell phone carrier to get her number changed and then Kit to give her a heads up.

While Baylee took a hot shower, Dylan kept an eye on Sarah and called the number for Karen Nash he'd gotten off the Internet, confirming the fact that they had the right woman. He then searched MapQuest for the directions to her address in Glendale and dialed Jake's number while he waited for the map to print.

Getting Jake's take on Connor's phone call and Cade's visit to Quinn was a little like fanning the flames of a bonfire. They both agreed that Connor tipped his hand. But why?

"I don't understand why Connor doesn't just leave her alone. And why does Cade go out of his way to make sure Quinn knows who got into her locker?"

"I said the same thing about Collin. It didn't take a rocket scientist to figure out that he's infatuated with Kit. If you follow the same logic, the same obsessive fixation could be true of Connor and Cade."

"Oh God. If that's it, and Connor's fixated on Baylee, he won't let this thing go. You still think it's a good idea to do the picnic thing tomorrow?"

"I couldn't derail Kit's Memorial Day train short of a natural disaster even if I wanted to. She's been planning this for a week. Just come prepared to spend the night. She wants everyone to have a good time, forget their worries, and that means stick around after they've had a few too many beers, no drinking and driving."

"Can you accommodate everyone like that?"

"Furniture was delivered yesterday. But they're still working on getting the electricity wired. The downstairs is good to go. Upstairs, that's another matter. But everyone will have a room and a bed. Worst case, you might have to take a cold shower upstairs, or stand in line to get a hot one down."

"Can't ask for more than that." When he heard the shower shut off, he told Jake quickly, "Look, I gotta run, so I guess we'll see you then."

Baylee fed Sarah and got her packed for the trip to see Karen Nash. Despite the failure of her visit nine years earlier, she was excited about talking to the woman again, excited about the prospect of gleaning some tidbit of fresh information that might have transpired over the past nine years.

The turn-of-the-century mission revival style house belonging to Karen Nash sat at the end of a palm tree-lined block in old Glendale. After unloading Sarah from the car, they were warmly greeted by a petite woman standing on the porch with graying blonde hair and a wide smile. Even though Baylee hadn't see her aunt in ten years, it was like she was looking at an older version of her mother. How had she managed to forget how much Karen resembled the woman she only remembered in old photos and bad dreams?

Over tea and cookies on the patio, Karen Nash took a walk down memory lane: ticking off funny stories, rehashing childhood memories, and funny anecdotes about the sister she hadn't seen in more than twenty-two years. When it grew warm, the three of them moved into the living room, where it was cooler, and once again, without too much prompting, Karen relayed the last time she'd heard from Sarah.

"As I recall, William had left the week before for San Francisco to start work on a new film. She called me on a Sunday morning because she phoned to wish me a happy Mother's Day. We talked about nothing in particular. She told me her plans to spend the day with you. The entire conversation was rather uneventful, just two sisters catching up on what each other's plans were for the week. It was the last time I ever talked to her." Tears ran down Karen's cheeks.

Baylee reached out to take hold of her hands. "I'm sorry, Karen. I should have realized how painful this would be for you. But I need to know. That day, did it sound like she was unhappy? Did it sound as if she was ready to take off for parts unknown?" And leave her only daughter in the dust.

Karen looked hard into Baylee's eyes. "I know the rumor, Baylee. And no, she said nothing about leaving. She wouldn't have done that. I told you that when you came here at sixteen. But you were very obstinate. Your father had planted an idea in your head and I could say nothing that would dissuade you from believing some ridiculous story about her running off with the tennis pro. I couldn't provide you with the info to back up William and you got upset with me, stormed out."

Embarrassed, Baylee softened her voice. "I remember. I'm sorry. But I was young and so very disappointed and downhearted from having made the trip. I admit I didn't respond very well to what you told me. But I was sixteen, Karen. What can I say? I just remember being so hopeful about finding you, wanting desperately to locate her, find out what happened, confront her maybe. I remember being exhilarated at that hope, and then I came here only to discover that you couldn't help me. I had to have someone to blame, so I blamed you for not having the answers. I was let down, Karen. I'm sorry I was rude. I know now that you weren't lying to me. Back then my judgment was clouded by youthful dejection and nothing more."

Karen nodded. "I felt bad for you, Baylee. I wanted to help and couldn't. Sadly there's never been a word from her. I haven't heard from Sarah in twenty-two years."

"Can you tell us anything about the tennis pro, this Luc Delaine?" Dylan asked hopefully.

"I can tell you I never believed that story about the affair. Sarah would never do that. Luc and Sarah were friends. They met at the country club and struck up a friendship. Nothing more. Now William," Karen's eyes darted over to Baylee, in sympathetic fashion. "I'm sorry, but your father had a roving eye. Sarah told me once about this one woman in particular he saw on a regular basis, a woman who refused to leave him alone even after he married."

Baylee shot Dylan a look. "Do you have a name? Did you know anything about her?"

"I know she was an actress, a blonde. Apparently she had worked with William a couple of times before. They had history together. Sarah said he was really hung up on her. I'm sorry, Baylee, that's all I can remember; it's been such a long time now."

"Thanks, Karen, you've actually been a big help." Even though it wasn't entirely true, Baylee wanted the woman to think so. This woman was after all; her mother's only living relative. They left shortly afterward with a promise to do a better job keeping in touch. But by the time they got little Sarah buckled into her car seat, by the time Dylan headed toward the freeway, Baylee sat there in the car, feeling just as dejected as she'd felt at sixteen.

&&&&&

In the dream, she was three.

She heard the angry screaming shouts coming from outside her bedroom. She knew she was scared. Were the mean people outside after her, too? She tried to block out the noise by covering her ears, trying to muffle the sound as the shouts got louder. She huddled under the covers. But the shrill voices wouldn't leave. There were two women yelling at her mama. Every so often she heard her mama's voice as she yelled back at both women to get out of her house. But it only made the mean people scream louder. And the women still weren't leaving.

Baylee thought the argument was about her daddy. But that couldn't be right because he wasn't even at home. She couldn't remember where he'd gone. All she knew was that her mother was home alone and arguing with two women.

While her three-year-old mind tried to figure out what was happening outside her door, the adults continued to scream bad words at each other. When the little girl heard hitting noises, her fear for herself turned to fear for her mama. She tried to work up her courage enough to crawl out of bed.

Finally she crept toward her bedroom door. She cracked it open enough to peer outside into the hallway. There she saw two women fighting with her mama as they stood on the upstairs landing. The woman with blonde hair slapped her mama. Baylee recognized her as Kit's mother. But she remembered that Kit's mother scared her, that she was big and mean. She didn't like Kit's mother.

But she didn't like the other woman either, the one with long black hair that was yelling mean things in her mama's face. And then all of a sudden Kit's mother slapped her mama again. Baylee tried to move; she wanted to run out into the hallway, to make them stop. But her throat tightened. Her stomach hurt and her feet refused to budge.

Just as she started to open the door further and creep toward the fight, the woman with black hair pushed her mama, and she watched as her mama fell in slow motion backwards down the stairs. Baylee remembered hearing the scream and her mama's cry, which lasted all the way down to the bottom step. She heard the dull thud hit the floor. And then nothing. She saw the two women exchange looks and then calmly descend down the stairs.

The little girl watching from the wings opened her mouth to cry. But no sound came out. Instead, she ran back to the bed and dived underneath just in case they came for her, too.

The adult Baylee sat up, remembering, reliving the moment in the dream when she'd been too scared to help. Perspiring, she fought for air. Reaching for the light on the nightstand, she fumbled in the dark, knocking over several items on the table. She heard something hit the floor. When she clicked on the light, she saw Dylan standing in her doorway.

"Ohmygod, you scared the life right out of me. What are you doing up?"

"You were crying in your sleep, thrashing around. Are you okay?" He went over and sat down next to her on the bed.

She scrubbed a hand over her face. "I had the dream. I saw the whole thing replayed again. I'm sure the woman in the dream is Alana. She's the first one who slaps my mom. The other woman looks like a young Jessica Boyd. She's the person who pushed my mom down the stairs."

She swept her hair back with her hand. "I don't know what's real anymore, Dylan. It has to be a dream. That's all there is to it. Why would my father tell me she left if she didn't? But if there's the smallest chance that she might have died that night I have to know the truth. Why would those two women do such a thing to my mother? And why would my father be part of it?"

Why indeed, Dylan thought as he reached out to touch her hair. He picked up a bottle of water from the floor, twisted off the cap. "Here, drink this. You want anything else?"

"Answers. I want some answers, Dylan."

But there would be no answers tonight, at least not until William decided to expunge the ghosts he had lived with for over two decades.

CHAPTER 13

Crandall House no longer looked like a ramshackle, boarded-up relic from the past. The stately Queen Anne Victorian with the wraparound front porch and bold columns draped with ornate ivy now looked like the showplace it had once been in its heyday back when it was a hotel, a stop on the Coast Stage Line in 1888. Actually, thanks to a team of workmen that had labored practically around the clock, the old house had been updated with all the latest and greatest gadgets.

Kit couldn't believe they'd actually moved in. Even if it were just for today, she didn't care. It was like a dream come true. Thanks to the team of electricians who'd worked up until eight o'clock the night before, they had electricity throughout the first floor and that included the kitchen. She looked around the room where everything gleamed brand new, from the stainless steel appliances to the new flooring.

Kit gazed across the room. Her eyes instantly locked on the smile Gloria wore prominently on her face as she stood at the marble countertop putting the finishing touches on the potato salad. Mother and daughter had been cooking and baking for hours, eagerly waiting for their friends to arrive, hoping for just one day where they could all enjoy themselves without worrying about anyone named Boyd.

Pepper, Kit's black-and-white Border collie, sniffed the appetizing smells in the kitchen then plopped down beside Kit's feet at the counter. Still a little slow getting around after the car accident weeks earlier, Pepper had made a tremendous recovery from surgery.

Kit set aside the marinade she'd prepared for the steaks and hamburgers Jake would grill later and watched as he stepped inside from the newly built deck onto the sandstone kitchen floor.

"Grill's got plenty of propane and is ready anytime you are."

"Where are they? It's almost ten-thirty."

Jake shot her a grin without asking who "they" were. All morning long she'd been like the proverbial kid waiting for Santa to come down the chimney on Christmas Eve. She'd been planning for this day all week and wanted nothing more than for everyone to get here, kick back, and have a good time.

When a car horn sounded from outside, she shot out of the kitchen like a runner at the starting line, running toward the front door so fast her shoes skidded on the newly laid hardwood floor in the hallway.

Gloria saw Jake smile and declared, "She gets like this when she throws a party, better get used to it. By the way, are we working on those grandchildren yet?"

He couldn't help but laugh. "That is none of your business, Mom. Don't get pushy, okay?"

At the word "Mom," Gloria's eyes misted over. She put her hand to her mouth before trying for some composure. Reeling in her emotions, she teased, "I always knew you'd make a smart-mouthed son-in-law. What was I thinking trying to get the two of you together all those years? I should have had my head examined."

"You love me, you know it, and you always have." He went over and gave her a kiss on the cheek. "There's no point in denying it. Even when I was a young upstart smartass, a pain in the ass, you loved me."

"Maybe a little. Even though you aren't so young anymore. That's why you need to start working on some grandbabies, lots of grandbabies."

Just then, Dylan came through the kitchen door hauling a Pack 'N Play. Kit followed, carrying Sarah in the infant seat with Baylee tagging behind, an olive green diaper bag strapped over her shoulder, and pushing a stroller that squeaked on the brand new floor.

Jake walked around the kitchen island and slapped Dylan on the back. "You guys sure don't travel light. You bring the whole house with you?"

"Laugh it up, pal. This could be you in nine months," Dylan shot back without rancor.

A stricken look crossed Jake's face at the realization of that statement. A hand went to his chest and stayed there as if the arrow had pierced right through his heart. "Point taken."

"Good. Then make yourself useful and get the cooler of beer out of the car," Dylan told him with mock contempt as he went about trying to find the best place to set up the port-a-crib so Sarah would have a place to nap later.

Jake disappeared down the hallway, considering Dylan's comment and realizing truer words were never spoken. In nine months, he could be hauling around a baby and all the trappings that went with one. Surprisingly, the idea didn't freak him out. He'd wanted kids once and, now that he had Kit, the possibility he might actually become a dad was more of a reality than it ever had been before.

By the time Jake reached Dylan's SUV, Reese was unwinding his lanky frame out of his sporty Lexus. Dressed in jeans and an ancient Nirvana T-shirt, he stretched his back. "Jesus, it's a long way out here. Traffic was awful. If you're planning to commute back and forth to Westlake Village every day from here you should think about getting one of these." He tapped the hood of his sporty hybrid 600.

"Good idea," Jake said absently. Any other time he'd like nothing more than to give the car a once-over, but at the moment, his mind conjured up the prospect of baby car seats and minivans.

Reese took a moment to look at the house for the first time and whistled. "Wow. This is some place." His eyes took in the angles and curves of the massive Victorian, the wide wraparound porch, and the curved balcony upstairs. He took in the view. Built on the top of a cliff overlooking San Madrid's little fishing village, he stared out into the ocean. "What did you pay for this?" Reese asked, as if being the man's lawyer entitled him to certain specifics.

When Jake threw out a ridiculously low figure, Reese whistled again. "You got a helluva deal. How much have you sunk into the place remodeling it though?" When Jake threw out another figure, this one not so low, Reese chuckled. "Well, let's see what that kind of money gets you."

They retrieved the cooler with the beer out of the back of Dylan's SUV, reminiscent of their college days at Cal-Berkeley, and started walking toward the house. They met Dylan on the wraparound front porch. He had a serious look on his face. "I know we agreed not to talk about this today, but before Quinn gets here maybe we should talk while the women are out of earshot."

Jake shook his head. "I don't think Quinn's going to be able to make it. Last I heard she had to work. But yeah, I think we need to talk, there's something I need to tell you guys and I don't want Kit to know about it yet."

"Actually, Quinn's coming, after she gets a little shuteye. But she's one of the reasons I wanted to talk to you. Cade showed up at the hospital yesterday morning after her shift ended. I thought Donovan was supposed to be keeping an eye on these guys. If that's true, I'd say he's doing a damn lousy job of it."

Reese stopped short and stared at Dylan, but it was Jake who offered, "I already chewed on Donovan some over what happened. He has a guy tailing after Kit and one on Baylee. As of yesterday afternoon, one's following Quinn now, too."

"That can't be. There's been no one around Baylee except me."

"Donovan says the guy's been there. If he's any good, don't you think it's better if you don't see him?"

"I don't like this. Baylee might've had the right idea after all. I should just get her out of L.A. and take her some place safe where Connor can't find her."

"And where would that be exactly?" Jake asked in mock irritation.

Knowing he'd been left out of the loop, Reese finally interjected, "Wait, back up here a minute, Dylan. What the hell happened yesterday between Cade and Quinn?"

Dylan went into a lengthy explanation about Cade's face-to-face threat, about his breaking into her locker, Connor's three a.m. phone call, and about the fact that Connor had heard Sarah over the phone. But before they could get into more specifics, Kit opened the front door and the conversation came to a screeching halt.

Assuming they'd probably been discussing the Boyds, she went on the offensive. "I thought we agreed to put this aside for today, just one damn day. Can we agree no more talk about them? Besides, it's time to get the meat on the grill. Quinn's about twenty minutes out."

Reese couldn't help it, at the mention of Quinn showing up, his pulse picked up. "I thought she was going to get some sleep."

"She said she got four hours. For Quinn that's a lot. I hope she's okay, though; she sounded a little strange. It's probably all those hours." At least Kit hoped that was the reason and not because Cade had threatened Quinn again. She turned accusingly to Jake, reminding him, "I want all of us to have fun today, not sit around discussing them, okay?"

Jake shot Dylan a reproachful look. "We got it. We'll get the grill going."

As they made their way inside, Reese turned to Kit. "How'd Quinn manage to get the day off?"

"She got off work Sunday morning around seven but got called back in around six in the evening to work another twelve hours for some guy who had more seniority and had a family emergency. Due to the hours she put in over the past forty-eight, she had downtime coming."

After stopping at the kitchen for a beer, the men collectively went outside to fire up the grill and do any talking away from the house.

But the festive mood had changed.

Thirty minutes later, Kit and Quinn stood on top of the well-worn path from the beach watching a relaxed Baylee walk side by side with Dylan. "I don't think she's looked this stress-free in all the months she's been back in L.A. And have you noticed, she's acting like her old self again." It did Kit's heart good to see Baylee enjoying herself.

"It must be the hair," Quinn said, as she watched a blonde Baylee, dressed in a pair of low rise shorts and a cropped sleeveless top, head up the well-worn path from the beach back up to the house, deep in conversation with surfer dude, who was toting the baby. "Can you believe how incredible she looks? She sure doesn't look like she's ever had a baby. She looks like she weighs the same as she did when she was about fifteen."

"I hope I look that good six months after childbirth."

Quinn almost tripped on a rock. "Is there something you want to tell me?"

Kit laughed. "I'm not pregnant—yet. But I'd be lying if I said I didn't want it to happen. I've got the nursery all picked out upstairs. When I give you guys the grand tour, I want you to tell me what you think."

"Right away? Don't you want to give it some time, see if this thing works out?"

"Oh, Quinn. I've been in love with Jake Boston my whole life. And he loves me. I'm so happy it's—scary. I can't ever remember being this happy before."

"You deserve it."

"Did you hear what he did?" Kit cocked her head in the direction of Dylan.

After the kind of shift she'd had that morning, Quinn was more than ready for some gossip, some down time, eager to spend time just hanging with her friends. "If you tell me the guy's into kinky shit, then I'm going to have to run up this hill, bitch-slap him upside the head, and then find her another place to crash."

Kit laughed. "Nothing kinky that I know of, Mom. No, he had Reese amend Sarah's birth certificate so he's listed as her father."

"Aww, that's sweet. Okay, so he isn't the pervert I thought he was. But that doesn't change his major player status. Who knew the guy would be such a boy scout with a heart of gold when it came to Sarah. All I know is he better not hurt Baylee. She has enough to deal with without having another guy take advantage of her."

At Quinn's tone, Kit turned to give her friend a long look. "Cade scared the shit out of you, didn't he?" She saw Quinn swallow hard and recognized the second the veneer dropped away. After all, they'd been friends since third grade, not as long as Kit had known Baylee, but long enough to know each other's moods and familiar with each other's temperament.

"Yeah. He got to me. He always does. But there's something I need to tell you, something I didn't mention to Baylee or Dylan."

Kit's radar went off. "What?"

"I got the impression—and maybe it's just that—but I got a sense that Connor's sort of hung up on Baylee, kind of like the same sick way Collin is hung up on you."

"What makes you say that?"

"The way Cade said Connor was looking for her, the way he said that Connor would eventually find her. The way he reminded me that Connor always gets what he wants. It was just—creepy. It reminded me of the weird way Collin always acted when he was around you, like that time he cornered you in the cabana house at the Enclave."

Kit remembered all right. If she hadn't screamed the house down, Quinn and Baylee would never have known where she was and come to her rescue. "I caught Connor once trying to get Baylee to leave with him. We were about fifteen at the time. It was during Collin's birthday party. He'd spent a considerable amount of time trying to get her to dance with him. He'd been drinking. He had to be in his twenties when it happened." She paused before adding, "And you know as well as I do that Cade hasn't gotten over you, not by a long shot."

"It's been four damn years."

"Yeah, but Collin and I were never together. You guys were actually a couple, you…"

"Go ahead, say it, we slept together. What can I say? It lasted for six weeks and I've regretted it so many times since. How was I supposed to know he'd beat the crap out of me?"

Kit cocked her head and gave her a disbelieving look.

"Okay, okay. You and Baylee tried to warn me. I was young and stupid. I admit it. But why can't he just leave me the hell alone?"

As they followed Baylee and Dylan from a distance back up to the house, Kit wondered that too. Why couldn't the Boyds somehow drop off the planet?

⚭⚭⚭⚭⚭

"**You don't have** to hold her, you know. You can put her down as soon as we get back to the house. That's why we brought the Pack 'N Play," Baylee pointed out as they made their way up the steep hill back to the house.

He knew that. Hadn't he been the one to load the thing into the car? But for now Dylan was content to hold Sarah as she slept and give her mother a little break from doing everything she usually did. He noted she looked so much more relaxed today than she had over the last forty-eight hours. And Dylan realized then and there that keeping

Baylee happy was something he very much wanted to do, one way or another.

As soon as they reached the grassy area where Kit and Jake had set up tables and chairs next to the grill on the lawn, he plopped down in a deck chair, adjusting Sarah to his shoulder. He watched Baylee drop in beside him for all of two seconds before she was bouncing up again asking, "How about a beer?"

"Do you ever just sit down and relax for five damn minutes?"

"Sorry." She grinned. "It's a habit." Then she charged off toward the coolers lined up on the deck. The coolers held an assortment of cold drinks, everything from mini bottles of wine to beer to soda. Watching her walk away, it dawned on him that all three women had the same boundless energy, some unnamed strength that seemed to originate from deep within and radiate outward.

Quinn, like any first-year resident, worked long shifts at the hospital. Kit owned her own business, and put in long hours, six days a week. As for Baylee, he'd seen her endless energy firsthand every day with Sarah. All three women were like energizer bunnies.

And whenever the three of them were around each other that same energy force seemed to get stronger, almost as if they fed off each other. Whatever had happened to them in the past, Dylan surmised, must have affected all three of them in such a way that whenever one was down the other two picked up the slack.

And then it came to him.

Their difficult childhoods had to have played a role in shaping that never-ending force field that seemed to drive them at high-speed. What little Baylee had said was enough to tell him that Kit's early years had been far worse than hers. And yet, he knew that after all these years, Baylee's early pain still haunted her dreams. He'd seen that for himself last night.

Admittedly, he didn't know much about Quinn's childhood, only that she was the daughter of the rock star

Nick Tyler and a globe-trotting, free-spirited artist named Ella Canyon. Quinn's parents never married, never lived together. But as he sat there holding Sarah, watching her sleep, he couldn't help but wonder what secrets Quinn held close to the vest. And she had to have a few.

He looked down at the bundle in his arms and then stared at her mother, who'd finally decided to have a seat next to him. Here was a life he held that could be his responsibility. One he could personally see would turn out for the good if he did this right. It was something weighty to consider.

Kit shoved an elbow in Jake's ribs as he stood at the grill, beer in hand, flipping a burger. "Would you look at that? Doesn't she look happier than you've ever seen her? Dylan wouldn't hurt her, would he?"

Jake reached around Kit's waist, drew her in to him before glancing over at the man in question, who was in an animated conversation with Baylee. Jake nuzzled Kit's neck, telling her, "He's a good guy, Kit. Dylan's been acting kinda funny ever since that night at the hospital, ever since he met her."

"But he has women crawling out of the woodwork," Kit pointed out.

Jake cocked a brow. What could he do, deny it? Willing to take up for his best bud, he said simply, "He takes care not to hurt anyone. Always has. Dylan's able to walk that fine line that says, 'We'll have some fun, but let's keep it light' and then somehow manages to stay friends with all of them."

"All I know is that Baylee seems at ease around him." As Kit continued to watch the woman and Dylan deep in conversation, she reminded herself it was simply a platonic arrangement designed to keep Baylee from leaving town. They had to get to know each other in order to share a house, didn't they? And Sarah's amended birth certificate thing was just a tactic to keep Connor from suspecting anything. "Do you think it'll work?"

"What? Them sharing a house."

"No. Amending Sarah's birth certificate."

"It should. After all, Boyd has no reason to go looking at Sarah's parentage."

About that time, Quinn meandered over, no longer wearing the wetsuit she'd worn to go surfing. She'd changed into white shorts and a red tank top, and held out an empty paper plate. "What's taking so long with the food? You've got hungry people here."

Without letting go of Kit's waist, with his free hand, Jake switched from a long spatula to a set of tongs, pinching a hot dog off the warmer and waving it in front of Quinn. Like a kid, she grabbed a bun and held it open while he dropped the meat inside. "This'll tide you over until the steaks and burgers are done, which should be in about five minutes."

"Finally," she said, as she took a generous bite and groaned. "Where were you hiding these? Are we roasting marshmallows later? Kit promised roasted marshmallows on top of melted chocolate and graham crackers."

"Where I come from we call those s'mores," Reese said tactfully, as he walked up behind them to the cooler sitting on the deck and pulled out a beer. Twisting off the cap, he watched out of the corner of his eye while Quinn devoured her hot dog in four bites.

"Yeah, well, whatever. Are we making those later over the fire the way we used to at the beach?"

Jake one-handedly flipped another burger as he rubbed Kit's back and wished he could get her alone, away from all these people. But that wasn't going to happen for hours yet. Not until this picnic had run its course. He patted Kit's rear end before turning to Quinn.

"Kit decided the s'mores were a tad on the messy side. But you get your pick of assorted cookies and brownies, and if you're really good, chocolate fudge cake."

Kit tacked on, "Slathered with lots of dark chocolate frosting the way you like it. You won't miss the s'mores, I promise. And you won't starve. Gloria made four different kinds of side salads."

Kit pointed to the table and Quinn followed her hand like a hound with a scent. She spooned out a generous helping of each kind of salad until she had potato salad, pea salad, pasta salad, and plain old leaf salad piled high on the double-duty paper plate.

Reese took a pull on his beer. "Now there's a woman with an appetite." Taking in her trim five-foot-seven athletic body, he added, "Where do you put all that?"

With a gleam in her eye, Quinn shot back, "So I've got a healthy appetite, sue me. You guys bitch about women who won't eat, then when we do, you make snide comments about it. Either way, we can't win."

Reese arched a brow and wondered why he was so intrigued with this woman who acted as if she couldn't stand to get near him for five damn minutes. Determined to get on the woman's good side if she had one, he conceded, "You're right. It's just that some women who work out in a gym for hours would kill to have your body." And energy, he thought.

That had her bobbling her plate. "Well, now I'm disappointed. I'd hoped the big-time lawyer might be attracted to my quick wit and brilliant mind instead of the way I look. How silly of me to think you could be that deep?"

When it came to this woman, he didn't seem to be able to win today, or any other day for that matter, so he took the path of least resistance. "That was a compliment."

"Was it?" She sighed. "Sorry, but I'm a little cranky." When she saw the skeptical look on his face, she chuckled and said, "Okay, a lot. But I had to work a straight thirty-hour shift and then got called back in for twelve more on top of that, didn't knock off until..." She glanced at her watch. "A couple of hours ago."

"I've heard horror stories from first-year residents about the brutal hours. You must be ready to drop."

What she could tell him about brutal hours wasn't for the faint-hearted. But she smiled and said, "I didn't want to miss the party."

She didn't tell him she'd needed to be around her friends, around people, after working on a four-year-old kid this morning for the longest twenty-five minutes of her life. Pulled from the family swimming pool, not breathing and without a pulse, the little girl had arrived at the ER for someone to save her life. It had fallen to Quinn. But she hadn't been able to save her.

After telling the family, seeing the sorrow in their eyes, the last thing she had wanted to do was crawl into bed and sleep. Her colleagues assured her she'd get used to that kind of thing. But she had a soft spot for kids. Where kids were concerned, she didn't think she'd ever get used to seeing children suffer or hurt. Or in this case die, drown. She could still see the kid's eyes.

She suddenly felt sick from all the food she'd just eaten. When she spotted Gloria setting the plates out on the picnic table, Quinn pulled herself back to the moment and headed off to see if she could help without a backward glance at Reese.

Kit saw the frustration on Reese's face and ambled over where he stood. "It isn't you she doesn't like."

"Could have fooled me," Reese retorted.

Kit shook her head. "She doesn't like lawyers in general."

"Mind clueing me in as to why?"

"Spending a lifetime communicating with your father through his lawyers makes a kid a little mistrustful when it comes to that particular profession. She doesn't mean anything by it, Reese. It's innate, a self-preservation tactic. Don't give up on her. She's a terrific person."

"A lifetime? But she's Nick Tyler's daughter." Nick Tyler, Ireland's proverbial rock legend, lead singer for Shatter, and the rock star he and every other kid his age had listened to and worshiped from afar, the guy *Rolling Stone* had once touted as the best lyricist of his time. "Growing up in Beverly Hills had to be a walk in the park."

Kit's eyes fixed Reese with a cold stare. "You'd think so. wouldn't you? But her father lived in Ireland." If she said more, would she betray Quinn's trust? Eyeing Reese's confusion, she decided she needed to set him straight. "Let's see if I remember my geography. Beverly Hills is way over here." She used her hands to illustrate her point. "While Dublin, Ireland is way over here." She had both arms extended out as far as they would reach in an exaggerated pose.

"Get it? She's never had a real relationship with Nick Tyler. Just lots of letters, notes, checks from his team of high-powered lawyers. Same goes for her mother." But Kit didn't intend to get into the Ella thing now while trying to explain Quinn's slippery relationship with her father.

"Tyler's string of lawyers handled what few birthday and Christmas cards she received over the years. Any money for school, for clothes, came through them as well. When she was a kid, any request for money had to be put in writing, no matter what it was for. When her mother wasn't around, the request fell to either Quinn or her stepfather. Being a product of a rock star and a free-spirited artist who didn't stay in one place for more than a couple of years had its own challenges, Reese. Sounds glamorous on the surface, but the lawyers take care of Tyler's financial responsibilities. That's all Quinn ever was to him, a financial matter."

Feeling small for what he'd been thinking, Reese wanted to know, "What about now, now that she's an adult? She's successful, smart. Doesn't she have a relationship with the guy now? I read somewhere on the Internet where the guy just divorced his third wife. You'd think he would've reached out to his daughter at some point."

"You'd think, but no. No reaching out for Nick Tyler. She tried when she was younger of course. All those times, she called and couldn't get past his personal assistants or wrote letters to him that went unanswered. He was just too busy touring or recording or living that rock star life, a world that didn't include his daughter. There are times when a kid just needs to talk to a parent about things that are happening at home, or at school, times when a kid just needs to hear from someone who cares, someone who thinks about them enough to ask how it's going at school, interested enough to see they get birthday presents. But then once you reach a certain age, around fifteen or sixteen when that rebellious streak kicks in, it's a little too late to have a relationship with someone who ignored you for the first fifteen years of your life."

"That explains a lot. Where was her mother during all this?"

Kit sighed. "Oh, Reese. Her mother ended up marrying Tyler's record producer. Quinn ended up moving here the summer before she started third grade. She was eight. But the marriage between Ross Jennetti and Ella Canyon lasted about as long as it took for the ink to dry on the license, no more than two years for sure. And then her mother took off, leaving Quinn here while she went in search of herself or whatever it is she does."

"Her mother left her with the stepfather and just took off? You're kidding?"

"I wish I were. From third grade on, Quinn lived in Jennetti's house, a strange man who didn't much like kids. But at least he gave her a place to stay and let her continue going to school here, knowing she couldn't count on her mother for stability. That's something, I guess." Kit left it at that. She bit her lip to keep from saying any more about Ross Jennetti, knowing she'd said too much already.

"Her mother left her with this guy? For how long?"

Opened up that door, didn't you? Kit blew out a breath. "She came back for visits at Christmas. Sometimes."

Reese narrowed his eyes. "This is a joke. You're putting me on."

"No, Reese. I'm not. I really hope you won't give up on her. Quinn happens to be a terrific person who loves children. After her residency, she wants nothing more than to become a pediatrician, open up a clinic. Ask her about it sometime."

Reese allowed himself another long look at Quinn. She was a woman with a prickly veneer. Why the hell she intrigued him was anyone's guess.

When Jake announced the steaks and burgers were done, everyone except Dylan and Baylee ambled over to the tables and dug into the food. As soon as Kit realized Baylee wasn't going to leave Dylan, she piled two plates high with a couple of burgers and walked over, handing them off to Baylee. "You can put her down, you know," Kit jokingly told Dylan, as she pointed to the port-a-crib they'd set up under one of the ancient oaks.

"That's what I told him, but he's afraid of waking her up."

Dylan hungrily eyed the food, but tried to play it cool. "It's no trouble holding her. I hate to wake up a sleeping baby."

"Well, you two need to eat," Kit told him, as she reached down and gathered the sleeping infant into her arms.

Making the transfer without waking up Sarah, Kit cradled her on her shoulder. "I'll hold her while you two go eat." She winked at Dylan and said, "You can't hog her all afternoon, you know. You have to share. And remember, I'm available to babysit anytime she runs you two ragged." She turned to Baylee. "I miss having you and Sarah at the shop."

"Now that I'm settled in at Dylan's, I could start back tomorrow if you want."

Kit looked uncomfortable. She and Jake had talked about Baylee making the trip every day back and forth to San Madrid and decided it might be asking for trouble. Knowing Collin had used that tactic to run Kit's Jeep off the PCH, they didn't want to take the chance it might happen to Baylee.

"Let's give it another couple of days before you come back to work, to try and gauge Connor's intent. That late night phone call isn't a good sign he's giving up." She saw the disappointment come into Baylee's eyes. "It'll just be for a couple more days. We just want to make sure he doesn't pay you a surprise visit and see Sarah." Holding the baby, Kit motioned to the plates she'd fixed. "Now both of you eat. There's enough food over there to feed a small army."

Jake watched Kit from twenty feet away. If it were possible, he fell in love with her just a little bit more. The woman had the sweetest nature of any woman he knew. Thank God she had come back to him safely. His hands fisted without even realizing it when he remembered how Kit had looked, bruised and battered, after Collin and his two thugs had pushed her Jeep off the road. She'd spent five days in the hospital. The memory reminded him of how close he'd come to losing her. There was only one man left standing who was responsible for hurting her. Jake intended to see the bastard locked up if it was the last thing he did.

He hadn't mentioned the e-mail he'd received that he hadn't been able to trace. At the first opportunity, he intended to tell Reese and Dylan, and get their take. He just didn't want Kit finding out and adding something else to the list of worries she had to deal with now.

As the group finished their meal, they kicked back and lazily watched the sun dip low on the horizon over the glistening, choppy water. They took pleasure in the fiery pink sunset and watched as the harbor lights from San Madrid twinkled to life in the distance.

Dylan conned Jake into helping him gather wood to build a bonfire, finding plenty of dry timber near the line of trees at the back of the house. But it took them close to thirty minutes to construct a makeshift fire pit with enough wood for a good fire that had any chance at lasting a couple of hours, at least until they called it a day and went inside.

When Baylee saw what they were doing, she gave them both a thumbs-up. "Can't have a picnic without a bonfire at the end of the day. Way to go, Surfer Boy."

When Sarah started to whimper in the Pack 'N Play, Dylan stopped what he was doing, ready to go over to the baby. But Baylee held up a hand and said, "You keep going. I'll get her. She's wet is all, needs changing."

After retrieving Sarah, she headed off in the direction of the house to get a dry diaper, and met up with Reese near the deck. "I've been meaning to talk to you all day. I'd like for you to draw up a waiver or something that says I won't hold Dylan financially responsible for Sarah's support in the future. He needs to know that I won't try to collect child support or anything like that."

Reese stared at the woman, wondering why she looked so different today and then realized it was the hair. "That's admirable, Baylee, but I don't think we need to put it in writing. I know Dylan isn't worried about it."

"But you are. You don't like loose ends hanging out there that might come back to bite Dylan in the ass later." When he started to say something, she quickly added, "I don't blame you for that. As his lawyer, it's your job to watch out for him. That's why I'd like for you to put it in writing. If you'll draw up the necessary paperwork using whatever words you want to use, send it over to his house, I'll sign it so he won't be on the hook, financially."

"I'm not sure how Dylan will take that."

"You and I both know it's for his own protection. It would make me feel better about him doing this."

Quinn sauntered up beside Baylee and said rather bluntly, "Is the barrister here giving you a hard time because he couldn't talk his friend out of that birth certificate thing?"

Baylee simply turned to look at Quinn and gave her a hard stare. "What has you in such a pissy mood today? Is it that thing that happened with Cade? You need to make sure hospital security doesn't drop the ball like that again and leave you vulnerable."

Quinn's bad temper plummeted. "I had a four-year-old kid die on me today."

Baylee and Reese eyed each other as if trying to decide which tack to take. It was Reese who blurted out, "Maybe if you talk about it you might lose some of that gigantic chip on your shoulder."

Quinn dropped down on the steps and told them the minute she'd seen the little girl she'd known it was too late to save her. "But despite her condition, I did everything I'd been trained to do to try to bring her back. It was just too late. I had to go out to the waiting room and look those parents in the eye and tell them their four-year-old daughter was gone. It was the hardest thing I've ever had to do."

"But think about all those others you've saved or will save, Quinn," Baylee told her, as she let her free hand rest on Quinn's shoulder. "I'm sorry that happened. It was a terrible thing, tragic. But you owe Reese an apology."

Baylee went around and sat on the step next to Quinn, settling the baby on her lap. "Dylan did a wonderful thing for me and for Sarah. Putting his name on that birth certificate might not have been the smartest thing he's ever done, but he didn't do it without acting on the advice of his attorney and friend. Reese did what any attorney, and for that matter, what any friend should do, he counseled him to do what was best for him. In the end, Dylan made up his own mind, came to a decision that benefited me and Sarah. And I'm grateful. But that's what friends do, Quinn. They stand up and say 'don't do this.' And you should know that better than most. I'm sorry you're hurting because of that little girl. But you knew when you decided to be a doctor there would be times when you wouldn't be able to save everyone."

Baylee got to her feet. "We talked about that, remember?" And with that she disappeared inside the house, leaving the new res feeling churlish.

When she'd gone, Quinn grumbled, "Well, she told me. She may be tiny, but she's pretty good at kicking my ass every now and again when I need it. She's right. I'm sorry for being so rude. I've had a bad couple of days. That's no excuse, of course, but…"

"Well gee, let me circle this day on the calendar; Quinn Tyler just used the S word."

"Oh, shut up. I just don't like lawyers."

Now that he knew why, he could tease her about it. "Lawyers in general or me in particular?"

"You're all right, I guess. You aren't completely without merit. You helped Kit out with St. John when she needed you. I'm grateful for that." She changed the subject. "Is that your hybrid parked behind Dylan's weird-looking Benz?"

"It is. I know Cade came to see you. Are you okay?"

Dylan must have blabbed. "I'm fine."

She didn't look fine; she looked exhausted, which prompted Reese to tease, "Want me to go beat him up?"

She laughed and it transformed her whole demeanor. "Would you?"

"It's been a while since I've come to blows with anyone, but I can certainly try."

Gloria listened as Quinn and Reese finally managed a civil conversation with one another without any sniping. She noted the longer the two of them talked the more Quinn's black mood lifted. She smiled. That was progress.

Now that it was getting dark, Gloria decided to light the tiki torches they'd placed around the yard. When she heard Kit's laughter, she looked over at her daughter wrapped up in Jake's embrace. The sheer wonder of it made Gloria's chest swell with the love only a mother could feel. Through it all, she realized how lucky she was that Kit wasn't angry with her, didn't hate her, wasn't even bitter about the kind of childhood she'd had.

Such a blessing, Gloria thought as she lit another torch. She glanced at the house that Kit and Jake planned to live in for a lifetime. She took in the growing night sky, the view from the cliff, and realized this spot would be perfect for an outdoor wedding. The image of Kit wearing a long white dress surrounded by Baylee and Quinn filled Gloria's mind as vividly as if the scene were happening before her. Enjoying the image of Kit's wedding, she wanted to remember that she had three girls who needed her now. She intended to be there for all of them.

And she wished Jake could find the son she'd never seen. Her eyes filled with tears at the profound loss of losing her twins. She felt cheated. After all the years she'd thought she possessed some psychic ability, the joke apparently was on her. Some psychic she turned out to be, she thought miserably. She hadn't even known she'd had a son. As she squeezed the tears from her eyes, she knew one thing for certain. There were tough times ahead. She could feel it in the air.

But then she didn't need psychic powers to know the Boyd sons were not finished with them yet. She might not be able to tell Jake where to find her own son, Ben Griffin, but she intended to use everything else inside her to make sure the three women she consider her girls stayed safe.

CHAPTER 14

Thirty minutes later, when the first blast of fireworks speared the night sky and lit up the San Madrid harbor, it was tough to say who squealed the loudest, Kit, Baylee, or Quinn. But it was Quinn who took off like a shot to stand at the edge of the cliffs to get a better view, telling her friends, "Come on, hurry up; you'll miss all the good ones."

Kit dragged Gloria to her feet, laughing at Quinn's enthusiasm, and both women followed her toward the cliffs. But when Kit noticed Baylee hanging back, struggling to make it up the hill carrying the infant carrier with Sarah tucked inside, she ran back, hefted it up and transported the baby the rest of the way.

After settling down on the ground, Baylee took a few moments to gaze at the sleeping baby nestled in her seat with her thumb in her mouth. Watching her daughter, a peace settled over her.

As she craned her neck skyward, taking in the show, she thought of how happy she was at the moment in spite of everything. She and Dylan were on better footing since Saturday. Here was a man she thought she could talk to, confide in.

She took her eyes off the show long enough to glance back over her shoulder at him, then watched as her friends enjoyed themselves. These people were her family. She wasn't going to think about anything worrisome tonight. She'd take pleasure in the fact that the people she loved were snuggled in around her, at least for the night.

While the women sat on the cliffs going ape over the fireworks, the guys hung back near the bonfire, never moving from their beach chairs, and cracked open another round of beers. This was the perfect time to finish their conversation from earlier, the one Kit had interrupted.

"There's something I need to tell you guys." Jake's tone of voice had Reese and Dylan turning in their chairs to give him their undivided attention.

"I got an e-mail Saturday morning. Sent anonymously. At least I haven't been able to trace it yet. And believe me, I've tried."

Dylan leaned over in his chair. If Jake couldn't trace it, no one could. "Okay. I take it this wasn't your usual spam."

"No. The sender said that if I'm curious about who killed Claire, I should find out where Connor Boyd was the morning she was killed."

Shock registered on Dylan's face. "Jesus. Do you think someone's just messing with you because of everything that's happened?"

"That occurred to me. But you know I always suspected something, something I never shared because it seemed too crazy, too implausible. But now, I've been doing a lot thinking back. Do you remember that party at The Enclave on Memorial Day about four years back? They called it the Boyd Bash. Claire and Connor were awfully chummy that day. I remember late that afternoon Claire disappeared for a couple of hours. When I went to look for her, I found her coming out of the cabana house. Didn't think much about it until I started going over that day in my head. That day, Connor followed her out. I never said anything until now. It's funny how you remember things when you have a reference point. It may sound crazy, I might just be grasping at straws, but I think the e-mail is legit. Of course, I know I'll need more before

I pay St. John a visit." Max St. John was the bulldog detective that had gone after Jake relentlessly soon after Claire's murder.

"You want me to put Donovan on it?"

"Yeah, I have something specific in mind. And then I need a meeting with Max St. John. Bring Holloway in on it if you can. I want you to set it up."

"Uh-uh. Not a chance, Jake. Not without your attorney present. You don't go near that man unless I'm there."

"Okay. But I want to know what evidence he has, Reese. I want to know what the son of a bitch has been sitting on for two fucking years. If the police are so reluctant to look at these high-powered people as suspects, we'll have to go around them or through them. One way or another, I want a meeting set up with St. John. I intend to apply my own pressure."

"I'll see if I can get him to give us some specifics beforehand. But don't hold your breath."

Dylan was curious. "What exactly are you looking for from St. John?"

"You didn't see Claire's bedroom that night, Dylan." He rubbed his temple. The memory of what he'd seen inside that room would stay with him for some time. "Someone went ballistic in there that day. There was a fight. And I believe Claire fought back, in fact, I know she did. That means there has to be blood evidence, DNA, something the killer left behind at the crime scene, under her fingernails, something concrete they can use to identify her killer."

Dylan and Reese exchanged looks. But it was Dylan who said, "When it comes time, how about we all pay St. John a visit? You know, if you're right. All it would take is a DNA sample from Connor Boyd to link him to the murder. We could work on that if St. John would cooperate. What I want to know, though, is who sent you that e-mail? Why now? Why not two weeks after it happened rather than two damn years?"

"That's what I'd like to know. And one I intend to work on. Look guys, I don't want you mentioning this to Kit. She has enough to worry about without wondering if I'm opening up a new can of worms. Plus, if Connor were responsible that just makes it—a more dangerous situation for Baylee. And remember, St. John isn't exactly thrilled about clearing Kit in Alana's murder. The guy could still make it tough on her. I want all of this behind us so we can move forward."

Reese blew out a breath. "I can't believe everything that's happened. It just keeps getting more bizarre by the minute."

"Talk about bizarre, there's something I've stumbled on that's pretty strange too, and believe it or not, it involves Alana and Jessica. It's about Baylee's mother."

Dylan proceeded to outline what convinced him Sarah Moreland never ran off with any tennis pro, including William's weird behavior every time Baylee was within earshot. "And I found out from Tanya that at one time William's personal attorney was Jessica Boyd. Not to mention William directed Alana in three different films, including one with Sarah. That means they all knew each other."

"And one night Sarah Moreland just disappears, takes off without a word?"

Dylan nodded in Jake's direction. "More like vanished without a trace, no letters, no cards, no calls in twenty-two years. The tennis pro leaves a promising career behind. She leaves her acting career. And get this, Baylee has been having this dream since she was a kid, a dream where she sees two women she swears looks like Alana Stevens and Jessica Boyd fighting with her mother on the upstairs landing. Then the one that looks like Jessica pushes her mother down the stairs."

"Have you been smoking weed?" Reese asked in disbelief, utterly convinced his buddy was high.

Dylan shook his head. "Geez, I haven't done that for a couple of years now, and you guys should know you were right there with me. Look, I know this is bizarre, but I think something really happened to Baylee's mom. I think this dream Baylee's having isn't a dream at all but rather a memory of the event."

Having been through a similar situation with Kit, when she had all but dreamed every detail about the Parker murders, Jake could sympathize.

"What does Baylee think happened?"

"She's beginning to think the same thing."

Reese once again felt he needed to be the voice of reason. "That's because you're planting the seeds in her head, Dylan. Look, women abandon their children every day. I had a conversation with Kit not four hours earlier. She told me Quinn's mother dumped Quinn with her stepfather and was never around much."

He stared out at the three women sitting on the cliff, who were watching the night sky light up with fireworks. "I'm beginning to think they had impossibly difficult childhoods I can't even imagine. And because of that, you can't foster this outlandish idea in Baylee's head. It's irresponsible. She has enough to deal with without your woo-woo conspiracy theory."

"You know, Reese, Quinn's right; you really can be a horse's ass when you want to be. Baylee hasn't had her mother around since she was three years old. I think her father force-fed her a bullshit story he's lied about for so long it's starting to eat him up inside. If what that little three-year-old saw actually happened that means Alana and Jessica murdered her mother. Why I don't know. But I do know that now that William is lingering at death's door, he feels guilty about it.

"And I'll tell you one other thing with certainty. After being in this for weeks now, after listening to what we think Alana and Jessica did to the Parkers, I personally think those two women were capable of the most evil, despicable things. Evil, Reese, and that includes pushing Baylee's mother down the damned stairs. What I can't figure out is why William went along with the story if they did something to her, unless he was in on it."

Reese blew out a breath. "At least you guys are consistent and crazy enough to believe in dreams."

Jake took immediate offense and fired back, "Yeah, hotshot, and Kit's dream turned out to be the backbone of what we have so far discovered happened to the Parkers."

"Okay, but it's a stretch to think Alana and Jessica might have killed Baylee's mother. Why? What was their motive?"

Jake looked over at Kit and the others as they continued to ooh and ahh over the fireworks. "Face it, Reese, when it comes to murder, Alana and Jessica didn't need much more of a reason than money and greed. We know for a fact they must have plotted and planned for months to take away Gloria's babies before they were born and it had nothing to do with money or greed but rather revenge for some slight.

"And I'd like to point out that their actions set in motion a childhood racked with abuse for Kit, the woman I'm crazy in love with, who had to spend sixteen goddamned years full of misery and pain with that bitch of a woman because of what Jessica and Alana did to Gloria. So, face it, Reese, Dylan's right. Those two were evil, plain and simple. The more we find out about them, the deeper the evil."

Jake turned to Dylan. "If you need anyone to buy into this theory about Baylee's mother, I'm right there with you no matter how ridiculous it sounds. Those two women didn't need much of an incentive to turn mean; they just were."

"Well, thanks for the support, Jake. But I don't think it sounds that ridiculous myself. I've seen Baylee's face after the dream. The panic there is too real." He swallowed hard thinking about a scared, three-year-old girl in that situation before he added, "I think she might've seen it happen. Imagine, watching in horror as someone pushes your mother down the stairs. She was just a baby."

"That's exactly the way I felt after seeing Kit's face every time she had the dream about the Parkers. Go with your gut, Dylan. Don't listen to Reese here. He has a tendency to think just like a stick-up-his-ass lawyer."

In response, Reese simply lifted his middle finger in the air at both of them.

Later, after they all dispersed to their rooms to get ready for bed, Baylee was sitting in a rocker, feeding Sarah in the room Kit had designated as the future nursery when someone knocked on the bedroom door. Dylan stuck his head in, and whispered, "How we doing in here, need anything?"

Baylee held up a finger to her mouth to shush him and whispered, "She's almost asleep." When he started to back out of the doorway, she shook her head and motioned for him to come further into the room.

"You don't mind?" He asked, as he moved closer, looking down at the sleeping baby with her eyes closed in slumber.

"Not at all."

Dylan went with instinct. He lowered his head and covered her mouth. The spark of heat from a simple touch shot through him like a firestorm.

The rocking chair halted its motion. He heard her intake of breath before she parted her lips to let him explore further. She tasted sweet like the juicy, ripe peach he'd watched her eat earlier in the kitchen. It was his last clear thought as he sunk into the kiss. With Sarah between them, he'd thought the kiss would be nothing more than a chaste exchange of skin, but flares of need sprang up in quick beats that soon matched the rhythm of his heart.

Tongues tangled back and forth. Their heads moved in time with the kiss. Dylan had a sense of something new, something he'd never experienced before, which was impossible, because he had experienced quite a bit. But he took in her scent. She smelled like fresh air, the air he needed to breathe. He imagined the smell of spring rain, the newly-mown grass of summer.

When Sarah stirred, they reluctantly broke apart.

"Want to put her down?"

"Sure." He took the baby out of Baylee's arms, eyed the Pack'N Play he'd carried upstairs earlier. Leaning in, he placed Sarah down on her back. Her mouth continued to make little sucking motions as she drifted deeper into slumber.

Baylee whispered, "Want me to walk you to your door?"

They began to move. Out in the hallway, his answer was to reach around her waist and bring her up against him. "What I want we can't do tonight."

"Soon," she promised, as she put her arms around his neck as they both fell into another mouthy kiss.

☙☙☙☙☙

Something was going down. Trevor felt it in his bones. The listening device hadn't been all that useful with Jankovic because the man spent most of his time away from The Enclave in search of him. How ironic, he thought now as he followed the goon north on the PCH. It looked like he was heading to San Madrid.

And the minute Jankovic's big Chrysler crossed the Ventura County line Trevor was certain of it.

By the time Jankovic pulled into the alleyway behind the Book & Bean, it was two-forty five in the morning. Trevor watched as the man got out of the rented vehicle, carrying something in his right hand. Trevor grabbed his night vision goggles, hoping he could make out what Jankovic held in his hand.

To Trevor it looked like some sort of explosive device. He sucked in a breath waiting until Jankovic made his way to the back door, watched as the man jimmied the lock and then slipped inside.

Trevor counted off one second, then two, before making his way to Jankovic's Chrysler. Finding it unlocked, he ducked into the back seat—and bided his time.

Fifteen minutes went by before Trevor heard footsteps on the pavement. Then the driver's side door flew open, and Jankovic clumsily slid in behind the wheel. Before the goon could start the engine, Trevor snuck his hand around to the man's throat from behind. The knife in his hand glistened in the darkness.

"I hear you've been looking high and low for yours truly. Good news, ace. Tonight's your lucky night. Looks like you found me."

"What the fuck?"

"Do exactly as I tell you. Drive out of the alleyway to the end of the street. Take a left and then head west through town, toward the harbor. When the street deadends, take another left, and head south."

The knife pricked Jankovic's skin. The tiny cut began to ooze red stuff. "Do what I tell you. If I were you I'd be doubly certain to miss any potholes in the road, or there could be a bloody mess. Get my drift?"

Jankovic grunted as he put the car into Drive, slowly making his way down the unlit alleyway.

"Now, I'm going to ask questions and you're going to give me the answers. What did you leave inside the Book & Bean?"

"Just casing the joint. That's all."

The knife put more pressure on the skin and deepened the small cut even further. Blood streamed from the cut. Jankovic's Adam's apple bobbed up and down as he swallowed hard, fear gripping his entire body.

"I'll give you a one more chance, but don't treat me like I'm stupid. You know and I know what this is all about. Now, I'll ask you once more: what did you leave inside the book store?"

"Explosive device."

"With a timer?"

"Set for tomorrow morning at eight-thirty. The timing makes certain that the targets will be inside."

"Where in the store did you leave it?"

With a knife at his throat, not surprisingly, Jankovic unburdened his soul, telling Trevor everything he needed to know.

By the time the car passed the city limits sign, Trevor commanded, "Pull over."

"What…what do you intend to do?"

"Sorry old pal, but it looks like I win this portion of the game. Round Two goes to me." With that, Trevor neatly slit the man's throat.

Ten minutes later, he dumped Jankovic's body in an isolated cove in the water. With a little luck, by the time anyone discovered him, his body would be too decomposed to render many clues. Whether or not they found it floating in two days or ten, it didn't matter much to him.

Trevor crawled behind the wheel of Jankovic's Chrysler and double-backed to the marina, pulling up in the parking lot near the boats. He cut the engine, retrieved the guy's cell phone from the floorboard. He pulled the keys out of the ignition, leaving them under the driver's side floor mat.

There were no security cameras here. He had already checked. It was the best place to leave the car because he could walk back to the Book & Bean from the harbor. And hopefully, the rental car company wouldn't take a week to pick up the car.

As he walked back to the Book & Bean through town, he used Jankovic's cell phone to dial the number of the rental car company he'd found on the rental agreement in the glove box. Even the lateness of the hour would work into his cover story.

When he got the leave-a-message-at-the-tone prompt, he spoke into the recorder, "This is Uri Jankovic." He rattled off the account information from the rental agreement needed before he continued with the message. "I've had a change in plans. My buddy and I are planning a fishing trip for a few days and as it turns out I won't need the Chrysler 300 after all. I'd like you to pick up the rental car Tuesday morning. It's in the parking lot at the marina in San Madrid. You can't miss it. The keys are in the car under the mat. Whatever charges there are, just keep them on the same credit card I gave you at pick-up. Thanks."

By the time he got back to the Book & Bean it was four-fifteen. He had to move his ass and get out of there before Griffin and Boston showed up.

He went in through the back door just as Jankovic had. His footsteps on the ancient hardwood floor creaked as he strode past the counter into the book store portion of the place, past the rows of bookshelves and made his way into the coffee shop.

He hurriedly walked behind the long, scarred oak counter and ran his hands between the commercial refrigerator and the gap along the wood. Bingo. He bent down and spotted the device exactly where the bumbling oaf had said he'd left the explosives. He slipped the entire mechanism into his backpack. Turning to go, he came to a sudden stop in mid-stride, as the painting on the wall caught his attention.

Just as it had the first time he'd laid eyes on it several weeks earlier, he was once again awestruck by how much the subject resembled his late wife. Kit had called it *Woman Rising*. Painted by the renowned artist Ella Canyon, the image of the semi-nude woman, draped only in a sheer white gown, had long flowing golden hair and stood in a greenish pool of water that seemed to show her rising out of the mist.

Now, as he stood there staring like a schoolboy, moonlight cast the woman in shadows and eerie shapes. His heart felt like it wanted to beat a double time out of his chest. He couldn't deny feeling a connection. In the blink of an eye, he made up his mind. He remembered Kit had dragged a stepladder from a storage closet to the left of the back door. He headed that way.

On the drive back to L.A., he couldn't help feeling a bit giddy. It had been an interesting night. He wondered what the stooges would come up with next. The ball was in their court. He wasn't sure how long it would take before they noticed Jankovic missing. And it was time to take care of Frank Geller. As he drove back to L.A., he began to devise a plan.

CHAPTER 15

At five o'clock the next morning, Kit quietly got up to do her usual baking for the day. Even with guests still sleeping, she made her way downstairs walking on air at her new surroundings. But as much as she wanted to stay cocooned inside the walls of Crandall House, she still had a business to run. And just because she'd enjoyed a nice couple of days off, she knew the morning rush after a three-day weekend would be both hectic and welcome.

The minute she sauntered into her spacious state-of-the-art kitchen, she felt like she'd hit the mother lode. For four years, she'd baked every day using the cramped kitchen in the small bungalow she rented from Gloria. As she turned the dial to pre-heat both of the commercial double ovens, she imagined all the delicious things she could bake every morning and with twice the room it would make for twice the inventory. She could try out new recipes and bake them twice as efficiently as she could have in her old kitchen.

Her thoughts drifted to last night and how they'd spent their first night in their new house, surrounded by all their friends. She couldn't have been happier. In fact, she was so happy she almost couldn't stand it. Almost.

By the time Gloria joined her in the kitchen at five-forty-five, Kit had her first batch of orange-cranberry scones and cinnamon buns out of the oven and on the counter cooling. Like a pro, she had a second batch waiting to go into the ovens and went to work filling the molds with more batter. Aromatic smells from the pastry began filling the room and the rest of the house.

"Smells wonderful in here." Gloria commented, right before she drifted over to the coffeemaker, still trying to wake up.

"Hey, Mom, how'd you sleep?"

The endearment caught Gloria off guard and caused her to bobble the decanter she held in her fist. She turned completely around to stare at her daughter. "Oh, Kit. Honey, that's the first time you've said…the word. It's so…"

"I figure the mother of two grown kids outta get used to hearing it more often. It's starting to roll off the tongue a lot easier now. Mom."

Gloria came over for a hug, dabbing at her eyes. "I'll never get tired of hearing it. You just keep calling me mom and it will make me the happiest person on earth. Now if Jake can just find Ben, I'll be all set."

Overhead, Kit heard footsteps on the ceiling. The creaky flooring of the hundred-and-twenty-year-old house revealed others were beginning to stir.

And when Baylee came through the door two seconds later carrying a bright-eyed baby on her hip, Kit left her batter long enough to pluck Sarah out of her mother's arms, telling her, "There's coffee. You look like you could use a cup. There's also bagels and cream cheese, plenty of cinnamon rolls and scones. Help yourself."

"She slept through the night again," Baylee announced through bleary eyes, pleased as punch that her daughter hadn't woken everyone in the middle of the night. "It's about a fifty-fifty shot. But the simple truth is she's been sleeping through the night a lot more often." Baylee grabbed a cup from the cabinet.

"That's a good girl, a big girl," Kit praised, playfully tweaking the baby's nose. Sarah giggled and contributed to the conversation by stringing together a bunch of babble, taking Kit's face between both of her chubby fists and pushing them together. When Gloria saw Kit holding the baby, willing to help with breakfast, she went to the counter where Kit had left off with the batter and began pouring it into molds to bake.

Baylee yawned and stretched. "She has a doctor's appointment this morning. We'll have to take off soon to make it there in what will probably be gridlock traffic."

When the oven timer dinged, Kit relinquished the baby to Gloria, who was already holding out her hands to take Sarah. Kit opened the oven door and took out another batch of scones, this time blueberry. "I have to get moving too. The time's gotten away from me. After being closed yesterday, I'll have a line out the door."

Jake walked in at that moment, rolling up the sleeves of his button-down Oxford dress shirt. "She always has a line out the door." He gave Kit a quick kiss before sniffing the air. "Are those scones?" He picked up one that had cooled and immediately broke off a big chunk, stuffed it into his mouth. "This is why I've gained five pounds. I need coffee."

Turning to Jake, Kit chimed in, "If you've gained five pounds, it's because you've parked yourself on your butt all day playing guard dog. I'll be ready to head out in about ten minutes." She grinned just before she gave him a mouthy kiss back.

To Baylee and Gloria, she explained, "Even if he is five pounds heavier, I have my own personal security detail right here. And you wouldn't believe all the cool perks." She wiggled her eyebrows up and down before adding, "I'm so glad we all got together yesterday. It was like old times, but not. Better."

Baylee agreed, "Thanks for a lovely day. I had a blast. And I love your house. Does this mean you'll be moving out of Gloria's house soon? Did Gloria mention I have dibs on that, by the way? I've decided to rent your house from Gloria."

"You have? You'll be living here in San Madrid? That's wonderful, we'll be neighbors." But all of a sudden she looked thoughtful. She sighed and rolled her eyes. "I can't explain it, but I just feel like those Boyds are up to something. I just know it. You be careful. Don't let your guard down for a second."

"Dylan sees to that. You should see him looking around to see if we're being followed like one of those TV characters on one of those cop shows."

"That sounds like the way Jake is now."

Kit turned around to start bagging the inventory of baked goods into food containers for transport to the store and saw a sleepy-eyed Dylan standing in the doorway looking a bit perturbed. "Hey, Dylan, we were just talking about you."

He headed for the coffee pot. "So I heard. I'm a regular Magnum PI."

Baylee laughed at his cranky mood. Then right in front of everyone in the kitchen, including her baby daughter, she walked over, tiptoed up to his chin, and gave him a quick kiss on his troubled mouth. "And we just love that about you."

Her bold demeanor had his lips curving. "As I remember it, that Magnum guy always did get the women."

☙ ☙ ☙ ☙ ☙

As soon as Jake got to the back door of the Book & Bean, he knew someone had been inside. The jimmied lock was a dead giveaway. When Kit started to rush inside, he grabbed her arm. "Wait a damn minute. Let me check the place out first." He didn't have a clue what he might find inside, but he wanted Kit to stay out here while he did.

"No way. We go in together or not at all. Do you think Collin did that? Or am I just being paranoid?"

Jake had no idea. It might have been nothing more than a couple of kids breaking in over the Memorial weekend just for kicks. But he wasn't taking any chances, not when Collin was out there somewhere lurking, waiting. "I suppose asking you nicely to wait out here isn't going to fly." When he saw the stubborn lock of her jaw, he got his answer. He decided it was too early in the morning to argue. Cautiously, they both made their way inside. "The least you could do is stay behind me. Got it?"

"Yes, I've got it," she said, looking around anxiously.

"It's a good thing we're both morning people, because right now you are really irritating."

"Right back at you."

Nothing seemed out of place in the bookstore, so they proceeded into the coffee shop. Jake wasn't surprised when he saw two customers he recognized as regulars standing patiently outside on the sidewalk waiting for Kit to open the doors. Nothing unusual about that. But at the moment he had other things on his mind than opening the damned shop. One slip up and Collin could be waiting to pounce. Jake wasn't about to be taken by surprise again.

Nothing looked out of place, as if the store had been robbed.

"What the hell? Look at that. *Woman Rising* is gone. Why would anyone steal a painting?"

Jake glanced up. Sure enough, the wall looked naked without the thirty-by-thirty-six canvas. "Didn't you say a couple of weeks back you had a customer come in interested in buying it?"

"Looks like he came back," Kit said, as she walked over to the counter, spotted a stack of bills on top of a note.

Jake picked up the money, started counting the wad of cash. "Two-thousand bucks. Looks like you made a sale and didn't even know it."

Kit turned the note around without actually picking it up. Printed in block letters it read: *Sorry about the lock but*

*at least the place didn't explode. Check your e-mail—
again.*

"Explode? What does that mean? Should we call the
police?"

"I think I get it now. But I'll know for sure after I check
my e-mail."

Kit gave him a curious look. "What are you talking
about? Does this e-mail have anything to do with what you
refused to talk to me about on Saturday?"

"Yeah."

"Okay, but it's time I read this e-mail. And Jake,
because I love you, you don't get any more free passes."

"I should have known," he told her later after he'd had
a chance to read his e-mail. The latest, also sent
anonymously, had arrived at five-fifty-six a.m. that
morning and claimed that a hit man named Uri Jankovic,
hired by the Boyds, had planted an explosive device timed
to blow up the Book & Bean with them inside at eight-
thirty that morning. "This same guy has to be the one who
sent me that bogus e-mail about Connor. I almost fell for
it."

"Wait. What makes you think he isn't on the level?"
Kit countered.

"Then again he could be a sick bastard harboring a
forty-year-old grudge. He's probably just messing with
us."

"Why claim to save us, unless…"

"Unless what?"

Kit looked pensive, then preoccupied. After several
long seconds, she tapped the computer screen and
declared, "He's the one who rescued me. That night at the
warehouse."

There was a certainty in her voice that sent the hairs on
the back of Jake's neck standing at full attention. This was
beginning to sound similar to the conversation he'd had
last night with Dylan about Baylee's mother. No wonder
Reese had been adamant about keeping it real.

"Kit, that's a helluva leap." But even as he questioned it, even as the words slipped past his lips, he somehow knew her conclusion made sense.

"No, he's the one who took the painting and the one who rescued me. It's the same guy. I know what he looks like."

Jake didn't like the sound of that. A man who'd killed as many people as this guy had would never leave anyone around to ID him later.

But Kit shook her head. "I know what you're thinking."

"I doubt that."

"No, you're thinking I'm in danger now that I know what he looks like. But he rescued me from Collin. There must be a way to prove it." She started to pace, to think. "Can you send a reply to the e-mail?"

"I've tried, but it bounces back every time. I've tried tracing the source, but the source is blocked." At that very moment, Jake's e-mail account dinged, signaling another e-mail in his inbox. They stared at each other for two seconds before Jake glanced at the sender. He sat up straighter in the chair when he saw that, it too, read Anonymous. The subject line read simply, *Hello*. Jake double-clicked the subject line and read:

Look in the commercial fridge. No, don't be scared. It's okay. Just look inside.

Jake checked his watch since the e-mail had suggested what was supposed to happen if Jankovic had his way at eight-thirty a.m. It was now seven-ten. He looked over at the woman he loved and made his decision. "You need to get out of here. Now. Go down the block as far away as you can and wait for me there."

"Are you nuts? You think I don't know what you're planning to do? I'm not leaving you alone in here."

"You're the one that's nuts, you know that. We could both be toast."

"For the second time, I might add. I'm not leaving. I think it'll be okay."

"If that's intuition talking, I hope to hell you're as right as you've been so far."

"It'll be okay. Let's do it."

And they did.

They ventured over to check the fridge out together, throwing open the door together. They both spotted it at the same time. A gold cowboy the size of a toy soldier stood prominently on top of a squatty carton of organic half-and-half.

CHAPTER 16

At the doctor's office, Baylee and Dylan stood next to the examining table like two anxious parents, watching with eagle-eyed interest as gray-haired Dr. Newman, the pediatrician, stretched Sarah out to measure her from head to foot. He measured the circumference of her head, then her chest. When he was finished, he made some notes in her chart, comparing her height to the weight the nurse had written down earlier. "I see she's gained almost two pounds. That's good, looks like she's topping the scales now at fourteen pounds," Dr. Newman reported to an elated Dylan.

"She's got a good appetite," Dylan commented. "How tall is she?"

"Looks like twenty-five inches, which makes her fall into the seventy-fifth percentile range." Over his glasses he looked at Dylan, anticipating his next question. "That's normal," Dr. Newman added before Dylan could ask. "Is she sleeping through the night?"

"It's about fifty-fifty," Dylan answered eagerly. "Last night she did, but she was worn out from the picnic."

"Introducing a little baby cereal might help her sleep longer. She's breastfed, right?" The doctor didn't wait for a response. Instead he began thumbing through Sarah's chart until he found what he was looking for. "Try mixing the cereal with a little breast milk; make it watery at first and then gradually increase the consistency. The cereal will provide her with the iron she needs too. Wouldn't hurt her to get a little vitamin D with the cereal." Dr. Newman made more notes in the baby's chart and took out his stethoscope, listening to her heart before moving around to her back. "Lungs are clear. She's sitting up, I take it."

Once again, the answer came from Dylan. "She sure is. And she rolls over too."

Baylee thought it sounded as if he were talking about a dog. But he looked so thrilled to be here, so excited to participate in this visit, she didn't have the heart to dampen his spirits with criticism. Instead, she enjoyed watching his reactions to everything that came out of the doctor's mouth as if hanging on to the doctor's every word Dylan could pick up some new and interesting tidbit about Sarah's development.

After feeling around Sarah's head, Dr. Newman said with certainty, "Soft spot in the back is closed up. The one on top's gotten smaller. That's good." He stuck a tongue depressor in her mouth. After looking around inside, he announced, "Two teeth. That's a good start. Is she reaching for things?"

"All the time," Dylan snapped out before Baylee had a chance to say a word.

"I see here it's time for her six month round of shots."

Dylan's face blanched. "A shot? She has to have a shot?" He looked accusingly at Baylee and grumbled, "You didn't say anything about her having to get a shot." He turned to Dr. Newman, pleading his case. "She's just a little baby. She isn't even sick. Why does she have to have a shot?" Without any more thought, Dylan promptly reached down and snatched Sarah up off the exam table in a purely protective gesture.

Baylee listened while Dr. Newman ticked off a list of diseases a mile long which the shot protected against and the importance of keeping Sarah from getting any of them.

When Dr. Newman left the room, Dylan grunted, "I don't like this."

"Frankly, I don't either. I think we should make a run for it."

Dylan's eyes narrowed. "You're making jokes? This is serious. They're about to stick this baby with a needle and you're making jokes. I don't believe how calm you are about this."

"Dylan. The first time she got her shot, I was right there with you. I researched the vaccines over the Internet and was so scared she'd have a seizure or some serious reaction that I almost didn't go through with it. And seeing that needle go in to her little leg when she was just two months old hurt me almost as much as it did her. Immunization shots are part of being a parent. What if she was exposed to influenza or hepatitis?"

"Seizures?" Dylan's face went white at the knowledge. "God, there's a lot to this. What did you do?"

"Sat up with her that night; gave her baby Tylenol, tried to make her more comfortable, and watched her like a hawk to make sure her fever didn't go too high and that she breathed normally. I'll tell you right now she'll likely run a fever tonight and be fussy."

"Well, that just isn't right."

"I agree. But the alternative is to put her at risk for all those diseases Dr. Newman mentioned. Do you want her to get sick?"

"Of course not." But he didn't want to see that needle go into her leg either. He didn't even want to consider the idea of seizures. "Let's think about this. Let me run out to the car, get my laptop, do a little more research on these vaccines, make sure they're safe before they stick her with that needle."

When the door opened and a middle-aged nurse walked in carrying a tray with a needle along with some oral medication, Dylan visibly winced and handed the baby to Baylee. "If you're set on going through with this, I can't watch."

"What do we have here, a nervous daddy?" the nurse scoffed, as she approached the baby, trying to get her to open her mouth so she could pour in some vile, red-looking stuff. Dylan glanced at the needle on the tray and made up his mind. While the nurse kept trying to get Sarah to open her mouth, he gathered up the diaper bag and infant carrier and stormed out of the room.

Later, when they got down to the first floor, Dylan steered them around the corner. Surprised at the direction he'd taken, Baylee wanted to know, "Where are we going?"

"There's a lab right around the corner of the building. If Sarah can suffer getting jabbed with a needle, so can I." And with that they walked into the lab to get the blood test he had promised.

While they waited in the reception area for Dylan to get his blood drawn, Baylee's cell phone rang. She glanced cautiously at caller ID. Relieved to see the call came from her father's number, she pushed the button. It was Tanya.

"Baylee. Hi. I thought you might want to know your dad is having an awfully bad day. He's been asking for you." And that was putting it mildly, she thought. The man had been ranting and raving since five that morning, mumbling something about Sarah. Tanya couldn't tell if he were talking about his ex-wife or his granddaughter.

"I can be there in thirty minutes. How bad is he?"

"Out of his head mostly. Talking crazy if you ask me."

They talked a few more minutes, Tanya assuring her that he would be fine until she got there. When Dylan came out of the back with a Band-Aid taped to his arm, she ended the call.

"How'd it go?"

"No problem." He reached to pick up Sarah. "How's Gidget here doing?"

"She's fine. Just so you know, I put off giving her the second round of shots until you felt more comfortable with the idea."

Unbelievably touched, he turned to stare at her. There was nothing she could have done that said she respected his opinion more, even if he had acted a little over the top.

"I might have overreacted."

"You think?"

"I'm new at this, okay. Be patient with me."

"I'm trying. After you've done your research, after you've weighed the benefits versus all the risks, we'll have time to make an appointment, bring her in next week to the doctor's office and get the boosters she needs."

"You don't think I'm out of line?"

"I think you're concerned. Getting babies immunized against a lot of nasty diseases is necessary and beneficial, but it's also a serious decision to make. And you're entitled to own that concern, know the risks. I think after your research, you'll come to the same conclusion I did that she should get the shots. But I want you to have that opportunity to judge for yourself."

"Baylee, I think that's the nicest way anyone's ever shown how much they value my opinion, especially something this serious. I'll get online when we get back and find out everything I can. When she got the first shots, did she get sick?"

"That night she ran a fever, it stayed around one-hundred degrees. She was a little lethargic and her leg swelled up some, stayed that way for about twenty-four hours. But the day after that the fever subsided and she seemed fine."

"I just don't want to do anything that hurts her or makes her sick."

Baylee smiled. "I know. And that is one of the nicest things you could do for me."

He threw his arm around her shoulders in a companionable way. "Who was on the phone?"

"Dad's having a bad day. I think we should drop by while we're out."

"Good idea. Let's get out of this place."

⚜ ⚜ ⚜ ⚜ ⚜

William Scott was indeed having a bad day. As soon as he spotted Baylee standing at the foot of his bed, his rambling escalated, and the man's words inexplicably became meaner. "Who asked you to come? Why won't you leave me in peace? You always make me feel bad, guilty. I didn't do a damn thing. Why is it every time I look at you I feel guilty for all those things I did wrong? I can't help what I did. I can't change what I did. I can't go back and make it right. Do you hear? I can't do it."

"Daddy, it's okay. Stop. Hush." Baylee thought he was talking about all the times he'd hit her, but then his comments grew nastier.

"Don't tell me what to do, Baylee Diane. You're just like your mother, just like Sarah. Sarah tried to tell me what to do. But she couldn't control me. I did what I wanted, marriage or not. Do you hear me? She couldn't stop me and you can't either."

Strangely, big tears formed in his eyes, he started to cry. "I didn't listen. I made a mistake, that's all. I can't change it, can't go back and make it right. It's too late, been too late for over twenty years."

"What are you talking about?"

But as quickly as the tears formed, he turned nasty again. "Don't question me. You've no right to question me. Just leave me alone, why don't you? I don't want to talk about it. It's over, done with; there's nothing I can do to bring your mother back. I made a mistake, that's all. I didn't know it would end like it did. How could I have known? But it's over. I can't go back and change the past. Leave me alone, do you hear? Leave me in peace." William put his hands to his head to cover his ears. "I can't take the voices. Leave me in peace."

Baylee tried in vain to get his hands down. "Daddy, what happened to my mother? Tell me. Did she leave on her own? She left, didn't she? Please tell me where she went."

William screamed, "Stop it. Get out of here. No one asked you to come here." He looked accusingly over at Tanya. "She called you. I didn't ask you to come here."

Baylee felt angry and confused. But she did as he asked and left the room, shaken.

Outside in the hallway, Dylan stood holding Sarah. He'd been standing at the doorway listening to William's tirade.

"Did you hear that? Did you hear him talk to me like that?"

"He's sick, Baylee. He doesn't know what he's saying." But Dylan thought it sounded like a man haunted by his own guilt.

She shook her head. "I don't understand why he's so mean. Why does he have to be that way? He's dying, Dylan, and I can't do anything to stop it. There may not be time for me to get the answers I want. But I think he's definitely acting responsible about something."

Dylan did his best to comfort her, to try and make her feel better about her father's odd behavior. It wasn't everyday your dying father made you feel small. But then again, Baylee seemed almost used to his caustic manner. In the back of his mind, Dylan thought William Scott acted like a very troubled man who needed to get a giant weight off his chest—the sooner the better.

🛆🛆🛆🛆🛆

Around the corner from William Scott's house, Cade sat in his Corvette relaying the information from his cell phone to Connor. "We hit pay dirt. She's here with the guy. Looks like they've got a baby, too."

So it was true. Baylee was a mother. The man he'd spoken to on the phone hadn't been lying about waking up the baby. "Boy or girl? How old?"

"I don't know a fucking thing about kids, much less a baby; the thing's little, that's all I know. The guy was carrying it around in one of those baby things, those carriers, so I couldn't see it very well."

"Did you get his license plate number?"

"I'm not stupid, Connor. Of course I did." He rattled off the plate number on Dylan's Mercedes G500 while Connor wrote it down.

"I'll get my buddy at the DMV to run the plate. What's the guy look like?"

Cade described Dylan to a tee.

"Good job, Cade."

☙☙☙☙☙

"What's this about you moving into Kit's old house?" Dylan asked, as he stood at the sink in the kitchen and poured spaghetti into a colander to drain while Baylee stood a few feet away at the stove stirring the homemade marinara sauce she'd thrown together.

"I need to start thinking about the future, my future, and Sarah's, start putting down roots. Kit's house is that first step. I need to get my jewelry design business back on track, so I can bring in a stable income. I've decided to take advantage of this downtime to launch a website so I can sell my jewelry online."

"You have a jewelry business?"

"See, it's invisible. Since I left L.A. it doesn't exist any place but in my head. Yes, I design jewelry. I do have a degree in art, and I decided about four years ago to turn my love of art into creating wearable jewelry."

"Sounds reasonable. Got any samples?"

"A few. I've almost exhausted my inventory, though." She went into a detailed account of how she'd had a successful booth at the local flea market, selling her jewelry there on the weekends up until the time she'd left. But over the past six months, she hadn't designed one new piece.

"But that's going to change," she promised emphatically, and realized for the first time in a long time, she actually meant it.

✤ ✤ ✤ ✤ ✤

After dinner, while Baylee got Sarah ready for bed, Dylan booted up his laptop, instantly digging up info about childhood immunizations. There were sites that touted the benefits, as well as sites that warned about the risks. And the risks were plentiful. There were sites that linked the vaccines to autism, seizures, abnormal breathing, high fevers; the list to Dylan seemed endless and scary.

But there were also plenty of websites that linked autism to the chemicals and toxins in the environment. It was a tough call to make, and a serious one. In the end, as Dylan sat there bombarded by both sides of the issue, his thoughts went to Baylee and how incredible it was that she had done her research, without a support system, and come to the best decision for her daughter, alone.

She'd had no one to lean on, no one to discuss the matter with in a partnership sort of way.

That fact moved something inside Dylan. The woman was incredible. There was no other word to describe her. He thought of what a difficult job she had as a single mom and didn't envy the responsibility, the weight of it all. He came from a pretty ordinary middle-class family from the Bay area. But it had been a two-parent proposition. He'd never once over the years realized how lucky he had been to have both of his parents around—until now.

As he sat there contemplating his own youth, he decided to check his e-mail. As soon as he accessed his account, one e-mail with the subject line Baylee, immediately got his attention. Double-clicking it, he read:

Boyd knows where you live. He wants Baylee dead. Be careful.

The e-mail had Dylan grabbing his cell phone and dialing Jake. As soon as Jake picked up, he told him about the e-mail and then said, "If this guy's legit, I have to take Baylee and Sarah and hit the road, get the hell out of here. I've changed my mind about her staying put. I think she needs to get out of L.A. for good."

Jake realized he couldn't stop the train of thought. But he muddied the picture when he told Dylan the equally bizarre account of what had happened that morning at the Book & Bean and the fact that their mystery man had e-mailed him as well. Much like Dylan, he felt like he needed to get Kit away from L.A. for good, but would she go?

"I think the guy's for real. He even left one of those gold cowboys at the store so we'd know he's the same guy who shot Collin and took care of Auslo and Taft before saving Kit. The guy's a regular Superman."

But Dylan wasn't yet ready to get on the guy's fan list. "So this hit man plants a bomb and he goes in and saves the day—again? Aren't you nervous? Kit knows what he looks like. How does this guy know when to show up? How does he know all this? Who does that? What's in it for him?"

"Of course I'm nervous. But Kit thinks he's looking out for her, and now it sounds like he's looking out for Baylee. She thinks it's because he doesn't like the Boyds or has some kind of grudge against them, probably because of the Parkers. He obviously knows about Collin's obsession, knows Collin doesn't want us to testify against him, and he's decided we're the good guys. Now, he's warning you about Connor. But what I don't get is why Connor wants Baylee dead? That's the other thing I don't understand."

"What's the statute on rape? Obviously, he thinks she could still burn him for some reason and he's worried."

"Either that or he's just a sick bastard right along with his brother."

"I vote for sick bastard. What should I do, Jake? I need to get her out of town. But where? Where will she be safe?"

"Will she want to leave her father? You forget he hasn't got that long to live."

Shit, thought Dylan, one more complication. "See, that's the thing; I'm not sure about anything."

"Hey, if you can convince Baylee to leave town, will you take Kit with you?"

"So you're saying I might not get her to budge at all," he muttered almost to himself as he tried to formulate a battle plan.

"Hey, I'm right there with you. I couldn't even get Kit to leave the store while I played bomb squad this morning."

"I've got to let Baylee know. This isn't exactly turning out the way I'd planned."

"You had a plan?"

"Look, I thought Connor would see us together and just leave us alone, leave her alone, go on with his life. End of stalker story. I didn't count on him wanting her dead. This was about not letting him know about Sarah, not Baylee's demise. I didn't count on him following us to her father's house. No, that isn't true. He didn't follow us. He must have been staking the place out this afternoon and I delivered her on a platter. Damn. That means I walked right into his net. He saw the baby. I got careless, Jake."

"Don't beat yourself up. If he saw anything, he saw a couple with a baby. That's it. I'm wondering how I can get Kit out of town, someplace safe. You want to bring them and stay at Crandall House?"

"Too much ground to cover. And they probably already know you've bought the place; they're just waiting for the moving truck to pull up. After all, you're already basically living there. I hate to break it to you, but Collin probably already knows."

That didn't make Jake feel any better. It did, however, cement his decision. But Dylan was too wound up.

"No, I need some place that's fortified, somewhat secure." At that moment, Dylan's e-mailed dinged signaling he had mail. "Wait a minute, looks like he sent a follow up." He double-clicked the message and read:

If you need a safe house for Baylee and the baby, take her to 12261 Contreras Court, Palos Verdes. Key's under the mat.

Dylan repeated the e-mail to Jake. "Okay, this is getting weird. Is he listening? It sounds like he has my house bugged. A safe house, is he kidding? This is a joke, right? This guy expects me to take Baylee to some house in the middle of the night on his say-so alone. He must be crazy as a crack addict. I'm not letting Baylee anywhere near this place on his word alone. I don't trust this guy."

"I'll call Jordan again, tell him we need help."

"Call me back." Dylan hung up the phone but continued to pace back and forth in front of the computer until he looked up to see Baylee standing in the doorway with her arms crossed, hugging herself, watching, listening."

"How long have you been standing there?"

"Connor knows where we are."

"Uh, then you heard everything."

"Pretty much. Connor must have been parked in the neighborhood waiting for us. Let's see the e-mail." Baylee walked over to the laptop, read the follow-up e-mail about the safe house and then the first one he'd sent in warning. "Who is this guy?"

"Gotta be Kit's hero. Somehow he's keeping track of the Boyds and it's like he's listening to us."

"That's freaky. Why does Connor want me dead, Dylan? I haven't made trouble for him. I did like he wanted. I didn't go to the police, didn't tell anyone and yet, he wants me dead."

"He's a sick bastard that's all there is to it. Pack a bag. We aren't staying here tonight. Just in case this guy knows what he's talking about, I'm not sitting here waiting for the bastard to make his move in the middle of the night."

"So Sarah and I are on the run again."

"All three of us are."

Baylee looked at him then. Drawing in a deep breath, she stepped over to him, wrapping her arms around his waist. "You don't have to do this, Dylan. He could just as easy kill you to get to me. I don't want you hurt."

"That's why we're running like rabbits in the middle of the night, getting off his radar for a while. But I'm in this Baylee, one way or another. I promise you I won't let him near you or Sarah. I'm just not sure where we should go."

"That's perhaps the sweetest promise anyone's ever made to me. As to where to go, an idea came to me while you were on the phone. My father has a place on Catalina Island, actually it's Avalon. We could stay there for a while. I need to call Tanya, let her know where she can reach me."

"Not if there's a chance anyone at BBG&G would know about the house. Is there?"

"I don't think so. When I was younger we'd spend the whole month of July there. A few times Kit and Quinn came along. As far as I know, the Boyds never knew we stayed there. I even considered going there when I left L.A. The only reason I didn't was because the island's fairly remote. They only have a twelve-bed hospital. For a first-time mother-to-be, for a first-time delivery, that was a little too small for my peace of mind. Even though the island has a healthy tourist trade, there's less than four thousand people living there year-round, and I didn't want complete solitude. Plus, I needed to be able to go where I could find a decent job. Blair assured me I would be able to get a good doctor, get a good enough job in Denver, so that's where I ended up. But Catalina is almost an afterthought, strictly a tourist destination most of the time."

"Then that's where we'll go." He picked up the phone to let Jake know their destination. "I need the *Sea Warrior*. If you can talk Kit into closing up the Book & Bean for a couple of days, you're both welcome to join us."

"Look, I need a favor, Dylan. And I haven't even talked to Kit about it. I need you to babysit Kit for a few days."

"Then meet me at the boat. We'll talk there. Two can play this cat-and-mouse game."

"Gotcha. Shouldn't we synchronize our watches or something?"

"Was that a joke, Boston? You pick a helluva time to get a sense of humor. You're a regular riot, you know that?"

⚜ ⚜ ⚜ ⚜ ⚜

On Jake's end, Kit had been listening to the entire conversation. She also had sensed all evening there was something he didn't want to tell her, talk about. And she still wasn't happy knowing he'd kept the e-mail their mystery man had sent to him about Claire to himself. She decided the best approach should be the direct one. As soon as he hung up the phone, she pounced. "Okay, what's up?"

With her arms folded across her chest, Kit looked at him like she wanted information. He assumed it was about the conversation he'd just had with Dylan.

So he told her about the e-mail sent to Dylan and that Dylan and Baylee planned on leaving town tonight.

She cocked her head to one side and waited for him to look at her. When he seemed to ignore her, she pushed the issue. "And?"

He finally looked at her, shrugged, and said, "I want you to go with them, close the store, and just go for a few days."

"And where will you be while I'm safe and sound hiding out with Baylee."

"Meeting with St. John to go over everything he has in his files about Claire's murder. Reese convinced him to meet with us. The meeting's tomorrow. I was planning to drop you off at Dylan's anyway. But now that we suspect Connor knows how to find Baylee, that isn't an option."

"Jake, when will you stop keeping things from me? You have to share. I knew something was bothering you all day. Why can't I go with you? I want to be there if for no other reason than to show my support."

When backed into a corner with her, he did the only sensible thing he could. He pled ignorance. "I'm new at this couple stuff, okay? I'm used to keeping things inside, not sharing what's going on. And this, this is so personal for me, something I'd very much like to close once and for all. Plus, I don't want you there reminding St. John that you were his primary suspect in Alana's murder. It's too risky to think about you walking into that police station where St. John might give you a hard time about Alana's murder. Even though Reese will be there, I don't want to chance St. John taking out his itchy trigger finger and doing something stupid."

"Like arresting me? But it's okay for you to go in there? What if...?"

He put his fingers to her lips. "He won't arrest me, Kit. Trust me."

"You know something, don't you?"

"He has DNA. He's always had it. Claire fought the guy. I just know she did. It isn't mine. I wasn't even there until after midnight that night. But I saw the room where she died, where she fought."

"Okay, I'll go with Baylee and Dylan. But call me the minute you walk out of there."

CHAPTER 17

Ninety minutes later, they met up with Dylan and Baylee at the San Madrid harbor in front of the *Sea Warrior*, the French-built, fifty-foot sloop that would take them to Catalina.

Dylan and Jake immediately started loading the boat with supplies they'd brought for the trip. Kit and Baylee unloaded the gear from the car and set it on the dock, waiting for the guys to lug it onto the boat, including most of Sarah's baby items. Jake took one look at the haul of stuff and said, "Jesus, there's a lot to this baby thing."

"You have no idea. If you're planning on getting Kit pregnant anytime soon, we need to have a serious discussion about doctor's visits and immunizations. You just won't believe what they do to the kid after it gets here."

In spite of the lateness of the hour, Baylee and Kit couldn't help but keep an eye out for anyone that might be watching them from a distance. Even though the harbor was relatively deserted and the place quiet, they were both aware that the day could have turned out much worse.

Baylee took Kit's hand. "On the drive up, Dylan told me about the bomb. I'm so glad you're safe."

"You and Sarah might have been there too. If that man, that stranger hadn't intervened, Jake and I might be collateral damage. Ka-Plewie! Blown to pieces!" Trying to lighten the stress of that idea, with a twinkle in her eye, Kit deadpanned, "Jake's dumping me."

Baylee gave her a hard stare, not buying it for a minute, before Kit added, "Dumping me on you guys, that is. He wants his freedom for a couple of days." When Baylee still didn't react to the lame attempt at humor, Kit said, "You're a tough sell tonight, Baylee." She then told her about Jake's plans to go see St. John.

"It is past time Jake confronted him and got some answers for his own peace of mind. He doesn't have a choice, Kit."

"I know. But I wanted to be there with him."

"Are you ready for that, to sit down with them and listen while they go over all the gory details about what happened to Claire? He couldn't share that with you, Kit. He doesn't want that part of his life tainting yours. Don't you see that? He's doing his best to separate that part of his life from you."

"He said almost the same thing. But hearing it from you, you always did see everything so clearly. That's why I don't understand how you couldn't have trusted Quinn and me to help you during what had to be the most difficult of circumstances."

"I know you don't. I'm sorry I disappointed both of you."

"You didn't, Baylee. But to go through childbirth without us to help, Connor must have really scared you."

Tired to the bone had her revealing what she hadn't been able to tell anyone. "He didn't just call, Kit. One night after I found out I was pregnant; he caught me off guard, outside my apartment. He had this crazy look in his eyes. He told me if I ever told anyone," she hedged, bit her lip. "He'd killed before and he would do it again. Those were his exact words. He'd killed before to protect what he had, that no one would take down what his family had built just because of a one-night stand. I had no idea what he was talking about. But he scared the crap out of me. So much that I knew I'd never tell him about the pregnancy.

Those crazy eyes told me if I said anything to you or Quinn about what happened he'd do something to both of you. And if…" She took a shaky breath.

"If one of my neighbors hadn't pulled into the parking lot about that time, I'm convinced he would have done something to me that night. My neighbor got out of his car. He came over and asked if I needed help. Luckily, Connor took off before I could answer. But the following day, he called to remind me again he'd hurt you or Quinn if I said a word. So I didn't. That e-mail Dylan got tonight said he wants me dead, Kit."

"Oh, Baylee, Jake thinks he's the one who killed Claire."

"Oh, God, really? I think he's certainly capable of it."

Seeing the pitiful look on Kit's face obviously there because she didn't want to leave Jake, Baylee tried to make her feel better and bumped her shoulder. "It's been ages since we were in Catalina. Remember how Dad always flew us over there in that little plane of his? Remember how we used to love going up and then looking down over the water? Didn't your father take you to Catalina once on a boat trip for the day?"

Kit nodded.

With no sign of a mood change, Baylee went on, "Won't it be fun to sail, even if we are making the trip at night?"

"We won't use the sails, Baylee. I'm sure Dylan will probably use the motor to get us there as fast as he can at this hour of the night."

"Oh. Well, you know more about that than I do. Remember that time the three of us found that old row boat that had washed up on shore? We wanted to make it into a pirate ship. That happened in Catalina."

"Okay, I get it. I'm making a big deal out of nothing. It's just a couple of nights apart. I should be able to deal with that."

"Think of it as a well-deserved rest after, you know, having so much…sex in the early stages." Baylee grinned.

"Not like I was peeking in the window or anything. But it's fairly typical early in the relationship. Not that I would know anything about having too much sex, or any, for that matter."

Kit laughed, bumping Baylee's shoulder. "So you and Dylan haven't gotten around to doing the bump and grind yet."

Baylee sighed. "I'm a mess right now. And this thing with Connor would scare anyone off. I don't want Dylan getting hurt. And we agreed to take it slow because of Sarah, you know, not just jump in the sack."

"But you want to…"

"Oh, God, yes. Yes, I do." The admission had her peering over at her wide-awake daughter sitting in the carrier playing with her hands. "I don't want to mess this up, Kit. Look at her. She's the reason I get up every day, the reason I've gotten through all of this. If it hadn't been for her…"

Kit reached out with her hand and took hold of Baylee's. "I can only imagine how difficult all this has been on you, but I'll help you any way I can. We all will, Baylee. You don't have to do this alone. Not anymore. We agreed to keep Connor from knowing anything about Sarah. We'll continue doing what we have to do."

Jake approached them slowly and announced, "She's all loaded, ready to go." His face had a look of pure dejection as he locked gazes with Kit. Baylee took the hint and left them alone to say goodbye.

Carting the baby carrier with Sarah tucked inside, she walked down the gangway to board and spotted Dylan standing at the helm. When he looked up and saw her hefting the infant carrier, he came around to take the thing out of her hands.

"Who do we have here?" he asked the baby in a jovial tone, as he easily swung her up to eye level. Sarah giggled at the movement, reaching out, trying to get her hands on Dylan's face.

He responded by shooting her a wide grin, letting her touch his nose. Instinctively, he kissed her hands. "Ready for your first boat ride, Gidget? It'll probably be a rough ride tonight. Sorry, nothing I can do about that." He made like he was chewing on her fingers and she cooed at the attention.

The scene made Baylee's heart swell at the way Dylan seemed to act as if Sarah were his own. If only...

Once they got underway, the sway of the boat as it rose up and down, skimming on top of the water at a rapid pace, kept them from too much activity. Kit had been right. Dylan didn't bother with the sails but rather gunned the motor with a speed she was sure he was at ease with.

In spite of the constant motion, Baylee located the galley and made a pot of much needed coffee for all of them. When the coffeemaker finished brewing, she found a thermal cup and filled it full, adding enough sugar to give Dylan a nice buzz, just the way he liked it. She left Kit sitting in the salon holding Sarah on her lap and took the coffee topside.

He was standing at the helm. She went around to face him, handing him the cup. "You look like you could use this."

Grateful, he took the steaming coffee all the while keeping his eyes on the black horizon. "It's a clear night, but we've got a head wind picking up. It'll take us longer than I thought."

The man looked windblown and tired but exhilarated as if he were in the middle of a race, competing against the elements. Gone was the fear she'd seen in his eyes earlier at the house, replaced instead by a fierce concentration. "You like going fast."

The intensity in his face softened into a smug grin. "Yeah. It's an adrenaline rush to go at top speed. But I'm careful, Baylee. The boat's equipped with GPS, a warning sensor, and radar. I won't do anything stupid, especially at night to put us at risk. Radar shows it's clear sailing all the way to Avalon."

She smiled. "I didn't think you would. It's a pretty rough ride, though."

"It is that. Tell me about where we'll be staying."

She told him about the old Spanish-style house built in the forties she remembered so well from childhood. The house backed up to the beach and looked out over the mountains. She described how far the harbor was from the house, and then went into a lengthy list of all the things they could do on the island. "I remember how the water used to be so clear you could see the fish swimming around. I hope it's still like that. But there's snorkeling, and diving, you can explore the caves in the area. You'll have fun. It'll be like a vacation."

He listened with interest, noting her exuberance. She obviously had fond memories of the place. He hoped she could settle in and relax there, maybe put the Boyd bastard out of her mind for a while.

Because for him this trip was anything but a holiday.

Two and a half hours later, Dylan had them docking in Avalon a little after three in the morning. As soon as Dylan killed the engine, Baylee helped him with the lines, getting the boat moored. Rubbing his eyes, Dylan told her, "We'll sleep on the boat. It's too dark to unload all the supplies anyway. And we need to get some sleep. How did Sarah do on the trip? Did she get seasick?"

Amazed that he would even think to ask about Sarah at this time of night as tired as he was, her heart dissolved into mush. If he continued to melt her resolve with all these simple gestures she'd have no choice but to jump his bones. "She's a good little sailor, but I kept her awake during the trip hoping she'd go back down as soon as we do."

"Good thinking. Tell me more about the house. How far is it from where we are right now?"

"It's just up the hill from Pebbly Beach. It won't take long to get there. Unloading will be a problem, though. It always is."

"I figured that. We'll use the dinghy to transport everything back and forth. You know, Catalina is one place where I haven't spent a whole lot of time. I came here some years back for the day and the place was so packed with tourists we left after only a few hours." He saw no reason to mention the cute little redhead who'd accompanied him on the trip.

"Good. It's nice to know there's one place I can show you around that you haven't already seen a dozen times before, someplace new where I can enjoy showing you the sights."

He cupped her chin. "As long as I'm with you, Baylee, as long as I get to spend time around you and Sarah, the where doesn't really matter." He brought his arms around her and pulled her into his chest. His lips met hers in a fierce, long, hard kiss, one that would have to hold them both for a while since Kit and Sarah were below deck. He brushed several loose strands of hair off her face and abruptly let her go. "You need to get some sleep."

"So do you."

Once they got below deck, Dylan noticed that Baylee, Kit, and Sarah had already settled into the foreword cabin. He headed for the aft stateroom where he promptly shed his clothes and crawled into bed. Five minutes later, he was fast asleep.

🔱 🔱 🔱 🔱 🔱

In Malibu, Connor Boyd couldn't sleep. Wide awake, he paced back and forth, unable to let go of the fact that Baylee had a baby. Could he be the kid's father? It was too much of a coincidence that they'd been together a year ago last March. He wasn't stupid. No matter what this Dylan Burke guy had said, he needed to find out more about the kid. Was it a boy or a girl? He wanted it to be a boy, a son. He could teach him everything just like his father had taught him.

When had the kid been born and where? Had she been pregnant when she left L.A.? That could be the reason why she'd disappeared. She wouldn't have wanted him to know about the pregnancy. For close to eight months, he'd looked for her and had come up empty. Okay, so he wouldn't admit that little tidbit to anyone that he'd actually spent a great deal of his time and money trying to track her down without success.

He would need to find out everything he could about this Burke guy. How long had the two of them been a couple? He shook his head. No, he refused to buy into the possibility the guy could be the baby's father. The more he thought about it, the more he decided the baby belonged to him. And if it did, that changed things, considerably.

"Goddamn it, why didn't you tell me, Baylee? Having a child could have turned things around for me. I can't believe you'd keep to yourself. You bitch," he uttered, as the black pain of a headache almost blinded him. At that, he hurled the glass he held in his hand against the wall, shattering the crystal into hundreds of pieces.

�※☽☽☽

The next morning in Pacific Palisades, Connor sat behind the wheel of his Hummer parked outside Dylan Burke's beach bungalow staring at an empty house. It appeared no one was home. No car in the driveway might mean Baylee and the baby had already taken off to parts unknown. Damn his contact at the DMV anyway. If the guy hadn't taken yesterday off, he might have caught her before she left.

In the passenger seat next to him, Cade watched his older brother with avid interest. Usually cool as ice on Mt, McKinley, Connor sat unshaven, wearing the same clothes he'd worn the day before. The guy looked like he was coming unglued.

"Why this interest in Baylee all of a sudden? Come on, level with me. What's going on? This is the personal problem you needed to take care of? What gives?"

"That baby you saw yesterday might be mine."

That's the last thing Cade expected him to say. His jaw visibly dropped. "You and Baylee. When?"

"Last March; the seventeenth to be exact, St. Patrick's Day. Get hold of someone in Vital Statistics, will you? I don't care if you have to dangle a shitload of money to get the information either. But I need to find out if Baylee Scott delivered a baby sometime last December."

Cade nodded, ridiculously touched at the idea of having a niece or a nephew. "I'll check November, too just in case it came early."

Cade watched as Connor got out of the car and walked up to the front door of Burke's house.

On the off chance that she'd just open the door, Connor rang the bell. When there was no answer he began to pound furiously on the wood. Angry, he took off around the cottage, looking through the windows, all the while wondering who had tipped them off. How had they known to run?

When he looked up and spotted a tall, attractive brunette wearing her wetsuit and carrying a surfboard heading out of the water, toward him, an idea formed. He automatically reached to straighten his tie and realized he wasn't wearing one. As the woman got closer, he turned on the charm. "Hi. I'm looking for Dylan Burke. Do you know him? Are you a neighbor?"

The brunette thought the guy staring at her was tall, dark, and dreamy, so she nudged up her flirt quotient. "Sure, everyone in the neighborhood knows Dylan. You're standing right in front of his house."

Annoyed at the stupid bitch but trying not to drop the charming façade, his voice tightened when he said, "Right. Maybe you could tell me something; does Dylan have children, a baby, perhaps?"

"Dylan? Funny you should ask," she said getting a huge kick out of the fact that she got to gossip about what she'd heard. "There's a woman that's been staying at his house for over a week now. Marilyn Harper, who lives across the street, told me she's seen them coming and going carrying a baby. And then over the Memorial weekend, Kendra saw the two of them eating out, and sure enough, Dylan told them the baby was his daughter."

Connor flinched at that. So it was a girl. He hid his disappointment. Boy, girl, did it really make a difference now after the fact? Suddenly, his head pounded. He forced aside the black thoughts swirling inside trying to cloud his vision.

Coming back to himself, he prodded, "But you don't believe it?"

"Actually, I don't. I suppose it could be true, I mean the way Dylan is with women, he's such a horn dog anything is possible. But let's face it, a single guy like Dylan isn't exactly the father type. He's lived here for five years, and trust me I've never seen him with a kid. Until now. Although..." She paused for effect and leaned closer, "...like I said, I guess it could be true, I mean the guy's a real player where women are concerned. And when you sleep around like that, well—it catches up with you eventually. If you know what I mean."

"But had you ever seen the woman before a week ago? Did this Burke and the woman have a history together that you know of?"

"Well now, it's hard to tell with Dylan. Could be she's one of the women who visit him frequently and I just missed seeing her."

"Thanks." For nothing, Connor thought as he headed back to his car, disappointing the brunette. And then he realized that wasn't true. He had a daughter. At that moment, he knew what he wanted. He wanted that baby. He'd find Baylee. He'd find the baby. Just then, his cell phone interrupted his thoughts. Caller ID told him it was good old Uncle Frank.

Connor could tell even over the phone that Frank was nervous. Something was wrong.

"Jankovic's disappeared. He isn't answering his cell phone."

"What do you mean 'disappeared'?" Connor asked, irritated, as the charming demeanor fell away for good, replaced by a heartless rage.

Unconvinced Jankovic was this professional hit man Frank had touted, he added, "He better not have disappeared with the money, Frank, without finishing the job, or it's coming out of your pocket, understand? I'm not paying for another screw-up. You got that?"

Frank tried to placate his impatient nephew. "I'm sure that isn't the case. Although I haven't heard from him since he was supposed to drive out to San Madrid to take care of Boston and the Griffin woman. I've watched the news but there's been no mention of an explosion out that way. I called the Book & Bean yesterday and a woman answered. So I know the place is still standing. I'm assuming it was Kit who picked up. Jankovic obviously didn't follow through. Maybe something happened or for some reason he couldn't get inside and had to abort the plan. I don't know for certain."

"Well for chrissakes find out. I thought this guy was supposed to be a goddamned professional."

"He is. He comes highly recommended. I assure you, Connor, the man knows what he's doing."

It didn't sound like that to Connor. "Well, get on it, man. Call me back. I want to know what's going on. We're paying this guy a fortune to get the job done. I want results, not excuses."

"I'm on it; trust me to find out."

"You'd better. If we can't rely on this guy, we need to know about it now. You take care of it, Frank. I have problems of my own to deal with," he chided as he climbed back into his Hummer, all the while snapping his fingers at Cade to hurry up and get back in the vehicle.

"What did you find out from the brunette?"

"It's a girl. Now I just need to know when she was born. Get on it, Cade. I need details. I have a daughter."

△△△△△

Across town at the East L.A. sheriff's department, six-foot-four ex-cop, Jordan Donovan pulled his SUV into the parking lot anxious to spend his morning with the cold case detective, Ron Blake, who had finally agreed to sit down with him and listen to what he surmised happened to Pete and Mary Parker.

True, most of what he had to share was pure speculation, developed by people with no formal police or investigative training. But the group of people, led by his friend, Jake Boston, had come up with an impressive timeline of sorts that showed a solid set of facts connecting their prime suspects, Jessica Boyd and Alana Stevens, to the Parker murders. He had to hand it to them it wasn't a bad first attempt at trying to solve a forty-year-old cold case.

As he walked into the substation, he thought about all the work he'd done for Jake Boston and Reese Brennan over the years. The two always managed to find him the most interesting cases. Throw in the fact that for two years he'd been trying to solve Claire Boston's murder, a murder still unsolved and heading quickly toward its own dusty, cold case box, he wasn't all that happy.

But just recently, Jake had asked him to take another look. He'd always felt bad about not being able to find Claire's killer. Maybe now after letting it sit for two years, he could start with a fresh pair of eyes.

But over the course of the last few weeks, it wasn't Claire's murder that had occupied most of his waking thoughts. The Parker murders had intrigued him enough to sit down with Kit Griffin and listen while she described the double murder of an old couple—in detail from a dream.

Well, they didn't call it La-La-Land for nothing, he supposed. The bizarre dream was only one reason his boss Reese had serious doubts and remained skeptical about the whole thing. From the beginning, Reese didn't buy all the guesswork because really, that's all it had been. Add in the fact that up to now, Jordan didn't even know for sure how exactly the couple had died other than what the newspaper article Jake had dug up at the library had told them. Both of the Parkers had suffered gunshot wounds and stab wounds.

Hopefully this meeting would put an end to all the speculation.

After going over the timelines, Jordan had become convinced that the motive for the murders had definitely been the money and the land itself. And no one could dispute the fact that the bloodsucking lawyers at BBG&G and Alana had benefited the most by the couple's deaths.

The timeline laid out all the specifics and more, including the fact that the moment the lawyers at BBG&G became aware that the Parkers' only son had gone missing in Vietnam, they'd filed a codicil to the couple's will making Jessica the sole trustee.

Reese had come up with that tidbit in old probate files.

Jordan intended to make sure he took full advantage of the meeting with Ron Blake. It was his job to make sure the cold case detective understood all the details pointing to his two prime suspects. As he walked up to the front desk, Jordan decided it would be a major victory if he could convince the detective that Alana Stevens and Jessica Boyd had at least a vested interest in the old couple's death.

A uniformed deputy escorted Jordan into a small ten by ten-foot interview room where he waited for Blake to make an appearance. After about ten minutes, Jordan's gung-ho resolve only grew stronger. Finally, the door flew open and a middle-aged man with brown hair walked in, eyed him carefully over a pair of reading glasses before offering his hand. "I'm Blake. So you're the guy with the insane idea he has something that might solve a forty year old murder."

"With that attitude, we may have a problem."

"Don't mind me I'm a natural cynic. Let's cut to the chase. Show me what you got."

Jordan opened his briefcase and took out a thick file folder, leafed through a stack of papers. Quickly, before he lost the guy, he went through the timeline showing the detective exactly how Jessica and Alana had the most to gain from the Parkers' deaths.

But it wasn't until he flipped open the briefcase again and took out the .357 the group had found in a mobile safe tucked away in Alana's attic that Blake sat up and took notice. Jordan placed the heavy weapon down on the table, watched as the detective eyed it with interest.

"I guess there's no point in playing hard to get. Let's take a walk," Blake offered as they left the interview room to head down a hallway into a much larger room, where a lone, beat-up, dusty brown box already sat on a conference table. "After your phone call I took the liberty of pulling this out of the Evidence Room, on the off-chance you actually brought me something."

Jordan stared at the carton. After forty years it had come down to a cardboard box. They stood around the table as he watched Blake dig through the carton, pulling out several pieces of paper.

Once Blake located the police report, they both went over the details, line by line. They soon learned that Mary Parker had died from a single gunshot wound to the head while Pete Parker had died from a single gunshot wound to the chest. According to the coroner, both had multiple stab wounds inflicted post mortem, after death.

Pictures from the crime scene revealed graffiti written on the walls of the couple's bedroom. Looking at the pictures reminded Jordan about Kit Griffin's psychic dream. At least that's what he called it. She had been adamant from the start about the exact words written on the walls. Standing there looking at the photos of the crime scene, he saw that her description had been eerily right on the money. How had she known the exact words written on the walls in the victim's blood, years before she'd ever been born? He didn't know anything about psychics or their dreams, but he did know how to read a police report. It confirmed the bullets retrieved from both bodies of the victims were believed to be those from a .357.

Goose bumps formed on his arms.

Blake stared at Jordan. "Bingo. That's significant." He held up an evidence bag from the box. "We retrieved bullet fragments from the scene. I'll send the gun off to the lab today. Put a rush on the ballistics."

Later, as Jordan walked to his car, he couldn't help feeling euphoric. Only a cop, or in his case, an ex-cop, knew how truly unusual it was to be able to solve a cold murder case, let alone one that had been sitting dormant for forty years, one that had killed a defenseless elderly couple in their beds.

He dug out his cell phone to give Reese and Jake an update.

But at that same moment Reese and Jake were crammed into one of the interrogation rooms at the downtown police station waiting for St. John to make his appearance. Jake sat at a table, drumming his fingers on the wood, nervous, while Reese sat there, the epitome of cool and collected, a fact that slightly pissed Jake off, until he reasoned that it wasn't Reese's ass that was on the line here.

After all, Reese hadn't been the one to marry a woman like Claire.

Determined to get out of this mess once and for all, to put it behind him and therefore move on with his life with Kit, Jake stiffened his resolve. He'd be damned if he took anymore crap from Max St. John. For the first time in two years, his chips were all in.

When the door finally opened and fifty-five-year-old Max St. John strolled in with a smug look on his face, Jake's resolution quickly turned to resentment, especially when he noticed Max's hands were empty. He hadn't brought Claire's case files after all. That one fact took Jake all the way past pissed.

"Come here to confess," Max chided, as he took a seat across from the two men.

So it was going downhill from the get-go. To hell it would, Jake thought, as he upped the ante. "I came here to find out why you never mentioned you had DNA on file; DNA that would have exonerated me two years ago."

Max's eyes widened a fraction. "Who told you that?"

Jake's body vibrated with anger. He stood up. When Reese tried to get him to sit back down, Jake simply batted his arm away. "Two years ago I took a polygraph and passed. I had an alibi for that day. The airline confirmed what time my plane landed at LAX. Witnesses at work told you what time I came through the door that morning and verified that I never left the entire day until eleven-thirty that night. I gave you a DNA sample. I did everything you asked of me. I cooperated fully until the day you told me I was the only suspect that made any sense.

"Damn it, St. John, I didn't kill Claire. I found the body that night, I was in that room, I saw all the furniture turned over, the mess, and the blood all over that bedroom. She fought with someone, Max. You know it and I know it. And it wasn't me. You have to have DNA from under her fingernails, something that clears me once and for all. And you're too fucking stubborn to admit it." Jake's fist slammed down on the table. "I want some answers from you. After all this time I deserve some goddamned answers."

"Where was this kind of emotion two years ago, Boston? I watched you sit there stone-faced, waited for you to get angry, and never saw anything but relief that your wife was dead."

Exasperated, Jake ran his hands through his hair. "Okay, you got me. Maybe something inside me might have been relieved. I don't know. She was sleeping with every man she came into contact with but me. How the hell was I supposed to react to that? You should know, Max. You're the one who sat me down in a room very much like this one and not so politely told me the facts about every one of her affairs. Let's see," he counted on his fingers, "there was her aerobics instructor, her yoga instructor, her personal trainer, her tennis coach. As I recall, you had a list. But you left someone out."

They stared at each other until Reese started to speak, but Max simply waved him away with his hand. "There was a list, a fairly long one."

"Did you name everyone on that list, Max? Or did you leave someone out?"

"What are you getting at?"

"Go get the file. I want to see the list."

Max got up and went to the door but before he turned the knob, he wanted to know, "You looking for someone in particular, Boston?"

"Yeah."

Five minutes later, Max was back in the room. It wasn't a file folder he carried, but rather a moving-size box. And he wasn't alone. Dan Holloway, his partner, joined them at the table. Max pulled the top off the box, pulled out a stack of papers, and started thumbing through the sheets until he found what he was looking for. "Now, you want to tell me whose name's on this list that I didn't mention?"

"Connor Boyd."

"Oh, come on, Boston. Man, you and the Griffin woman must have one major personal vendetta against this particular family. No wonder they kidnapped Kit and tried to get back at you. Connor Boyd? You must be crazy."

"Check it out. I believe Connor and Claire were having an affair. I missed it two years ago because I concentrated on the list you put in my head. But there had to be neighbors who saw him come and go at the house—more than once. If you interview those neighbors again, show them a picture of the man, one of them might remember seeing him come to the house the day she died. Maybe they might remember how often he came to the house. Of course, I'm not stupid. I know that only proves they were having an affair. But then there's the DNA evidence, a ton of which must include blood and semen samples. It wasn't my DNA you found there, Max, but that of the man who killed Claire."

Dan Holloway stared at Jake in disbelief. "Let me make sure I understand this. After everything that's happened to Kit at the hands of Collin Boyd, after he kidnapped her, you want us to reopen your wife's case, start digging around, go talk to your neighbors in Westlake Village, get them to ID Connor Boyd as the man Claire was seeing, and then go after him?"

"Actually," Jake said, as he jerked a piece of paper out of Reese's hand. "We have someone who has already done the legwork for you guys. He's already talked to the neighbors, showed Connor's picture around.

"It just so happens, the names on that paper are several of the neighbors who remembered him and identified him from the photo Jordan Donovan showed them. It seems Connor Boyd was someone who visited my house on a frequent basis. A few estimated the guy in that picture came and went from my house as long as a year before she died."

Jake handed the piece of paper off to Max, let him study it. "All you guys need to do is present him with that fact that he was having an affair with Claire, gauge his reaction, and then ask him where he was the morning she died. Ask him to submit to a DNA test."

Max shook his head. "That's all we have to do, huh? Look, Boston, you have the bucks to spend any way you choose, but..."

Jake interrupted him. "And that just chaps your butt, doesn't it, Max? I don't give a rat's ass about your petty vendetta against me. All I'm asking is for you to do what the taxpayers pay you to do, what you should have done two years ago. Find Claire's killer."

"It isn't quite that easy, Boston. I respect the fact that you came here today. I'll even tell you this much, the DNA we have on file did not match yours." He gave him a rueful look. "Okay, I owe you one. But so often in these cases, trust me, it's the husband."

Reese stood up, lawyer taking over in place of a supportive friend. "So officially he's no longer a suspect."

Max looked irked for about two seconds. Then glad to have this chance to clear the air, he admitted, "You're right. We have semen samples. Plenty. And your wife had blood and skin under her fingernails. She put up a helluva fight. There's plenty of DNA to go around. We swabbed every person on that list I gave you. There were no matches. I didn't know about the affair with Boyd. If and I emphasize if, the affair ever happened." He pointed to Reese. "You of all people should know that I can't just go knocking on Connor Boyd's door and say, 'hey there, how about you open up your mouth and I'll swab it for DNA?' I have no official cause to do that."

Reese countered, "Hypothetically, if we could get you a DNA sample would you compare it, use it? Would you send it to the lab?"

Max lowered his voice. "This conversation never happened, got that?"

Reese nodded. "Of course not. We were never here."

"If we were having this conversation, we're talking about a sample from Connor Boyd, right?"

Jake nodded. "That's the plan."

"Okay, if you could manage it, and I don't know how you could, I'd send the sample to the lab just like I would anyone else's you brought me, if for no other reason than to shut this one up." Max gave Jake a brief glare and then smiled. "But if you tell anyone that, I'll deny it all the way to retirement."

Fifteen minutes later, they'd left the building and were standing outside in the parking lot. Jake turned to Reese and asked, "How do you think it went?"

"Good on two fronts. First, we found out your DNA doesn't match anything they have, which we already knew. And second, we got them to say they'd compare a DNA sample if we got one. I'd say that's a win-win."

As he opened the door of his car, Jake took out his cell phone. "I need to call Kit, let her know how great it went."

CHAPTER 18

On the *Sea Warrior* Dylan woke to sunlight dripping down through the skylight above the bed. A glance at his watch told him he'd slept until almost ten o'clock. For him to do that, he must have been wiped. He crawled out of bed, stopping to listen for any signs of life outside his door in case the others had been just as exhausted and were still sacked out. But all he heard was the water lapping at the sides of the boat and the sounds of the harbor slowly coming alive around him.

As quietly as he could, he made his way into the adjoining head and turned on the shower.

Fifteen minutes later, fully dressed and ready for the grueling task of unloading their gear into the dinghy and hauling everything up to the house, Dylan walked out of his cabin surprised to find the salon deserted.

As he absently counted how many trips he would have to make to get everything to shore, he slowly opened the door of Baylee's stateroom only to find the bed made, the place neat and tidy but empty. At a complete loss, an uneasy feeling started to creep up his spine. It was then he began to look around the boat for all the gear they'd brought with them and discovered it already gone.

How had two women with a baby unloaded all that crap into a dinghy? How had they motored to shore without him hearing their every move? And had they hauled the stuff all the way up the hill to the house on their own while he slept like the dead?

His stomach rumbled. He peered into the galley, sniffing the air. For the first time, he noticed the fresh fruit and cinnamon rolls on the counter, smelled the hot coffee already brewed in the pot.

It was then he spotted the note taped to the front of the refrigerator door. Ripping it off, he learned that Baylee had taken the dinghy, was already at the house, and would come back to pick him up at ten o'clock. An arrow at the bottom of the note told him to turn it over.

He read: We let our captain sleep late.

Underneath the simple line she'd drawn a huge red heart. For some inexplicable reason, the red heart moved him like nothing had in years. He walked over and poured himself a cup of coffee, reached for the sugar, loaded it up, and brought it back to the little bar area. He sat down, picked up a sweet roll, and shook his head in appreciation. Baylee was so unlike any of the women he'd dated. Most L.A. women wouldn't go near pastry if you paid them for fear they might gain an extra ounce if they so much as inhaled sugar.

But not Baylee.

His beautiful Baylee. She cooked and ate real food. Thinking about her like that had him smiling into his coffee. God bless her, he thought, as he took another tasty bite. Just as he put the last crumb in his mouth, he heard a woman's voice yell out, "Ahoy matey, permission to come aboard."

He headed topside, grinning like a fool. When he got to the deck, he peered over the side of the railing. Looking down into the water next to the boat, he saw Baylee, sitting in the dinghy, bobbing up and down on the water. She'd left her hair loose and the wind lifted it wildly in the breeze. Dressed in a sleeveless red cropped shirt and khaki shorts, she looked tan and happy. A wild thought ran through his head that the woman looked good enough to eat for breakfast. His mouth watered.

"Hey, sleepyhead, we were getting worried about you."

"Hey. What happened to all the gear?"

She gave him a quizzical look and noticed his hair was damp and pulled back in that stubby ponytail that made him look like a seventeenth century pirate, standing on the deck of his ship rather than a software geek. "Everything's at the house. I'd have been back sooner, but we've been scrubbing the house clean. The floors are absolutely filthy and every piece of furniture has at least seven layers of dust in spite of the dust covers. We all started sneezing the minute we set foot inside."

"How? How did you move the gear?"

The quizzical look turned almost comical. She smiled up at the serious look on his face. "We're resourceful. Now are you staying on the boat or are you coming with me? Since I've got the dinghy, if I leave, you'll have to swim in and it's farther than it looks."

Sensing a challenge, he stated flatly, "I haven't finished breakfast yet. You wouldn't want me to leave on an empty stomach, would you? And I have to get the stuff in my room. Come on up here, Baylee." He motioned to her with his index finger that he wanted her to climb out of the motor boat and join him on deck. "Keep me company while I finish those cinnamon rolls you left for me. And thanks for breakfast."

She knew he was up to something. She could see it in his eyes. But she didn't really care because since waking up that morning, knowing they were in Catalina, knowing they had put some miles between the baby and Connor—it felt good to be on the water, sitting outside in a motorboat looking up at Dylan, relaxed without a care in the world.

With a cloudless June sky overhead, the harbor around her coming alive with people, the island's birds chirping a song to summer, the air itself seemed to stir with energy, maybe even optimism. It felt good to say silly things, kid around with each other, and be normal for a change. Baylee felt almost giddy, like a kid again.

For the first time in months, she felt hopeful.

Wishing it could stay like this forever, she decided to join him. Stretching her arm up to reach the side ladder on the *Sea Warrior*, she struggled to grab hold of the lowest rung. Sometimes it was hell being short, she thought, as she finally managed to latch on and pull herself up, climbing toward the top.

Halfway up though, all at once, she saw Dylan's arm snake out and pluck her off the ladder as if she weighed no more than one of the island's orange garibaldi dangling on a hook.

"God, you look good this morning," he called out, as he plopped her down on the deck.

His arms immediately found her waist. His mouth connected with hers like a fierce magnetic pull. Their tongues touched, drawing hers into a playful rhythm. Their bodies hummed with pent up need. When they came up for air, he sucked in a deep breath. A blitz of images flickered through his mind. Baylee holding Sarah; Baylee feeding her. It was broad daylight. He tamped his lust down a notch, deciding to keep the mood teasing. He backed her up against the railing, leaning into her; body pressed against body, his arms still circled around her tiny waist.

She smelled like flowers, jasmine maybe, or lavender, he wasn't sure which. Whatever it was kicked the lust up again. It was all he could do to pack it back down. "Now spill it, woman, how did you and Kit move all that gear by yourselves?"

"You don't intend to let this go, do you? We're not helpless, Dylan. We have our resources. Besides, Kit's an Amazon with superhuman strength. Haven't you seen her in action? And I might be small but I have strong muscles." Despite his lock on her, she flexed an arm. "Then there's Sarah; she carried most of the heavy stuff."

"So that's the way it's gonna be, is it? How about if I kiss it out of you? How would that be, hmm?" He kissed her forehead, her nose, each corner of her mouth and then zeroed in on those moist lips again. He lowered his head. She tasted like wind and sea.

Baylee's lips parted, anticipating his skilled moves. She dropped into the kiss. Longing nipped at her belly. She held on tighter. On tiptoes, she floated upward as their bodies bumped.

What was supposed to be a quick morning kiss soon built to red-hot want. They stood tasting, sampling, nipping as hunger began to race through both of them. The tongue tag went on and on, creating streams of white hot light that warmed her from the inside out.

Sinking deeper, the heat speared up to brilliant orange flame. Caught up, she felt like her feet left the deck. She was flying, as if her entire body rose higher, higher in his arms. Suddenly she was aware they were both moving. She realized she'd left the ground for real.

Dylan carried her down the steps going below deck.

"Where are we going?" she moaned huskily.

"I got my test results via text. Everything checked out. What's your stance on morning sex?" he asked as his mouth moved to nibble that tender spot along her throat before moving to her ear, before coming back to her mouth in a fierce persuasion.

"I'm all for it. Everyone knows morning sex is the best."

"Mmmm, my kind of woman," he whispered, as he stood in the middle of the salon with her hugged up against his chest. "I want you, Baylee. But if you aren't ready for this, tell me now, and I'll put you down right here, right now, and we won't go any further."

She wrapped her arms tighter, nuzzled his neck. "I want you, Dylan."

"Thank God," he growled, and swept her into the stateroom. He laid her down on the bed and went down on top of her.

He sought her mouth. Their tongues sampled then greedily devoured. He began to shed her clothes. When her top flew off, Baylee sought flesh too. She wrestled to get his T-shirt over his head. When it finally sailed through the air, her fingers roamed over bare chest, appreciating the feel of his athletic shoulders.

His fingers expertly worked to get rid of the bra. The bra went flying. They tumbled over one another until Baylee straddled him. His hands reached up to take advantage of her perfect, supple breasts, her pebbled, rosy tips.

He reared up to lave and taste, lingering over the swell of one breast all the way to the nipple and back again. He suckled one, then the other, nibbling each peak into his mouth until they hardened.

"Baylee, you taste so sweet."

Her hands fisted in his hair, guiding him, nudging him back to her breasts then further down toward the searing heat.

He tugged at her shorts and found her bare-assed underneath. His fingers went wild, plunging into her moist hot center. She bucked. They rolled again. He came out on top. His fingers probed, toyed, played. As she climbed, he watched her eyes change from glaze to dark, then flicker with pleasure as it built slowly, layer by layer.

His mouth connected with hers, took in her short breathy groans.

The orgasm rocked through her, sending her body into waves of little quivers and quakes. As soon as the tremors played out, he began to move down the length of her, tasting every curve of nipple and ridge again, savoring every touch of smooth skin. He leisurely, deliberately laved his way past her navel, past her flat stomach, past a landing-strip-patch of feathery light hair, hair that proved without doubt she was a natural blond.

His tongue dipped to play at her moist core.

Baylee wanted to thrust, propel him further toward the satin heat. Her hips moved to the beat of his tongue as he feasted until she came in a burst of dazzling colored rockets.

He trailed back up her body, tasting skin, licking his way until he got to her mouth. He nipped her lower lip before sucking her tongue.

Coming out of her satiated state, surrender came easily, sweetly. She began to move beneath him. At some point he rolled to his back, retrieved a foil packet from somewhere, and sheathed on a condom.

Eyes closed, Baylee missed the weight of his body on hers. Lazily she tried to lift her head. She opened her eyes in time to see him settle between her legs. She felt his lips on hers again then hot moist tongue. He slipped a finger in between her folds, began to stroke again, working her to another fast quake.

But just before she came again, he knelt between her thighs, eased gently into her. She wrapped her legs around him and began to move again, plunging him deeper, driving him further. He fought against greedy release, fought for control, fought to hold back. But when her rhythm increased, he quickened his thrusts. When he saw her eyes change, he simply let himself go, dropping into the depths of the blissful wave.

$$\triangle \triangle \triangle \triangle \triangle$$

She traced a finger along his spine as she lay there, content as a puppy lapping cream, with him still inside. If there were anything that could have made this morning more perfect, she couldn't think of what it might be.

He let out a sigh and pressed his lips to hers. Reluctant to move, he rested his forehead on hers. "That was incredible. You're such a little thing. I must be crushing you."

"You're fine. No, more than fine. You're amazing. After such a long drought I had four. Fabulous four." She threw her arms out wide in celebration.

He rolled to his back, bringing her with him. Still buried inside her, with his arms locked around her, he pushed her hair out of her face so he could see her eyes clearly. "You have the most incredible shade of eyes, the color of the ocean. Promise me something."

"What?"

"You won't ever again believe I couldn't be attracted to you. You are beautiful."

"Oh, Dylan. You say the sweetest things."

"Now," he prodded, "tell me how you and Kit got all that stuff into the dinghy by yourselves."

She giggled, still high on afterglow. "We did it the old-fashioned way. Catalina has all manner of people you can hire to transport your stuff to shore. Kit and I simply got online, found a company who specializes in unloading a boat, picked up the phone, and paid someone to show up with a big boat of their own, load up our stuff, and cart it to the house in one trip. We didn't want you to have to spend half a day by yourself lugging all that crap around after having such a difficult night."

"Aww, that's sweet." He started moving his hands up and down her slim body, exploring things he'd missed earlier in their haste to make love. Then with his teeth, he tugged lightly on her lower lip. "That must mean between the two of us we should still have enough energy left to go another round." Smoothly, skillfully, he rolled on top of her again and began to feast on her mouth.

℺℺℺℺℺

It took Dylan and Baylee another two hours before they finally made it to the Spanish-style two-story villa, tucked up against the harbor. Like two randy teenagers coming in from a date, reluctant to say goodnight, they snuck up to the porch and stood at the front door, locked up in each other. Neither wanted to end one of the best mornings they'd had in some time.

From the living room, Kit thought she heard someone on the porch. With Sarah poised on her hip, she went to the front door and threw it open. Still wrapped up in each other, Dylan and Baylee stood entwined in each other's arms and didn't even bother breaking apart.

"What took you guys so long?" One look at their goofy faces and Kit had her answer.

After all, Baylee had been gone for almost three hours.

"What took you guys so long?" Kit repeated like a parrot, forcing them to look at her, but neither bothered to acknowledge her existence.

"Ran into rough seas," Dylan finally admitted without sparing Kit so much as a glance.

"Almost a squall," Baylee added, all innocent, standing there with her arms locked around Dylan as if she were under a vampire-like spell and couldn't tear herself away.

"Definitely bad weather," Dylan persisted.

Kit sighed. There wasn't a cloud in the sky. Snapping her fingers with her free hand, Kit said without rancor, "Hey, snap out of it. We still have to put all this stuff away, like the groceries, unpack our clothes, finish cleaning this place up. I can't even put Sarah down to crawl on the floor without giving it another swipe with the mop."

Mentioning Sarah finally had the desired effect. It got them both moving. Once they let go of each other, Baylee headed straight for Sarah, plucking her out of Kit's arms. "Hey, angel-face, did you miss Mommy? Did you eat your cereal for Auntie Kit?"

"Chowed down just like Dylan here does. Put cereal in front of her and it seems she's just like this big guy with food." Kit playfully tugged on Dylan's shirt sleeve. "It was like watching Pepper zero in on his Dog Chow."

"Even though I resemble that remark, I'll take it in the spirit it was given, and say, I'm glad Sarah's taken to her cereal—like her Daddy," Dylan boasted, lips curving into a wide grin.

Kit looked him up and down with hands on her hips. "I could use some muscle to get things cleared out of the living room." She rolled her eyes, then smiled. "Daddy.

Those moving guys dumped the gear right here. I've checked out the bedrooms, all five of them. We can use the middle one upstairs as the staging area. If we store most of the stuff there until you guys get around to unpacking it, I think we can get most of this stuff out of the high traffic areas. Although, at some point we may have to cram some of it into one of the larger closets at least for now to get it out of the way. I checked the closets in this place, even the ones in the hallway. All five bedroom closets are filled to the brim with junk."

She turned her attention to Baylee, "I never realized your father was such a pack rat or the sentimental type. Take a gander in those closets and it doesn't look like the man ever threw anything away." Remembering the mess Jake and Dylan and Reese had found in Alana's attic when they went looking, she added, "What was it with that generation about keeping everything they ever laid their hands on?"

Focusing on Dylan, without skipping a beat, she gave orders like a drill sergeant. "Start with the guest room further down the hall. We designated that as Sarah's room. Then grab the bags with her clothes. Haul them upstairs like a good boy. Daddy."

"Yes, boss, right away, boss, anything you say, boss," Dylan mocked, his eyes lighting with merriment. Picking up a bag, he heaved it up onto his shoulder before heading down the hallway toward the staircase.

"Oh, stop it. You slept the day away and now it's time you made yourself useful," Kit yelled after him.

"You sure are bossy without Jake around," Dylan declared, jovially.

At the mention of Jake her drill sergeant demeanor softened into a puddle of marshmallow crème. To Baylee she merely said, "He called after the meeting. St. John agreed to send any DNA sample from Connor to the lab. They have DNA from the crime scene, Baylee, and it doesn't match Jake's. He's no longer a suspect. Yay for our side!" Kit did a little happy dance.

"You mean if we can get Connor to take a DNA test, we could find out if he's the one who killed Claire?" Dylan asked, picking up a box of groceries and heading into the kitchen.

"Yep. Jake said there's a ton of DNA."

"But that would just prove they had sex, not that he killed her," Baylee pointed out.

"Not if his DNA matches what's under her fingernails. Claire fought her killer, put up quite a struggle. So there's evidence from the fight."

Hearing that grisly detail sent chills up and down Baylee's spine. Her face went white. Slowly, she dropped down on the sofa with the baby on her lap. It was Dylan who saw her face, set the box of supplies back down on the floor, and came over to kneel down in front of her. "What's wrong?"

"Tell him, Baylee. I already told Jake what you told me." When Baylee looked horror-stricken, Kit added, "I'm sorry, but he needed to know what Connor said to you that night because it might be relevant to Claire's murder, although I'm not sure he mentioned it to St. John this morning. But Dylan needs to know because he's caught up in all of this." Noting the concerned look she saw on Dylan's face now, that seemed to be an understatement.

"What are you not telling me? Something else happened with Connor, didn't it?"

She told him what she'd told Kit on the dock about Connor's showing up at her apartment before she had left L.A. "I took the threat seriously. It was more than just trying to scare me. You should've seen the look in his eyes. He was glassy-eyed, empty, like he wasn't all there."

"My God, I thought maybe Jake was reaching, you know, just grasping at a last straw in Connor's direction, that maybe that e-mail he received pointing to Connor was some kind of a joke, but... I understand now why you didn't go to the cops. Look, I know this is overwhelming. I know you're scared. But you have to try and relax while you're here. You can't keep up this stress level for long without it taking a toll health-wise. It isn't good for your immune system or for Sarah's, especially since you're still breastfeeding. You need to work on putting this mess out of your mind while you're here."

He kissed the top of her head and then leaned down to kiss Sarah's. "I'll do everything I can to keep him from getting to you and Sarah. I promise you that much here and now. You have my word. Whatever it takes."

"We all will, Baylee. That's a given," Kit assured her.

"I know that. But has it escaped either one of you that if he suspects Sarah belongs to him, if he pushes that, he'd be forced to take that DNA test and bingo, Jake would have his proof. Or…it could…backfire completely and…" Her voice trailed off. She couldn't even bring herself to say what she'd been thinking.

Dylan did it for her. "A DNA test would prove paternity, prove once and for all Sarah's his, and it would open up a huge can of worms for both of you, especially if the DNA came back showing he wasn't the one who killed Claire. I get it, Baylee. You'd have everything out in the open about Sarah's paternity, a custody battle on your hands, and he'd have unfettered access to this baby."

"Exactly," Baylee huffed out. "And he's an attorney with all kinds of power at his disposal. It's too scary to even think about. Look at what Jessica did to Gloria." She drew in a breath. "I'd have to leave; Dylan, take Sarah away and hide. Costa Rica here I come."

Dylan gave her a weak smile. "Let's take it one step at a time for now. Keeping you and Sarah safe is the first priority. Right now, Connor taking a DNA test for any reason is down the road. I'll say it again, try to unwind while you're here. You deserve a break. I'm not suggesting that you lower your guard."

"I know what you're saying." She took a deep breath before puffing it out. "I'll try. That's all I can do."

Kit looked at her watch. "I'm meeting Jake at the harbor at one-thirty. He took the ferry over from the mainland. I've got to get going. I don't want him wandering around Avalon looking for the house. Can you two behave yourselves while I'm gone?"

Plucking Sarah from Baylee's arms, Dylan looked wide-eyed and innocent at the comment. "Hey, we wouldn't think of doing anything in front of the b-a-b-y. Shame on Aunt Kit for thinking like that. She has a dirty mind, doesn't she, Sarah?"

"Oh please," Kit shot back. "I'm trusting the two of you to act like mature adults and not like the naughty teens I caught standing on the porch earlier. I'll be back in thirty minutes. Do you think you can keep your hands to yourselves for that long in front of the b-a-b-y?"

Baylee laughed. The intense mood lifted. "Get out of here and go make out with Jake. You aren't fooling anyone. So go. You're on the clock."

Kit had just disappeared out the front door when Sarah started rubbing her eyes like she was sleepy. "Okay, somebody's ready for a nap. Let's get you all tucked in, sweetie."

Baylee headed upstairs and Dylan trailed behind her carrying Sarah. "Do I need to set up the port-a-crib?"

"Nope, all taken care of," Baylee told him as she approached the bedroom down the hall, one of the smallest of the guest bedrooms upstairs but the one that used to belong to her. The room suited Sarah perfectly. The walls were painted a cheery yellow and decorated with some of Baylee's own artwork, colorful paintings of different kinds of animals she'd done in high school and hung years earlier to brighten up the room. She reached over, plucked Sarah out of Dylan's arms, and put her down on the twin bed to change her diaper before sitting down in the wooden rocker. Baylee looked around the room. "Could you maybe find her baby monitor so we'll hear her when she wakes up?"

While Baylee fed Sarah, Dylan dug around in several bags that had already been brought upstairs until he found the monitor. By the time Baylee put the baby down in her crib Dylan had it up and running. He stood in the doorway patiently waiting for her to back out of the room. As soon as she closed the door, Dylan pulled her into his chest, kissed her full on the mouth.

"Mmmm, you taste good. We've got twenty minutes before Kit comes back. Let's make the most of it."

His touch, his kiss, sent her reeling. She covered his mouth. Dylan cupped her rear, picked her up. and whirled around, leaning his back up against the wall. She pressed her body into his. They were both on fire

But then they heard the front door burst open. Even with the need hanging between them, they recognized the voices downstairs in the entryway. Kit had returned with Jake.

"Damn, that was fast," Dylan protested. "I thought we'd have more time."

"We might have if I'd been quicker putting Sarah down."

"Couldn't be helped. We have the next few days." He touched her cheek. "I think I understand now why you were so upset that first night at my house about moving so many times. It takes a lot out of you—out of Sarah. I see that now. We'll get through this, Baylee. I won't let him hurt you."

Baylee smiled. This was what she liked about him, his ability to pick up on how she felt, see her predicament, and appreciate the circumstances. The mention of "him" made her breathe out a sigh. But she was determined not to let Connor wedge himself into her thoughts. "I know how uncomfortable my meltdown the other day made you. But you handled it very well."

He chuckled, tucked a strand of her hair behind her ear. "I'm getting used to having women around. You and Sarah are growing on me." He looked further down the hallway wishing the two of them could make use of one of the bedrooms. "Which room is yours?"

"The one with the balcony, the one closest to the ocean."

"Tonight then." He gave her a mouthy kiss and rested his head on her forehead. "That will have to hold us both for a while," he whispered, as they both started moving toward the stairs, hand in hand.

⚭⚭⚭⚭⚭

For the rest of the day, the four of them stayed busy getting Baylee and Dylan settled in their new digs for the long haul. That meant a thorough cleaning and dusting of the place from top to bottom.

Even though Jake and Kit weren't staying, they did their part unpacking boxes, scrubbing down the kitchen, putting away the groceries they'd ordered, and unpacking stuffed-to-the-gills suitcases.

Kit had not underestimated the amount of junk William had stored in the closets. To cover more ground, the four of them split up, each taking a bedroom to strip the sheets off the beds and prepare for a massive laundry detail.

But no matter the bedroom, each of them encountered the same problem. The bedrooms were cramped, crowded with furniture.

There was no way to clear anything out because every closet was in the same condition, stuffed to the brim with years of outdated clothes or stacks of old magazines, everything from ancient copies of *Life* to *Reader's Digest* to *Harper's Bazaar*, along with a ton of old hardcover books and just plain junk. It soon became clear they couldn't unpack anything until they'd made room in the closets for all the stuff they'd brought.

Baylee had taken the master suite at the end of the hall near Sarah's room for her own. She opened the windows to let in some much-needed fresh air. The breeze right off the ocean felt cool as she stood there a moment enjoying the view of the glistening water and the pristine sandy beaches below before turning to strip the sheets off the bed.

After choking from the dust, she took the linens and dumped them in the hallway.

It was time to tackle all the useless stuff in the dreaded closet. The minute she opened the door, she scanned the overflowing mess inside and groaned. She stared at her father's old clothes. Every stitch of clothing smelled like mothballs. But she had to make room for her things. And if Dylan decided to put his clothes in here they'd definitely have a storage problem. One by one, she started taking down shirts and pants still on hangers. She toted them into the unoccupied bedroom, which had become the staging area, and tossed them on the bed for now. She'd deal with them later.

On her third trip back to the closet, she eyed a couple of boxes stored on one side of the shelf and plied back the lids. One contained more magazines. Another held an assortment of men's tennis shoes. She shook her head. Going through these would take a while. She didn't have that kind of time to waste. She decided to move these into the catch-all bedroom. After making a couple of trips back and forth, she stood just inside the walk-in closet appreciating the space she'd created. But there still wasn't enough room for Dylan's stuff. She turned her attention to the other side of the walk-in closet.

It was then she noticed some clothing hanging in the back that looked out of place. There were women's dresses hanging at the end of the rack.

Curious, Baylee stepped further along the rod holding hangars to get a better look. Instinctively, she started going through each piece of clothing, one by one, pulling back each dress, each blouse, each sweater, giving them the once-over. As she studied the outfits, she decided they were from at least two decades earlier, probably the 80's.

When she plied back a section of dresses, she suddenly spotted what looked like a crease in the wood hidden behind all of the clothes. To take a closer look, she had to remove several outfits from the rod. Creating a sizeable gap, she took a step toward the crevice in the wall.

Feeling along the seam, she realized it was a recessed panel that was supposed to slide. She tried moving it to the left then the right. It was rough going at first. The track seemed to have rusted from lack of use. When she finally managed to work the piece of wood all the way open, she saw what looked like an old, dusty, leather-bound book propped up at an angle. Tentatively, she picked it up, swiping off cobwebs and dust with her hand. She felt the gold embossed words on the cover that read simply, *My Diary*.

In the warmth of the small space, chills ran down her arms.

Feeling a little like an intruder who'd just stumbled on someone else's hidden, forbidden treasure, she took her find over to the bed and dropped down on the bare mattress to get comfortable. With a sense of dread, she sucked in a breath and slowly opened the book to the first page.

She realized the book belonged to her mother.

The first entry was dated the day she'd married William Scott.

Curious, Baylee flipped through more of the pages, skimming each daily entry. At first, her early writings covered the mundane, ordinary reflections of a young woman in love. Then she realized some of the statements referred to the seventeen-year-old girl's obvious smitten state with a much older man. It seems Sarah Moreland had been infatuated with William Scott from the minute she had walked on to that first movie set years earlier. The entries revealed that the teenager had obviously fallen in love with him long before they'd actually gotten together.

Reading her mother's heartfelt words, Baylee discovered William had taken Sarah's virginity on her eighteenth birthday, three years before they'd tied the knot at the altar.

Some of the paragraphs painted the picture of a naïve, young woman who had poured everything she had into building the relationship with him from the beginning, even when it meant trying to please his every whim in bed. A little disgusted with some of the detailed descriptions, Baylee read on about how frustrated Sarah had grown at what he insisted she do. Who knew her father had been into bondage?

As she read more, she discovered the marriage had been in trouble almost from the start, especially since William's proclivity for kinky sex became more of a demand. According to Sarah's own words, a mere two months into the marriage, she had suspected William was seeing someone else.

That confirmed what her aunt, Karen Nash, had said about her father's wandering eye. It seems William's infidelity hadn't fooled his naive wife for a minute despite her young age.

As Baylee flipped through more pages, she learned her mother had eventually come to the conclusion that there was one woman in particular, an actress, that William couldn't seem to stay away from, even during the course of his wife's pregnancy, which apparently had happened by accident, certainly had not been planned, a mere month after their marriage.

According to the entries, William had not been thrilled to discover he'd soon be a father. In fact, Baylee read in no uncertain terms how unhappy he'd been about the prospect. At one point, according to Sarah, he had demanded she end the pregnancy.

A disillusioned Baylee sat there on the bed, feeling her mother's pain. As she read the words, tears welled up in her eyes. As young as Sarah had been, she had stuck to her principles and had refused to give in to William's wishes.

As a woman, not to mention Sarah's daughter, Baylee felt particularly outraged at her father's callousness and infidelity. His betrayal during his wife's pregnancy had to have been especially hurtful, since more than likely Sarah had been at her most vulnerable.

As Baylee continued to read further, the journal left no doubt the cheating had never stopped. Instead, there were nights when William hadn't come home at all.

Totally absorbed in the story, Baylee thumbed forward through the book, looking for a name. Surely, Sarah had discovered the name of the woman that had played such an integral part in ruining her marriage. When one name finally jumped off the page, stunned, Baylee flew off the bed. She tore down the hallway so fast she turned over several cartons of old books, spilling the contents all over the hardwood floor. She didn't even stop to pick up the mess but rather took the stairs two at a time, looking to share what she'd found with everyone else.

🜨 🜨 🜨 🜨 🜨

"**According to what** my mother wrote, the entire time they were married he was caught up in this affair with Alana. There wasn't one day that he actually spent trying to make his marriage work. He was playing around from the start," Baylee railed, as she paced back and forth in front of the stone fireplace in the living room.

"Your father and Alana were involved," Dylan stated again, incredulously. "I thought they hated each other. You said there were times when he tried to keep you and Kit apart because they had some kind of private war going on between them and you two kids were caught in the middle," Dylan pointed out, genuinely perplexed.

"The war obviously came later. Like you said, they must have had a falling out at some point. According to her journal, the two of them were hot and heavy during the entire course of the marriage. Read some of her entries; read how many times he saw Alana over the course of three years. Some nights the man didn't even bother coming home. It's disgusting, he's disgusting. He even spent time with Alana when my mother was pregnant. It's obvious to me he never even made an effort to make the marriage work. And when he found out she was pregnant, he badgered her to end it. Poor Sarah."

"But why would she leave her journal behind?" Dylan wanted to know. "That makes no sense. And why leave it hidden here instead of the house in Beverly Hills?"

"Maybe by the time she made the last trip to Catalina, spending any time in this house, she probably thought, 'Okay, it's over for good. There's no need to bring my diary along because it reminds me of the lousy, cheating bastard I'm married to.'" Kit shot a compassionate look at Baylee. "Sorry."

"Why? That's exactly what he was, a lousy, cheating bastard and with Alana of all women. I feel sorry for my mother. All these years I blamed her for walking out, for leaving him, for leaving me. Now, I know why. Could you just imagine how that made her feel knowing she never really had his attention, not even from day one? That he was never really committed to the marriage. No wonder she turned to someone else."

But Dylan wasn't convinced. He thumbed through the journal. "So far, I haven't found any mention of Luc Delaine at all."

"This book only covers the first year of marriage."

"It still doesn't make sense. Are you sure this was the only book inside that hidey hole?"

Baylee looked bewildered for about two seconds before she took off like a shot out of the room and raced back upstairs. By the time she reached the master bedroom, Dylan was hot on her heels.

"I didn't even consider there might be more, didn't even look," she admitted to Dylan as she stumbled around in the closet, stepping over some of the clothes now strewn all over the floor before falling to her knees and reaching into Sarah's cubby-hole, hiding place.

She took a deep breath. Sure enough, there in the back were two more leather-bound books, one covering the second year of marriage, the other, the third.

As Dylan thumbed through the books, he commented, "I'll say one thing for your mother, she was meticulous in detail."

"She was. She obviously poured her heart and soul out in these."

"Where do you suppose the last one is? By my calculation, she kept these starting the first of every year she was with William. She was five months into another year when she went missing."

Baylee gaped at him. She hadn't even thought of that. "Good question. I guess I'll need to turn Dad's house upside down to find out."

"Maybe it's somewhere in this house."

She kissed him on the mouth. "Dylan, you think of everything. I guess we start here and tear this house upside down first."

But after several hours of clearing out closets, tearing through drawers, rearranging book shelves, none of them discovered the final journal belonging to Sarah Moreland.

Although they didn't locate the last diary, it was clear in the ones they had read that Sarah cared for Luc Delaine. Time and again, she had declared her love for him, but never as a lover.

Because it seems Luc had hoarded a secret.

Luc Delaine, the tennis player ranked number four in the world, had been gay.

CHAPTER 19

"So if Luc was gay, that pretty much puts William's story in the fictional category," Dylan said as he flipped a burger on the outside grill while Baylee whirled together frozen margaritas a few steps inside the patio door of the kitchen.

"Maybe she ran off with him in spite of that just to get away from William? Maybe it was her only opportunity to escape," Baylee offered the minute the noise from the blender ceased.

Dylan sent her a dubious look. After believing a lie which her father had propagated for twenty-two years, what did he expect? He'd known she might be resistant to the truth, but he didn't think she'd continue to hang on to her father's phony story when faced with hard facts.

As soon as Baylee appeared outside with the pitcher, Kit got up to pour the mixture into goblets. She handed one off to Jake as he sat at the outdoor table, holding the baby on his lap.

"I've got a ton of questions about William's story too," Kit said, eyeing Baylee the same way Dylan had. "But first, how did William and Alana come to despise each other? Because they did."

Dylan flipped another burger and pointed out, "Not only that, but how did the man come to purchase a home five houses down from her then switch gears and decide she was off-limits to his daughter? Sometimes going off the deep end so much about it, he'd forbid that child from stepping foot inside Alana's house."

Maybe now was his chance to get Baylee to see how William's story didn't add up. "I just don't buy the fact that Sarah's married to the guy for three years, puts up with his cheating ways and then one night she decides to pack up and leave her daughter behind with him. Plus, she leaves those journals behind, especially when she makes it clear in between those pages that the only reason she didn't divorce his ass in the first place was because of you, Baylee. She's trying hard to make the marriage work in spite of William's infidelity because of you. She's doing everything she can, putting everything into the marriage."

And there was one point Dylan could not get past. "I just want to say that every time I've been around your father, he's acted like he's carrying around a lot of guilt—about something." Dylan shrugged before adding, "Just a personal observation by an outsider looking in at the situation with a new perspective. This ongoing affair he had with Alana might be it." But he didn't think so. "Or, it could be something more sinister."

A couple of feet away, Kit stopped in her tracks and stared at him at the grill.

The image came quickly, like a blur across her vision. It made her dizzy. Everything and everyone around her ceased to exist as she focused on the scene as it played out and she was sent back in time to that night inside William's house, watching in slow motion as it happened.

While the others continued to chat, Kit had taken a side trip to the night Sarah went missing.

Baylee went into detail about how Dylan thought William had done something to Sarah until she glanced over at Kit and noticed she'd turned pale as a ghost. Kit had a pained expression on her face. Baylee turned to look at Jake, who was also staring at Kit, watching her every move.

Baylee saw Kit abruptly drop into one of the lawn chairs, white as chalk.

"What's wrong, Kit?"

Kit drew in a deep breath as the images remained constant, like a movie on DVD, as she watched two women, the woman who'd raised her, and the woman's best friend, Jessica, standing together at the top of a staircase, arguing with a petite blonde woman.

Having seen pictures of Baylee's mother, Kit winced as the event became sharper, clearer, as if someone fine-tuned the picture.

Kit swallowed the bile that rose in her throat. "That night Sarah demanded Alana and Jessica leave the house. She wanted them out. They hadn't been invited. Apparently, Alana had used a key she had to William's house. That's how she slipped in that night, she and Jessica. Alana strolled right in, bold as brass. Wait. Alana had sold William his house and had copied the key, kept it without William's knowledge. The key allowed the two of them to simply walk in the front door that night and right up the stairs, where they confronted Sarah on the landing just after she'd put Baylee to bed. Hmm, that's exactly the way they entered the Parkers' home the night they killed the old couple."

Even though Dylan stood at the grill, he turned to meet Baylee's eyes before he stared over at Kit in disbelief. The three of them eyed Kit as if horns had suddenly sprouted from both sides of her head right before their very eyes. But Kit didn't even notice. She steamed right on.

"That's it. That's exactly right. Dylan is correct; something sinister happened." From the lawn chair, Kit glanced up at Dylan. "You've hit the mother lode. Only it wasn't William."

Kit picked up Baylee's hand and gripped it so hard, it hurt. "Your childhood dream is fairly accurate. You did see Alana and Jessica. Both of them were there that night, both of them fought with Sarah. Sarah didn't stand a chance against both of them. They towered over her, over-powered her."

"You remember my dream from therapy? How? Even I don't remember all of it."

"I do. But I'm not projecting what I heard in group. I'm sure of it. Of course, I remember your discussing what happened in the dream with Strasberg. And you know why? Because there were so many times I saw both of those women do such despicable things it branded me for life. Things that for the longest time I couldn't put together, didn't understand fully what was happening. We were just kids, Baylee, trying to survive our own personal anguish. How could we know the adults around us were such evil people? But I obviously didn't let go of the images, couldn't for some reason get them completely out of my head."

Kit sat up straighter. "But what you remember wasn't a dream. It happened. It was real."

"Intuition again, Kit?" Jake asked in wonder.

"It's something. I'm just not sure what. But we should confront your father with the journals; find out the truth once and for all, the sooner, the better."

"Do you think he even knows about what they did?"

Kit's brows drew together in concentration. After some time, she concluded, "Oh, he knows." And wasn't that a kick in the pants, she thought. But then she took in the stricken look on Baylee's face. "Dylan's correct that William's carrying around a ton of guilt. It's eating him up inside. I'm sorry, Baylee."

"Don't be. Somehow it doesn't surprise me," Baylee said solemnly. "What else did you see?"

Kit described the entire scene, reiterated her idea. What little three-year-old Baylee had witnessed that night was Alana fighting with her mother, and then Jessica Boyd had stepped in to finish the job by pushing Sarah down the stairs. When she finished, Kit recognized their skeptic looks.

"I'm telling you it wasn't a dream. What Baylee saw was the real deal," Kit insisted.

"Baylee's been having this dream as long as she can remember," Dylan pointed out, as he plated the burgers. "That has to be significant in the bigger picture."

"How can you be so sure?" Jake asked Kit, wanting to believe what she saw as fact.

"The same way I knew the dream about the Parkers was significant, as if it had already happened exactly the way I saw it."

"But that was your dream," Baylee pointed out. "How can you possibly see what my dream is like? And it's been years since I've spoken about it in group."

"I don't know. I don't have all the answers. All I know is what I see coupled with what I remember from group. I remember it freaked me out just as much then as it does now that the women you saw looked like Alana and Jessica. I believed it back then, Baylee. But who would have believed either one of us, even if we'd pursued it? I might not have said anything at the time, probably didn't, as a matter of fact, but just because I stayed quiet doesn't mean I forgot how you described what happened, how terrifying it was for you.

"But don't you see I saw the sequence of events as they killed the Parkers in my head, I saw them in gritty detail, just like now; I see grainy images, but I recognize Alana and Jessica. And they're fighting, arguing with a woman with blonde hair, who was wearing jeans and a gray sweatshirt at the time. They were yelling at each other. And then all of a sudden Alana moved in, hauled off, and slapped her. Jessica swoops in like she's coming to Alana's rescue, gets into the middle—and wham—she pushed Sarah, the much more petite woman, down the stairs."

Baylee gasped. "Did I tell you that? That's exactly what happens in my dream. My mother had on jeans and a gray, long-sleeved top. It could have been a sweatshirt."

It was Dylan's turn to act as cynic. "Maybe you see it that way, Kit, because that's the way Baylee described it to you in group therapy, in the beginning. Power of suggestion."

Kit shook her head. "No. No. The woman wore her blonde hair in a long layered look, like they did in the eighties. Big hair. I don't remember Baylee describing the hairstyle she saw that night."

Undeterred, Kit added, "You look a lot like her, Baylee. I can see what she looks like dead, lying at the bottom of the stairs. Her body's twisted…unnaturally, as if she might have broken her neck." Kit trembled slightly at the image.

Dylan looked at Baylee's face, which had gone white at Kit's words, and then he shot a glance at Jake as if to say, 'can't you get her to shut up?' but Jake just shook his head.

Jake reminded Dylan, "What can I say? She was right about the Parkers, I vote we go ask William Scott about all of this, see what kind of reaction we get from him."

"God, I'm so confused," Baylee said as she wearily put her head in her hands. "It's harder to deny all this what with Kit seeing it too. My father has his faults, but how could he keep this a secret all these years? This whole thing is a little too fantastic to even think about."

"I think we're all more than a little blown away as to how she's able to do this. But I sat there that day in the library when we went looking for some newspaper article in the archives that I really didn't believe we'd find." Jake gave Kit a look as though he believed in her one-hundred percent before adding, "Then there it was in black-and-white, elderly couple found slain in the Hollywood Hills. That's something I won't forget, or the chills that went with it. I don't know how she does it, only that she's been right so far."

Baylee's shoulders slumped. She looked at Kit with genuine resignation. "I've known you all my life. I'm not saying I doubt what you're seeing, of course I don't. It's just that, this is my dream, not yours. But how could you possibly know that kind of detail, what my mother looked like, especially that night? You've seen pictures of her that I hid from my father and would take out every now and then just to look at her, keep her image alive in my head. But in those pictures her hair was different, like the one in her wedding dress. She wore her hair up the day of her wedding. That night, the night in the dream, that layered look was new. I'm pretty sure she hadn't worn it that way for very long. I always thought she looked a little like Farah Fawcett. See, I'm getting the memories mixed up."

"It's okay, Baylee. I know what you mean. This is new to me, too. These visions are new. But I'm not going to lie and say I don't see what happened because I do. Clearly there's something going on here."

"Yeah. And some days it's all too much to take in," Dylan suggested as he passed around the plates Baylee had yet to set out on the table. "This whole thing is getting a little too weird. But while you're at it, Kit, maybe you could look into the past and tell us where the hell Sarah hid that last journal."

Kit laughed and threw a potato chip at Dylan's head. "Very funny. For that I might need my crystal ball."

Afterward, while they cleaned up the kitchen and Jake was at the sink loading the dishwasher, Baylee turned to him and announced, "I just want you to know if you have to get a DNA sample from Connor to close the case on Claire's murder, I won't hold it against you. I know how much you need to put it behind you once and for all. If that's the only way…"

"Baylee, I'm certain he killed Claire. I'm as sure as Kit is about what she said happened to your mother. I want to put Claire behind me. That much is true. But that isn't why I think the DNA is a good idea. If Connor did it, then we can put him away for a long time, get him out of your life and Sarah's for good. I want him to pay for what he did to Claire, and that also means he pays for what he did to you. The Boyds have a history of getting away with things. I want an end to all of this once and for all. The DNA may be both our tickets at doing that."

"Jake, you have no idea how much I wish you could send Connor to jail with one little sample of DNA. But what if…"

"Let's take one step at a time, Baylee. Just one thing at a time. Try not to worry so much about the results."

She wondered if he really understood the implications of what he was suggesting. It wasn't that easy to forget Connor Boyd. They didn't know him like she did. Sure, it was easy for everyone to tell her to relax but a lot more difficult to put it into practice. She knew it would take a bloody miracle to get him out of her life, out of Sarah's. Merely wishing him out of sight, out of mind wasn't going to work. He wasn't simply going to go away. But she gave Jake a weak smile anyway. "That's exactly what Dylan told me. I only hope you both know what you're doing."

$$\triangle\triangle\triangle\triangle\triangle$$

That night as Baylee lay in bed, she worried about all of it. What would happen if it turned out Connor wasn't Claire's killer after all and he'd be free to fight for custody, or at the very least for visitation? What if it turned out he was Claire's killer but somehow managed to pull legal strings and get away with it? Nerves tangled her up in knots, filling her with fear and doubt.

When she heard a light knock at the door, it opened before she could respond and Dylan stuck his head in the room. "You want to talk about it?"

She cocked her head to stare at him. "I may be relatively out of practice, but something tells me you did not come to my room—to talk. And besides, we had a date. For a minute there, I thought I'd been stood up."

He walked over to the bed and sat down beside her, rubbed a finger down the side of her face to her chin. "You wore your worried face to bed. I had to come see if you were okay. If there's a side benefit…" His voice trailed off as he took in the way her hair tumbled to her shoulders, watched those aqua eyes, saw the worried look fall away, and fill with anticipation.

"Oh, there is. Come here, Dylan. I need you tonight."

That eagerness he saw in her eyes, knowing she wanted him as much as he wanted her had him pulling her greedily into his arms. "I thought it would take forever for everyone to go to bed."

He felt her pulse thump each time his lips nuzzled another area of throat.

The hunger gnawed between them.

She entwined both arms around the back of his head. "I was hoping we could go hiking while we were here, but I think Jake and Kit are going back to L.A. tomorrow. That means we lose our babysitters."

"Good." He slid his hands under her hips and tugged. "We can be alone then, run around naked in the house if we want," he told her with a twisted grin as he pressed his lips to hers.

She looked into his eyes, saw craving. Her juices flowed. "You want to run around naked," she asked as she nibbled back along his shoulder.

"We could stay naked all day if we want. I want you naked now, Baylee."

"You first," she demanded as she lifted his shirt over his head, tossing it onto the floor. Her fingers drifted to the button of his shorts. She worked it open and then slid down the zipper. Willing to oblige, he shed his shorts and underwear, stood before her.

She took a long measured look down his body and gestured with a curve of her finger to come closer. As he moved to her, over her, Baylee felt a warm liquid pooling between her legs.

"Let's get you out of these," he suggested. He worked to pull off her pajama top, his fingers spreading over silky skin. He moved his mouth down to her bared breasts, and began to nip and suckle generously with teeth and tongue.

A jolt of pleasure swam through her as she ran her fingers through his golden locks. At the idea they'd get to spend the night together, lie together in each other's arms, Baylee opened up, feeling sexy, bolder than before. She consumed his mouth again in a slow seductive tease before rolling over him. She began to make her way down his body, using lips and tongue to caress, to fondle, to stroke.

It was torture, thought Dylan, as he watched her move slowly down his upper body. He did his best to be patient, to let her explore, let her set the tempo, since she seemed so determine to play and take her time.

But when she continued to use mouth and tongue to lick and taste as she slowly made her way back up to his mouth, patience became difficult. "Come on, Baylee," he groaned in quiet desperate need. "Now."

Running her hands along his body, she slicked along at a leisurely pace. "I want you, Dylan."

With that, he sought her core. He began to work her, slowly at first. Stroke for stroke, she became hotter, wetter. He watched as her eyes heated, watched them change and darken, and sent her up, soaring through the bliss.

She rose up from release, still glassy-eyed. She pushed him back on the bed, straddled his hips, lowered herself onto him and began to ride, up and down, fast and furious, then slow, deliberate strokes, taking her time, but working toward that ultimate goal.

As soon as he felt her body began to quiver, he grabbed her hips and slammed into her, thrusting faster, deeper, bringing them both through the wave at the same time.

Sated, his brain struggled to form a single, coherent thought. He couldn't move. He couldn't remember the last time sex had been like this for him, completely gratifying on every level.

Baylee lay on top, boneless. "I know I need to move, but I'm not sure I can."

"Mmmm, know what you mean. Let's just lie here—and recover."

She rested her head on his chest. "Sure. Recover and then try it again. Maybe next time we'll get it right."

He laughed. "That's the spirit. We wouldn't want to waste a minute of our first night together."

Baylee smiled down at him. "Let's see whatcha got, Surfer Boy."

"Ah, a challenge," he muttered as he drew her down to him, began nuzzling and chewing on the soft curve of her neck again. "I'm good, but even I might need a twenty minute reprieve."

She responded by wiggling around on top of him—and felt him go hard inside her.

"Okay, I guess I've got super powers and didn't even know it," he joked as he tried to think if he'd ever felt this way before. But how could he concentrate on the past when Baylee kept doing all manner of creative things to his body.

And once brought to life, he decided to make the most of it.

After going at each other for a third time, they lay entangled in the sheets, spent, exhausted. Unable to move, he said, "I guess I know what to do in the future to get that worried look off your face."

Too relaxed to move, she laughed and moaned, "You have my permission to do that as often as necessary."

"I intend to as soon as I find another ounce of strength. Right now, I feel like Superman ran into a big dose of kryptonite."

She laughed and rolled into his sweaty chest. "I feel so—tingly."

He busted out laughing. "You should. I know how to turn you to mush now, woman."

"Then I like turning to mush."

His mouth met hers. The kiss had the heat building once again. "God, you're so incredible. But I honestly don't think I can manage it a fourth time." He grinned and pushed her hair off her face. "Give me a couple of hours though and I promise I'll deliver."

She chuckled, sucked the sweat off his neck. "Okay. I'll let you sleep."

"I slept late this morning, thanks to you. How about we talk about what Kit believes happened that night, her vision, for lack of a better word?"

She sighed. "It's possible, I guess. She's seeing what I see in my dream. And we know those two killed the Parkers. So there's that. But I'm having a tough time with my father's part in all of it."

"It must have been difficult for all of you growing up with parents, you know, like that, so cold and calculating."

"I don't want you pitying me, Dylan."

"It isn't pity exactly. It's—"

"Sure it is. You can't help it. It's human nature to feel sorry for someone who had the kind of childhood the three of us had. But why is it that a lot of people would rather believe child abuse occurs only in the lower economic echelon and doesn't think it happens in places like Beverly Hills? If you have money, live in a big house, you couldn't possibly abuse a child, right? If you think about it, the opposite is true. A person with money can hide it better, lie with conviction, make people believe what isn't true and then go to great expense to cover it up.

"I mean, just look at the school nurse, Mrs. Abbott. The woman knew every time I showed up at school with black and blue marks on my face. She'd ask what happened, all concerned. I'd tell her and yet when Dad showed up at school he had a good story at the ready like I'd run into the door or something. And then the same thing happened when Kit would come to school with bruises. Alana would show up at school; she'd tell her version, put on a stellar performance, something like, 'Oh, my little Kit is so uncoordinated. She's just the clumsiest little thing on two feet.' And yet, Mrs. Abbott must have believed my Dad and Alana rather than us because not once did the woman report the abuse to the authorities. Mrs. Abbott had to know the truth. She did the exact same thing with Quinn, too. Ask yourself why the woman wouldn't just make a call to Protective Services? The three of us decided that the only reason Mrs. Abbott would call home instead of the authorities is that they had to be giving her money, money to keep quiet. And if Dad paid her that meant Alana and Quinn's stepfather did too. But then what's a little blackmail in Beverly Hills between parents and the school nurse just to keep a little thing like child abuse a secret from Child Protective Services?"

Dylan couldn't believe what he was hearing. "The school nurse knew and did nothing? My God, how could she violate the law like that, live with the fact, sleep at night? How'd you guys get through all of it?"

"We tried not to go home, only when we had to."

"Oh, Baylee."

"And once we got out on our own, we eventually got the help we needed. For three years, sometimes twice a week, we'd meet for group therapy. Group therapy was cheaper for us than individual treatment, and we were on a tight budget back then. But that isn't the only reason group worked. Initially, we went together because, let's face it, we were our own support system. And we just didn't think anyone would believe us. Mrs. Abbott hadn't, so why would anyone else? Our parents had money. My father the well-known director, Quinn's stepfather, an influential man in the music industry, and of course, there was Alana, a successful businesswoman with Sumner and Jessica Boyd for friends, very powerful friends. But after our first couple of visits together as a group, Dr. Strasburg gave us a validation we'd never had, accepted what we had to say as fact. Except for the three of us, no one had ever done that before."

He stared at her angelic face, looked deep into those aqua eyes, saw the pain there. He wasn't exactly sure what to say. But he knew what would get her mind off the door he'd unintentionally thrust open. He moved to her mouth, began to leisurely run his hands down her body.

Sure enough, he discovered he had more energy than he thought.

☖ ☖ ☖ ☖ ☖

The sun filtering in through the window had her squinting into the morning light. Without moving her sore body too much, she reached an arm out to feel the other side of the bed. Empty. So he couldn't even bother to stay and snuggle, she thought lazily as she rolled to glance at the clock. 6:50.

My God had she really slept that late? She yawned and stretched. Her body felt thoroughly used. Dylan's lovemaking had her feeling more relaxed than she had in a year.

Sliding out of bed, she grabbed for her robe and smiled as she thought back to the kind of night they'd had. Marathon sex could be draining. She needed coffee. But as she tied the belt on the robe, she wondered why the house was so quiet.

She headed down the hall toward Sarah's room. Before she ever reached the open doorway, she heard the giggling first, then a genuine belly laugh from her six-month-old daughter. Her baby sounded happy, babbling in the way of all infants, content.

She pushed open the door wider and there, lying on the floor, was Dylan, stretched out on his stomach, stacking wooden blocks into a tall tower while Sarah sat in front of him taking delight in knocking them all down then clapping her little hands together.

She watched them from the doorway for a moment, the scene tugging at her heartstrings. Dylan looked like a proud father, spending precious alone time playing on the floor with his little girl. Could she pretend and make it true? Or was it a ridiculous fantasy she needed to stop weaving?

When Sarah spotted her mom, she began clapping her hands together. Dylan turned to catch her gaze. They stared at each other as desire sprang up between them in spite of the baby.

Sarah reached over, put both of her small hands on Dylan's cheeks, trying to get his attention, trying to get him to play with the blocks again.

Baylee watched as Dylan took the hint, slowly turning his face toward Sarah's. With his long frame, he playfully rolled into the blocks, knocking them all down for her benefit.

He scooped up the infant, the movement causing Sarah to giggle with glee. "I let you sleep in, thought you could use the extra hour after—the big night we had."

"Thank you. The extra sleep was appreciated. You changed her diaper." It wasn't a question.

"Piece of cake. No poop, just dripping wet. Took me a while to get it taped together with her squirming around, though, but then I'd watched you enough, thought I could handle it."

Baylee grinned. "Looks like you did an excellent job. She's gotta be hungry by now."

"Probably. But she's been a doll since we got up."

"I need coffee. Want me to bring you a cup when I come back up?"

"I'd love a cup."

"Breakfast in twenty minutes," she said as she turned to go and head downstairs, her heart feeling lighter than it had in months.

As she rounded the door in the kitchen, Baylee smelled freshly-brewed coffee and knew Kit was already there whipping up something tasty for breakfast. When Baylee walked in, sure enough, Kit stood at the counter, stirring batter in a bowl. She stopped long enough to look up at

Baylee. "Well, don't you look...rested." She wiggled her eyebrows up and down.

"What we did didn't exactly resemble rest," Baylee confided, as she took down a cup from the cupboard and walked to the coffeemaker. "You do get up early, don't you? Couldn't you at least sleep in today, let me take care of breakfast, while you take care of Jake?"

"Habit. And just so you know, I took care of him...twice. I took the initiative and threw together some pancake batter."

"By all means, your pancake batter is legendary. Believe me, Dylan will appreciate it. Where's Jake?"

"On the phone to Ireland again. He's relentless in trying to find Ben."

When Baylee turned around from the coffeemaker, Kit was grinning at her. Baylee went over and promptly wrapped her arms around her waist.

Kit reciprocated, leaning her head down on the top of Baylee's head. "It's about time you had sex. Just be careful. Don't get in over your head."

"Okay, Mom. I promise I'll be careful."

"Don't look at me like that. You know what I mean. That man's a player, Baylee. But God, he is a hunk. Besides, I wanted to talk to you. Alone. Without the guys. We didn't get much of a chance to hash out my..."

"Vision?"

"No. Yes. I need to explain a few things. First, it was different somehow when the people I saw Alana and Jessica murder were...strangers. I had never met the Parkers. That didn't come out right. But you know what I mean. I care that the Parkers were murdered, of course. But...well, this is after all, your mother I saw...pushed down the stairs...killed...murdered. Somehow, this seems more personal, even though I didn't know her I've seen pictures you've shown me from the time you were very small. These images in my head are—disturbing. The Parker murders haunted me for weeks, still do, but now..."

"You see my mother dead and it wasn't an accident. Alana and Jessica were involved. What no one's talking about, what you didn't mention, what none of us mentioned last night is why my father didn't do anything about it? I thought about this. He had to play some role in it. It's the only thing that explains why he ignores those women murdering his wife and doesn't bother reporting it to the police. But then he takes it a step further and makes up a story to cover for them."

"Maybe he didn't know right away."

"Oh, come on, Kit. You don't really believe that do you? Even though in my dream or memory or whatever the hell it is, I didn't see him when it happened. Do you really believe those two women didn't gloat at some point, didn't brag about what they'd done? Do you think for a minute they kept their secret from him? I don't believe that and neither do you."

"No. But I had to give it a shot. He might have found out after the fact. How long, I'm not sure." Kit frowned. "Maybe I'll work on that angle, see what I can...you know, see."

Baylee tilted her head to study Kit's face. "That is so weird, the way you do that I mean. Last night you went dead pale when it... Does it just pop into your head like that or what?"

"I think there has to be some motivation to go back into the past and see, back in time to view what happened. Alana's murder triggered the Parker dream. Once that surfaced it sort of opened a door. And I guess talking about your mother prompted this particular door to pop open." Kit shrugged. "Hey, I can't explain it any better than that."

Baylee heard footsteps overhead. "Do you know he let me sleep in this morning while he got up with Sarah?"

Kit smiled. "Not only a hottie but thoughtful."

"He is." And wasn't that a surprise. "You guys going back today?"

"Got to," she said, grinning. "I left the shop in Gloria's care. She says everything's running smoothly, but the truth is, I have a business to run. I won't let the Boyds ruin something I've put my life savings into."

"Just be careful, Kit. Collin is too much like Connor. And they're both like their mother."

"Insane," Kit agreed as she poured another cup of coffee.

By the time Dylan walked into the kitchen with the baby on his hip, Sarah was ready for her own breakfast. He took a long look at Baylee standing at the stove pouring pancake batter onto a griddle. He could get used to this. That brought him up short. When had he come to feel like that?

She turned and saw Dylan holding Sarah. Her breath backed up. He looked so natural with her, the resemblance between the two uncanny. Their same coloring made them look like father and daughter. Caught off guard by those thoughts, she simply waved Dylan into a chair until she could find her voice. Knowing his love for food, she finally squeaked out, "How many pancakes for starters?"

"Forget about me. I've got a hungry baby here. She's getting fussy, wants her momma."

Kit stepped to the stove to take over as Baylee took Sarah out of Dylan's arms. She immediately went to the kitchen table and sat down.

As Sarah began to nurse, Baylee's eyes drifted to Dylan's. Their eyes locked, held.

Dylan's mouth went dry. He forgot about everything else and saw only Baylee, the way the sun filtered through the kitchen window and fell on her golden hair.

Baylee saw him swallow, saw him move toward her, and felt him plant a gentle kiss on her forehead before moving to cover her mouth.

Dylan heard Kit clear her throat, heard the clang of a plate on the table. In spite of the distraction, he found it difficult to pull his eyes away from Baylee and the baby. When had they both snuck into his heart like this and taken over? Had he ever felt this kind of punch to the gut? Certainly not that he could remember. Understanding came slowly, like measuring the fierceness of an initial wave, before bracing for it to bash your head and take you under.

He heard Kit saying something.

"Go ahead and eat, Dylan, while they're hot. I'll go remind Jake that he wanted to leave this morning. He's probably forgotten all about the time."

But she might as well have been talking to herself for all the good it did. Kit left the kitchen wondering if that talk she'd had with Baylee might have come just a little too late. It looked as though her friend had already gone down for the third time.

CHAPTER 20

On his fourth day back at work in his Beverly Hills fifteenth-story corner office, Frank Geller sat at his desk trying to catch up on his month-old messages. Despite the early hour, despite the pot of coffee he'd already had, his mind was not on the job. At sixty-seven, Frank was more than ready to move on to retirement. He was tired of the daily grind, weary of the constant arguments with his law partners. Jessica and Sumner might have been dead, but they lived on in their three callous, cold sons.

Disgusted with his heavy caseload, litigations that had been stalling even before he'd taken time off, he wanted nothing more these days than to have some free time to spend with his new thirty-year-old bride, the woman who made him feel twenty years younger.

He wanted that simple life he'd been promised back in 1969. The life they'd lied and cheated and killed to get. The life he believed he would have had when he went along with what his two sisters, Jessica and Eva, and his brother-in-law had so meticulously planned out. And no one could forget the role Alana played in the whole thing. It had been a stroke of genius how she'd manipulated that poor sap, Forrester, into unwittingly providing those all-important documents they'd needed during the Parker's lawsuit. Who could have predicted McKetrick would have agreed to fork over fifteen million to those cattle-raising hicks?

Lady Luck had been on their side and continued to be when the Parker's son, Noah, went missing in Vietnam. That had been opportunity. And a Geller never let opportunity knock without answering.

They'd plotted and planned and stolen until even more millions had fallen into their laps. If those plans happened to include murdering said hicks, so be it. He'd been in on the strategy, the calculation, had even contributed his share to how it would all go down.

But he hadn't murdered anyone. At least, not that night.

The old couple had been distraught over their missing son in Vietnam, probably wouldn't have lived much longer anyway. They were old, at death's door. They'd have been dead inside of a year, Frank reasoned now.

The couple's trust fund had certainly provided all of them with a nice tidy life. You couldn't deny luck like that, or how all the stars had lined up, how everything had so neatly fallen into place. When it was meant to be, it was meant to be.

Certainly, none of them could have predicted the firm's overnight success from that moment forward over winning one little lawsuit. If it had brought fame and fortune to their door, they had gleefully reaped the rewards. When opportunity knocked, you certainly didn't tell it to go away.

Of course, along with all that fame and fortune, along with all that money, had come a heavier caseload, a lot of pressure, a great deal of stress. It had not been easy dealing with his overbearing sisters, Jessica and Eva, and Sumner, his controlling brother-in-law, on a daily basis. Every one of them could be pains in the ass and that was on a good day.

But that was in the past.

Frank had no doubt the firm was about to take a one-hundred-and-eighty-degree turn, a new direction under the leadership of his three brash nephews, Connor, Cade, and

Collin. He winced at the thought of his sons, Garrett, Scott, and Taylor having to deal with those three on a daily basis. The very thought made him break out in a cold sweat.

The Boyd sons were too hot-tempered and unpredictable to lead. Not to mention, they lacked that essential innate drive and ambition you couldn't teach, something that came from knowing lean, hungry years. Neither Connor nor Cade nor Collin knew anything about lean years. Their parents had seen to that. Now, they'd inherited the firm. With Sumner and Jessica no longer around to reel them in every now and again, there was no telling how far off the deep end they'd dive.

But it was no longer his problem. It was time to escape. No question, he deserved that simple life he'd been promised so very long ago.

As he shook himself back to the present, he was glad he'd taken his nephews' warning to heart. Frank wasn't stupid. He wasn't taking any unnecessary chances. He'd hired two of the best rent-a-cops he could get to watch his back, accompany him to and from work, stand guard at the door, make sure he was never alone. Even now as he sat here trying to get into the groove of work, he felt fairly safe.

It wasn't even seven-thirty yet. Trevor's plan couldn't have been simpler in its approach. If it all went the way he thought, there would be that certain element of surprise that always gave him that extra boost of adrenaline. The bodyguards Frank had hired weren't the brightest. They weren't in shape. They weren't even real bodyguards but rather glorified security guards used to walking around a parking lot marking tires. And that, of course, was a plus on his side.

But a true professional never took anything for granted or left anything to chance.

On cue, Trevor pushed the button on the recorder he held in his hand.

He watched from one of the vacant offices as the two-way radio strapped to the heaviest of the rent-a-cops crackled to life. The muddled voice, the garbled language, came out as something intelligible.

"Come back. I didn't copy that."

Again the distorted message filled the air. The message that wasn't meant for anyone to decipher, broke the silence. Suddenly, the rent-a-cop abandoned protocol and said simply, "Hey, Mike, is that you? I can't understand a word you're saying."

Clearer, but breaking up every third or fourth word or so, Trevor pushed the recorder again. This time the message coming over the two-way radio hinted at a disturbance on the fourteenth floor. "…Cory…got…trouble…floor fourteen…breaking glass… Cory… need…help…intruder… Cory…need…assistance…do you …copy? We've…got…trouble…need assistance."

Cory, who had been on the job for less than six months, never thought for a moment the call was fake. Trevor watched as Cory deserted his post outside Frank's office to go help out his buddy Mike.

Trevor grinned. Another plus in his favor. Well-intentioned, Cory had left poor Mr. Geller clearly unguarded.

A few minutes later, Trevor opened the door to Frank's office and stepped inside. Talk about feeling secure, the man never even so much as glanced up from the papers until Trevor walked up to the man's desk.

"Such a twit, did you really think they'd be able to keep me away?" He saw the shock register on Frank's face.

That boost kicked in.

Frank's eyes locked on Trevor's and froze. Automatically he reached for the phone.

Trevor placed a gloved hand over Frank's to still the motion. "I'm afraid it's too late to phone a friend."

"Who are you? Why are you killing my family?"

"Well, now, it's like this. Let me tell you a story."

"I don't have time for stories. Look, I have a fortune in a Swiss bank account. It's yours, just don't kill me."

Trevor shook his head and laughed. "Can't do it, mate. It wouldn't be fair to the others. Besides, Frank, they need you to argue leniency with the Devil. Even as we speak, they're waiting for you at the gates of hell."

"Wha…what are you doing?" Frank's eyes grew wide when he saw Trevor reach into his pocket and pull out a .22 Smith and Wesson.

"It's small but effective when fired from close range. And it never misses from a few inches away." He saw Frank swallow nervously, watched as his mouth went dry in fear.

"I'll give you anything you want. Look, I'm writing down my Swiss bank account number and the code you'll need as we speak." He shoved the piece of paper frantically toward Trevor.

"Sorry, mate. There's no bargaining in your future. That will only buy you a very quick suicide."

Ten minutes later, Trevor had just made his way out of the elevator to ground level when he felt the earth begin to shake. He saw the building sway, heard breaking glass above him and looked up in time to see broken shards rain down on his head. The quake had him taking off running through the parking structure as fast as he could to reach open space.

⚭ ⚭ ⚭ ⚭ ⚭

Connor, on the other hand, had made a side trip to Agoura Hills. At the same moment the ground stopped shaking, he was parked in his Hummer outside Gloria's house staring at Baylee's Range Rover which was parked in the driveway. It hadn't moved in days. He knew that for certain because he'd hired private security to stake out not only William Scott's house twenty-four-seven but also to babysit her car here in Agoura Hills. But she'd made no more slip-ups showing up here or at her father's house.

He'd been up most of the night. The trip to Gloria's house he now realized had been made on impulse and a mistake. He glanced over at the man sitting in a Chevy at the end of the street. Was that his security detail? he wondered as the two locked stares. It better be, he thought bitterly. The bitch was costing him a fortune and not for the first time.

His head pounded like a mutha. No one was getting him any results. Why couldn't anyone find one fucking woman with a little baby? If the answers weren't coming to him, he'd by God find his own. He opened the car door and climbed out. Maybe she was holed up inside the guest cottage after all, he decided, as he crossed the street and walked up the driveway between the Range Rover and Gloria's Honda Accord. He'd check the inside of the cottage for himself.

Walking her dog, Gloria saw him cross the street from the end of the block. For a bit of security, she reached down and snatched up Morty, her Chihuahua, from the pavement. She had no intentions of backing down from the likes of Connor Boyd. But as she got closer, she saw the vacant look in his eyes. Alarm crept up her back.

"Gloria."

"What are you doing here, Connor?"

"Where's Baylee?"

"You think I would tell you? Humph, I wouldn't, not even if I knew, which I don't."

When he got close enough, he reached out to grab her arm, but the dog had other ideas. Morty bared his teeth, growling. Connor jerked his hand back just in time. "Tell me where she is."

"I have no idea. I suggest you leave now, Connor, before I call the police."

With the dog in one hand, Gloria reached in her pocket with the other and pulled out her cell phone. "Do I make the call Connor, or do you leave? You don't frighten me for a minute."

"Look, old woman, you should be scared. But I'll leave, this time. Your threat to call the cops isn't why I'm going. I know plenty of cops. Answer me one thing, though. Is Baylee in that guest house around back?"

Gloria forced out a laugh. "Of course not. You're welcome to look and see for yourself."

Connor started walking to his car, jingling his keys, but turned back. "You know and I know that baby is mine. I intend to find her, Gloria. And when I do, I intend to get sole custody. Be sure to tell her that the next time you two talk. She can't hide from me forever." With that, he climbed back into the Hummer, started the engine, and barreled off down the street.

Gloria watched him go. "Oh, Baylee, I do hope Dylan has you well hidden. If not, we may have to get you out of the country…and fast."

⚛ ⚛ ⚛ ⚛ ⚛

At that very moment on Catalina, the not-so-well-hidden Baylee enjoyed a leisurely pace along the boardwalk in the sunshine with Dylan by her side as he pushed Sarah in her stroller. Headed down to the harbor to see Kit and Jake off to catch the ferry back to the mainland, the four of them watched the boats come and go as they kept up a steady stream of chatter before they reached the landing where the ferry waited.

"I miss having you and Sarah at the shop," Kit told Baylee.

"I miss the work. I even miss waiting on the cranky customers, even the commute into San Madrid every day. I guess I got used to that little fishing village more than I thought."

"When this is all over, you'll move into Gloria's house and make San Madrid your home."

"I can't wait. What is it you aren't telling me, Kit?"

"Be careful, Baylee." Kit glanced over Baylee's shoulder at Jake, who was deep in conversation with Dylan. She hoped Jake was doing what she could not, warning Dylan about Connor.

Just before the last call to board, Jake pulled Dylan aside and told him, "Stay on your toes. Kit got a call from Gloria before we left the house. Connor came by. She said the guy looked strung out, started ranting how Sarah was his, threatened to get sole custody."

Dylan's knees wanted to buckle. "Shit. This is exactly what Baylee feared. Jesus, Jake." He ran his hands through his long locks of hair. "I want to keep her safe. I'm not sure Catalina is going to get the job done, not far enough away, not by a long shot. How do you feel about me taking off for parts unknown? Because right now, I'm not so sure that isn't the best thing I can do for her."

Jake slapped Dylan on the back. "Dylan, I've known you since the first grade. Are you by any chance in over your head here?"

Dylan didn't have to ask what he meant. He rubbed his chin and looked over where Kit stood talking to Baylee. His world seemed a whole lot brighter. "I'm pretty sure I'm drowning, maybe going down for the last time."

"You couldn't have picked a better human being, and those eyes."

"Her legs aren't bad either," Dylan offered, but even the distraction couldn't lessen the tension. "Maybe I should take her to Canada."

"I know just how you feel. I've got a hearing coming up in less than a month that's supposed to put Collin away for a measly five years."

"That's not enough."

"You're telling me." He glanced over at Kit saying goodbye to Baylee and Sarah. "You let me know if you can talk Baylee into leaving her father. I'll use whatever you come up with to pack Kit off with you."

⚶⚶⚶⚶⚶

On their way back to the house, Dylan wondered if he should mention Connor's visit. But glancing over at the peaceful look on Baylee's face as she took pleasure in their walk, he decided to at least postpone the bad news until later, maybe after Sarah went down for her morning nap.

As they explored the shops along the boardwalk, Baylee itched to check out each quaint little store she passed along the narrow cobblestone pathways. The whole village looked as if it belonged along the Mediterranean.

Noticing Dylan had been exceptionally quiet, she decided to share her Catalina stories with him, ones about all the celebrities who had made the Island home over the years. "Not many people realize that Norma Jean Baker, aka Marilyn Monroe, lived here during 1942 while she was married to James Dougherty, who was in the merchant marine. The Island had been taken over by the military during the war and Dougherty was stationed here. While they were here they lived in an apartment overlooking Avalon harbor."

"I didn't know that."

"Not many do. But there's a museum here dedicated to all kinds of interesting tidbits, like the fact that *Mutiny on the Bounty* was filmed here, the one with Clark Gable. And John Wayne used to bring his family here for vacations. Charlie Chaplin used to come here to fish."

She looked so cute Dylan thought, as she talked and searched each store, each one selling their own version of touristy T-shirts, mugs, and a generous assortment of tacky souvenirs. Although she didn't buy anything, she was like a kid at Christmas. Watching her take pleasure in the hunt, he did his best to enjoy the ambiance of the place, but the conversation he'd had with Jake on the dock kept coming back to him in spades.

Connor knew Sarah was his. No, Dylan corrected, he suspected. Suspicions would only get you so far. But it seemed he was hot on their trail anyway.

Dylan began to deliberately check out their surroundings. They were virtually trapped here. Great places to hide, thought Dylan, as he scanned the gentle slopes and rolling hills of the place. Because most of the island fell under the protection of a conservancy established by the heirs to the Wrigley fortune, a good portion of it consisted of either natural habitat areas or designated campgrounds. Not that Connor was the type to ever get his hands dirty at a campsite or for that matter check out any natural habitat but his own, Dylan thought now.

• There were virtually no vehicles allowed on the island. A decade wait for permission to own a car here tended to put people off getting one. Most residents, as well as visitors, used golf carts to get from one site to another.

That was great if you had all the freaking time in the world, thought Dylan. But if Connor showed up unannounced… What the fuck good would a golf cart do if Connor paid them a surprise visit in the middle of the night and they needed to get out fast?

Dylan began to prepare an exit strategy.

But Sarah's fussiness interrupted his escape plans. Nap time. It took them all of three minutes to walk back up the hill to the house. Ten minutes later, she was snuggled down inside the Pack'N Play fast asleep.

As they stood there looking at the sleeping infant, a quiet settled over the house. The next couple of hours belonged to them. Dylan looked at Baylee. Heat flared between them. "What do you say we take our own version of a morning nap?"

Without saying a word, Baylee took his hand, pulled him out of the room and down the hall to the master bedroom.

☙ ☙ ☙ ☙ ☙

Head cocked to one side, Max St. John stood next to Frank Geller's desk, studying the position of his body. He didn't mind anyone settling old scores with these guys. From what he'd learned over the last month, they'd had their fingers in a lot of dark places. But it didn't really matter who the victims were, whether a hooker or a high-profile, highly paid attorney, no one murdered on his watch and got away with it.

He'd seen a lot over the years. In the old days this might have been deemed a suicide, plain and simple, and no one would have been the wiser. God, how he missed those days. How many more months did he have until retirement anyway? Too many, he thought sadly. Looking at the blood splatter on the wall, he knew one thing for sure. Whoever was out to get these people might possibly be the best he'd ever seen. And he'd seen a lot. He glanced up just in time to see his partner, Dan Holloway, stride into the room.

"I'd say it was suicide except for one small problem. We're standing in the office of the last original law partner and he's just become victim number..." Dan counted off the victims on his fingers. "By my count. five. This guy's good."

"Just thinking the same thing myself. But there's also this." Max held up a gloved hand, turned a gold cowboy the size of a toy soldier over for Dan to inspect. "He's also consistent. Five victims, five crime scenes with different caliber weapons used, including one where he used a knife. There are no patterns to speak of, except for leaving this gold cowboy at each scene."

"Five that we know of," Dan reminded him. "And the guy almost got Collin, the lucky SOB."

"Yeah. That we know of. We'll have to see, won't we? What it looks like and what it is are entirely two different things."

"Coroner's report and forensics will tell."

At that moment, Garrett Geller, the victim's son, appeared in the doorway.

"Get him out of here," Holloway bellowed to the uniform standing guard.

"He wouldn't have killed himself," Garrett yelled in protest when the guard tried to manhandle him back into the hallway. "He'd just gotten married, just got back from his honeymoon for God's sake. Can't you see that the same bastard who killed my aunts and my uncle did this? Can't you see that? What kind of morons are you? Anyone with a brain could figure this out. Don't go calling this a suicide."

"Get him out of here," directed Max. "And if you can't contain this crime scene any better than that I'll find someone who can."

With that, the uniform grabbed Geller and backed him forcibly out of the room.

Dan shook his head. "Even we morons know that our guy is responsible for what's starting to add up to a very impressive body count."

"You got that right. I'd say this is a personal vendetta. That's a given. You know, I got a curious phone call from a cold case detective, a Ron Blake, over at the Sheriff's Department. Double murder. 1969. An old couple named Pete and Mary Parker." He relayed the information to Dan about the couple's connection to the law firm, the lawsuit they'd won, the fifteen million at stake, and the codicil of the will where Jessica Boyd had been appointed the sole trustee of the estate, essentially removing the couple's son, Noah, out of the inheritance picture.

"I remember hearing about the lawsuit. The paper ran some kind of anniversary addition once, about how the case had essentially put Boyd Boyd Geller & Gatz on the map. Why'd he call you?"

"To confirm his prime suspects were my dead victims. Alana Stevens and Jessica Boyd."

Dan's mouth dropped open. "You're joking?"

"I wish I were. It seems Boston and his lawyer did a little end around, had a private detective deliver a .357 Magnum they found in the Stevens' attic. Ballistics match made in heaven."

"Son of a bitch. That might explain this whole thing."

Max nodded. "Looks like someone came back forty years later to settle a score. Any ideas?"

"Geez, the son, this Noah Parker would be my guess. But the guy would have to be in his sixties by this time, wouldn't he? Be easy enough to check. Run his name through the computer. That's why we live in the technology age."

"I did that. The son died two years ago. Looks like we'll just have to go where the wind takes us on this one, Dan."

⚜ ⚜ ⚜ ⚜ ⚜

Baylee's eyes flew open. She realized she was in bed. She glanced at the clock and stretched catlike. Not yet noon. When was the last time she'd had a morning nap? Inclining her head, she listened to the quiet of the house. Lazily, she rolled over and saw the empty side of the bed where Dylan had earlier done absolutely, amazingly sinful things to her body.

She ran her hand gently across the sheets—and smiled at the memory of each glorious one. The man had wonderful technique, skilled hands with long fingers; not to mention, he had an even better mouth.

Leaving her alone in bed was becoming a habit of his, she thought. So he wasn't the kind of guy who liked to stay in bed and snuggle. Well, there were worse things about a guy, she guessed, as she got up and threw on a pair of shorts and a cropped T-shirt.

She padded down the hall to check on Sarah. Expecting to see the baby still sleeping, she was surprised to find the crib empty. She headed downstairs, stopping long enough to listen when she got to the bottom step. The house was too quiet. Despite her relaxed state, nerves started to jangle along her spine. Where were they?

But then through the open windows, she heard Sarah giggle and Dylan's calming voice coming from outside on the back lawn. They were sitting on the grass playing with a large bright red ball. Where the ball had come from Baylee had no idea. But Sarah was having fun attacking it as it became clear Dylan was using the rubber orb as incentive to try to get her to crawl.

So far it was working. The baby kept trying to reach the ball, one little scoot at a time, and then up on all fours. Obviously, she hadn't yet gotten the hang of putting the whole motion together. But it wasn't for lack of trying.

Dylan glanced up, saw Baylee standing there in her little shorts and top, and sucked in a breath. She met his gaze. Dylan moved to scoop up Sarah, but Baylee shook her head and joined them on the grass. "It's beautiful here, peaceful. I like watching you with Sarah. You're good with her, Dylan."

"She's a joy to be around. So are you." He put Sarah back down on the grass.

Their eyes remained steady as they stared at each other, until finally Sarah squealed in delight as the ball rolled to her, breaking the trance.

"Anyone ready for lunch?" Baylee asked, lightheartedly.

"I could eat," Dylan said casually, trying to forget the punch to the gut he seemed to constantly feel around her.

"You can always eat." As she took off for the house, over her shoulder she offered, "I'm thinking thick grilled ham and cheese Paninis with lots of yummy cheese. Okay with you?"

With that itch in his belly, he watched her stroll back to the house. "You're making my mouth water."

Just before she stepped inside the kitchen, Baylee grinned to herself, knowing neither one of them was discussing food.

She dragged Sarah's high chair outside on the patio so the three of them could eat and watch the boat traffic come and go in the harbor. While she set the table and put out the food, she noticed Dylan had booted up his laptop. The intense look on his face told her something was wrong. He had already mentioned Connor's visit to Gloria. What now?

When she saw his face tighten yet again, she couldn't help it, she asked, "Okay, spill it, Dylan."

"Just another e-mail from our mysterious friend, giving us an update on Connor."

Dylan read the e-mail aloud, "Connor's on the prowl. Wherever you are, lay low. Remember don't use any credit cards for purchases. They can be tracked. Use cash only for everything. Don't make any slip-ups."

"Oh. I'm glad I didn't buy anything this morning. He really seems like he cares, this guy, this stranger, whoever he is. The question is why?"

"I don't know. But we're going to do exactly as he suggests and not use a single ATM or credit card transaction that can be traced back to either one of us."

Baylee noticed Dylan's thoughtful look and how he stared longingly at the water.

"Why don't you go surfing, Dylan? It'll relieve some of that stress. The water here is crystal clear. There isn't much of a wave to speak of, but you can go swimming. It's high time you enjoyed all the benefits the Island has to offer."

"I'm enjoying the best benefit of all." He shot her a wicked grin. "Let's all go down and sit on the beach."

When he leaned over in front of Sarah, he added, "What do you say, Gidget?"

"Sarah says it's a deal."

"What about Sarah's afternoon nap?" If anyone had suggested to him two weeks ago that he'd be concerned with anyone's nap but his own, he'd have laughed in their face. But now, he looked over at the baby sitting in her high chair. Funny how he'd done a complete one eighty in such a short amount of time. And no wonder. These two were his world now. But how would he ever convince Baylee of that?

"She'll sleep no matter where we are, at the beach or in the stroller. The important thing is you follow your own advice and try to relax, enjoy the time here. Who knows what the future holds for any of us?"

As he watched the sea breeze ruffle her hair, he realized truer words were never spoken. They needed to take advantage of the now. He moved to her then, sat beside her at the table, took her hand in his, brought it to his lips. "I'm crazy about you."

"You're just caught up in all this. It's easy to get drawn in, Dylan."

"Why do you do that? Why do you refuse to see what's happening between us when you know it's true?"

"I'm not saying I don't feel something. But it's a little soon, don't you think? I have Sarah to think about. I can't just..."

"Fall for a player. I got that, Baylee. But this is different. I'm different. The sooner you see it, the better off we'll both be." He stood up in a huff and started cleaning off the table, carrying the dishes back inside.

Baylee sat there looking at her daughter. "Men are complicated creatures, Sarah. The sooner you realize that, the easier life will be."

🔱 🔱 🔱 🔱 🔱

In order to lessen the chance they were being followed or tracked, Jake and Kit had taken the ferry from Catalina into Santa Barbara instead of docking at San Pedro. As they stood on the deck, Jake's arm went around Kit and he said, "We're playing the percentages. If by some chance Connor gets wind we were in Catalina, I'm hoping he'll think it was just for an overnight jaunt. The

Sea Warrior left in the middle of the night so there's not much chance he picked up on that."

"This is all so clandestine. I hope Baylee and Dylan remember to keep a low profile. I'm not even sure I should use my cell to call her anymore. What if Connor is keeping tabs on Baylee through me?" Even as Kit said the words from the ferry railing, she scanned the dock for any sign of a Boyd lurking about. "I won't kid you, Jake; I'm worried about Baylee. After talking to Gloria, that man isn't going to give up."

"Sick perverts rarely do. And something tells me the guy's getting more desperate by the day."

❧ ❧ ❧ ❧ ❧

After spending the afternoon at the beach, Dylan and Baylee came back and fixed supper together, thankfully back on solid ground again. Neither dared bringing up the earlier strained conversation about their "feelings."

As she bathed Sarah and got her ready for bed, Baylee reasoned that two people couldn't spend as much time together as she and Dylan had been doing lately without bumping heads every so often. It wasn't normal to think they could agree on everything, least of all how they felt about each other.

So what if she hadn't been honest? She knew she was falling for the guy. But it wouldn't do for him to know that. She might be rusty at the game, but she hadn't forgotten the rules. When all this was over, she was headed to Gloria's beach bungalow in San Madrid. He would pick up his game in Pacific Palisades as if they'd never shared this time together. End of story, Baylee thought, as she prepared to put an exhausted Sarah to bed.

Later that evening, settled at the dining room table with Dylan's laptop, heads huddled together in fierce concentration, they tried to come up with a website design for Baylee's jewelry business.

"Baylee's Beads, catchy title. I like that. What's your favorite color?"

"Soft blue, I guess."

"Of course, the aquamarine eyes," he said, as he let his fingers fly, tapping keystrokes in rapid fire succession.

"What?"

"Your eyes are the first thing I noticed that night at the hospital. They're almost the color of turquoise, only bluer, softer. Beautiful color. Since the goal is to get orders online, we'll make it easy to navigate, easy to sort through the catalog by category, bracelets, necklaces, earrings. Anything else?"

"Rings."

"Right. Got it." He hit the keyboard a couple of more times, and voila, her catalog appeared.

She sat back and inspected the screen. This was her first foray into owning a legitimate website. "You are amazing."

"That I am. Marvelous, actually. Glad you finally took note."

"And conceited of course. Did I mention over-inflated ego?"

"Let's not get carried away. My sensibilities might get bruised."

"You have no sensibilities," she said lightly.

With that, he drew her onto his lap, nuzzled her ear, then her neck. "I bet I can find each and every one of your sensibilities in a matter of minutes. Want me to prove it?"

She nuzzled back. "Mmmm, let me show you. Besides, I need to pay my web designer. It seems he did all this incredible work getting me online."

She picked up his hand and led him to the stairs. As he followed her down the hall to the bedroom, Dylan let her take the initiative. She seemed to thrill at taking the lead. When they got to the bed, she pushed him back and began to undress him. She pulled his T-shirt over his head and tossed it aside. She began to work the zipper on his shorts. When he was down to his underwear, he reached to undress her, but she pulled back just far enough and said, "I'll do it while you watch."

He liked that idea. As she began to move, to dance without music, he watched as she slowly, seductively started removing her top. She then ran her hands down her own body until she fingered the waistband of her shorts, began to shimmy out of them. By the time her hands moved to unsnap the bra, she had his mouth going dry. She slithered out of her panties. That was it for him. He'd used up all the patience he had. He reached for her. She pushed him further back on the bed, straddling him. She brought her lips down on his and whispered, "I want you, Dylan. I want you inside me. Now."

Baylee moved her hips. She flexed her muscles, continuing the dance, moving to an imaginary beat. She seemed determined to do the work. He took her lead, tried to hold back, waiting out her climax. The minute he felt her body start to tremble, he starting moving, began to build his own rhythm until a frenzied pace sent them both sailing through the glassy dune.

CHAPTER 21

In the dream, they were twelve, spending the last lazy days of summer vacation on Catalina, playing on the beach, running carefree along the sand.

With her long black hair flying loose in the sea breeze, Quinn as usual was out in front leading the pack, darting in and out of the waves, running at full throttle, her only speed. "Come on you guys, hurry up. We found it. It's ours. We need to claim it and drag the thing up here before the Fallon brothers see it and try to capture it as theirs. It's our ship."

Quinn had spotted the beat-up, old, wooden dinghy from the front deck of the house. She had taken off like a shot, encouraging Kit and Baylee at the top of her lungs to follow. They had been hot on her heels in pursuit ever since, trying to catch up with her to get a glimpse of Quinn's find.

"It wasn't here yesterday. I'm sure of it," Quinn yelled over her shoulder. "It must have washed ashore sometime during the night."

"It was that thunderstorm we had last night," Kit reasoned, as she caught up with Quinn just as they reached the vessel.

Out of breath, Baylee came up behind them. She looked down at the ten-foot rowboat with peeling green paint and rotten planking, listing badly at Quinn's feet. The poor thing had seen better days at sea. But to Baylee and Kit and Quinn, the old boat held the promise of hours and hours of something to do besides listen to grownups bitch and moan about their lives, watch on the sidelines as they drank booze, smoked weed, and take hit after hit of blow.

"Dad keeps some tools in the garage, paint too. We could fix that planking and repaint it."

"That's the idea," Quinn agreed. "But we need to pull it up to the house before someone else comes along and takes it. Like those Fallon boys. They're always getting in our business. You never know when they're out sneaking around, spying on us."

"They spy on us because Eric has a major crush on Kit."

"Bull. They spy on us 'cause they're dirtbags," Kit decided.

"That too," Baylee agreed. "But even when we get it back to the house, we'll need to keep it out of sight until we can get it seaworthy."

"Good thinking," Quinn said, as she reached down to grab hold of the bow. "You get the stern, Kit. Baylee and I will take the bow."

"Why do I always have to get one side all by myself?" Kit complained.

"Because you're a good head taller and stronger than both of us put together," Quinn told her emphatically. "Quit whining. The sooner we get the boat up to the house, the sooner we can start work on it. A little elbow grease and we'll get it back in the water inside of a week then christen it with a bottle of wine from William's stash."

It wasn't lost on either Kit or Baylee that it might take a lot more than elbow grease to make this broken-down tub seaworthy ever again. But neither girl felt like dampening Quinn's enthusiasm.

But just then, Kit let go of her side when she spotted Quinn's mother walking toward them. It wasn't quite eight o'clock in the morning and the way she walked gave Kit every indication that Ella was already plowed or maybe still high on the blow from the night before. Either one was enough of a reason to dread the woman's sudden appearance.

"Please tell me you are not bringing that disgusting piece of junk up to the house," Ella screamed at the trio.

With that, Quinn dropped her side as well, which caused what was left of the bow to bounce and land on Baylee's foot.

"Oww," Baylee moaned. "I think I got a splinter."

"See, that's the reason you do not need to be playing around with this broken-down piece of shit. Honestly, did it ever occur to any of you that you are girls, as in female? For chrissakes act like girls instead of like a bunch of heathens and grubby little boys. You should be playing dress-up or playing with dolls, maybe even getting into makeup, not out here on the beach with some nasty piece of garbage that floated in with the tide. How many times have I told you, Quinn, dirty and filthy is not an attractive feature?"

"Neither are drugs or booze," Quinn muttered.

"What did you say to me, you little shit? That's uncalled for. I'm the grownup here. You aren't. You'll do what I tell you when I tell you. Got it?" She turned to Kit then. "And for God's sakes, Kit, look at you. Your mother would faint if she could see you now. You have grime all over your face and you're all sweaty. You're all three disgusting."

Baylee saw Quinn wince while at the same time watched Kit take a step back in retreat at the harsh words. She knew that look on Quinn's face, the one that said, "I know I should have kept my mouth shut. But she makes me so mad, I can't help it."

Baylee understood that completely.

Ella's words had slurred then, the words coming in slow motion as the dream began to fade. What had Ella Canyon been doing on the beach in Catalina? Why was she there? Why had she intruded on the trip in the first place and why had she come along to ruin their adventure?

⚜ ⚜ ⚜ ⚜ ⚜

Dylan noticed Baylee tossing and turning in her sleep. When she started moaning, he leaned over and gently touched her arm. "Baylee, you're dreaming. What's wrong, baby?"

She sat upright in bed so fast she bumped heads with Dylan. "Whoa there, it's me, honey. It's me, Dylan. Relax now."

"I was dreaming," she squeaked out, sleepily. "We were kids, Quinn, Kit, and I."

"What was it about?"

"I'm not sure exactly. Nothing really." She rubbed her forehead, not sure if she understood why the dream had upset her.

"Baylee."

"Just an incident from childhood. It's nothing." But she needed to talk to Quinn and Kit.

"If it's nothing, why did it upset you?"

Even though sleep still muddled her thoughts, she managed to sputter out, "I'm not sure. But I remembered Quinn's mother, Ella Canyon, was with us here in Catalina. I hadn't remembered until now she made the trip over with us one summer." She told him about the scene on the beach. "Why would I dream about Quinn's mother? I haven't seen her in years. For some reason it was unsettling."

To Dylan, it didn't sound so bad. But he could tell she was upset by the way her entire body tensed. "I think you're on high alert, so much that any little thing is worrisome. Let me see what I can do to take your mind off your troubles."

Despite her frame of mind, the snicker slipped out. "Oh, Dylan. You're the best."

"I know. But you're supposed to reserve praise for after," he drawled, as he began to place kisses on her throat before moving to her mouth. "Luckily, I don't need much incentive."

"So I've noticed."

They made love, and afterward, Baylee spent a restless night, so much so that around five-thirty, she finally crawled out of bed, leaving Dylan snoring softly into his clump of pillows. As quietly as she could, she crept out of the room and down the hall to Sarah's room. Finding her daughter still sleeping, she headed downstairs to make a much-needed pot of coffee.

As she made her way into the kitchen, she decided she could get used to this sleeping through the night thing. It's a shame the dream had gotten in the way of enjoying it.

She couldn't figure out exactly what disturbed her about a dream when they were kids. There had been no violence, no argument, just the typical callous words from one of their parents. And for what? Ella had gotten offensive over an old dinghy.

Why would Ella's nastiness bother her after all these years?

She hadn't thought about Ella Canyon in years, and certainly not the brief time the three of them had spent on Catalina. The trips there that included her friends had always occurred during the summer. But if it weren't the harsh words from Quinn's mother that disturbed her, what was it? Had the scene actually taken place? Had Ella Canyon ever been on Catalina Island? And why did it matter?

After putting the coffee on, Baylee picked up the phone to call Kit. She would have called Quinn but knew if she weren't on duty at the hospital and had any downtime at all, she might not appreciate a call this early in the morning, especially about Ella. But one thing Baylee knew about Kit, you could always count on the woman being awake this early in the a.m.

She dialed Kit's number and waited for her to pick up.

"What's wrong?"

"You don't say hi anymore?"

"Not when you call this early. What's up, Baylee? Is it Connor?"

"No. I have a question. Do you ever remember Ella Canyon coming with us to Catalina? It would have been in August, I think."

"Well, that came out of left field. Whew! Let me see, weren't we twelve when she tagged along with us and your dad that summer? She was having some problems around that time."

"When wasn't Ella having problems?"

"Good point. As I remember, she horned in on our trip. None of us wanted her there, especially Quinn. Why?"

"So, she was there the day we found that old rowboat washed up on shore and she made us leave it there."

"Sure. She pitched a fit for no good reason and the Fallon brothers scooped it up out of nowhere and claimed our pirate ship for theirs. That pretty much ruined the rest of our stay while we had to watch them fix it up and get it in the water. What's this about Baylee?"

"I'm not sure. Do you think there was something going on between her and my father?"

"Oh, Baylee. Of course there was. They shared the same bedroom the whole time we were there. The woman had major drug problems around that time. She was using and drinking. For that matter, so was your dad."

"Ah, that's what I thought. Thanks, Kit. I just needed to kick-start my memory."

"Did you hear the news? Ballistics came back on the slugs they found at the crime scene back in '69. That .357 according to the Sheriff's Department was definitely the murder weapon used to kill the Parkers."

"Wow. You really did it, Kit. You solved a forty-year-old cold case."

"We all did, Baylee. And Jake thinks he's located Ben Griffin living on a farm in the countryside on the outskirts of Galway. He's sending an overnight package to the address he found. Maybe just maybe this is him and we'll finally get lucky."

Baylee could hear the excitement in Kit's voice. "You let me know when you and Jake make your travel arrangements. Don't take off in the middle of the night and head for Ireland without saying goodbye."

"Huh? The plan is to get him to make the trip over here. We discussed heading to Ireland and realized in the midst of all this it just isn't feasible. I'm not leaving you, Baylee. I may want to meet Ben, but I'm not going anywhere while Connor is on this obsession kick and Collin is waiting to pounce."

"Thanks, Kit. You know, I haven't said this in a while, but I love you."

"I love you, too. You're my rock. Always have been."

"Right backatcha." When she heard Sarah's voice over the baby monitor, Baylee told her, "I gotta go start breakfast. I want to make Dylan something special."

Kit chuckled. "Is that what you're calling it these days?"

Baylee hooted with laughter and hung up.

Fifteen minutes later, Baylee had the waffle iron going and the table set. Without a microwave, bacon sizzled on the stove, the old-fashioned way. The smell of breakfast cooking gave the house a homey feel. It reminded her of the many occasions growing up when she'd walked into the kitchen and found Tanya preparing breakfast. The memory made her smile.

She heard Dylan overhead, knew by his footsteps that he was more than likely taking Sarah out of the crib at that very moment.

A couple of minutes later, Dylan appeared in the kitchen doorway, carrying Sarah on his hip. Despite holding the baby, he looked sleep-tussled, like he needed coffee while little Sarah looked wide-awake ready for a brand new day. Baylee watched as he slipped Sarah into her high chair and walked to the coffeemaker, saw him stir in enough cream and sugar to choke a horse.

"Morning, Baylee." He leaned over and touched his lips to hers.

She smiled. "Breakfast is ready."

"It smells wonderful. But then so do you." With one hand, he pushed her hair back off her neck and placed a chaste kiss there.

"I smell like bacon."

He laughed. "That must be it then. I'm starving."

This seemed so easy, Baylee thought, as she forked a waffle onto a plate. She could visualize this scene playing out day in day out. Turning around at the stove, she noticed Dylan had already started mixing Sarah's cereal. Her breath caught. Her stomach fluttered and flip-flopped. When had that happened exactly? Oh. My. God. She was in love with Dylan Burke, all the way in love. Stupid. Stupid. Stupid. How could she have fallen in love this fast? Just because the man could charm panties off a mannequin didn't mean she had to take the fall like a love-struck teen. Okay, okay, she loved the guy. So what? It didn't mean she had to confess her every thought to him, did it? No, she had no desire to make an ass out of herself in the middle of what passed for her messed-up life. She would just have to bide her time. When this chaos was over, she'd somehow work on getting Dylan Burke wedged out of her heart. Even if it took a damn crowbar.

☙☙☙☙☙

It wasn't until later that day Baylee managed to reach Quinn at the hospital where the res was into her seventh hour of a twenty-four-hour shift.

"Hey, can you talk? I don't mean to interrupt your work but…there's something I need to ask you."

"No prob. Just finished putting fifteen stitches into the forearm of a guy who got a little too close to a switchblade."

"That sounds...horrible," Baylee said, her stomach pitching a little at the idea.

"Well, he said he had it coming since he made a play for his brother's woman and should have known better."

Baylee gasped in horror. "His brother cut him for making a pass at his girlfriend? That's barbaric."

Quinn snorted. "More like sliced him open. But that's life on the streets. Apparently. What's up?"

"I have a question about Ella Canyon."

"What has she done now?"

Through the cell phone, Baylee could hear the self-assurance go out of Quinn at the mere mention of her mother. "It isn't that. It's about...one summer. Were you aware she and my father were sleeping together during our trip to Catalina that summer we were twelve?"

"Sure. Who didn't Ella sleep with? That would be the short way to go. As I recall, your dad was her go-to guy for snow and weed that summer and her meal ticket for a month or so. Why? What's this about, Baylee?"

"Nothing really. It's just that I had this dream about that summer when we found the old rowboat that washed ashore. So Ella made the trip to Catalina with us then?"

"Yeah. She wormed her way in all right. Messed up the whole month of summer vacation, too. And then the minute we're back in L.A. she hit the road again, this time I think it was with a bodybuilder who happened to be into speed and ecstasy. But then I could be wrong. The bodybuilder might have been a couple of years later. The men came and went like a revolving door. It was hard to keep up with all the different men. After I turned ten, I stopped trying."

Baylee heard a beeper go off in the background. "Sorry, Quinn, I didn't mean to bring it all up again."

"No prob. Nothing like walking down memory lane chocked full of potholes. But I gotta go. Looks like I've got an accident victim coming in with a ruptured spleen. Cool. I haven't done one of those yet."

Baylee couldn't help it; she laughed. "Good luck then." When she ended the call she continued to be a little awed by Quinn's enthusiasm over ruptured organs. And didn't have a clue how her friend had chosen such a profession where she routinely worked with all that blood and sewing up people's limbs.

CHAPTER 22

For days he'd had someone searching the records in Vital Statistics. So far they'd come up with nothing, a great big fat zero. Connor was aggravated and growing edgier, if that were possible. He sat back in his desk chair and stared at Cade, who was in the process of trying to prove how industrious he'd been at hunting for any tidbit of information about Baylee and the baby.

"So far there's nothing at Vital Statistics. There's no birth certificate on file here in California. Could she have gone out of state?"

"Well. Yeah. Genius. The stupid bitch could have gone to any of the other forty-nine states. Why didn't she just tell me she was pregnant?"

To Cade the answer was pretty much a no-brainer. But he chose his words carefully. "If I had to guess I'd say it's because she knew how persuasive you can be at times when you want to get your way." He held up his hands when Connor gave him a look of contempt. "She might have thought you'd make certain she got rid of it."

The disdain left his face but was replaced by sheer indignation. "Well yeah, but that didn't happen, now did it? I might be a father and for months now she's denied me the right to my own flesh and blood. Any judge would see that as a father I deserve time with the kid." He slammed his fist down on the desk. "If that baby's mine, I want custody. To hell with what she wants. I wouldn't have the bitch now knowing she's been with that dildo Burke. If that's my kid, I want her. I want what's mine."

Cade looked into his brother's face, saw he needed some buoyancy. "With the right incentive, a judge might be persuaded to rule in favor of the father and give him full custody, especially if the woman in question is deemed unfit to be a mother."

Connor's demeanor brightened. "I could arrange that."

"Sure you could. Now for the bad news, bro. What if you're not the father? What if the baby actually belongs to this Burke guy? Have you thought of that?"

Connor shook his head. "I feel in my gut the baby's mine. And if it is, nothing will stop me from getting my daughter. I need to find her, Cade."

"Look, why don't you just ask her old man?"

"What?" Connor looked baffled at the idea.

"Taylor is the old man's attorney, has been for years. Send him in to do recon. Get him to visit the old guy under the guise of talking to him about his will or something and ask him pointblank where Baylee is. While he's at it, have Taylor grill him about the baby. From what I understand the guy's got one foot in the grave anyway."

"Cade, you're a fucking genius. All this time the answer's been right in front of me." He picked up the phone. "Taylor, get your ass in here. I need a favor. Now."

⚜⚜⚜⚜⚜

"**Just get the** old man to open up about Baylee or his granddaughter, anything at all just get him talking about them and keep pumping him for information." Like a broken record, Taylor Geller listened once again as Connor struck the same chord. Stuck on the same groove, he continued to harp on Taylor about how to talk to Baylee's father as they pulled into the driveway at 15202 Bel Green Drive.

Connor stared at his cousin, so like him in looks. Taylor had always been a bit of a goody two-shoes when it came to things like bribing a judge. But for a thing like this, he was the perfect stooge for the job. "You're good at shit like this. Just stick to the story about adding the new grandbaby to his will. Updating the will was a stroke of genius, and we should be home free."

Taylor looked agitated. He didn't like the idea of coming here to harass William Scott. The guy was dying, and he actually liked the aging director. But anytime Connor entered the mix it always turned into a disaster. You never quite knew if the man would blow up and hit something or you. Taylor'd gotten roped into this because he was the old guy's attorney, but he didn't like coming here acting like the eight-hundred-pound-gorilla, not one bit.

Connor absently adjusted his tie as he reached to ring the doorbell and reminded Taylor, once again, "You know these people better than I do, just don't fuck this up. There's a lot riding on finding out where that baby is."

When a small black woman opened the door, Taylor went into charm-mode. "Hi there, Ms. Lincoln, I called earlier about seeing William this afternoon. Is he ready for us?"

Tanya eyed the two men carefully before deciding to open the door wider and allow them inside. "When you called you didn't say anything about bringing anyone else with you, Taylor. You usually come alone. What's this about?"

"Well, it's like this, Ms. Lincoln. This is my cousin, Connor Boyd, who's in charge of the firm now that we've had a series of deaths in the family. We were doing some checking, going over some of our high profile client lists, William's name of course popped up. As we went through some of his papers, just routine stuff really, Connor here happened to mention that William's daughter, Baylee, had recently added a baby to her family."

Tanya eyed Connor suspiciously, giving him the once-over. "How did you know that?"

"Saw her the other day, Ms. Lincoln. Pretty as a picture, both mother and daughter, that is."

Taylor went on, as if nervous. "A birth is always a good excuse to go over the will, make sure everything's updated with the latest information and is in order, ready for anything. I just need a little more information, a date of birth, where the baby was born, and we can take care of this right here, right now, today, get the new grandbaby squared away in the will."

To Tanya the guy sounded too much like a used car salesman trying way too hard to close the sale before she walked off the lot. But the man was William's attorney. If they needed to add the baby to the will, so be it. She would see to it that they took care of every detail while William still had the energy and the time.

But as she showed them into the study, skepticism began to seep in, something she hadn't considered before she'd let them both in the house. Why did it take two attorneys to add a little baby to a will? These guys seemed a little too eager. "If you'll wait here, I'll go get William."

But when she told William about their visit, told him who was waiting for him, his eyes changed into cold fury. "Push me into the room and then leave us alone. I'll take care of this, Tanya."

When they got to the study, as soon as William heard Tanya close the door behind her, he turned a furious glare Connor's way and pointed a bony finger, demanding, "I want you out of my house. You think I don't know you. You think I don't know what you are. You're Jessica's oldest son. Trash is what you came from; trash is what you are now. Nothing can change that. Now get out of my house. Your mother ruined my life. That bitch ruined my fucking life. Now you get out of my house this very minute and never darken my door again."

"But sir," Taylor did his best to keep up the ruse for his cousin's benefit. "Your will. We understand you recently had a granddaughter. She isn't in the will. We need to add your granddaughter…"

William turned his cold, furious eyes on Taylor. "You aren't hearing me. You aren't adding anything to my will. I'll get new attorneys. Today. Now. Tanya, Tanya, where are you?" When the door flew open as if she'd been listening at the door, William turned in his chair. "Get these bastards out of my house, or I'll call the police." His face went white. His breathing became erratic, difficult. Tanya stood like an iron statue and demanded, "You heard the man, move. Get your asses out of here."

Taylor moved toward the door, but Connor stood planted where he was. "When did that bitch of a daughter deliver, William? When was your goddamned granddaughter born? What is her name? I'm not moving an inch until you give me some information, old man."

Despite the ashen gray look on William's face, he shook his head and managed to gasp out, "Then you'll…wait until…hell freezes over. Don't…" His wheezing grew worse. "Tanya, don't tell this son of a bitch…anything. Don't…say a word. Call… the… police. Now." As the air went out of his lungs, with each word, William gasped for breath.

Connor stepped to the wheelchair and grabbed William by the shirt. "I hope you die, old man. That baby is mine, and there's nothing you or anyone else can do to change that fact. I'll find out what I want to know one way or another with or without you. And when I do, I'll see to it that bitch of a daughter of yours is deemed unfit to raise my child, my daughter." He leaned further over him and taunted, "Do you hear that? Are you listening? Now, take that to your grave, you stupid, fucking old man." Connor stormed past him, leaving Tanya trembling. As soon as she saw William's condition, she grabbed for the phone and dialed 911.

△△△△△

Hours later, Tanya stood in the private room looking out the window at the night time traffic below. She watched the lights of the cars from the twelfth floor, as sadness swept over her. For thirty years she'd worked for William Scott. She'd kept secrets she had no business knowing. Now, it was time for all those secrets to see the light of day. Her sweet Baylee needed to know the truth. But even she didn't know all the particulars, no, not every detail. She'd had questions. She'd asked so many times and gotten no answers. She was just the housekeeper, the nanny, the one who tried to provide a decent home for a little girl left without a mother.

If William died without ever revealing the truth, Tanya knew Baylee would turn to her, ask all those questions all over again, and she wasn't the one who could provide the answers. Tanya had done everything she could do for William. She glanced over and looked at the man lying in the bed. He was rambling again, had been since the doctors had admitted him. Even the nurses said it wasn't the medication, since he'd refused anything for pain except what they'd given him when he got here.

An hour ago, during his latest round of outbursts, William had demanded to see his daughter, telling Tanya there was something he needed to tell Baylee before he got worse. His rants were difficult to understand because he kept going in and out of consciousness, from present day to the past. None of it made any sense to Tanya. And that was the problem. Baylee needed to know the truth about her mother and she needed to hear it from her father. Despite the lateness of the hour Tanya checked the time on her watch. Maybe William's revelation could wait until morning, but she couldn't be certain of that. There had already been enough time wasted. She pulled out her cell phone. No better time than now for William to unburden his guilt.

△△△△△

On Catalina Island, Baylee's cell phone rang.

Dylan sprang up out of bed like he'd been shot, immediately going on alert. But when he realized it was simply a ringing phone, he scrubbed a hand over his face and reached over to the bedside table. When he saw Tanya's number displayed in the digital readout, a number of scenarios ran through his head. At two in the morning, this probably wasn't good news. He glanced over at Baylee, who was just now beginning to stir from the sound of the ringing phone.

"Dylan, I hate to wake you. But you need to get Baylee here fast. There's no good time for this. I don't think William has much longer. He's in a bad way. You'd better prepare Baylee for the worst. And Dylan, Connor came to the house. He's going crazy trying to find out where she is. He was furious when William wouldn't tell him anything. William made him leave the house. Connor went into a rage."

Dylan blew out a breath. "We're on our way." He looked at Baylee's face and sighed. "We need to go. I'm sorry Baylee. It doesn't look good."

For the next twenty minutes, Dylan put his exit strategy into play, which really amounted to nothing more than calling in a favor from a friend. Thanks to a surfing buddy he knew who flew helicopters for one of the major corporations in Los Angeles, Dylan and Baylee and Sarah were airborne within forty-five minutes after Tanya's phone call.

Thirty minutes after that, a taxi picked them up from Santa Monica Airport and took them to the Medical Center. With Sarah still tucked into the infant carrier fast asleep, Baylee and Dylan walked into the hospital a little before dawn. They took the elevator up to the twelfth floor where Tanya was waiting for them in the hallway. She ushered them in the direction of William's room.

"How bad is it?"

"He's been asking for you. There's something troubling him, has been for months now, Baylee. He needs to unburden himself. I want you to keep an open mind."

"You know, don't you, Tanya? It's about my mother, isn't it?"

"I don't have the answers, child. But he does."

"Will you keep an eye on Sarah for us? I need Dylan to come with me. I don't want to do this alone."

But as soon as Baylee and Dylan pushed open the door, they saw bedlam. Doctors and nurses surrounded William's hospital bed, a crash cart to one side. One doctor worked frantically on him, paddles still in hand. Baylee heard the loud bleep of a heart monitor. She felt Dylan's arms go around her. She stood back watching, wondering if her father would make it. Suddenly she was torn, filled with concern about her father but upset that she'd come so close to finding out the truth about her mother only to be denied yet again.

It seemed like an eternity before the team got him stabilized, got him breathing on his own. The lead doctor took one look at the visitors and motioned them back out into the corridor.

⚛⚛⚛⚛⚛

William fought for his life. He stared down a bluish white light shining brightly from a dark, elongated tunnel.

He remembered a wild night of sex, the booze and cocaine flowing plentiful. Not a party exactly, but he couldn't get rid of the image of a hotel room with a king-sized bed where he lay naked with two gorgeous females, one stunningly blonde and the other equally beautiful with silky black hair down to her ass.

The three of them were wrapped up in each other, enjoying each other. They had been at it for hours. He remembered the two women bickering, gossiping, both trying to one-up the other with how much they'd spent on jewels, clothes, cars. The list was endless, the competition between the two always fierce. But he recalled how the talk always returned to their two favorite subjects, sex and money.

As they all three lay sprawled among the sheets, the conversation came back to William in sickening clarity.

"What did I tell you? Didn't I say he was worth it?"

"I had to try him out for myself, didn't I? He has terrific stamina."

"Now that he's single again, we can do this as often as we like." Alana turned to William. "I told you the little prude was no good for you. I'm the only one you need, William, the only one who knows what you like. You know that."

The black-haired beauty laughed at that as she moved out of bed, naked. "Oh, I wouldn't say that. We both can make William happy. Three is a lot more fun than two; two's boring. Alana and I know how to do all kinds of things much better than the little wife ever could."

"Let's have some more champagne and celebrate William's newfound freedom." Alana crawled out of bed to pour the wine and picked up an overturned glass off the floor in the process. Stumbling in the direction of the bottle of champagne still on the room service cart, she bumped into the wall. "The way Jess and I took care of things, you won't even have to get a divorce."

"Why's that?" William asked, still dazed from the sex and the lines of blow he'd inhaled.

Jess staggered over to where Alana stood, tried to help her with the pouring. "Because, you idiot, you can't divorce her when she's dead."

The hairs on the back of William's neck stood up as he stared at the two women. But it wasn't their nakedness that had his attention. "Alana, what the fuck is she talking about? What did you do?"

"Oh, William, don't be so dense. Jessica and I took care of your whining little problem, that's all. Well, our problem, really. No more bitchy little wife to nag you. It's as simple as that." Alana giggled. "You won't have to worry about a custody battle or paying that bitch any kind of alimony, no settlement. She's gone. And she isn't coming back." Alana laughed at her own joke.

"What did you do? You told me she was having an affair with Luc. That she ran off to Europe with the tennis pro and left Baylee alone in the middle of the night."

"Oh, William, how stupid you are. You told me you wanted out of your marriage. You've been telling me that for years. What did you expect me to do? I got impatient. Jess and I made that whole story up. We're the ones who started the rumor at the country club." She giggled again, which set Jessica into full-blown laughter. "We got rid of Sarah and Luc in one fell swoop."

Lana waved her arms in the air in an exaggerated fashion. "We had to start the rumor about the affair. Little goody two-shoes Sarah was too tight-assed to ever cheat on you. Don't you know that? She was too concerned about spending time with her little brat to spend any time with Luc. So we got creative."

"We're an amazing team, aren't we? Lana and I make sure we get what we want." Jess put her arm around Lana and they did a little dance, giving each other high-fives.

William had a sick look on his face. The blow was already starting to wear off. Were they joking? Alana was always kidding around about all kinds of stuff. That was it. They were just kidding him, trying to get a reaction. It was a bad joke; that's all it was. Suddenly, he was aware of the pounding in his head. He slowly got up out of bed, reached for his robe. "What did you do to Sarah?" he asked, half expecting them to confess they weren't serious.

"Jess pushed her down the stairs."

William staggered back against the wall.

"Yeah, but not before Lana here gave her a wicked right cross that sent her reeling. That gave me the chance to finish her off."

"Hey, she was no match for me, petite little bitch." Alana flexed her arms in a power stance that had William feeling like he was about to throw up. He took a step toward the bathroom, away from the faces of evil. He had to know, had to ask. "What about Luc?"

Jess tossed back her hair. "Oh, Luc was easy. We lured him back to Alana's place, offered him a sample of our best disco biscuits—and boom! Next thing you know, he's sprawled on the floor, dead as a doornail."

"Okay, so I gave him a little too much shit." Alana laughed wickedly. "Since we were on a roll, we went over to your house, paid a visit to your darling little Sarah. The little woman had the nerve to get all indignant, had the audacity to ask us to leave, threatened to call the police if you can believe that. Jess here took it personally."

Stunned, William wanted to know all of it. "Where are they?"

"Don't worry about it. They're dead and buried. No one will ever find them. Trust me."

William threw off the robe and started putting on his pants.

"Where do you think you're going? We aren't finished with you yet."

"I need to go check on Baylee."

But Jessica sensed something was up. She narrowed her eyes. "Don't even think about it, William."

In the blink of an eye, Jess turned on her best friend. "You just had to open your big fucking mouth, didn't you? He's going to blab first chance he gets."

Jessica whirled around to William. "You say anything to anyone, anything at all, you so much as breathe a word of what we said here tonight and I'll make sure the police know it was your idea. They go really hard in this state on husbands who solicit murder for hire. Oh, yes, Alana and I will simply tell them you wanted your wife out of the picture. We'll both testify against you."

Alana grabbed Jess's arm. "But he won't do that, will you, William? We're in this together. You'll keep our little secret because if you don't, you know you might be next. Isn't that right, William, my love? You say anything to anyone and that daughter of yours might suffer a terrible, unfortunate accident."

The memory came to him in clarifying detail how he'd run into the bathroom just in time to throw up.

"You say anything to anyone and that daughter of yours might suffer a terrible unfortunate accident." For years those words had haunted him. It played over and over again like a bad movie, his worst.

Even now lying on his deathbed, William still heard those words, those shrill, harsh words he would never forget no matter how long he lived. It came to William then. He didn't have all that much longer. Life for him was almost done.

Baylee touched her father's cheek. His eyes flew open. "Daddy, I'm here now. It's okay; don't worry, I'm here now. Daddy, look at me. Do you hear me?"

When his eyes settled on his daughter's face, it took him a few seconds to come back to the present. His body felt like he was still in that hotel bathroom after a night of drugs and booze. His gut burned; his chest hurt. He still remembered the way he'd thrown up. His eyes glanced around the room. He remembered then that he was hooked up to machines in a hospital room.

Things were as bad as they could get.

"Baylee," he croaked out. He tried to remove the oxygen tube from around his nose. "There's something I have to say, to tell you…before I leave. It's hard to tell." He wheezed, his air closing up. "But you need to know the truth about your mother, hear the truth from me." The words were raspy. "Sarah never left, at least not the way I led you to believe."

God help her, she knew what he was about to say and couldn't hear this from him by herself. She started backing toward the door. Dylan had gone to find Tanya, tell her what was happening. But now, she had to find him. She couldn't travel down this path without him.

"Dylan, get in here," she yelled frantically, keeping her eyes glued to her father. She watched as William tried to sit up in bed. She went to him then, attempted to get him to lie back down. It wasn't difficult to do. One push and he was flat on his back again.

Dylan came into the room on the run. He took one look at Baylee's struggle and then stared at her father. Noting the alarm on William's face, Dylan went to help. "Has he said anything?"

William motioned for them both to come closer. "I can't...talk so loud." His rheumy eyes searched Dylan's. "She's...upset with me. She has a right to be. I've been a lousy father. And I'm about to upset her even more. It's about her mother, my lovely, gentle Sarah. She died, Baylee. Your mother never walked out on you."

No matter how much she'd talked about it with Dylan and Kit and Jake, she wasn't prepared to hear the words. Her knees locked. She felt weak and sick to her stomach. "What are you saying, Daddy? I want to know all of it."

Whispering the worst of it now, he rasped on. "I'm saying...Alana and Jessica...they killed your mother. Alana wanted us to be together. She took it upon herself..." He saw the doubt in Baylee's eyes. "You have to believe me. I had no idea she would hurt Sarah, let alone... It's the last thing I wanted. It happened while I was out of town. While I was in San Francisco, Alana and Jessica went to the house...they confronted Sarah. There was a struggle. Jessica pushed her down the stairs. Before, before Sarah, they lured her friend, that tennis pro, back to their house, gave him enough drugs to make sure he OD'd. I'm not sure of all the details. All I know is they killed Sarah; they got rid of Luc. Sarah and Luc were never a couple. They're both...dead."

"Daddy, why didn't you do something? Why didn't you go to the police? Why did you allow them to get away with doing something like that? Why?"

Breathing labored, William winced, "They said if I told anyone, they'd see to it that the police would think I was in on it. They threatened you." William started to sob. "If I said anything, Alana assured me she'd see to it that you had an accident. I made a mistake, Baylee, a big one. Alana and I had known each other for years, for years, Baylee; we had a history. After I married your mother, I kept the affair going with Alana." If it were possible, the shame and guilt had William's voice growing weaker. "The woman wouldn't leave me alone. I'm not making excuses. But she was...relentless. Alana was my weakness. Alana and Jessica were my weaknesses. I'm sorry, Baylee. They took Sarah away from both of us."

Baylee felt numb. She'd already known most everything he'd admitted. Thanks to Kit, thanks to Dylan, she'd been prepared for the fact that her mother was dead. But it didn't make hearing the words out of her father's own mouth any less horrendous. Validation after all these years seemed rather pointless, anti-climactic even.

As if he understood, it was Dylan who carefully framed his words. "Where are they, William? What did Alana and Jessica do with the bodies?"

"I...I...I'm not sure exactly, buried them...somewhere."

Dylan knew he was lying. His disgust came out in his tone. "William, you were married to the woman; she was the mother of your only child and you didn't bother to find out what those women did with Sarah's body? I'm not buying it."

"Don't judge me. I...I...I was weak. I know that. I let Alana and Jessica get away with murder. They were evil. I didn't want any harm to come to Baylee. Don't you understand that?"

He turned his head to look at Baylee. "That's why I never trusted her whenever you went down to Kit's. Within the year, we stopped seeing each other. It was over, done. I stayed away from her; she stayed away from me. That was the deal."

All of a sudden fury ran through Baylee like a blazing, out-of-control wildfire. "My God, all this and you could have just gotten a divorce. You bastard. I found her journals. She hid them away. She tried to make the marriage work from day one, but you never did. Her journals paint a very disgusting picture of what she endured during her marriage. You didn't deserve her. You didn't even want me."

William's eyes went wide with shock. Rasping he explained, "That was a gut reaction. After you…were born, after…I held you for the first time…I changed."

"Obviously, you didn't change…at all…you continued seeing that evil bitch the entire time you were married. She and Jessica killed my mother. I hope it was worth it, Daddy. I hope every time you fucked her it was worth my mother's life." With that, Baylee turned and flew out of the room, away from William's bedside.

But Dylan stayed rooted to the spot, boring holes through the man until finally William felt his stare and reluctantly looked away. But Dylan was determined. He took William's face and turned it back to force the man to look at him. Certain Dylan had his attention, he leaned in, and whispered, "Where are the bodies, William? What did Alana and Jessica do with Sarah and Luc?"

Dylan saw William swallow hard before the man started to sob again. But Dylan refused to be moved by the man's display of emotion. He thought of Baylee. Another wave of disgust hit him. Making sure his tone was more forceful this time, Dylan met the old man's eyes. "It's just the two of us here now, William. Tell me where they buried the bodies."

☸☸☸☸☸

Dylan went in search of Baylee. There was no doubt in his mind it would fall to him to tell her what he'd learned from William. He needed to make a couple of calls first, one to Reese to make sure they had the legal aspects covered, and then he'd have to make the necessary calls to the authorities, make them aware of the situation. If that meant a phone call to Max St. John or to Dan Holloway, then maybe he'd have Reese take care of that chore as well.

What arrangements did one make in order to begin the process of digging up bodies buried on the sprawling grounds of a private residence in Malibu? How many acres did the Boyd compound cover anyway? Would they be able to rely on William's description of where the bodies of Sarah Moreland and Luc Delaine had ended up? No, they'd probably use cadaver dogs for that job, thought Dylan, as he added another call to his mental checklist.

Dylan shook his head thinking about his conversation with William. He'd practically had to force the old man into spilling what he knew. As he walked toward the waiting room, hoping Baylee had sought out Tanya for comfort there and hadn't gone farther, he realized it was a shame William couldn't have been a little bit more specific. But so help him God, Dylan knew one thing, if it took days or weeks or months, he would not rest until he found the remains of Baylee's mother. Sarah Moreland deserved a proper burial. Luc, too, for that matter. But more than that, Baylee deserved to find her mother, to know where she was once and for all, and if possible, put all of this behind her so they could move forward to a future together.

When Dylan spotted Baylee wrapped up in Tanya's embrace in the waiting room, he breathed a sigh of relief. Approaching the two of them with caution, he waited for a sign that it was okay to intrude upon their moment. He didn't have to wait long. The second Baylee spotted him, she all but melted into his arms.

"When do you think they did it, Dylan? When did it happen?"

But Tanya didn't give him a chance to answer. Tired to the bone, she spoke up and said, "May, Mother's Day. It was a Sunday. I had that day off. That's when she disappeared, Baylee."

Dylan held out his arms to take Sarah, and she grabbed on to his shirt. "Karen said the last time she talked to your mother it was Mother's Day. So, I'm thinking it was sometime after she put you to bed that night."

"I came to work the next morning at seven. You were distraught, upset. You thought you'd had a bad dream. You told me someone pushed your mama down the stairs. Child, I thought you'd had a bad dream. I swear I did."

"My God, Tanya. Did you know? Did you know then what they'd done and didn't say anything either?"

"How could you think that? Of course not. I suspected something bad had happened, yes, that's true. Because I knew your mama. I knew she wouldn't have just up and run off like they said she did. But I didn't know what exactly had happened. I knew William had affairs. And I knew that Alana was one of the women he wouldn't stop seeing because that woman called the house night and day sometimes. And I suspected Jessica Boyd was another one he saw frequently. But I didn't have proof about anything, just my suspicions. I never thought your mama left with that Luc fellow. Not in a million years.

"For years I listened to that man rant and go on about what 'those two women' did to his Sarah. But it was always during times he'd been drowning himself in a bottle or two of whiskey. Then he'd get the shakes, pass out, and then the next day when I'd ask him about what he'd said, he'd claim he didn't remember a thing about his ranting and raving. But I knew your father acted guilty about something. I just didn't know what it was.

"But there's something I want you to keep in mind about that night, the night those two women hurt your mother. They left a three-year-old child alone in that house all night long by herself. Those two women didn't have the maternal instincts of an alley cat between them, if you ask me."

Disgusted, Baylee stared at Tanya. "You got there that morning. I'd been hiding under the bed. And together we went looking for her all over the house. We searched the entire grounds for hours and hours. I remember how I cried and cried. Oh, Tanya. What kind of evil would make those two women kill her like that? They took my mother from me. And my father helped them lie about it."

"I wasn't sure what happened between your father and Alana. But I do know she stopped calling about six months after. That would have been around Christmastime. Your father's drinking got worse then, Baylee. During those days he never brought women home with him, but he stayed away for weeks at a time, like he didn't want to be in that house.

"I would have quit, Baylee-girl, if not for you. But I just couldn't leave my baby for William to raise when I knew all the man would do is hire some stranger in off the street to take care of you. I couldn't do that."

Tanya broke down then and Baylee went to her, wrapped her up.

Dylan simply let them cry it out because he'd never seen a situation as sad as this one. And when she was ready, he made sure he held on to Baylee as if his life depended on it.

Because he was beginning to think it did.

🜋🜋🜋🜋🜋

Getting Reese involved was the best idea he'd had in days. Reese handled all the calls, all the details so that by noon the wheels were already in motion. While Dylan and Jake waited outside William's room in the hallway Reese was inside with Max St. John and Dan Holloway taking the old guy's statement. It was no surprise that William had hired Reese, especially since Tanya had mentioned he'd fired Taylor Geller.

When the door finally opened and Reese emerged with the two detectives, Reese motioned for his friends to follow them down the hall to the waiting room.

"I'm pretty sure you have enough to get a search warrant," Reese said to Max.

Max nodded in agreement. "I'll make the call to the DA. Getting a court order from a judge is the next step."

"Lots of luck with that. You'll have to find a judge that isn't in their back pocket."

"Cynicism there, Mr. Brennan?"

"Maybe. But I've been up against them in court; I know what they're capable of. Where are you in the rest of this?"

Max bristled at the implication. "I'm doing my job, counselor. You let me take care of it. I'll work on finding a judge if I have to go through a dozen to do it. If I can get the court order today, I'll have the cadaver dogs in there first thing in the morning to search all sixty-five acres."

"So William couldn't be more specific than that?" Dylan asked.

Max shook his head. "No. And there's the problem. He thinks Jessica told him the bodies were either buried next to the reflecting pool near the main cabana, or where the old pool house used to be. He isn't exactly sure. To make matters worse, he claims he hasn't been on the property for over twenty years. His memory isn't all that good."

"Do you think he's lying?" Jake asked. "Trying to cover up his part in all of this?"

"That's something that will have to be determined, to be checked out. Later. He's agreed to talk to us again tomorrow. We're taking advantage of that before…"

"If he's able you mean. Do you think he has that long?" Reese asked. "The man looks like he's on his last leg."

Dan chimed in, "We'll see. I'm headed now to talk to his doctors."

"There's always a chance that Jessica could have been lying about where they buried the bodies in the first place," Dylan pointed out. He gave Reese and Jake a tight look. "Why do I get the feeling Jessica and Alana were probably lying to him?"

"From what I've discovered about the two women, I'd say that's very likely," Max agreed. "But we'll start in the direction he gave us and spread out from there."

Holloway threw in, "It really doesn't matter if they were lying. We'll know soon enough when the dogs go over every inch of the place. There are no less than seven main houses and four guest bungalows near the cliffs. We'll leave no stone unturned."

And Max added, "I hope you know this is going to take some time. Don't expect miracles, people. This process is slow. Don't expect answers any time soon. It's a very large estate, a lot of ground to cover."

"That's what I was afraid of," Dylan said miserably.

CHAPTER 23

"**W**hat the fuck is this?" Connor railed, as Max St. John handed him a piece of paper. When he realized it was a search warrant, he ran his hand through his hair and stared hard at the detective. "You have no right to come in here and do this. This is bullshit. I'll have your badge for this, you son of a bitch. I'll make sure your retirement comes next week. I'll get a judge to squash this before you've gone thirty feet."

"Are you finished, Mr. Boyd? Because until you do all of those things, we're going to turn this place on its end."

"Just what the fuck do you think you'll find?" Cade demanded.

"Read the warrant. We're looking for two bodies."

"Bodies? Are you fucking nuts?" Collin fumed, as he stood flanked by his brothers. "You won't find bodies here. This isn't a cemetery for chrissakes."

"Then you have nothing to worry about," Max insisted. He motioned for the uniformed officers to get the cadaver dogs ready. "All of you will need to find another place to stay until we're done."

"And when exactly will that be?" Connor demanded.

"Until we're done. We'll also search every house on the grounds, which includes the one you're now standing in." Max turned back to his search team, shouted out orders. "Start with the cabana house and then move on to where Mr. Scott indicated near the reflecting pool. And try to locate the groundskeeper. He may be able to provide us with additional information as to how long these buildings have been here."

"Old man Scott did all this? You'd believe anything that doddering old fool told you?" Connor accused.

"He's implicated your mother in a double murder. You're an attorney, Mr. Boyd, all of you are. You know how this works. This is a legal, court-sanctioned search."

"We'll see about that," Connor said before warning, "My mother is fucking dead. Or have you forgotten that, you stupid bastard? It may be legal, but someone's going to pay for this."

Max watched the three brothers as they stormed off in the general direction of the circular driveway out front. "Those are several pissed off people. We better hurry this along. They might make good on their threat to find the right judge to squash this thing. Let's get to work, people. Let's make every minute count while we have the chance."

Inside William's hospital room, Baylee hadn't left his bedside for almost twelve continuous hours. During that time, the man's condition had deteriorated. His blood pressure had dropped, his pulse was weak. William hadn't uttered another word since his deadly revelation to Dylan and then went through it all again for Reese's benefit, as well as, the two detectives.

They'd recorded and transcribed William's statement officially. Reese had agreed to make the changes to his will effective immediately, which seem to please the old guy. But because he'd slipped into a coma, the last hours had dragged by without any more shocking disclosures.

Quinn had been darting in and out all day, checking on Baylee and Sarah whenever time permitted, whenever she wasn't tending to people in the ER. Kit and Jake had just left to go grab a shower and a meal at Gloria's and had promised to come back to look after Sarah while Tanya took a breather.

Everyone had been keeping vigil by Baylee's side, but it was starting to grow wearisome and tedious for all of them. She didn't like hospitals and didn't see how Quinn literally lived in one.

Concerned for her well-being and trying to be supportive, Dylan watched Baylee like a hawk. She had to be exhausted from the entire ordeal. Not only did she have to deal with William's slow slide into death, she was now awaiting word about her mother's remains.

As William's lawyer now, Reese had made the trip to The Enclave so he'd be on site just in case there was any news to pass along. The last time he'd called he'd told them the cadaver dogs had gotten a hit near the cabana house. But that had been hours ago.

"You look tired."

"I guess I am a little," she declared, as she rubbed the back of her neck.

Eyeing the droop to her shoulders, Dylan moved behind her chair and started rubbing her aching muscles.

"Mmmm, you have magic fingers, Surfer Boy. If you ever wanted to give up software code and make a living as a masseur, you could hire on to one of those cruise ships, change your name to Alejandro, and set up shop."

For the first time in two days, he busted out laughing. "Now there's an idea. But don't forget how terrific I am at coloring hair. I'd hate to give up my hairdresser's license."

And for the first time in as many days, Baylee laughed as well. She almost blurted out how much she loved him, but at that moment, Dylan's cell phone rang.

He looked down at the display and recognized Reese's number. "Anything yet?"

"Jackpot. But you aren't going to believe this. They didn't find two bodies near the cabana house William described but three human skulls along with some tattered clothing, some denim jeans, something that looks like an old athletic sweatshirt, and various shoes. The remains weren't really buried all that deep down, maybe three feet at the most. There's no way to ID the bones yet with what we have though. I'll know more later. The coroner's here. The bones are headed to the morgue. Everything's down to a crawl. They've brought in a forensics team, including a couple of anthropologists to look for more bones. I'll keep you posted."

Dylan tried to ignore the fervor he heard in Reese's voice and disconnected. He turned back to Baylee, saw the stricken look on her face, and knew he didn't need to say a word. Baylee did it for him. Tears ran down her cheeks. "They found her, didn't they?"

"They found three skeletal remains, Baylee."

"Three?"

"Yeah. It's too early to tell who they were. I'm sorry, baby. It'll take another couple of days at least before they get any kind of answers. It might not even be your mother." But as he wrapped his arms around her, held her, he was pretty sure the forensic team had just discovered Sarah Moreland and Luc Delaine's final resting place.

When Tanya came through the door with the baby, she looked ready to drop. "Sarah's getting fussy, needs to nurse, I think."

"Give her to me. Come here to Mama, baby."

"How about I go get us some coffee?" Dylan asked, rubbing his tired eyes. "I could use the caffeine."

"I could use a sandwich and a glass of milk," Baylee said, as Sarah started to nurse.

"I think I'll go along with Dylan, and get me a bite to eat as well. I could use the exercise," Tanya said.

"You could both use the break," Baylee pointed out as they both turned to leave.

"I'll be back in ten minutes, Baylee," Dylan promised. "And Quinn's shift ends in less than two hours. She'll be up here to hover. And Jake phoned earlier. He and Kit are making preparations to get Ben Griffin over here within the week. As soon as they grab a quick bite they'll be back within the hour. And Gloria's on her way, too. She and Kit want to sit with William for a bit to relieve you so you can get some rest."

"That's fine, Dylan. Get some food into Tanya first. She looks like she's about to drop."

If she were honest with herself, she enjoyed the peace and quiet spending a little alone time with Sarah. The past couple of days had been brutal. She'd waited twenty-two years for an answer to what had happened to her mother. She could wait another day or two, maybe even a couple of weeks, if that's what it took to get the answers.

She had provided St. John with a DNA sample for comparison to anything the forensic team might find. Getting swabbed had brought a chilling reality full circle. All those times she'd visited The Enclave with Kit, only to learn now her mother may have been buried within yards of where she'd eaten birthday cake and ice cream during a party for ten-year-olds. That was truly disturbing.

How could her father have kept that awful secret and let her attend a social event at the Boyds' year after year? For Baylee, the depth of her father's secret wasn't just heartbreak, but broken trust. Her father had betrayed the memory of her mother, never once attempting to set the record straight. How could she forgive him for that even at death's door?

For the first time in years, she realized that tonight she could go to sleep knowing her mother had not abandoned her but had been cruelly taken from her by two evil creatures that didn't have a heart or a soul between them.

Baylee gazed down at the miracle in her arms. Watching Sarah nurse, she realized how lucky she was. She had named her daughter Sarah in spite of the fact that she'd spent years bitterly angry believing her mother had abandoned her in favor of a tennis pro, believing William's story unconditionally.

His lies, she thought now, had covered two decades. How many times had he repeated that lie?

Even with that, when it had come down to naming her baby daughter, she'd gone with her heart. Sarah Moreland would live on through her namesake, her granddaughter.

All at once, the door burst open. Connor Boyd stepped inside William's room. The heavy hospital door banged hard against the wall. The noise startled Sarah. She puckered her lips and began to cry. Baylee quickly tried to button her shirt, but Connor closed the distance and got right in her face. "You bitch. You should have told me I had a daughter."

"What…are you talking about?"

He grabbed the front of her blouse, jerking her up and out of the chair. "Don't even try denying it. I know she was born December sixteenth, one day shy of exactly nine months from the night we slept together. Her birth certificate was amended two weeks ago. You think I'm stupid? Think again. She's mine."

He tried to wrestle Sarah out of her arms, but Baylee held on for dear life, struggling, fighting him with everything she had while the baby wailed in protest.

"What are you doing? Connor, she's just a little baby. Don't do this, Connor. You're wrong. Sarah belongs to Dylan."

"We'll see about that, won't we?" He hauled off and slapped Baylee across the face. Despite the blow, she tried to fight back. With fists clenched, one hand clutching Sarah, she repeatedly hit him in the arm, in the chest, anywhere she could land a blow. But at five-three, she was no match for a man several inches taller with a longer reach. The second slap sent her reeling. And so did the punch he threw to her mouth. The jab knocked her to the floor.

As she fell backward, Connor quickly snatched Sarah out of her arms. He used that moment to rush out of the room with the baby bawling at the top of her lungs.

By the time Connor reached the elevator, Trevor had come up to stand behind him as if he were just another visitor waiting for the door to ding open. Once the elevator car slid apart, Connor stepped inside. Trevor followed. Trevor waited until Connor hit the button to ground level before turning to eye the terrified infant. As the car began to rumble downward, Trevor looked over, stared at the screaming child. His heart broke a little. But he had to stay centered.

A nervous Connor told him, "She's hungry. She'll calm down when I take her to her mother."

"Right," Trevor retorted as if unimpressed. He calmly asked, "How old?"

"Six months."

"Cute little thing."

"Yeah."

"Funny, she must look like her mother. She doesn't look a thing like you."

Irritation flitted across Connor's face for about two seconds, but then he nodded his head a fraction toward Trevor and said nothing else.

Once the elevator door opened at ground level, Connor bumped his way past other visitors, increasing his pace, rushing to the bank of elevators in the lobby that led down to the parking garage.

The entire time Sarah protested as loudly as her lungs allowed.

Trevor desperately tried to stay on his heels while at the same time staying back far enough to keep Connor from becoming suspicious. They joined a small group gathered waiting for an available car to open up to take them down to the parking structure. Trevor watched as the double doors opened and a stream of people filed past, gawking at the wailing infant.

Annoyed that she was making a scene, Connor clumsily tried to bounce Sarah up and down in his arms. When that didn't work, he tried to put his hand over her mouth to keep her quiet, which only seemed to infuriate Sarah further. Resisting his efforts, her head moved back and forth, and she struggled in his arms in complaint.

As soon as the last person emptied the car, Connor impatiently hopped on, quickly pressing the button several times in rapid succession to get it to start moving. Calmly, Trevor waited for the last possible second to board the car himself, making sure he didn't allow Connor an opportunity to change his mind. They rode down a couple of floors, making stops for a few other people, who seemed grateful to get out of the car away from the screaming baby.

Trevor didn't bother to make small talk but listened instead to Sarah's wails of protest as they became more and more pronounced. When the elevator door finally reached Level Five, Connor hurried out, heading beyond the first row of cars at a fast clip.

Trailing behind, Trevor scanned the parking lot until he spotted the familiar Hummer in the distance, parked several rows away. Knowing Connor's destination made it better, but this was hardly the ideal place for a coup. And no matter how he wished otherwise, it wouldn't be bloodless. He reached down, pulled the knife from his boot.

With no time to consider the security cameras or anyone who might be lurking, Trevor gauged the situation and realized he didn't have much of a choice. He couldn't let Boyd reach the Hummer and make off with the baby. It had to be here or not at all. And it had to be quick and clean.

With Sarah screaming, Boyd never noticed Trevor come up behind him. The baby was the perfect diversion. In a movement that lasted no more than five seconds, the six-inch blade Trevor held sliced deeply through Connor's neck, severing his carotid artery. Connor's free hand instinctively flew to his throat before trying to grab for the weapon. With blood spurting and streaming down his neck at a rapid rate, he soon began to falter. The second his momentum waned, Trevor snapped Sarah out of his clutch. With his left boot he pushed the weakening man to the concrete.

Trevor took off for the stairwell. He descended two floors down before he stopped to try and quiet the baby. "Shhhh, shhhh, little one, it'll be okay. You're okay. You're just frightened. Everything will be fine. Shhhh, now. I'll get you back to your mother." An Irish lullaby popped into his head from another time, another place. Memories of holding another infant, his baby daughter, flashed through his brain in a montage of scenes that came fast and hard and painful.

He began to softly sing to the baby in Gaelic. His heart melted when she placed her weary head on his shoulder, as if she knew her ordeal was over. She did her best to try and calm down, all the while hiccupping and sniffling into his chest. Patting her back the way he remembered, the way he'd done a lifetime ago, he used his thumb to wipe her runny nose. Swaying back and forth, he rocked her gently until she quieted, falling into exhaustive slumber.

☙ ☙ ☙ ☙ ☙

When Dylan came into the room with the coffee and spotted Baylee lying on the floor, he flung the carton holding the coffee cups aside and bent to where she lay. She was still out cold. The bruise on her face was already turning purple, her puffy and swollen lip looked twice its normal size, and blood from her nose trickled down to her chin.

He looked around for Sarah. Terror engulfed him. A wave of nausea clutched his stomach. While he ran to the bathroom sink to grab a washcloth and wet it with cold water, he dialed nine-one-one on his cell.

It felt like he waited fifteen minutes for anyone to pick up.

As soon as the dispatcher answered, Dylan's composed manner evaporated. With every word, his panic grew. "There's been a kidnapping at the Medical Center, a six-month-old baby, Sarah Burke, was taken less than five minutes ago by a man named Connor Boyd. You need to put out an Amber Alert. Now. Get the police here! The suspect is driving a black Hummer. I don't know the plate number, but you should be able to cross-check the name to the plate."

After getting the specifics, the dispatcher told him, "The police are on their way. Do you want to keep the line open?"

"Sure, but I have…the baby's mother has been injured. She fought the guy and she's out cold." He stuck his head out the door and wondered why no one had heard the commotion. He yelled down the corridor. "I have an injured woman in here. Hello? Could someone get me a doctor? Now."

By the time he knelt down beside Baylee again, she began to come around. "Baylee, honey, talk to me, what happened?"

She attempted to gain her feet but slunk back down to the floor when her head spun. "Connor. Connor has Sarah." Baylee pleaded, "Go, Dylan. Go find her. I'll be fine. Hurry, please, don't let him take her. Don't let him get away."

The nurse came in, just in time to see Baylee throw up.

Dylan was torn between running and staying. But when he saw the look of pure panic on Baylee's face, he knew he had no choice. He took off down the hallway, not knowing for a minute where he was going or what he intended to do when he got there.

☙☙☙☙☙

In the parking structure stairwell, Trevor took off his jacket, unbuttoned his shirt, and slipped it off. He used it to wipe some of the blood off the baby's face. When he'd done the best he could, he took the shirt and bundled the baby firmly inside. If he didn't get out of here soon he'd have a shitload of swarming police all over the place.

He shrugged back into his jacket, zipped it up, and opened the door of the stairwell leading down to the third level parking. He stuck his head out and looked around. He saw no one. With the coast clear, he headed straight for the elevator, hoping like hell that when the car opened it would be empty. Luck had been riding with him up to this point. Now was no exception. When the double doors dinged open, a sigh of relief escaped his lips. The car was vacant.

He stepped inside momentarily to pull out the red emergency stop button so the doors wouldn't close. He took the time to place a kiss on the baby's forehead. Gently, he put the sleeping Sarah on the floor still wrapped in his shirt. Trevor hated letting her go, but time was not on his side. He pulled a gold cowboy from his jacket pocket and slipped it into the front pocket of the Oxford shirt. Reluctantly, he re-engaged the emergency lever and stepped outside the elevator, watched as the door closed and baby Sarah disappeared.

⚛ ⚛ ⚛ ⚛ ⚛

By the time Dylan reached ground level, a crowd had gathered around the bank of elevators leading to the parking garage. Five police officers converged on the scene about the same time Dylan waded into the throng of people.

A man yelled, "Look at that, there's a baby with blood on her in the elevator."

Dylan's heart sank. A sickening feeling washed over him as he maneuvered his way to the front of the crowd, pushing and shoving for space. Then he heard Sarah start to fuss. The sound was the most wonderful sound he'd ever heard in his life. Before he ever laid eyes on her, he knew she was at least alive. By the time he inched his way through the crowd, he watched as a police officer reached down and scooped her up off the floor.

Specks of blood smeared her face. The shirt that wrapped around her little body bore red stains as well.

Sarah started to cry for real.

It was music to Dylan's ears. Knees weak, he reached out his hands to take the baby and told the officer, "Oh God. She's mine. She's hurt. Give her to me."

"Now wait a minute…I can't just…do that…who's to say… We don't even know whose blood this is. This is a crime scene."

Dylan didn't give a shit about a crime scene. He wanted to get Sarah back to her mother. With shaky hands, he reached around to his back pocket and pulled out his wallet with his driver's license, flashed it to the officer. "I'm the one who called you guys. I'm Dylan Burke. This is Sarah Burke. She's mine. Now give her to me." He reached out his hands again, and when Sarah saw him, she held up her little arms and babbled something that sounded very much like a long drawn out, "Daaaaaaaaaa."

"Well, okay then," the officer said as he handed Sarah into the waiting arms of her father. "You lead the way. I'll need to follow you upstairs and get your statement."

The minute Dylan clutched her to his chest, Sarah laid her head on his shoulder and stopped crying. With the cop in tow, Dylan raced toward the elevator to head back upstairs, holding on to Sarah for dear life. He had to wait for an available car, and while waiting he began to unwrap the shirt from around Sarah's body, trying to examine her for injuries, trying to figure out why she was wearing it in the first place and why it had so much blood on it.

But while loosening the shirt, a small gold cowboy slipped out of the pocket and hit the tile floor with a ping.

Bending to pick it up, he had a sick feeling what that meant. Their mysterious stranger had obviously, once again, shown up out of the blue and rode to the rescue. Dylan didn't know why and didn't care. If he ever came face to face with the man, he'd kiss him on the mouth right before he bought him a round of beers.

But right this minute, he needed to make sure the baby wasn't hurt. He handed the bloody shirt to the officer and took turns examining her arms and legs for anything that looked like a cut or a scrape. Even though she'd stopped crying, he checked her as best he could for any outward signs of trauma. Relieved to find she didn't have so much as a cut or a bruise on her anywhere, he clutched her to his chest.

When the elevator finally opened he didn't realize tears were streaming down his face until he saw his reflection in the mirrored glass inside the car's sidewall.

As it rumbled upward to the twelfth floor, he leaned his weight up against the opposite wall and cried like a baby right in front of the cop.

The minute the elevator doors slid open, he looked up through teary eyes and saw Baylee standing at the nurses' station wringing her hands with a swollen face and puffy lip, bruised and battered, her heart ripped out waiting for any word about their daughter.

Their daughter, thought Dylan, relief and joy running through him.

As soon as she spotted Dylan holding Sarah, she threw herself into his body. "Oh, my God, you found her. She's safe. Oh, thank God. You brought her back to me. Thank you, Dylan. I love you."

"Is that for me or for Sarah?" he asked in wonder.

"It's for both of you. You did it, Dylan. You found her and brought her back to me."

As she plucked the baby from his arms, Dylan wrapped both of them up. Kissing the top of Baylee's head, he told her, "We've found each other. I love you, Baylee. I love Sarah. And I'm not letting either one of you go."

Dear Reader:

If you enjoyed Deeper Evil, please take the time to leave a
review. A review shows others you've liked my work.
By recommending it to your friends and family it helps spread
the word.
Please Tweet/share that you've finished Deeper Evil.

If you do write a review, by all means let me know via Facebook
or my website.
I'd love to hear from you!!

For a complete list of the author's other books visit her website.
http://www.vickiemckeehan.com/

Want to connect with the author to leave a comment?
www.vickiemckeehan.wordpress.com/ blog
www.facebook.com/VickieMcKeehan

Go to the next page for a preview of
Ending Evil
Book Three of the Evil Secrets Trilogy

ENDING EVIL

Darkness descended and caused shadows to fall around him, helping to conceal his movements. He quickened his pace as cop cars passed him on the street on their way to the Medical Center.

It seemed to him the LAPD was moving into the area in record time from every direction. From the corner of his eye, Trevor Dane watched as uniformed cops blocked off the main entrance and scurried to get the hospital in lockdown mode in a matter of minutes.

At least he had made it off campus before that had happened, he thought, as he kept his head down and continued putting one foot in front of the other toward his Chevy, which he'd parked several streets over in a residential section of the neighborhood.

He wasn't far enough away though, not by a long shot. He kept his pace brisk as he dared not steal a glance behind him. He didn't have time to worry about security cameras and what surveillance images he'd left behind. Too late for that, he thought, wearily.

He'd worn gloves though, and he had another name to check off his list.

That list was getting shorter by the day. He'd taken care of the viper, Alana Stevens, right out of the box, driving a knife through her black heart and enjoyed every second of it.

From there he'd moved on to Jessica Geller Boyd, where he'd taken a 9 mm Glock and put it to her temple. He'd ended those soulless dark eyes once and for all. Her sister, Eva Geller Gatz, had met a similar fate except he'd used a .38. With Sumner Boyd he'd stayed with that same trusty .38 caliber although he had switched weapons, wouldn't do to use the same gun.

But with sleazy Frank Geller, he'd gone with the standard suicide gun, a .22 caliber Smith & Wesson.

Now, the boot knife that went wherever he did had taken care of Connor Boyd.

That left two brothers still standing. He'd missed taking out Collin Boyd once before. He didn't intend to miss a second time.

Because he wore no shirt beneath his jacket dusk made the June gloom marine layer cooler than it had been just an hour earlier. He'd left his shirt behind, the shirt he'd used to wrap up little baby Sarah, which obviously had Connor Boyd's DNA all over it. But it couldn't be helped could it, he reminded himself.

And the baby was safe now and for all time, back in the arms of her mother, Baylee Scott, away from the violent and unstable man who'd fathered her.

The baby.

It had been a long time since he'd held an infant, especially one so young, so dependent on the adults around her. He remembered her smell, her little face, her little puckered mouth, the hiccupping, and her eyes brimming with so many tears.

Tears she should never have been forced to shed.

Not twenty minutes earlier, he'd slit the throat of the baby's father and left him on the dirty concrete of the fifth floor parking structure to bleed out. He would not soon forget Connor Boyd's cold eyes as he died beneath his feet.

Nor would he forget the man's attack on the young mother. He had used his fists to bring her to her knees. If he'd let the man escape with Sarah, he wouldn't have been able to live with himself.

Trevor heard even more sirens grow closer. He needed to put as much distance between this place and the crime scene as quickly as he could. Even a professional, he reminded himself, with his years of experience, sometimes had to take risks.

He sighed. No sense beating himself up. Not every kill could be as meticulously carried out as one could hope or plan, he thought bitterly. Even though there was no chill in the air, he pulled his jacket collar up around his ears. He hurried on.

From the moment Connor had kidnapped Sarah, ripped the baby out of her mother's arms, he had left Trevor few options. As he saw it, he'd been fortunate Connor had made his escape route via the parking garage. The place had been deserted enough that he had been able to take the man down without bringing much attention to himself or to the area.

When his rented Chevy came into view, Trevor pressed the remote key lock. Good thing he hadn't parked near the hospital. He hadn't spent years working as a hit man for nothing. He thought of his bumbling counterpart, Uri Jankovic, and wondered if the Pacific Ocean had yet to give up his body to the land. Probably not, he decided, as he slid neatly behind the wheel of his car, quickly threw the vehicle in gear, and took off down the quiet, residential side street.

As he drove toward the 101, he contemplated his next move.

He could simply leave L.A. now, wad up his list, discard it in the nearest trash can at LAX and be on the next flight to Buenos Aires. He could find the first available warm body and spend the next two months fucking anything with a heartbeat.

Or, he could finish what he'd started, put an end to the evil, once and for all. He still had two more names on his to-do list. He was certain Cade and Collin Boyd weren't yet finished. He didn't know what their next move might be, but he knew for certain there would be one.

He pressed the accelerator, shot into the lane to access the 101, and made his decision.

Ending the evil, once and for all, was the only thing that made any sense.

Noah Parker wouldn't have wanted it any other way.

• • • • •

Two months into her first year of residency, Quinn Tyler realized chaos was about to erupt inside the ER.

Having just finished stitching up a thirteen year old skateboarder's sidewalk meet lip mishap, she quickly shed her pair of latex gloves and stepped back out into the common area of the ER.

She caught the triage nurse taking the call from the paramedics and knew they were bringing in a White male in his late-thirties who'd had his throat slit. He'd been found bleeding out on the fifth floor of the hospital parking garage.

Quinn heard the overhead pager repeat the same alert several times. "Code Trauma Now!"

The litany brought every available shift resident on the first floor running, along with the respiratory nurse and most of the ER staff including, Harold Mendenhall, chief of emergency surgery.

They all hovered near the ER doors—waiting.

Minutes later the doors whooshed open and paramedics wheeled an injured man inside. Quinn grabbed another pair of gloves, slipped them on and prepared to go to work. It wasn't until the man had been transferred from the gurney to the table that Quinn recognized him as Connor Boyd.

But he didn't look anything like the dark brooding man she remembered from her youth. This man was white as the sheets around him. And dark blood already congealed around the six inch long slice to his neck.

As the paramedic reported on his vitals and what up to now they had done for him, Quinn listened, keenly aware the man looked more dead than alive. "He had a faint pulse when we first got him loaded." He shook his head. "But I think we lost him on the way inside."

Dr. Mendenhall went to work, sizing up the man's condition and snapping out orders. "Jesus, this man's carotid artery has been severed. He's lost too much blood. But we'll give it our best shot. Lopez, get me a blood workup. Stat! He's not breathing. Angie, intubate him. Ms. Tyler, don't just stand there. Once Sullivan has the tube in, try to put pressure on the wound and get that bleeding stopped." To him it pretty much looked like a lost cause, but they might get lucky.

Quinn watched with a certain amount of envy as Angie Sullivan, third year resident and Mendenhall's favorite underling, manually intubated Connor trying to get him to breathe. Together they worked the airbag compressing air into his lungs.

Even though she'd been ready and willing to apply pressure to the wound the minute he began to show any signs of life, Quinn waited for the signal that never came. Despite the fact that Angie and Quinn and Mendenhall worked frantically to get the man to breathe, after a long twenty minutes, even a brand new resident like Quinn, knew it was too late. He'd lost too much blood.

Connor Boyd was gone.

He had more than likely bled out in a matter of minutes. Whoever had done this to him had known what they were doing, at least in Quinn's mind they had. After another several long minutes, Mendenhall simply said, "I'm calling time of death at," he glanced up at the clock, "8:25, even though it was more like twenty minutes ago. By any chance, is there any next of kin around?"

"You goddamned right there is. Don't you dare stop working on him. Do something. You can't let him die."

Quinn whirled around at the sound of Cade Boyd's voice and saw a disheveled man, standing holding the curtain that separated the attending rooms. He gripped the fabric like a drowning sailor held onto a life raft. Unlike his brother, Cade wasn't pale but stood defiant and red-faced.

A pair of cold, black stormy eyes met hers.

Don't miss these other exciting titles by bestselling
author

Vickie McKeehan

The Evil Secrets Trilogy
JUST EVIL Book One
DEEPER EVIL Book Two
ENDING EVIL Book Three

The Pelican Pointe Series
PROMISE COVE
HIDDEN MOON BAY
DANCING TIDES
LIGHTHOUSE REEF
STARLIGHT DUNES
LAST CHANCE HARBOR
SEA GLASS COTTAGE
LAVENDER BEACH
SANDCASTLES UNDER THE CHRISTMAS MOON
BENEATH WINTER SAND

The Skye Cree Novels
THE BONES OF OTHERS
THE BONES WILL TELL
THE BOX OF BONES
HIS GARDEN OF BONES
TRUTH IN THE BONES

The Indigo Brothers Trilogy
INDIGO FIRE
INDIGO HEAT
INDIGO JUSTICE
THE INDIGO BROTHERS TRILOGY BOXED SET

ABOUT THE AUTHOR

Vickie's novels have consistently appeared on Amazon's Top 100 lists in Contemporary Romance, Romantic Suspense and Mystery / Thriller. She writes what she loves to read—heartwarming romance laced with suspense, heart-pounding thrillers, and riveting mysteries. Vickie loves to write about compelling and down-to-earth characters in settings that stay with her readers long after they've finished her books. She makes her home in Southern California.

Find Vickie online at
https://www.facebook.com/VickieMcKeehan
http://www.vickiemckeehan.com/
https://vickiemckeehan.wordpress.com